THE STRONGHOLD

SEBASTIAN BENDIX

THE STRONGHOLD
Copyright © 2017 by Sebastian Bendix

ISBN: 978-1-68046-590-7

Fire & Ice Young Adult Books
An Imprint of Melange Books, LLC
White Bear Lake, MN 55110
www.fireandiceya.com

Published in the United States of America.

Cover Design by Caroline Andrus

CHAPTER ONE

The Exercise

I RUN, BUT NOT BECAUSE I AM BEING CHASED. I RUN BECAUSE I WANT TO. My legs are powerful and ache to be put to the test, so I test them. My clothes—olive fatigues patched with stressed leather—make the running easy. I slip through the forest, quiet as a cat. Not that I would know a cat if I heard one. The cats are all dead, either from plague or from being hunted for food during the famines. They've been extinct further back than I can remember. But I know they were quiet.

Rafe thinks he will catch me, but he's been wrong about that too many times to count. It's not that Rafe is slow or that he's not capable. It's that he is arrogant and thinks he deserves to be captain, and he assumes that's all it takes to earn it. And maybe he would be captain were it not for me. But I am better than him—I have always been better than him, and he knows it. As long as I am alive and able, I will be captain, so it isn't paranoia when I say that Rafe would like to see me injured or dead.

I hear movement in the forest behind me. The ground is dry, the way it gets before the winter, thirsty for the snow. The snap of brittle pine branches makes for a noisy pursuit. Any root that could trip me, any slick rock I could slip on, I avoid. I even try not to step on the crunchy needle beds, for our ears are attuned to the sound. But Rafe isn't thinking about these things. He's thinking he has to be fast if he's to catch me, and catching me is all he will need to win. That's Rafe's fatal flaw—everything is a contest to him; it's not about survival. To me it's not a contest. To me it's life and death.

I come to a clearing and stop. There are trees here with low-hanging branches that look alive and sturdy. Easy to climb. I could keep running, for several klicks at least, but this place is perfect. Sooner or later the chase has to end, and I'd rather it be on my terms, not Rafe's. So I go to the nearest tree, which happens to be the sturdiest. I only need to test the branch for a millisecond before I can tell it will handle my weight. Then I grab hold and swing my legs up, scissoring the branch to leverage myself into the tree. Beyond that the branches are closer together and the climbing is easy. I climb as quiet as I run.

By the time Rafe enters the clearing, I am at least seven meters above him. Directly above him at a dead drop, by my assessment.

I can tell by the way Rafe freezes that he senses I am near. But he doesn't look up. Rafe has what my father calls "tunnel vision" in that he gets so focused on what he is after that he doesn't look for clues, doesn't read the signs. Not that I left any signs.

I stand stock-still on the branch, Rafe's head no bigger than a doll's beneath the toe of my laced leather boot. If I spit, it would land in the part of his oily black hair, which he wears tight and spiky because he thinks it makes him look like a badass. My hair is lighter, "sandy blond" my mother calls it, and I wear it shaggy and loose. I guess it doesn't make me look like as much of a military badass as Rafe, but the girls like it, and besides, I have not lost a single exercise yet because of my hair. And I don't intend to start losing today.

Rafe continues to stand alert and unmoving, and I begin to fear that he may break from his usual pattern and look up. If he looks up, I will be trapped in the tree, and he can claim victory. To lose in such a humiliating fashion will result in endless ridicule—not just from the cadets but from the Old Guard as well and even Papa Byrne. Rafe will certainly never shut up about it. That's just one of the many ways he and I differ. He likes to brag endlessly, and I don't. It's not that I don't think highly of myself. I do. I just don't run off at the mouth about it every chance I get. My father taught me that. My father and I don't agree on everything—in fact, we don't agree on a lot of things—but we agree on that. We let our actions speak for themselves.

But none of this matters because I am not going to let Rafe win.

I reach down to my thigh for a special leather sheath that has been stitched into my well-worn fatigues. I don't need to look, because I know it's there, and sure enough I feel the cool, smooth kiss of the wood. I can't help but smile. I slip the boomerang out of the sheath, feeling the weight of it in my hand. A gift from Papa Byrne. He's not my actual father, but I often wish that he was. He is the man I want to become, a good soldier and great leader. Papa Byrne sees himself in me and believes that I will one day take his place at the head of our militia. I want nothing more than to prove him right.

He told me the boomerang is a weapon from Australia. I do not think Australia exists anymore, at least not as a nation, and even if it did, I would not go there. I don't intend to go anywhere outside of Deacon's Bluff. The bluff is my home, and I will fight for it and maybe even die for it one day. Papa Byrne says it's only a matter of time. That is why I train, every day, preparing for the inevitable war to come.

If Rafe were more vigilant, he might recognize the sharp, whipping sound of my weapon as I throw it. It spirals in a lazy dance, clipping the low canopy of branches, creating a distraction before returning to my hand with a slap. Rafe tenses and goes for his pistol, which, considering the circumstance, is a cowardly move. I keep this in mind as I drop from the tree, landing directly behind him.

In one move I have Rafe's throat hooked in the curve of the boomerang. The curve is deadly sharp—I know because I sharpened it. I bet Rafe didn't know that a boomerang could double as a blade. He knows now.

"You fight like a hostile," he hisses through gritted teeth.

I pull the boomerang tighter. "You went for your gun," I say.

"I thought I saw a zombie."

That's a lie. Rafe didn't see a zombie. No one on Deacon's Bluff has seen a zombie in nearly twenty years. None of us who are under eighteen have ever seen one. Rafe's lying makes me angry, angrier than I'd be if he just copped to pulling his gun for no good reason. But I rein it in because that's what a leader does.

"Blow," I say. Then I push him away before I'm tempted to cut him.

Rafe shoots me a hateful look, practically begging for a scrap. But he knows that I'm not going to give him the satisfaction. The exercise is over, and anything he tries to pull now will be reported as insubordination. He may have the stones to draw his gun when I'm not looking him in the face, but he sure as hell doesn't have the stones to draw on me now. My eyes tell him in no uncertain terms that I am done messing around. Rafe wises up, puts two fingers in his mouth, and whistles.

We stand there, and he spits on the ground between us, as if the terrain is to blame for his failure. I don't spit. I don't waste saliva. There is a rustle of brush as Gunnar steps out into the clearing. Gunnar is big and tall and blonder than me. When he smiles, his teeth are so large they remind me of the clay tiles we keep in the storage bins.

"Neville for the hat trick," Gunnar says.

I don't smile. Not yet. Not until it's official. "Call it," I say.

Gunnar pulls a stopwatch from his pocket. It's the old-fashioned kind with a clockface, not the digital kind. Digital is what people were using when the world all went wrong, which is why we don't trust it. Not that it matters much—most of the digital stopped working years ago. Gunnar clicks the button on the watch, stopping the timer.

"Called! Eight forty-eight! Neville!"

Gunnar's voice booms through the forest like a cannon. The first cadet to answer the call is Jessup. He skulks into the clearing, a scowl plastered on his rat-like features. I saw a rat when I was very young, so I know what they look like, but they seem to be all gone now too. It's too bad. Jessup could be their king.

"Seriously?" he whines. Jessup is on Rafe's team because he and Rafe are best friends, thick as thieves. You'd think he'd get tired of being on the losing team by now, but I guess even rats have their loyalties.

"Like you were some big help!" Rafe is clearly in no mood for Jessup's crap. The smaller boy wisely keeps his mouth shut, but behind Jessup's eyes I can see that he is looking for an angle he can work in this losing scenario. I don't trust Jessup entirely and sometimes wonder if he is secretly the most dangerous of the group. Rafe is the aggressor, but Jessup is the one who has the most to prove, and those are ones you really need to watch out for.

We find the others half a klick away, gathered in the ravine. We hear them before we see them because Devon is yelling. I'd recognize the shrill sound of that voice anywhere.

The yelling is directed at Seth, a boy all skin and bones who has the misfortune of being Devon's younger brother. The poor kid is stranded atop a high boulder, one of many that make up this vast and treacherous artery of stone. How he got there, I do not know, but I wouldn't be surprised if his fatass of a brother was the one to put him up there in the first place. And now the fatass is pissed because Seth is afraid to jump down and possibly break his ankle.

"Hurry up," Devon shouts. "They blew the signal five minutes ago!"

"I can't! It's too high!"

Immediately my blood begins to boil. Seth is the youngest of us and so far has proven no great shakes as a cadet, but Devon just enjoys bullying him. Devon is the kind of boy that you don't make a leader, because you know he's going to be cruel to his subordinates. There are men back at the Fort like Devon, men like Marcus Nagel, but Papa Byrne is too smart to make those men leaders. Papa Byrne is a kind man, but he's stern and forceful when he needs to be. That's the sort of leader I aspire to be. I don't suffer squabbling among my soldiers, and I certainly don't suffer brother-on-brother cruelty. Which is why I get even angrier when Devon picks up a rock.

His chubby arm is just drawing back when I catch him by the wrist.

"What the hell are you doing?" I shout at him. But I know damn well what he was doing. He was intending to bean his brother with that rock.

"He's my family; I'm entitled!" Devon's voice cracks, the child peeking through the bluster. I squeeze his arm, making him whimper. I've got a strong grip. He drops the rock.

"On patrol we're all family," I say, even but stern, like Papa Byrne would, "and out in the field family don't squabble. We clear?"

Devon looks in my eyes like he wants to protest further, but then he looks to Rafe and Jessup, his cronies, for support. Their faces give him nothing. Devon is mean, but he's not an idiot, so he drops the rock.

I go to the foot of the boulder and look up at Seth. He smiles down at me, face spattered with freckles. He's missing a front tooth—he should have lost the last of his baby teeth years ago. I suspect Devon had something to do with that.

"All right, Seth, it's not that high," I call up. "Jump down. If it goes bad, I got you."

The boy thinks it over for a second, then nods. He takes a breath and steps off of the rock.

He makes the jump just fine.

We take the path back, coming along the shoulder of the southern river.

The water is running low now, lower than it was last winter at this time. My father expects the river to dry up altogether eventually, but Papa Byrne thinks he's just being paranoid. "Paranoid" is a word that gets thrown around the Fort a lot, usually when two parties have cause to argue. But mostly our people wear the word like a badge of honor. Better to be a little paranoid, they say.

I'm pretty paranoid these days, but I've got good reason to be. I'm the best cadet on Deacon's Bluff, and you don't get to be the best without making a few enemies.

CHAPTER TWO

The Stronghold

THERE ISN'T MUCH TALK ON THE JOURNEY HOME, WHICH SUITS ME FINE. As we pass through the woods, I am struck with the pang of sadness I always feel when fall is drawing to a close. I look up at the patchwork of red and gold leaves that still cling to the branches. All gone soon. Winter is a tough time at the Fort—rations are tight, and people get pent-up and squirrely. The adults tend to argue, and the kids tend to scrap. I try to spend as much time outside the walls as possible, but there are always restrictions, especially when the snow comes. And these last few winters, the snow has come hard. My father says the snow will only get worse on account of what the government did to the atmosphere; the winters, longer and longer. No one at the Fort has nice things to say about the government, but the government is gone now, so I don't see much point in harping on it. But harp on it they do.

The forest thins out where we cut down the trees, and I can smell vegetables roasting. It's lunchtime at the Fort. Exercises make a cadet hungry, and we're all ready to grub down. By now the last of the summer vegetables are being eaten, and soon our suppers will be poured out of jars and chipped from blocks of ice. None of it will have the flavor it did when the weather was warm and the food was fresh. And people wonder why I tend to get thin in the winter.

Through the last of the trees, I first see the towers, then the great wall. I

7

feel a rush of pride whenever I return home, and today is no different. We built Fort Thunder—at least our parents did—out of wood and whatever pieces of the old world we could carry with us onto the island. Our parents wanted a place where we could be free from the world's evils, so they raised the great wall and killed all the zombies and hostile marauders that tried to rush at our gates. None of them got through. We have Papa Byrne and his brave militia to thank for that.

We reach the gates, which are carved with the symbol of Fort Thunder. It's a pyramid with an eye in its center, caught in a circular target as if you were looking at it through the scope of a rifle. Ever since I was a kid, that eye gave me the spooks. Papa Byrne explained to me that the pyramid represents the government and its worship of money, and the eye represents the way the government kept everyone under surveillance with cameras and satellites. We view those things as symbols of oppression, and our rejection of them is the true foundation on which Fort Thunder was built. Every last one of us would fight and die to preserve it.

As we approach, I see Wilkes stationed in the southern watchtower crow's nest. That's a common sight this time of day, Wilkes looking down at you, spitting brown gobs of chaw from beneath his patchy grey-and-white beard. Wilkes is one of the Old Guard, the original militia that, along with the council, started it all. Some of the kids steer clear of Wilkes on account of his gruffness and the intimidating scar that creeps up the left side of his cheek. Not me. I like Wilkes, and I like his scar. I'd be proud to have a scar like that one day.

"Who won?" Wilkes hollers down, shouldering his rifle. Sentries get to use the best rifles, the high-caliber ones with the high-powered scopes. I've been pulling sentry duty since I turned seventeen and have already proven myself a crack shot with a 22-50 and a 30-06. I bet I could peg a deer at sixty-odd meters, if there were any deer left.

None of the losing team wants to step forward to own up, so Gunnar does the honors for the winners—my team. "Team Neville," he says, not without a hint of pride.

"Looks like Team Nagel's on latrine duty yet again," drawls Wilkes in his usual world-weary fashion. Rafe, Devon, and Jessup's faces droop at exactly the same time, three sad-sacks in a row. I want to laugh, but I don't. It's not nice to be a sore winner.

8

"That's not fair," Devon protests. "Seth spent the whole exercise scared on top of a rock. He should be put on latrine duty with the rest of us."

"That's not how it works, and you know it." That's the end of the discussion as far as Wilkes is concerned. When a member of the Old Guard hands down a verdict, very rarely is it questioned. Certainly not by any cadet that wishes to stay on duty.

The familiar grinding of the winch signals the opening of the main gate, and seconds later we are all inside. Returning from a patrol makes me feel like a conquering hero, and winning the day's exercise only heightens the feeling. At this time of day people like to mill about the square, talking about the weather or other such trivialities. The square is a gathering place, a rare oasis of open space before our dwellings—tight clusters of wood and rusty scrap—take over. When I was a kid, the square seemed huge, but the older I get, the smaller it seems.

The centerpiece of Fort Thunder is a tall building with a high, pointed steeple. It was built the year the Fort was founded, 2019, a year before I was born. We call it the armory on account of it housing our supply of firearms—and we have a lot of firearms. My father thinks we put too much stock in guns and not enough in learning and agriculture and other things. The men argue about this a lot, but nothing ever seems to change. And the armory stands there in the center of it all, not saying a word, like a great towering sentinel.

Only the other kids take a real interest in us. They are gathered anxiously around the water pump, waiting to hear tell of today's exercise. Tessa is there, looking at me in that way she does, all hungry eyes and wet lips. I get a nervous feeling every time I see her. I find the idea of her more frightening than any zombie or hostile, but I'd never tell the other boys that. I have a reputation to uphold, after all.

"Come to claim your prize?" Tessa purrs. She walks right over to me, swaying her hips in a practiced manner. Tessa just turned sixteen, but she likes to present herself as a lot older—sexy, sophisticated, and of her own mind. It's not something girls are supposed to do, but Tessa is Papa Byrne's daughter, so she tends to get away with things the others can't. She's been putting on this vampy routine ever since her body grew curves and the boys all started to notice—and boy, do they notice. Rafe, for instance, can barely keep his tongue in his mouth.

"Hello, Tessa," I say, and she slinks up right next to me. I can feel her breath, warm and sweet-scented. She's beautiful in a way that makes me ache to my roots, but there's something so cold and unknowable about her. Her beauty is a weapon, hard-edged and cruel, and heaven help anyone who gets in the way of it.

"We don't have to wait," she whispers hotly, just loud enough for the others to hear. I can feel Rafe shooting jealous daggers with his eyes. "You could sneak me out late one night, take me to the old ranger station..."

"I don't think your father would approve."

"Daddy doesn't need to know. Besides, he *loves* you. You're his favorite."

It's true; I am Papa Byrne's favorite. He doesn't have a son and likely never will as his wife, Tessa's mother, passed in the winter of twenty-two. I was a toddler then and don't remember her, but by all accounts she was a good woman. My mother and she were close friends. Mother says that after his wife died, Papa Byrne became a different man, colder and more withdrawn. But I don't see that. He's always been warm and open with me. I suppose I am the closest thing to a real son he will ever have.

I should be grateful that Tessa was chosen as my betrothed, but in truth I am not. I should love her; I should want to take her out by the old ranger station, but I don't. Though I can see that she is very beautiful and I feel a burning need for sex, the truth is—and I would never admit this to anyone—I am afraid of it. And it doesn't help that in my heart I do not love Tessa, the person she is on the inside. She is cold and cruel, and when I imagine the long years together raising children, I begin to feel sick to my stomach. But this is what is expected of me. I am the eldest living child of the Lucky Thirteen, the original thirteen families to settle on Deacon's Bluff, and as such it is my sworn duty to continue our people. Tessa and I will be the first of our generation to procreate, and it is an event our elders, my parents included, are anxiously awaiting.

"In the spring," I say, hoping that the thaw never comes, "when it's warmer."

Uninvited, she wraps her arms around my body. "I'll keep you warm." The boys all giggle, all except Rafe. Giggling irritates me—it's a behavior expected of girls, not soldiers. I push Tessa away, but gently. My gut tells me that I don't want to ever see her truly angry.

"*Bowie* Neville," Tessa says, using my name like the knife I was named after, "you are a no-good tease!"

"And that's why you love me." I give her a flirty smirk. It's true; she does love me.

That's what scares me the most.

There's a commotion at the water pump that mercifully ends our flirtation. Emily and Amy Erickson, seven-year-old twins, are quarreling. One of them—Emily or Amy, I can never tell them apart—grabs a brimming bucket of water and throws it at her mirror image of a sister. It's not a good throw. The bucket hits the ground, splashing up and soaking an unlucky bystander come for her morning water ration.

The bystander is Maya, and she is understandably pissed. "You little beasts!" she screams, putting the fear of god into the knee-highs. Maya is Wilkes's daughter, and she is not like the other girls of Deacon's Bluff. She's tough, for one. Not in the way Tessa is tough, with her words and her walk. Maya has got real stones. I've seen her out back by the latrines, shooting at the recycling glass with a slingshot she made from a branch and an old bungee cord. She's not a bad shot either. She does it in secret because girls aren't supposed to handle weapons, not even blades or slingshots. They aren't allowed to be soldiers—not with the way things are now. If it were up to me, Maya would train as a cadet, but it's not up to me. Not yet, anyway.

"You're one to call someone a beast," Tessa says. She doesn't like Maya because Maya doesn't fit in, doesn't behave the way girls ought to behave. And in Tessa's world, disapproval amounts to ridicule. "A little water wouldn't hurt you."

"Sorry I don't meet your standards of cleanliness, Tessa." It's clear from Maya's tone that she's not at all sorry.

"I'm not ashamed to have standards." Tessa dismisses Maya with a smug flip or her hair and directs her gaze back at me. "I want the best, and I get it."

Maya rolls her eyes, but she knows not to take things too far. All of the girls learn that lesson with Tessa sooner or later.

A voice cuts across the square like a raw nerve. "Rafe! Goddamnit, boy!" We all turn, knowing full well to whom the voice belongs. Marcus Nagel stomps over, a seething knot of aggression, compound bow gripped tightly in hand. He's coming from the firing range, where he has likely put arrows in many a bullseye this morning. The way he's looking, you'd think he'd just as soon put an arrow in his own son. "Did I hear right? That you lost again?"

Rafe looks like he's ready to crawl into a hole and die. I actually feel sorry for him in these moments, and these moments come with ferocious regularity. It all traces back to Rafe's brother Ryan, who was two years older than me and nearly the soldier I am. He would have been in the militia by now if he hadn't been killed. The official story is that a jammed pistol went off during an exercise, but everyone knows better. Ryan put a bullet in his own skull because his father pushed him too hard. And now Marcus is pushing Rafe twice as hard as if to make up for it. Rafe is a pain in my ass, but with a father like that, I can't blame him for being a jerk.

"It's not my fault," Rafe says, throwing his teammates under the bus. There goes my sympathy. "Devon and Jessup wouldn't follow orders." This is a load of crap, and we all know it, but if it saves Rafe from a public beating, so be it. But judging by Nagel's sickened look, he isn't buying it. His chest heaves beneath his tanned leather vest as he pulls his scraggly hair back into a tight ponytail, the telltale sign of a beating to come. We all tense nervously, waiting for the fists to start flying.

Nagel sees the looks on our faces and changes his mind. "Go help your mother. It's all you're good for," he spits. Rafe nods at the command and takes his leave on the double. His father looks at us, dishing out the stink eye, wishing none of us were here so he could whup Rafe's ass with impunity. "What, none of you shits have afternoon chores? Go on. Git."

I DON'T HAVE ANY AFTERNOON CHORES, BUT I HEAD HOME ANYWAY. I'M just glad to be getting away from Nagel, and if I'm being truthful, Tessa too. Upon my return to the five-room cabin that serves as our home, I am greeted by the familiar smell of my mother's curry hanging thick in the air. There is no meat, of course. Game has been gone from the island for so long that I barely remember the taste of it. But I remember that it tasted good.

My mother is forty-nine but carries herself younger, despite the hard years she wears on her face. Her name is Callie, short for Calista, which means beautiful—at least according to my father. Oftentimes, when he looks at her from across our tiny living area, I can tell he still means it. But when she looks at him, I see something else. Respect, loyalty, and certainly some form of love, but her eyes do not long for him the way his long for her. I believe it is because my father is a brilliant man, an important man, and being the wife of an important man comes with a heavy cost. I feel the weight of it in her every gesture toward him, every loaded glance.

"Curry so soon? It isn't even cold yet." She smiles at my chiding, and I land a kiss on her cheek. I grab a stray carrot from the carving board, and she playfully swats at my fingers with her knife. The only knives women are allowed are the ones used for cooking.

"Your father is in the study," she says. As if there were ever any doubt.

Most Fort Thunder dwellings are not afforded the luxury of a study, but my father is the keeper of the Fort library, so it was incorporated into our home when our cabin was built. It is a cramped room lined on all sides by shelves of dusty, weather-worn books. My father, the great Harlan Neville, spends most of his time there, seated at an old maple-wood desk, his nose in a novel or charter or even some silly religious text. He says I should feel free to sit in there and read whenever I want. To this day I have not taken him up on this offer.

"How was the exercise?" he asks, removing his glasses and rubbing his temple. He's been rubbing his temples a lot lately, and I don't think it's just out of habit.

"We won," I answer proudly.

"That's good," he says. I can tell he's not impressed. The fact that I led my team to yet another victory is not a source of pride for him. It makes me angry, but like a good son and good soldier, I bottle it. When I have a son of my own, I'll be proud when he tells me about winning his training exercises. I certainly won't save my enthusiasm for musty old books.

My father puts his glasses back on, straightens in his chair. He hides the pain well, but I can see it there, written on the hard lines of his face. Pointing it out to him won't do any good. Even if he has been to see Doc Seaver about it, all we have left in the way of medicine are the homemade remedies Frankie Seaver whips up in their kitchen. Powders mostly, ground from the herbs we grow and roots she finds in the forest. Nonsense, really. But sometimes when people take them, the remedies make them feel better. I think it's all in their heads, but whatever works. I wish there was something that would work for my father. We disagree sometimes, a lot of the time actually, but I don't like to see him in pain. And I really don't like that he hides it.

The thought causes me to look away, to the overstuffed shelves crowding me in every direction. All these books, written by people who have fallen to dust.

"See anything you'd like to borrow?"

My anger rises back to the surface. "That's three times in a row we've won the exercise," I snap at him, "and you tell me to go read a book."

"What would you like me to do, Bowie?"

"I don't know. Congratulate me?"

"Congratulations."

It rings hollow to my ears. "I shouldn't have to ask for it."

"I'm sorry that you feel that way, Son."

My father is not the kind of man to freely admit fault, so this conditional apology is the best I will get. "Papa Byrne says that at this rate I'll be head of the militia by twenty."

Bringing up Papa Byrne was stupid. He and my father disagree over the direction of my life, and on more than one occasion heated words were exchanged on the subject. If I was hoping to win fatherly approval, this was the wrong way to do it.

"I am your father," he says, not for the first time, "not Patrick Byrne."

Wisely, I choose not to argue. My silence is sufficient apology.

"Bowie, I have no doubt that you are going to be a great leader one day," he says, leaning back in his chair. "But leadership isn't just training for a hypothetical war. It's compromise and debate and doing what's best for your community. It's about understanding the big picture."

"I think I have a pretty good understanding of the big picture," I say.

My father's smile says that he doesn't agree. "You have one understanding. But there are layers on top of layers. Many shades of grey. You need to be able to see them, identify them. To navigate them with caution. And the best way to do that is to be informed. Gather information and try to look at things from all possible sides."

In my mind, there is only one side—ours. But I nod anyway.

"All I ask is that you balance your training with education."

My father loves that word. *Education*. Before the Great Leavening he spent some years as a teacher, a professor at a respected university. As a learned man, he understood the corruption that ate away the old world, and when the house of cards fell, he and my mother fell in with like-minded people who wanted to leave it all behind. But still, he clings to these relics of the old ways. His beloved books. As a gesture of appeasement, I scan the spines, and my eyes fall on a particular title. Smiling, I take it down.

"I'll borrow this one," I say.

My father glances at the book I have chosen. *The Art of War* by Sun Tzu.

ACROSS THE RANGE, THE FEATURELESS MAN DANCES IN A HAIL OF BULLETS. I fire a final round and nail his head back, knocking it clean off of his shoulders. It dangles there loose, still tethered to the neck, bobbing like a deflated balloon.

"That's some shooting right there, son," Papa Byrne says. He's lying beside me, flat on his stomach, his own rifle propped on the row of sandbags. I put down my M16 and smile.

Papa Byrne takes aim at the man, an articulated dummy that stands thirty meters downwind on the firing range. He tests the breeze, which is blowing a faint ruffle through his white-streaked hair. He's on the far side of fifty now, and his muscular body has settled into a powerful, husky bulk, but he doesn't carry himself like a heavy-set man. He still clocks a four-minute kilometer and can take the whole of the obstacle run better than cadets half his age. Still, his time as militia leader is drawing to a close, as all things must. That's why I'm here.

He pulls the trigger of his trusty AR-10, and I cup my ears from the skull-rattling boom. Bullets strafe the dummy like a surgeon's knife, clipping the sinewy cords that tether the limbs to its torso. Byrne targets the left arm first, then the right, the left leg at the hip, then the right. He nails the cord every time, dropping limbs like autumn leaves. Naturally he saves the head for last. With one crack shot he severs the neck cord, freeing the head from the body. It falls, hitting the ground with a sad, comical bounce.

Papa Byrne sits up, satisfied. "Now that's how it's done!"

I look at him, unable to hide my admiration. "You even nailed the headshot."

"Had to," he says smugly. "A zombie with arms and legs is still a zombie."

Technically, the dummy was meant to be a hostile, not a zombie, but I'm not one to argue with Papa Byrne. His point stands—if you aim to kill your target, you take the headshot. Every soldier knows that. I've never killed a man as I've never had cause to. But in my heart, I know the time will come, and when it does, I hope I can operate with one-tenth of Papa Byrne's skill.

He leans up against the sandbags and takes out his chaw pouch, stuffing a brown pinch under his lip. Chewing tobacco is the preferred vice of militiamen, but I find it disgusting. Still, if I have to suffer the taste to gain the respect of my men, I will.

"Heard about the exercise today. Good work."

"Thanks," I say. It's nice not to have to ask for approval.

"What's the status on the other cadets?"

"They're all doing well."

"All of them?"

I know what he's getting at. "Well, Seth needs a little work..."

"More than a little from what I hear."

"And where did you hear it, I wonder?"

Papa Byrne scowls at me. He doesn't like sarcasm. "Don't get sore over a little healthy competition, Bowie."

"Healthy for Rafe," I grumble. "He shouldn't be coming to you behind my back. It goes against the chain of command." I know that falling back on protocol will strengthen my position. Our leader is nothing if not a stickler for protocol.

"Fair enough," he concedes, "but he has a point. If Seth is a problem, he needs to be relieved of duty."

"Seth's not a problem."

"You know, not everyone is cut out for the militia," he says, knees popping as he stands. "There's plenty of other things Seth can do to make himself useful. Farming, for instance. It was good enough for his father, when he was alive."

"You sound like *my* father," I say as I shoulder my rifle and stand.

"Harlan Neville is a good man." I'm not used to Papa Byrne speaking highly of my father, even though they share a healthy, if somewhat chilly, respect. "Fort Thunder needs scholars and thinkers. I've never denied that. But we also need soldiers and generals. You are an exceptional soldier, Bowie. And one day you will make a great general. Your father will come to admire that eventually. Give him time."

I want to tell him that I'm not so sure my father has a lot of time left, but I don't. It would feel like a betrayal and could jeopardize my father's standing in the council. Weakness is never taken lightly here at Fort Thunder, and some would be quick to call for his resignation. So I just sigh discontentedly and look back down the shooting range.

He puts an affectionate arm on my shoulder. "We can't live our lives trying to please others. Ultimately you have to do what feels right for Bowie Neville. Even if that goes against what your parents might want for you. After all, what is the founding principle of Fort Thunder?"

My answer comes in less than a second. "Be the captain of your own ship."

Papa Byrne smiles, teeth stained yellow from tobacco. "That's right. All you need to do is keep your head down and your eyes on the target. If you do that, there's no way you can fail."

I smile at him. "I won't fail, Papa Byrne. I promise."

"I know you won't, Son," he assures me.

Maybe it's because of my father, or maybe it's the weight of his expectations, but his endearment does not comfort me. Not today. We pack up our gear and head out of the range, and as we part ways, I feel the first chill of winter invading my bones.

IN AN ATTEMPT TO SHAKE OFF THE FEELING, I WALK THE PERIMETER OF the Fort. Since I intend to rise to the role of leader, I see it as my duty to understand the inner workings of the community, even the aspects of it I will take little part in. I love my home with all my heart and am proud to be a part of a community that is so strong and self-reliant. Walking the compound makes me feel like one of the knights in the stories my father read to me as a boy, a champion of the people, Lancelot or Galahad. I only hope that when the time comes, I can live up to that promise.

The recycling area borders the shooting range, which makes sense as it is unoccupied most of the time. Here is where we keep the glass, plastics, and other salvage items that have a regular use. Processing can be as simple as washing the items for reuse or as complex as melting them down to be reconstituted into something else entirely. It's a job that falls to the farming and maintenance families, and as such I have spent very few work hours in this section of the Fort. But I have a healthy appreciation for recycling and understand how crucial it is to our survival, a sentiment I express to my cadets whenever they want to waste bottles on shooting practice. Most of the time I get an eye roll or a grumbled "killjoy" for my efforts.

Beyond the recycling are the latrines—several rows of fiberglass outhouses tucked under camouflage netting. The plastic receptacles under the outhouses—we call them "crap buckets"—have to be removed regularly and emptied into a peat moss pit just outside the southeast wall, then rinsed and returned. It's not so bad during the winter because the cold air keeps the smell isolated, but in the summertime the heat and ocean breezes waft the odor right back over the wall. All the peat moss in the world couldn't cover that stench. The custodial family, the Clarks, handle the latrines most of the year, but I assign insubordinate cadets the duty as punishment. Rafe has spent quite a few hot summer afternoons dumping crap buckets, unsurprisingly.

Past the latrines is the farming area, which has a compost heap designated for the small amount of food that spoils or doesn't get eaten. You'd think that the smell of rot would make farming unpleasant, but once the crops come in, the air is naturally sweetened by the ripening vegetables and fruit. Agriculture is crucial to our survival, of course, just as important as, if not more than, the militia. Soldiers can't fight on empty stomachs. But oftentimes there is friction between the farming families—the Ericksons, Haverfords and Kassidys—and the militia, usually over water rations and other resources. Most of the time my father comes down on the side of the farmers, saying that the Old Guard treats them like second-class citizens. I don't think that's true; it's just that the militia has a lot of responsibility resting on their shoulders. Papa Byrne and his men have bigger things to worry about than celery and pumpkin squash.

I walk down the long rows of corn, brushing the stalks with my fingers. At the end of the rows, I see Whitney Erickson and Laura Kassidy pulling carrots out of the ground. The twins are playing in the wheat field beyond, and their mothers are laughing and enjoying their daughters at a distance. Soon I will be raising children of my own, a thought that I should find comforting. Looking at the girls twirling blissfully in the wheat, it saddens me that I only feel dread.

After the farm the dwellings begin, laid out in neat, tight clusters. I've seen the pictures of the way homes used to look, and I know that our houses are modest by those bygone standards. Ours are comparable to the homes built by settlers back before the world went crazy. As far as I'm concerned, we have all the space we need. I don't like to spend time indoors anyway and stay out all day when I can, even in the dead of winter.

The narrow alleys that separate the dwellings don't allow for much privacy between neighbors, so I move quickly through them and do not lurk about. It's pretty easy to catch wind of a conversation if you're inclined to eavesdrop, which I am not. The girls all make sport of it, as do some of the boys, but if anyone tries gossiping to me, I just tune them out. You have to be very careful of what you say in a place like this, so I make it a policy to keep my thoughts to myself. "Closed mouth catches no flies," my mother likes to say. The saying is rather gross, but I agree with the sentiment.

Adjacent to the housing sector is the mess hall, the largest building in the Fort aside from the armory. It's essentially a long log cabin with a few small windows and a stovepipe jutting from the roof. Our home kitchens have stoves, but the one in the mess hall is big and can handle a lot of food, so big community gatherings usually take place there. We have harvest celebrations in both the spring and fall, remembrance days when we honor our dead, and even parties that the parents allow us kids to have now and again. Inside is nothing special, just a few rows of benches and tables, but some of my fondest childhood memories—birthdays and awards ceremonies—have taken place inside that modest hall.

Last but not least is the armory. The tallest building in the Fort, you can tell the time of day by marking where its shadow falls on the ground. When I was a kid, its crooked steeple and constant, lording presence used to scare me, as it did all of the kids.

One rite of passage as a Fort Thunder youth is to sneak into the armory when the parents aren't looking and steal a bullet or an arrowhead as proof you were there. But that isn't easy. The armory is guarded most of time, and even when not, it's secured with a complicated system of locks. Only the militiamen have keys, so the trick is to steal a set and break in during the wee hours of the morning. I did it for the first time when I was twelve, and it was Gunnar who stole the keys from his father, August. I can still recall the first time I saw inside the building, guns hung from floor to steeple, silent and lethal. I convinced myself that I heard a ghost, and we ran out without locking up and then had to sneak back and secure the padlocks before first watch. We scared ourselves silly, but it's something Gunnar and I laugh about even to this day.

My father doesn't like the armory. He says that it reminds him of a church, and churches spread ideologies that made the world a volatile place. All who founded Fort Thunder agreed that this would be no place for religion, so it's forbidden to worship any sort of deity, which is fine by me. I can hardly believe that people used to kill each other over an imaginary man who lived in the sky. Father says we do have a religion—that we worship the almighty gun—but I think he just likes saying that to make people feel guilty or something. I have yet to see anyone praying to a Magnum 57 or assault rifle. I suppose if they did, they would do so in the armory.

Dinner is ready by the time I get home. It's potato stew with cornbread, my favorite. Mother made it because I won the exercise, so at least one person in the family appreciates my accomplishments. There is the usual small talk about the day's events, about Father's arguments with the council, and about the farmers' complaints about the noise from the firing range.

I eat my food and don't really listen. Like Mother, I just politely nod along to my father's diatribe, not contributing to the conversation. We've been doing that for as long as I can remember.

After supper my father excuses himself, suffering another one of his headaches. I help my mother with the dishes and ask her about his health. She says that it's fine, that it's just the stress of dealing with the council's bickering, but I can tell she is lying. We are no strangers to sickness here on Deacon's Bluff—most of those we have lost have fallen to illness. The Seavers do the best that they can, but without real medicine it amounts to very little. Often, I have thought about stealing away to the mainland to find one of the buildings where the sick were treated in the old times—*hospitals*, they were called. But Papa Byrne assures me that such places are gone, all of the medicine used up by addicts and people who refused to work. My blood boils at the thought of such people, and I'm glad we would never allow freeloaders to live at the Fort.

When the washing is done, I go to my room and leaf through the book I borrowed from Father. It was written by a Chinese man from long ago who was apparently a great warrior. There are no Chinese people living on

Deacon's Bluff—in fact, there are no people of any ethnicity other than white. It wasn't supposed to be this way, my father says. The bluff was intended as a safe haven for people of any race provided they were useful and copacetic with our chosen way of life. But many on the council, Papa Byrne included, felt that other races couldn't be trusted, that they were too accustomed to help from the government and had become complacent and lazy. An exception was made for one family, friends of my parents—but that ended badly. Now when I learn about other cultures, I read it in a book. I don't think I'd like other cultures.

I try to immerse myself in the book but find it difficult. There is a lot about waging war, and I've never wanted to be a conqueror. We founded Fort Thunder to be left alone, not to take land from others. The book also stresses how important it is that soldiers never question their government. I can't abide with that sort of thinking. I do understand that Fort Thunder has its own government of sorts, as much as we'd all like to deny it, but every society must have laws.

The government the Chinese warlord is talking about is the kind that invades and enslaves, and that was the kind of government we rejected when we settled here. There are other settlements out there in the wilderness, warmongering people, but we want nothing to do with them. All we want is to be left in peace, to live our own way of life—that is the cause that we fight for. To that end, *The Art of War* has little to offer.

I put the book down on my nightstand, next to the toy soldier who has stood sentry there ever since I was a boy. He's not a toy soldier really; he's an *action figure*—that's what my father calls him. We used to have a lot of action figures lying around for the kids to play with, but over the years they were all broken or destroyed. I caught Devon lighting one on fire once and gave him a punch on the arm for his trouble.

This action figure is a muscle man in army fatigues and an armored vest. He is brown skinned, an African American, but seeing as there is no America anymore, Papa Byrne would just call him "black" and say it with a slight look of disgust.

I pick up the figure and hold it in my hands, moving the arms, then the legs, back and forth, back and forth. Making him march. It's the only sort of playing I do with him. I'm too old for toys as it is, so who knows why I keep this thing around.

That's not true—I know why I keep it. But I don't like to think about that.

I put the toy down and ready my brain for sleep. My room is small, really more of a compartment, but I like it that way. Tight spaces comfort me. But tonight, it's suffocating, like the world is crushing down on me. Maybe it's the events of the day bothering me, this nagging sense that I'm standing on unstable ground. Or maybe it's the coming winter, or my father, or my dread of marrying Tessa.

I breathe deep, relaxing my body and mind, a technique I've mastered through years of training. A soldier must be able to sleep in the most uncomfortable situations—there are no featherbeds in foxholes, as the saying goes. After a few minutes of steady breathing, I begin to drift off, and my mind teeters on the edge of a welcoming dream...

A howling shriek snaps me awake. Then follows a crashing rumble, and the world starts to shake. I roll off my bed, landing crouched at the ready.

As a soldier, my first thought is that we are under attack. My ears are attuned to the sounds of war, gunfire, and mortar—this is the moment I've prepared for my entire life. But following the noise, there is only an unsettling silence.

My next thought is that it was an earthquake. There were several natural disasters that contributed to the downfall of society but none as legendary as The Great Shake, an earthquake so powerful that it sunk a good chunk of the coast into the ocean. It happened before I was born, so I did not experience it, but many of the Lucky Thirteen did and have horrible memories of the event. Occasionally one of them will share such a memory, and it usually results in bad dreams for the youth unlucky enough to hear it. I steady myself, hoping that if this is just such a dream—of which I've had many—I'll wake up before the ground falls out from under me.

But I do not wake, and the ground remains firm. I hear my parents stir in the next room, followed by excited voices outside my window. People are leaving their beds and homes to gather in the square. I don't know what happened, but I know that whatever it is, it's big.

I pull on my boots and race out the door.

CHAPTER THREE

The Plane

OUTSIDE, EVERY MEMBER OF FORT THUNDER HAS GATHERED, SOLDIER AND civilian alike. They talk among themselves in hushed, frightened tones. I, however, am not frightened. I'm ready to face whatever's coming. Heck, I welcome it.

Papa Byrne arrives on the scene, his presence settling the crowd some. The Old Guard gather to him, flanking their leader as loyal soldiers should. Wilkes and Nagel are there as well as Jessup's shifty-eyed father, Mitchell. Rounding out the ranks is August—Gunnar's father. His nickname among the Old Guard is The Viking due to his height and Nordic appearance, a trait his son shares. The Christiansen family—August; his wife, Tif; their sons, Gunnar and future cadet William—are close friends of our family. Many nights we've spent in their company, playing games and enjoying Tif's cooking. My father likes to joke that her stews are better than my mother's, which is probably true. I envy the Christiansens—they always seem so happy to be in each other's company, and they never seem to squabble like we do. Sometimes I wish I was born into their family rather than mine, but then I feel guilty for wishing it.

The crowd grows quiet, anxious for answers. Papa Byrne steps forward, arms extended in a gesture of calm. "Easy, everyone," he assures. "No cause for alarm."

Alan Erickson, husband of Whitney and father of the twins, steps anxiously out of the crowd. "It sounded like a plane!"

This causes renewed worry and frightened mutterings, but all I feel is excitement. The thought of seeing a plane—those mythical machines that flew people across the skies—is enough to keep me up for days. And a plane actually landing on Deacon's Bluff? That was something I never imagined I would ever see.

And I yet may never see it. "We haven't had a plane fly over for nearly twenty years," Papa Byrne says, crushing my hopes while dampening the fear in the square. "There are no planes. Even if there were, there wouldn't be any fuel left to fly them."

Erickson doesn't seem convinced and mutters something to his wife. I catch Nagel eyeing him venomously. Nagel holds contempt for any man who isn't one of the Old Guard; if you're not a soldier, he's not interested in your opinion. Erickson's lucky that Nagel's not in charge because Nagel would probably knock his teeth in just for asking questions. Despite being a soldier myself, I'm grateful Nagel is not in charge.

"Probably just plates settling," Papa Byrne continues, sounding completely unconcerned. "Nothing to get worked up about. Go on back to your homes."

It doesn't wash with me one bit. We've had several minor quakes over the years, and that was not the sound of plates settling. What's worse is that I can tell Papa Byrne doesn't believe it either. He's lying, and the others are so desperate to believe it that they're taking his word at face value. There's a little more relieved talk, then the good citizens of Deacon's Bluff disperse and go back to their homes and their not-so-comfortable beds.

One person who seems as unconvinced as I am is my father. He and my mother share a questioning look, and my mother just shrugs and turns back to our home. Father catches me reading him and tries to distract me with a smile. "Come on, back to bed," he orders kindly.

He follows after my mother, and before I join them, I hesitate, scoping out the Old Guard.

Papa Byrne has gathered them off to the side, out of earshot, and is addressing them in a low, serious tone. Even from across the square, I can tell he's giving them classified orders.

On top of that I can tell that he's worried.

It is even harder to fall asleep than before. My mind is fixated on the noise and its questionable origin. Zombies are mindless and cannot fly planes, so I'm not worried about them. But marauders can fly planes— hostiles who would invade our island in the dead of night and try to breach our walls. I imagine that exact scenario, running defensive strategies in my mind, over and over, well past the point of drifting off to sleep. In my dreams men come at me in waves, rusted blades in hand, mouths full of stone-sharpened teeth. And I kill every last one of them.

I'm chewing the last of my breakfast cornbread when I arrive in the square the following morning. My cadets are there waiting.

"Papa Byrne says we gotta wait," Rafe reports.

Glancing up to the crow's nest, my heart sinks. Papa Byrne is up there, binoculars trained on the horizon. This can mean one thing only—that the Old Guard has taken first patrol from us. Whatever happened last night definitely has our general spooked.

"Did he say what's going on?"

"No, he didn't," Rafe answers flippantly. "Why don't you ask him?"

Rafe knows that I'm not going to ask Papa Byrne. Cadets are on a need-to-know basis when it comes to Old Guard maneuvers, and there are harsh consequences for asking too many questions. But Rafe sure would love to see me slip up.

Papa Byrne puts down his binoculars. "Gates!" he hollers. I nod to Gunnar, and we hustle to the iron winch that cranks open the main gates. Cranking the double-handed lever takes two men, assuring that no one can open the gates on their own. Gunnar and I are the only cadets strong enough to do it, and even for us it can be pretty hard.

The Old Guard shuffle in, looking tired. They're loaded down with serious hardware—AKs, M16s, StGs, Glocks. Except for Nagel, of course. All he carries is his compound bow.

Papa Byrne climbs down from the tower to debrief the men. Hushed words are exchanged, cautious glances thrown our way. Whatever is out there, the men don't want us to know about it.

"OK, boys," Papa Byrne says to the men, loud so we can hear. "Grab some grub. I'll join you in a minute." The Old Guard head for the mess, ready to chow down. Papa Byrne comes over to us, smiling. But I can tell he's got a lot on his mind.

"Is everything all right?" I ask.

"Fine," Papa Byrne answers. But I can tell he doesn't like that I'm asking. "All the same, no patrols for the cadets today. You're free to run exercises, but I don't want you straying far from the Fort. I don't want anyone slipping into a crevice kicked up in last night's tremor."

We've never had a tremor that was bad enough to form a crevice. He's hiding something, but I know better than to challenge him. "Roger that," I say.

He pats me warmly on the shoulder. "Normal patrols will resume in a day or so, after the men have done a thorough inspection of the area. Until then, stay close, and report to me if you notice anything out of the ordinary."

"Of course, sir."

He smiles, nods to the others, and goes to join his men in the mess hall. The cadets look to me for further instruction.

"Report back here at twelve hundred hours," I tell them.

I leave like I'm making for home but duck into an alley and double back around, coming up behind the mess hall. The windows there are always open as the kitchen gets really hot, even in winter. I hear the men talking inside, but I can't make out what they are saying. I crouch under one of the kitchen windows, nearest the voices.

"...passengers, it looked like."

That's Wilkes's voice—I'd recognize his sleepy drawl anywhere.

"...no survivors. All dead."

The words give me an excited chill. I have never set eyes on a person who was not a member of our community. The thought that someone could be out there—even a dead someone—is very exciting. And a little bit scary.

"Where?" I hear Papa Byrne ask.

"The bridge." Wilkes again. "As in stuck in it, on our side. Just hanging there like a goddamn Christmas ornament."

The bridge of which he speaks—the Densmore—is on the southeast tip of the island. I have never seen the Densmore or been to the southeast tip because it falls in the restricted zone. Cadets are absolutely never allowed to go to the restricted zone for any reason—hence the word *restricted*. I have always wanted to go there, of course, but I am a good soldier who does as he's told. But I am also curious, and today my curiosity might get the better of me.

"Well, did you take care of it?"

"It's jammed in real good. We'll need explosives," August says.

"So do it," Byrne says. "I want that thing gone."

"Right now, in the middle of the day?" Judging by the sour tone, I identify that voice as Nagel. "They'll hear the blast clear across the island."

"You have a better plan, Marcus?"

"Yeah, we hold off till early tomorrow, before sunrise. Tell them it's an aftershock. Hell, most of them will be too asleep to notice."

There's a silence as the plan is considered. I creep up toward the windowsill, straining to listen, intending to not miss a word.

Maya comes around the corner and sees me. She starts to open her mouth, but I raise my finger to my lips. Thankfully, she takes my cue to stay quiet.

"Fine, tomorrow at oh four hundred. And be quick about it. I'm running out of plausible explanations."

That's all I need to hear.

I slink away from the window and over to Maya. She clearly has questions, and I don't intend to answer them within earshot of the window. I take her by the arm and lead her into the maze of alleyways that separate the dwellings.

"What were you doing?" she whispers excitedly. "Spying?"

"Mind your own business, Maya."

"Like you were minding yours?" Maya is clever, which I appreciate when she isn't being a nuisance. She has steel-grey eyes and a wide, upturned nose, but I wouldn't say she is ugly. If she did something with her hair other than letting it hang in a tangled mess, she might even be pretty. But winning the attention of boys has never been important to Maya. "It's about the noise last night, isn't it?"

I give her a sharp look but only because I want to get her off my case. "I don't know what's going on, Maya." And it's the truth. I don't—but I do intend to find out. "If I were you, I'd be a little more careful about how I spend my free time."

"What's that supposed to mean?" she demands, hands on her hips.

"It means I've seen you out by the latrines, practicing with that slingshot."

She scowls and looks at her feet, knowing she'd catch hell if I squealed. I would never squeal—I'm not a rat—but others would. Rafe and Devon for certain. "Look, I don't care what you do," I say, keeping my voice low. "I think you're a pretty good shot, truth be told. But just watch out, OK? I'd hate to see you land yourself in hot water."

She gives me a smile, but it's not the flirty kind Tessa gives me. It's a smile of respect. I respect her, trust her even, but I don't want to fill her head with any silly notions. We exchange nods, I go my way, and Maya goes hers.

THE REST OF THE MORNING PASSES PAINFULLY SLOW. I CAN BARELY KEEP my mind on my job, retarring the roof in preparation for the coming winter. Several times I almost burn myself, and at one point I spill hot black goo on my newly resoled boots. But I don't care about the spill or the roof or my boots. All I care about is what I'm planning for later this afternoon.

After lunch I am excused, and I meet the other cadets in front of the gates. I tell Wilkes that we are going out for a game of capture the flag. He tells us to stay close to the Fort. I agree that we will. Satisfied at my word, he and August open the gates, and I march the cadets into the woods and out of the sightline of the south tower.

By a cluster of trees, I stop to brief my squad. "Change of plans. We're going to check out the southeast quad today."

This sends out a nervous wave, like an electric jolt from the generators we keep tucked behind the armory. Rafe steps forward in a huff. "But that's restricted."

"I'm well aware of that, Rafe."

He looks to the others for support, but they don't know what to make of my orders. "You're out of your mind. Papa Byrne specifically ordered us to stay close to the Fort."

"I know what Papa Byrne said." I stand tall to project the confidence of my conviction. I'm not the tallest of us, that distinction would fall to the junior Viking, but I'm broad shouldered and can look imposing when I want to. "If we're going to show the Old Guard that we have the stones to lead, we're going to have to start acting on our own initiative. Sometimes that might mean disobeying the occasional restriction."

"It wasn't a restriction; it was an *order*."

Rafe is going to fight me on this, as I knew he would. In fairness, I'd do the same if I were him. So I change my approach. "Aren't any of you the least bit curious to see what's out there?"

You don't live on this island your whole life without getting curious about the restricted zone, especially if you're a boy. By the excited looks on most of their faces, my appeal to their sense of adventure is working.

But not on Jessup. "We know what's out there," he protests, trying to mask the cowardly rise of his voice. "Nothing."

"So why is it restricted?"

"You know why!" Jessup's heart is practically leaping out of his throat. "That's where the jetty is, and there's been zombies spotted out on the jetty!"

"Have you ever seen a zombie, Jessup?" I scan down the rest of their faces. "Have any of you ever seen a zombie?" Glances are exchanged; heads are shaken. Of course no one has.

"Wouldn't you *like* to see a zombie?"

An awed hush comes over them as they consider my challenge. I sense excitement, but I also sense what Jessup has been so desperate to hide—fear. The challenge is to their manhood, and that's the one thing that might be able to trump the word of Papa Byrne. A soldier must prove that he is a man, that he is worthy of the cause, and a man must show courage. Fear is the enemy, more than any hostile, zombie, or marauder.

It's a risky play should Rafe choose to squeal on me. Thankfully, no one has respect for a squealer, and Rafe knows it.

"I'll go it alone then." Proving that I have the stones to do as I say, I make south toward the jetty. I'm fifteen paces into the woods when a voice pipes in behind me.

"I'll go," says the voice. Distinctly female, but boyishly cocky. I turn to see Maya step out from behind a tree that stands between myself and the cadets. The boys are slack-jawed to find a girl roaming free outside of the Fort.

"Jaysus, Maya." Cursing will land you in real trouble with the elders, so we've gotten into the habit of making new words out of the forbidden ones. Not that anyone gives much a care for Jesus at Fort Thunder. "How'd you get past the gate?"

"She dug a tunnel out by the latrines that goes clear under the wall," says Seth. Maya shoots Seth a glance that is equal parts venom and shame. The thought of tunneling into the soft, soaked ground by the latrines is enough to make the toughest gut queasy. Not to mention the godawful smell. It seems Tessa's criticism of Maya's personal hygiene wasn't that out of line.

"Look, don't rat, OK?" Maya doesn't have the warmest relationship with her father, especially since her mother passed a few years back. Old Wilkes has been a frosty presence ever since then, even on the best of days. His dreams of a proper son died with Marcy Wilkes, and his daughter was poor consolation. The fact that Maya is such a tomboy only seems to make matters worse, as if her masculinity only rubs salt in the wound.

"Get outta here, dyke." Leave it to Devon to be the first to open his fat, stupid mouth. The other boys snicker at his name-calling, but I don't find it the least bit funny. That's the sort of tossed-off remark that leads to rumors, and rumors lead to accusations, and accusations lead to banishment. I shoot the bastard a look so withering it makes him flinch, quivering his jowls.

"Maya can stay," I say in no uncertain terms.

Rafe's eyes widen with protest. "You can't be serious!"

"She's more a man than any of you." I look to Maya to see if I've offended her, and judging by the smile on her face, I haven't. There might even be a hint of pride. "Come on," I say to her. Then I turn and head south into the woods. Maya follows. Like a good soldier.

I don't look back, but I hear the sound of boots falling in line behind us. Less than a minute later, we are a unit fully on the march. I push us forward, head held confident and high, showing no fear or falter in my stride.

But there is a part of me—a tiny part—that is just as afraid as the others.

THE JOURNEY TO THE SOUTHEAST QUAD IS NOT AN EASY ONE. THERE IS A trail, but years of disuse have left it overgrown and treacherous. Not even the Old Guard comes this way very often. But I can tell they have recently because of freshly hacked branches and underbrush. I don't carry a machete, but Rafe does and is only too happy to hack at anything that gets in our way. He's welcome to it if that's what he needs to work out his aggression, but I'm sure he'd be even happier to swing that blade at my neck.

We come to the rock ravine that webs across our island like a burst capillary. Up near the Fort the rock takes the form of mighty boulders, but farther south it diminishes into loose shale, jagged and brittle, crunching beneath our boots as we walk. I like the noise—it accentuates the steady drum of our march. If we were bombed-out savages, like the people on the mainland, we might use the shards of shale for weapons, spears and clubs and such. But we aren't savages, and if there's one thing that isn't in short supply at Fort Thunder, it's weapons.

We follow the shale up an incline, which is dangerous as the crumbling rock tends to shoot out from under your feet. Gunnar is reminded of this the hard way when it does just that, landing him hard on his ass. No one but me dares to laugh. Surprisingly, the one person who never seems unsure of her footing is Maya. She takes the incline like she's been climbing all of her life, scampering effortlessly to the top. Some of the boys grumble as she goes, muttering "show-off" under their breath. All I can do is smile and admire her.

Catching up to Maya, the rest of us reach the flat terrain that waits at the top of the incline. Here we reach our last stop before the restricted zone, a small cluster of cabins that have fallen into disuse. Only one of them still has all four walls standing, the old ranger station. It was a government outpost back in the day. At least, that's how Papa Byrne tells it. Even in its heyday it couldn't have been much, and now it barely qualifies as a structure. Most of us boys have wanted to explore here at one time or another, but our parents only allow it under their supervision. This place is used as an example of everything we fled from, and going on past this point is strictly and passionately forbidden.

Beyond the ranger station is the road—or what's left of it, at least. Standing before its cracked and crumbling pathway, I feel a sense of unease I know is shared by the others. This is the point of no return. As far as any of us has ever gone.

"This is it," I say to the others. "There's no turning back after this point."

To my surprise I get no objections, not even from Rafe. "All right then," I nod.

Together, we walk down the road. Around us, the woods are quiet except for the sound of leaves being rustled by the wind. We travel long minutes, no hostiles or zombies leaping out to attack. After all these years it's strangely anticlimactic. It's really just a road.

Ahead of us, the sound of crashing waves signals the coming of the cliffs. Soon the forest gives way, opening up to a wide expanse of sky. We arrive at the cliffs, coming to stand before a sheer sixty-foot drop into jagged, angry rocks. Ocean waves crash against the cliffside only to be sucked back into the crevices, the sound of a giant monster smacking its lips. One look over the edge is more than enough for me, but some of the others can't seem to resist, laughing and making a game of it. Devon scares Seth by pretending to push him over, but one look from me and he doesn't do it again. This is no place to fool around.

To the south, along the cliffs, a rust-brown monolith beckons. Even though none of us have seen it before, there can be no mistaking it. The mere excitement of it picks up the pace of the march, rushing us toward its ancient glory. A legend we have only known in whispers.

Maya speaks for us all when she says, "Wow."

What stands before us is a monument to a world passed into ruin. The Densmore Bridge connected Deacon's Bluff to the mainland by a kilometer of concrete and steel cable, and from what I know of bridges, it was not particularly impressive. But it survived the Great Shake well enough to allow our trucks and conveyances to pass over from the mainland, and when we were safely on this side, our parents blew the thing sky high. With the threat of zombies and invading hostiles, it was the sensible thing to do. Destroying the bridge severed our ties to the old world, and if any of the adults regret that decision, I have never heard it voiced. What remains of it is a tangled ruin of metal and cable, a frame of girders rising into the air before plummeting into the bay. Seeing it at last fills me with a sense of awe, but that awe soon gives way to wistfulness. I wish I could have seen the bridge in its true glory, carrying cars across its proud thoroughfare.

I signal for the others to hang back as I approach what was once the on-ramp and is now just the crumbling stump of a severed limb. Through the shroud of bay fog, I can barely make out the shadow of the mainland and the wreckage that sits on the other side. I cannot see below, not from this vantage point, but I know what's down there—a treacherous jetty of ruined bridge that snakes across the bay, petering out before reaching the far shore. Our campfire stories tell of zombies, flesh-eating lepers who lurk on the jetty, but stories don't scare me. I grab hold of a jutting piece of rebar and lean over the edge, ready for whatever horror waits below.

Not horror, but unexpected nonetheless.

At first, I don't know what it is I'm looking at. A massive, silvery cylinder is wedged into the cliff, held in place by a cradle of gnarled girders and metalwork. I lean out farther, craning to get a better look, noting the long, flat panels that hang there, tethered to the body by remnants of wire and frame. The tip of the cylinder is tapered to a dull point where a flat black windshield sits, cracked but unbroken. I try to get a look inside, but the sunlight glints off of it, blinding me.

A plane. What's left of one, anyway. I've seen pictures of them in Father's books.

Despite my not giving the go-ahead, the others approach the drop. I am too dumbstruck to reprimand them. The bravest of them, Gunnar and Maya, join me right at the edge.

"What is it?" Gunnar asks.

"It's a plane," I answer.

Excitement spreads like a nervous fire. Before anyone can do anything risky or stupid, I address my unit, stone-faced. "Nobody makes a move until I say, understand? Don't even get too close to the edge. The last thing we need is for someone to fall."

"We need to go back," Rafe says. "We need to report this."

"But we're not supposed to be here," whines Devon. "We're gonna be in so much trouble when they find out."

We all exchange looks. None of us have been in a situation like this before, and I need to assert my leadership before dissention is allowed to take root.

"Papa Byrne already knows," I say. Stunned silence follows.

"What do you mean he already *knows*?" Rafe scoffs out the words, as if the very notion that our elders would mislead us is beyond ridiculous.

"Why do you think the Old Guard took first patrol this morning, Rafe? This was the noise we all heard last night. They know about this plane. I heard them talking about it."

Rafe would like to challenge my assertion, but he knows what I'm saying makes sense. The only question now is what we do about it. I am of a mind to keep it a secret, to make the cadets swear an oath of silence and let the Old Guard handle it without ever knowing we were here. But then Maya points to the plane, and everything is out the window.

"There's something moving down there!"

Again, I gaze over the edge. At first I notice nothing...

Then I see it—a shadow moving behind the glass. The cockpit behind the windshield is dark, and I can't get a good look, but there can be no mistake.

There is something moving inside the plane. Something alive.

The cliffside is composed of loose soil and rock, so I test it with my boot to make sure I can make the downward climb. Confident that it will hold, I begin my descent, but before I can get far, Rafe grabs ahold of my arm.

"What the hell do you think you're doing?"

"There's somebody in there." I yank my arm away. "I'm going to get them out. You just wait here and do nothing. That's what you're good at."

My words sting enough to release his hand from my arm, and with no further protest I lower myself over the edge of the cliff. It is only a couple of meters down to the plane, but the drop is nothing to laugh at. The odd girder and jutting piece of rebar help with the descent, and where there is no skeleton to navigate, I find crevices in the rock. Still, I am careful not to get cocky. One false move and I am pulp on the jetty below.

A few heart-jumping moves and I arrive at the plane. Through the cracked windshield I see a pair of figures slumped in the cockpit. Two adults —a man and a woman. Their eyes stare blankly back at me from the shadows, and I know that I am looking at a pair of corpses. Death is not something the youth are sheltered from at the Fort, and I have seen a handful of dead bodies over the years, but never the dead bodies of outsiders.

Any hope of this being a rescue mission begins to fade. Maya and I must have seen something moving in the settling plane. Crestfallen, I begin to climb back up...

WHACK! Something slaps against the passenger window, nearly causing me to lose my hold on the cliff. Steadying myself, I turn to the sound. A few meters down the fuselage is a small, round window, presumably for a passenger. Inside, pressed up against the glass, is a bloody hand. It moves slowly downward, smearing a five-fingered trail of red.

The fuselage is smooth and featureless save for a hatch near the cockpit. I reach for the small lever recessed in the hatch and pull, opening it. A hiss of air escapes from the cabin, and I flinch back reflexively. The hatch lifts open.

A blast of odor hits me, the nauseating smell of decay. My every instinct screams not to enter, but the thought of someone in danger presses me forward, into the darkness of the plane. My eyes adjust, and I am able to make out some semblance of the interior—clean lines, smooth plastic, and gleaming metal. To my left I can see the cockpit and the bodies slumped there, heads cocked at unnatural angles.

To my right is a narrow row of seats, and one of them has a body strapped into it.

A girl.

My heart jumps several beats. The girl is unconscious, her hand pressed absently against the window. She appears to be close to my age. From the rise and fall of her chest, I can tell that she is breathing, that she is alive. Injured, in shock, but very much alive.

The plane shifts, and I steady myself against the smooth, concave walls. I move toward the girl, and the plane groans, the ballast of my weight pulling it free of the girders, inch by inch. With every step, I risk pushing it right out of its cradle and off the cliff.

But I won't abandon my mission. I will not leave her to die.

Step after step I move—slow, cautious—down the aisle to where the girl lies strapped in her seat. One step more and the fuselage pitches forward, sending my stomach to my throat. I am sure we're going down, right to the jagged floor of the jetty. But the plane pitches back, rebalancing, righting itself like a seesaw. I draw a quiet, grateful breath.

A quick step farther and I am crouched before the girl, close enough to feel the faintness of her breath. She smells sweet, like the berries my mother picks in summer.

She is buckled in by some sort of strap, and it takes me a moment to free it from her narrow waist. I pull her into my arms, feeling the strange quality of her clothing. The jacket she wears is pink and soft and has a hood built into it; it feels comfortable enough to sleep in. Her pants are sleek and formfitting as if made for her alone, not passed down and repurposed like what I am wearing. For the first time in my life, I recognize the crude functionality of my faded, well-worn attire.

The plane groans again, and I curse myself for losing focus. If I don't get us out of here soon, we'll be trapped in the plane as it falls. I pull the girl out of her seat, sling her arm over my shoulder, and walk the both of us slowly toward the hatch. With every step, the plane protests like a waking beast, moaning its displeasure at our movement.

We reach the hatch, stepping through to the waiting cliffside. No sooner have I pulled my unconscious cargo through than the plane pitches forward, coming loose from the girders and starting to plunge. My free hand grips a rock jutting from the wall of the cliff, and the plane falls with a thundering protest. I don't look down.

Four heartbeats later—I feel them hammer in my chest—and there comes a deafening crash of metal on rocks. I pull my body and the girl's close to the rock, praying that the crash doesn't start an avalanche. Seconds pass. The cliffside holds.

The girl stirs in my arms, moaning in the grips of a dream. For some reason, this makes me laugh. I think I'm just thrilled to still be alive.

I look up and see the astonished faces of my cadets (and Maya) looking down at me. Looking down at *us*, I should say. They look as surprised at our survival as I am.

"A little help," I croak.

At Gunnar's lead, the cadets quickly form a human chain, and Maya, being the lightest, is sent down to be my link. She doesn't hesitate a second. She repels down nimbly, reaching where I cling, and I let go of the stone to grab hold of her hand. Maya catches me, and we lock elbow to elbow. I give her a grateful smile. "Thanks," I say.

"No problem," she answers.

Gunnar calls to pull, and after some serious grunting they manage to pull me and my living cargo up the cliffside to level ground. Once the girl is taken from my arms, I collapse onto my knees and laugh. I have never been so grateful for steady earth. I want to kiss it.

The others are gathered around the girl, gawking, understandably curious. I collect myself to stand and push through them to get a better look at her myself.

My first thought is that she is beautiful. In the soft light of afternoon, her hair seems silver, like a halo fanning out around her head. I have never seen hair that color before. Her skin is a deep, even tan and free of any blemish, except for the dusting of freckles across the bridge of her nose. Her cheekbones, high and rounded, give her the appearance of a sculpture or painting. Her lips are full and perfectly pink. I've been looking at her for almost a minute when I realize that I've forgotten to breathe.

"She's alive," I inform the others. "Gather some wood to make a stretcher."

Rafe shoots me a furious look. "We are *not* bringing her back!"

"Yes. We are."

"This is insane! You can't do this!"

"I can and will. And if you fight me on this, I'm going to report you for insubordination." I turn to the others. "Does anyone else have an objection?"

They don't. A team immediately sets out to gather wood for a stretcher. Even Jessup and Devon seem willing to help. Recognizing that he has no support, Rafe grumbles and joins in with the others. Minutes later and we are ready for the journey home.

I can only imagine the trouble we'll face when we get there.

CHAPTER FOUR

The Girl

THE TRIP TO THE RESTRICTED ZONE WAS A CAKEWALK COMPARED TO THE trip back. Our dead-to-the-world passenger adds an extra challenge to the journey, making it difficult to navigate the cliffs and ravines, boulders and densely forested areas. On a high hill Gunnar nearly loses his grip and sends the stretcher tumbling, but thankfully Maya steps in to assist. Rafe insists on taking over at the head of the stretcher, so I agree to swap Gunnar out, and I can tell it bruises my friend's ego a bit. I remain at the foot of the stretcher the whole way as this entire rescue mission is ultimately my responsibility. Rafe does a good job of navigating the terrain, but I suspect his desire to get close to the girl is his primary motivating factor. That and to prove himself my equal.

By the time we near the Fort, my arms and shoulders are hurting bad, and I'm afraid that I may have pulled a muscle in my back and neck. Before we are in eyesight of the tower, I call the unit to a halt and lower the stretcher. I give Maya a look, and she nods, leaving us and sneaking off, back into the Fort the way she came. If she is spotted with us, she'll be in deep trouble, and nothing I might say will be of any use. But one thing is for sure—if I had respect for Maya Wilkes before today, I have twice the respect for her now.

"Now listen up," I say to the boys. "I don't expect anyone else to take the heat for this. This was my call, and I will face the consequences alone."

"Yeah right, that'll happen," Rafe grouses sarcastically. "We'll all take the fall for this, and you know it."

Unfortunately, he is probably right. A quick read of their faces tells me what I already know—that no one is too thrilled by the threat of punishment. But we have been trained to accept consequences as a team, and I see a sense of resolve travel from person to person. It is Gunnar, my brave Viking friend, who finally speaks up.

"We couldn't have left her there. She would have died for sure. I wouldn't want that on my conscience."

His words carry weight with the cadets, even the ones who don't like me. He could probably inspire more loyalty in them if he was chosen to be leader or if he wanted to lead. But he wasn't, and he doesn't.

"Fine then," Rafe concedes. "We stand together on this. But this was Bowie's call; we were all just following orders."

"Agreed," I say. I look to the others. "Are we good?"

The others nod, silently accepting the pact. Rafe and I pick up the stretcher, and with the last of our strength, we press for the gates.

Wilkes is manning the crow's nest, and his eyes nearly fall out of their sockets when he sees what we're carrying. He lets loose a shrill whistle, and seconds later the gates are cranked open. An air horn sounds, a signal for the militia to meet us inside the gates. Dread ties a knot in my stomach. The air horn is always a bad sign.

We haul the stretcher the last leg of the journey, laying it down just inside the gates. There is a buzz in the air almost immediately. It's been years, more than a decade, since anyone here has laid eyes on an outsider. Kids swarm around us excitedly, grasping at the girl's hair, wanting to touch her pleasantly textured clothing. I swat them away with my hands and harsh words, shooing them off like frightened little animals.

The nearest of the adults drop their duties and rush to our aid, but when they realize that the injured party is a stranger, they devolve into an anxious mob. There's a lot of fearful whispering of "hostiles" and "intruders" as panic spreads like wildfire. Some insist on crowding, and I am forced to shove them away. Thankfully, Wilkes climbs down from the tower and assists me in controlling them.

Before things can escalate further, Papa Byrne is on the scene, flanked by August and Nagel. The crowd sees him coming and wisely clears a path. It takes his militia-honed mind only a moment to realize what is going on. After a hard-nosed inspection of the stretcher and its female occupant, Papa Byrne directs his steely blue eyes at me.

"What the hell is going on here, Bowie?"

There aren't many people who can truly intimidate me, but Papa Byrne is one of them. "We found her on the bridge." My voice betrays me, cracking like an adolescent. "There was a plane. We pulled her out of it..."

The anger rises in his face, and I can tell that he wants to yell, dress me down in front of everyone. But his words come out measured and calm. "What were you doing at the bridge?"

"Papa Byrne, sir—"

"Don't *sir* me, boy." I have never seen Papa Byrne this angry, never heard such disappointment toward me in his voice. "You are not to go into the restricted zone. That has always been a standing order, not to mention that I expressly stated that you were not to wander far from the Fort. You disobeyed a *direct order*. What possible justification could you have?"

I open my mouth to make more excuses but think better of it. The best strategy now is to keep my mouth shut and let this admonishment run its course. "This girl is a hostile, Bowie," he continues, "and by letting her inside our gates, you may have given away our position. Did you even think of that?"

"No," I admit. Shame flushes my face.

"Clearly not." He ends the sentence with a withering scowl, and I see that something has changed in his eyes, the way he looks at me. I am no longer the son he has always wanted, and he, no longer the father I wish mine could be. Now he is just my superior. Now he is just Byrne.

He turns to his men. "Take her outside," he barks. "She's not staying here."

August and Nagel are moving in to lift the stretcher as my father and mother arrive on the scene. At the sight of the unconscious girl, my father goes right into crisis mode.

"What's going on here, Patrick?"

"*Your son* brought a hostile through our gates," Byrne answers sharply, as if Father is complicit in my actions. "Now step aside so we can take her back outside."

My father does not step aside. "She looks injured!"

Byrne is getting visibly annoyed. "Her injuries are not our problem," he says dismissively, "and I intend to keep it that way."

Knowing better than to challenge Byrne in front of his men, my father takes him gently aside. "Patrick," he says, keeping his voice low, "this girl is Tessa's age."

"I'm sure there are plenty of hostiles Tessa's age. Younger even! What do you propose we do, Harlan? Take all of them in? Let them set up camp inside of our gates?"

"That's not what I'm saying, Patrick."

"Then what *are* you saying?"

"I'm asking you to show some *compassion*," my father implores. "At least let the Seavers have a look at her before we turn her out into the cold."

Patrick Byrne is not known for his charity, especially where the safety of the Fort is concerned. But he also doesn't want to seem needlessly cruel in front of his people; he has often told me that cruelty is not the best way to lead. "Fine. But this is on your shoulders, Harlan. You and your boy's. Are we clear?"

My father looks to me, and I accept my responsibility with a nod. There is a glint in his eyes that I haven't seen often of late—pride. It catches me off guard, but I'd be a liar if I said that it didn't make me feel good.

Byrne pivots back to his men. "Change of plans. Bring her to the infirmary, and let the Seavers have a look at her. Let's see what we're dealing with here."

Nagel and August lift the stretcher, Nagel muttering curses. Under Byrne's watchful eye they carry it to the infirmary, where Doc Seaver is already waiting at the door, his hard-lined face a perpetual mask of worry. The stretcher is carried inside, and the door closed quickly behind it. Byrne stands outside, fending off the crowd of gawkers.

"All right, everyone, that's enough excitement for now. Go back to your duties. We've got the situation well in hand."

As the crowd gradually disperses, my mother comes over, taking my hand. We stand together, mother, father, and son united as a front. I can't remember the last time I felt this close to my family. It gives me a strength I never knew I needed. It gives me the courage to face the judgment of my peers.

And judgment will be severe, of that there is no doubt. I can see it on Tessa's face, glaring from across the square.

Before going inside the infirmary, Byrne assigns Mitchell, Jessup's father, to stand watch at the door, and he takes to the task with puffed-up authority. The infirmary has a small window that opens out into the rear alley, and I consider sneaking back there to eavesdrop, but too many eyes are focused on me right now, two of them belonging to Tessa. As the crowd awaits more news, she corners me, riddling me with questions. *Why was I in the restricted zone? Who is this girl?* All questions I do not have satisfactory answers for, nor would I give them to her if I did. I'm just about to lose my patience and possibly say something I will later regret when Byrne storms out of the infirmary, eyes blazing. He motions gruffly for his daughter to come away from me, and I wonder if he is reconsidering our betrothal. That is one silver lining to this cloud that I hadn't considered.

Tired of everyone throwing me dirty looks, I make for the firing range. I'm not really in the mood to shoot, but I need something to take my mind off of things. Cutting through the alleys, I run smack into Maya, who still reeks from crawling back in by the latrines. After giving her a brief recap, she asks the seven-dollar question.

"So. Are you in hot water or what?"

"I reckon so."

"Do you think Papa Byrne will demote you?"

"Couldn't say. That'd sure make Rafe happy though."

Maya's jaw clenches, and she nods in commiseration. Rafe's ambitions are no secret to anyone with a pair of eyes. "Watch out for that one," she advises. "Tessa too."

It's no surprise that Maya has no love for Tessa—what's surprising is that Maya has correctly identified Tessa as a threat. "Tessa has no authority," I say dismissively.

"She has her father's ear. If daddy's little girl feels threatened, she can put ideas in his head, get him to do things he normally wouldn't." Glancing around quickly, paranoid, she lowers her voice. "You don't know how girls can be, Bowie. Boys fight with their fists, but girls find ways to hurt that are far worse than brawling. We fight dirty. Cut deeper."

She's got a good point. I don't have the greatest grasp on the way girls think, but I'm a fast learner. And it helps to have a friend on the inside. I don't want to insult Maya, to pry where I shouldn't, but I can't help but be curious about her. "Tell me something," I ask. "Why are you so different from the other girls?"

She shrugs, not bothered by the question. "Born that way, I guess. I just never cared about the things girls care about. Dolls. Dresses. Boys."

I am not attracted to Maya, but it's not because she is ugly. If she cleaned up and did something with her hair, she'd be as pretty as most of the girls on the bluff. Maya is like a little sister to me, but more importantly, she is a friend—I would never want sex and all of that messy stuff to come between us. I'm glad that she has no interest in me, but I do wish she would show some interest in *someone*—a nice guy like Seth for instance—even if it was just for show. It could be very dangerous for Maya if it got out that she didn't like boys, a fact that I'm sure she's aware of. All of the children are expected to pair off and eventually mate, and anyone who rejects that decree stands the risk of being declared *redundant*.

And trust me, you do not want to be declared redundant at Fort Thunder.

"You're the only one I could ever trust with that information," she tells me. I'm glad she realizes that, glad she trusts me. "I can't even tell my own father."

It's a sad fact, but she's right not to tell him. Wilkes is a good man, and I believe he loves his daughter dearly, but he also is a man who believes deeply in the law. And redundancy is the law that we hold high above all others, even the law of the gun. All members of Fort Thunder must be useful to the community; there is no room for freeloaders and those who won't carry their weight. For women, unfortunately, the chief duty they are assigned is the proliferation of our people. They must reproduce. If a woman is unable to reproduce, or if she refuses, she is banished from Fort Thunder and sent out into the wilderness. I have never witnessed this in all my years, but there is a first time for everything, and I don't want the first time to be Maya.

Then again, if any girl could survive out there with the zombies and the hostiles, it would be this one. But that doesn't mean we should push our luck.

"One day, things could be different, Maya. Our parents won't always be in charge. If I play my cards right, I'll be running this place in a little while."

"Yeah, well, right now I wouldn't be so sure," she says with a ribbing smile, "but if anyone *could* change things, it'd be you, Bowie."

I smile back and offer her a closed fist—the gesture cadets use to express our bond and solidarity. This is the first time, in the history of Fort Thunder, that it has been shared with a girl.

Maya makes a fist, and we bump knuckles. Then we go our separate ways without another word.

I come home to find Mother waiting for me, as anticipated. She is worried about the predicament I am in but understanding as to why I chose to rescue the girl.

"We have to tread lightly here, Bowie," she advises. "I know your heart is in the right place, but this is a delicate matter. The last time strangers came to Fort Thunder, things did not go smoothly. It nearly tore our community apart."

"This is different," I say. "These aren't some savages coming at our gates. This is a girl. She's alone. She didn't mean to be here—"

"I understand that, Son. But it doesn't matter what her intentions are or how she got here. It doesn't matter that she looks pretty and seems harmless. To the others she is a threat."

I start to say something but decide that it isn't worth the effort. My mother looks at me with eyes that seem to understand something that I don't. It's not a look I enjoy. "She is pretty, isn't she?" Mother continues.

"Yeah, I guess."

She smiles, and now I understand that look. "There's nothing wrong with what you're feeling. She's something different than what you're used to. That can be a powerful thing."

"I'm not attracted to her," I say defensively. "She was hurt and was going to die if we didn't help. I made the call, and I'll live with the consequences. How she looks has nothing to do with it."

That seems to satisfy Mother, even if neither of us believe a word of it.

Father arrives home a little over an hour later, fresh from his meeting with the council. He looks more exhausted than usual, painful lines etched into his face. He plays it off as just the usual stress that comes with council meetings, but Mother and I both know that the headaches are part of it. But truthfully, right now, I care more to hear what is to become of the girl.

"She'll live," Father reports when I ask. "Doc says her wounds are superficial, just some cuts and bruises. He thinks that she'll regain consciousness by morning."

"Do you think she'll be able to stay?" I'm trying not to sound too interested, but judging from my mother's raised eyebrow, I am failing.

"I think I can negotiate a few days for her," Father answers, wearily taking his seat at the head of the table, "but it's liable to get ugly. Patrick is none too thrilled with this, to say the least. And the Old Guard will stand with him."

I take a seat at the table. "And what did they say about me?"

"Whatever your punishment, I don't think it will be too severe."

My father reads the relief on my face. "No one questions your motives, Son," he assures me. "You saw someone in trouble, and you acted. But you broke the law to do it, and that has consequences. You may be on latrine duty for the better part of your eighteenth year."

While the prospect of hauling human waste is no treat, it is hardly the worst hand I could be dealt. "And what about my standing as captain?"

"I wouldn't worry too much about that." My father pushes an auburn lock back on his head. "Rafe Nagel is rash and impulsive. It's no oversight that he wasn't promoted to captain over you. Some boys just aren't fit to be leaders. Gunnar is a more suitable replacement, but he doesn't have the passion or tactical mind that you have. It would be foolish to strip you of your rank over this, and Patrick knows it. Nothing matters more to him than the militia, and the cadets are the militia's future. I can't say for certain, but I am fairly confident that your standing as cadet leader is secure." Then he added, "For now, anyway."

I catch myself breathing a sigh of relief. My father seems glad, even though I know he wouldn't mind if my military career was sidelined. I appreciate him putting his personal feelings aside for the sake of my happiness. We seem to be making some progress on that front.

Still, there is no cause for celebration. "Bowie, all eyes are on you now—not just Patrick Byrne but the council as well. The entire community. None of this is being taken lightly. If you push this further than you already have, there won't be a second chance. Do you understand?"

"Yes, Father."

"Good." He smiles, but it seems forced, strained. The headaches again, or maybe he's more afraid than he lets on. Either way, our conversation has ended.

We have supper, then I go to my room and spend some effort trying to sleep. All I can think about is that strange hair, spreading like a halo, so silky and silver. How would it feel to run my hands through it? I wonder. My wondering fades into a dream of the woods and a soft hand in mine as we pass among the trees. I don't need to see a face to know it is her.

THE FOLLOWING MORNING, I AM UP AT THE CRACK OF DAWN. MY PARENTS and I arrive in the square to find most of the others already gathered. There is a lot of whispered talk about the hostile in the infirmary, that she has regained consciousness and will face interrogation. It would appear that my mother's prediction of fearful mistrust has proven spot on.

Byrne arrives flanked by the Old Guard, looking ready for a military tribunal. His eyes are fixed on me, still judging me harshly, and the pit growing in my stomach drops even deeper. Seeing this, Father puts a supportive hand on my shoulder, letting me know that whatever comes, we stand together. But he cannot shield me from that eviscerating glare.

The door to the infirmary opens, and a hush comes over the crowd. Doc Seaver and Frankie emerge, leading the girl between them like a frightened child. Awake, her face shows an intelligence I couldn't see before, a mind that is working and alert, taking in the situation and trying to make sense of it. Her clear blue eyes scan over our faces, like a spotlight rooting out invaders in the dark, and I wonder if she recognizes me from the rescue, even though I know that is highly unlikely. That hair, still as shiny and silver as I remembered, is pulled tightly back from her face in a knot. Her arm is bandaged, and there are some superficial cuts and bruises on her face, but otherwise she seems in good health. That's good because if there's one thing that earns you respect in Fort Thunder, it's being a survivor.

Byrne, however, does not seem impressed. He steps toward her, hand on the holstered pistol at his hip as if ready to draw. The girl swallows nervously at the sight of the gun. From what I know of the savage tribes, they do not possess the sort of superior firepower we do, so her reaction is understandable. But then I think of the plane, so refined and sleek, and have a tough time imagining that thing piloted by savages. The formfitting clothes she came in with have been traded for some of the girls' castoffs, but even in fatigues and patched leather, this girl comes off as otherworldly, sophisticated. If this is what the savage tribes look like, the picture I have carried in my mind all these years has been very, very wrong.

All Byrne seems to see is a potential enemy. To her credit, the girl tries to stand tall as his shadow falls over her. As we all wait for Byrne to speak, the square is silent.

"I'm told you speak English," he states flatly. "Is that correct?"

"Yes," the girl answers.

Immediately the crowd begins to chatter, but Nagel turns, intimidating them into silence. He has that effect on people. Byrne gives him a silent nod of approval before continuing.

"What is your name?" he asks the girl.

"Alexis. Alexis Jarrell."

Alexis. Now the mystery has a name.

"What are you doing here, Alexis Jarrell?" Byrne's voice has taken on exasperation, as if his time is being wasted by this intrusion. "Why did you trespass on our territory?"

"Trespass?" There is genuine confusion in her voice as well as fear. "We weren't 'trespassing' anywhere. We were on our way north to visit my grandparents. They are getting really old, and we're thinking it's time to—"

"There's nothing north of here but snow and cannibal tribes," Byrne interrupts. "I think that you're lying and that you've been sent here as a spy."

"What are you talking about?" Alexis says defiantly. "And where are my parents?"

Byrne holds his cold eyes on her, then turns to address me. "Bowie, why don't you tell your new friend here what you found when you rescued her?"

I am suddenly flush with nervousness. Not because my superior is putting me on the spot but because my first words to this girl are going to greatly upset her. Somehow, without even knowing her, I find myself not wanting to make her sad. But I step forward, stern-faced, and do what I am asked.

"There were two other bodies in the plane. They died in the crash. Even if they hadn't, once the plane came loose from the bridge and fell to the jetty, they would have." I look to Alexis and do my best to soften my face. "I'm sorry."

Alexis looks into my face, but her eyes don't seem to register me. "Oh god," she stammers, falling to her knees. "Oh god..."

The sobs come freely, and they only seem to further irritate Byrne. But the rest of the crowd—save Nagel, of course—are visibly affected. Most of us are hardened, but there aren't many among us who enjoy the sound of a woman crying. It's a sound that reminds us of the times we've had to bury our own.

This goes on for uncomfortable minutes. Byrne remains unmoved; he probably thinks that it's all for show. "That's enough," he says, grabbing her arm and hauling her up. "If you think a show of crocodile tears is going to save you, think again."

But the truth is even the Old Guard, Wilkes especially, are showing signs of distress at the crying. You know it's bad if tough old Wilkes is upset. "Is all this really necessary, Patrick?" he asks.

This earns him stink eyes from both Byrne and Nagel, and it looks like things could get ugly between them. I want to step in and side with Wilkes, but I remember my mother's warning and stay quiet. My father, however, has no such compunction. He steps forward.

"It's clear this poor girl has arrived here by accident and has suffered trauma, not to mention tragedy. There is nothing to indicate that she is a spy or means us harm in any way."

"Wolves in sheep's clothing," is the answer Byrne has for my father.

"I wish you could hear how paranoid that sounds," Father fires back.

"Paranoia has kept this community safe for nearly twenty years, so I'll take that as a compliment."

Byrne's words get nods and mutters of support from the crowd. More of that sort of grandstanding and any ground my father hopes to gain will be lost. "Be that as it may," Father says by way of deflection, "we do not settle matters in this community through interrogation and fear. This matter demands a full meeting of the council, so I'm calling one immediately. In the meantime"—he looks to Alexis, offering sympathy—"get this poor girl something to eat."

CHAPTER FIVE

The Meeting

ALEXIS IS WHISKED AWAY BY THE WOMEN, MY MOTHER INCLUDED, WHILE the men adjourn to the armory for the council meeting. This leaves me with my disgruntled cadets and an even more disgruntled girlfriend, Tessa. She immediately starts in.

"She's not as ugly as I expected, for a hostile. But that hair is gross."

"She's not a hostile, Tessa," I say sharply.

Her eyes flash with rage. "You like her, don't you?" Her hands tense, her fingers curling as if readying to claw out my eyes. "I could see it written all over your face! You *like her*!"

"Don't be stupid."

That does nothing to calm her. "Don't treat me like a child, Bowie. I'm sixteen now, and I know a few things about boys. I get more than my fair share of attention." She glances at Rafe when she says this, and he looks away, afraid that I'll catch it. It doesn't surprise me that Rafe would make passes at Tessa when I'm not looking, and the truth is I don't really care, but my ego bristles at it anyway. He should know to stay away from Tessa.

"You're making a big deal out of nothing," I tell her. "I saw someone in trouble, and I helped. I would have done the same if it had been a boy, or a man even. Everyone seems real bent out of shape over it, and maybe they're right, but I made the call, and the last thing I need is you questioning me about it." She folds her arms and looks away from me, huffing. "We aren't married yet, Tessa. You don't have a say in what I do."

"Fine," she says, the word sharp and bitter on her tongue. "You do whatever you feel like doing, Bowie Neville. See if I care."

She storms off, into the alleyways, and I catch Rafe, Jessup, and Devon exchanging smirks. "Something funny?" I ask them.

"Wouldn't catch a girl talking to *me* that way," Rafe mumbles.

"I doubt I'd catch a girl talking to you *at all*, Rafe."

Making like I have something better to do, I walk off, leaving Rafe with my burn. I hear Gunnar and Seth chuckling behind me, and it gives me a satisfied smile.

As I walk the alleys, I know I should just head for home, but I can't shake my thoughts of Alexis. It kills me that she's sitting in the mess hall, awake, and I'm not allowed to be in there. It should be my right as her rescuer to at least get to talk to her. Maybe she'll tell me things she wouldn't tell Byrne or any of the adults. I did save her life, after all. The more I think about it, the more I feel that this is my mission, and I should be allowed to see it through to the end. Yes, that's it. It's not that I want to be with this girl like a boy with a crush; it's that I should be the one to interrogate her. It's really the right thing to do.

Keep telling yourself that anyway, Bowie.

Doubling back, I make for the mess hall, creeping under the windows to see what's going on inside. As luck would have it, the women are in the kitchen, preparing some food, and Alexis is alone at a table. Fort women are more trusting than the men, so it doesn't surprise me that they've left the girl unsupervised. Besides, there isn't anywhere to run even if she wanted to.

I figure this gives me a five-minute window. I sneak in the front, careful not to be seen, and close the door quietly behind me. I throw the latch quickly so no one will come in.

Alexis looks up at the sound of the soft click. I put my finger to my mouth, signaling for her to be quiet. She does but seems a little wary of my presence.

Now comes the hard part. Summoning my courage, I pad softly across the hall and take a seat at the table across from her, trying not to let the wooden bench squeak. "Hi," I say softly. "I'm Bowie. Bowie Neville."

"Yeah, I know," she answers, matching the low volume of my voice. "You're the one who pulled me out of the wreck. I guess I should thank you."

"It was nothing," I lie. She smiles at me, and I feel like I am going to jump out of my skin. I look around nervously, anxious that one of the women—my mother or Candace Mitchell, who is in the kitchen with her—will come out and catch me in the act. Or maybe I'm just anxious to be talking to this strikingly beautiful girl. So anxious, in fact, that I really don't know what to talk to her about. So I say, "I'm very sorry about your parents. I swear there was nothing I could do for them."

"Thank you," she says. But her eyes are guarded, apparently dry of tears. She glances toward the kitchen, to the sounds of pans clanking. "Are you sure you should be in here?"

"It's fine," I answer. She seems anxious to get rid of me, and it kind of stings. So what do I do? Brag, of course. "I'm head of the cadets. That means I pretty much do what I want."

She cocks an eyebrow. "I see. You're a big man on campus."

"Campus?"

"Yeah," she says. "You know, like college."

"Oh." *College* is a word I recognize, from my father. "You mean like learning. Books and stuff."

Her lip curls, bemused. "I take it you're not a big reader."

"My father would love it if I was," I confess, "but I'm more of a soldier than a reader."

"I see." She glances around nervously, as if the mess hall is a cage. Which I guess it sort of is as far as she's concerned. "And what army do you fight for?"

"What do you mean?"

"You said you were a soldier. Soldiers typically belong to an army."

"I belong to the militia," I answer, "or at least I will."

"OK, I get it now." Her face grows cold. "I've been taken in by the crazies."

Anger starts to worm its way up from my stomach. I do not like the tone this girl is taking. "We're not the crazies," I say defensively. "The crazies are out there." I point to the window, as if that clarifies what I'm saying, which it doesn't. "I mean outside the Fort."

"You call this shantytown a fort?" She laughs, and I don't like the sound of it. "Trust me, dude, you have no clue as to what's out there. No clue."

Now the anger has taken root, causing my throat to hitch. "I have a pretty good idea of what's out there. Zombies and marauders and hostiles. In fact, I think we may have a hostile in our midst right now."

"What?" She chuckles. "Me?"

I rein in my temper, hardening my face into an icy mask. "Where are you from? What settlement?"

"I'm not from a settlement. I'm from a city."

"There are no cities. Not anymore."

"You wanna bet?"

"You're lying."

"I'm not."

"Then prove it."

We sit there a long moment, glaring at each other, locked in a stalemate. I'm still trying to process her outrageous claim of being from a city. She has to be lying. It's the sort of thing a hostile spy would say, so I shouldn't be surprised. Still, coming from such a pretty face, it has me twisted. Maybe Byrne is right about this girl.

Alexis looks at her clothes, the baggy, ill-fitting fatigues she's been saddled with. It seems to bother her more than being a hostage. "I can't prove it to you now. But if you can get me back to the plane, I'll show you proof."

"I'm not going to do that. The plane is in the jetty, and I'm in enough hot water as it is for pulling you out of it."

"I thought you were a big man who made his own rules?"

The anger again. "I'm a soldier who follows orders!"

"You're not a soldier," Alexis spits back. "Soldiers fight for a cause! Soldiers fight for a country! You don't have a country! All you have is this stupid, backward shithole!"

Rage. I stand, slam my hand on the table. "I fight for Fort Thunder!" She reels back, startled. "This is my home, and I'll die for it! And I won't hear any more of your lies!"

"Bowie, that's enough!" I turn to see my mother standing in the door, Candace Mitchell beside her, holding a steaming bowl of mush. "You shouldn't be in here!"

"I was just leaving," I say to them. "Papa Byrne is right; this one is a hostile. Don't believe a word of what she tells you."

Alexis scoffs, and I pin my furious eyes back on her. "Enjoy your mush, spy. If I were you, I'd eat it before it gets cold."

I storm out of the mess hall. Mother does not follow after me.

I've been at home for over an hour, lying in bed staring angrily at the ceiling, when Father comes in. "I heard about what happened in the mess," he says. "Stupid Candace. She should have been watching the door. Probably too busy boring your mother with her gossip."

I don't care about Candace Mitchell. All I care about is the girl, who is likely our enemy, and what happened at the council meeting. I sit up in bed, put my boots firmly on the ground. "I interrogated the girl. She's definitely a hostile. We should inform Papa Byrne."

"Now hold on, Son," Father says. "This situation is extremely sensitive. Before you go off half-cocked to Byrne, telling stories, I need to know exactly what she told you."

The truth is I'm having trouble remembering exactly what she said. My anger is confusing my thoughts. "She said she was from a city and that we were the crazy ones. Or something along those lines."

My father sighs, runs an anxious hand through his hair. From the way he is squinting, he is either suffering a headache, or he is scared. Maybe a little of both. "Son," he says, "I think you and I should go for a little walk."

Leaving the Fort is no trouble when you are accompanied by an adult, though Nagel looks at us a little cockeyed when we ask him to help with the gate. Outside, my father chooses the path we will take, and I know immediately where we are going. We used to go there a lot when I was younger, but we haven't been there together for years.

Callie's Peak, named after my mother by my father, is a small mountain not much bigger than a hill, but it is the highest point of elevation in all of Deacon's Bluff. From here you can see the entire island: the Densmore to the south; the fracture of jetty beyond; the ravine peeking through the trees in a spiderwebbing scar pattern; the long finger of the pointe, reaching for the mainland but always falling short. And of course, the endless blue expanse of the Pacific Ocean to the west. This has been my world for my entire life, and I have never had need for anything more than I could see from this hill.

Maybe that's why Father brings me here, to remind me of that. Or maybe he just misses coming here himself.

We take our favorite spot, a slab of rock that juts out far enough to let us dangle our legs over the edge. I take a loose rock and toss it down into the pines below, gently swaying on the breeze. The stone skitters as it lands, a satisfying sound.

"Beautiful, isn't it?" Father says, stating the obvious. I hope he didn't bring me here just to talk about the view.

"Yes, it is," I answer.

He sits there a while, taking it in, and I'm glad that the view seems to take away his pain. Then he looks to me, and it returns. "Son," he says, "I hoped the day would never come when you'd be confronted with the world outside of Deacon's Bluff. But it appears that day is upon us."

"I'm not interested in how things are outside the bluff," I lie. "Don't worry about what that girl said to me. I don't believe a word of it."

"But that's the thing, Bowie. One way or another, you are going to have to deal with it. With the larger world. This girl—she's a problem that's not going to just go away, no matter how much Patrick Byrne wants it to. Somehow, someone is going to come looking for her. And when they do, when they find us, it could mean the end of all this." He gestures to the vista that sprawls out before us. "It could all be taken from us."

This sort of talk pisses me off, reminds me of why Byrne and my father so often come to words. When my father talks like this, he sounds like a right coward. "Let them come," I say. "I will fight whoever comes at us, to the death if I have to. I will never allow Fort Thunder to fall to the hostiles, not while I'm alive."

"That's very honorable, Son. And I want you to fight for whatever it is that you believe. But don't die for Fort Thunder, Bowie. That was never what I wanted for you."

I can't believe he is saying this. Of course I would die for our home! "What better thing is there to die for?" I ask.

"A family of your own," he answers. "A life you make for yourself when you truly know what your options are. Not just the options we give you."

"I'm fine with those options," I say. But for the first time ever, I'm not quite sure I believe it.

My father sighs and looks to the northeast, to where the pointe reaches for the mainland. It's as if his mind is reaching for the mainland as well. "When we came here, I honestly believed that this was our best option," he starts. "Hell, I believed it was our *only* option. I know you've heard all this before, from better storytellers than me, but things were *bad*, Son. Really bad. Three pandemics in as many years. Wars breaking out on every continent. Then, after the Big Shake, the country went under martial law. You know what that is."

"When the military takes over," I confirm. I know I'm supposed to think it's a bad thing, but if the militia is good, like our militia, it shouldn't be bad, should it?

Father seems to sense my thoughts. "Trust me, Bowie, it was ugly. And I have to say, I am grateful for knowing Patrick Byrne at that time, grateful to call him my friend. Because he had been preparing for a day like that to come. Myself and some of the others, we were talkers—we could get together and talk about change, talk about breaking free and cutting off ties, but Byrne was ready to actually *do* it. He galvanized us. Helped us to organize into the core group that would make up the Lucky Thirteen. And it was Byrne's contacts and cleverness that got us off of the mainland before it seemed like the worst was about to go down. He knew about this island, knew that with the right equipment we could make the crossing and then cut ourselves off. None of us really believed it would work, but Byrne believed, and here we are, almost twenty years later, independent. Free.

"But like everything, freedom comes with a price. People used to say that a lot back in my day, and I used to think they were full of crap. But here I am now, saying it."

"It doesn't sound like crap to me," I say.

"Yes, well, over the years I've begun to feel that the price was too heavy. I know you remember the Logans and what happened to them." A hitch rears in my throat, but I force it down, as if swallowing the memory will make it go away. "But there was another incident. One that happened when you were a toddler, too young to remember. See, for the first few years after we settled, I kept waiting for the other shoe to drop. I thought for sure the planes would start flying over, and someone from the old government would spot us, see what we were doing here. But Byrne had chosen this spot well—we were clear of flight patterns, and only occasionally did the roar of an engine boom distantly over the water. Then, after a few years, even that pretty much stopped. Still, I figured sooner or later someone would come.

"Eventually, someone did come. But not from the government. They were just people, refugees like you or I. Hardscrabble people who had tried to do the same as we did, run off into the wilderness while the country tore itself apart. But they weren't as prepared as us. They didn't have our supplies, they didn't have our ingenuity, and they didn't have our guns. All they wanted was some food, something to help them get through the winter, which was proving brutal. Byrne didn't believe them. He turned them away, told them to get off our island, and when they didn't leave, he turned the militia on them, guns blazing. And you know the worst part, Bowie?"

I shake my head, not knowing, not wanting to know.

"It's that I didn't have the stones to stand against him. I just stood there and let him and his men mow those poor people down. People who only wanted our help."

His lip trembles, and I can tell he is forcing back tears. I don't think I can stomach the sight of my father crying. "Maybe you were wrong," I say. "Maybe they were hostiles."

"That's the thing, Son." He steels himself, regaining control, and I'm glad for it. "When you start seeing the world in those terms—people as hostiles or zombies or whatever—then they cease to be human. And in doing so, you make yourself *less* human. Does that make sense?"

It doesn't, but I nod anyway. "What does this have to do with Alexis?"

He looks at me and smiles, recognizing that she is what I've been wanting to talk about this whole time. "Son, that girl is just a girl. She's not a hostile, she's not a marauder, and she's certainly not a zombie. Just a girl. Now, that comes with a whole other set of problems, of which I'm sure you're aware. But worrying that she's the enemy isn't one of them."

"So what she said back in the mess hall," I ask, "all of that was true?"

"I don't know what is true and what isn't," Father answers. "In case you hadn't noticed, we're living on an island cut off from the rest of the world. I haven't set foot on the mainland in twenty years. But judging from her clothes, judging from the fact she flew here in a plane, I'd have to say she's from someplace with some sort of restored infrastructure. What that is, I can't rightly say, and I certainly can't say that I trust...whatever it is. But I do know that she's not from a settlement that's worse off than ours."

It hurts me to hear him diminish Fort Thunder that way—I've been raised to believe we have it better than anyone else. "I don't trust her," I say.

"That's fine, Son," Father says. "Be frugal with your trust. But while you're at it, don't believe everything people will tell you. Especially not the cadets and especially not Papa Byrne. Be careful, Bowie. That's all that I'm saying."

My father's words—more of a warning really—settle over me like troubling weather. I don't like living with uncertainty, don't like it when things become so unclear. Everything that I have known and believed in all my life seems suddenly thrown into question, and frankly, I resent it. I'm beginning to wish that I never went into the restricted zone, beginning to regret pulling that girl out of that plane, beginning to regret all my damn courage.

Troubled, I turn to my home, to familiarity and comfort. But now, from this vantage point, it's somehow not the same. The armory, the highest point in the stronghold, watches us with that single eye, unblinking, staring at us from across the wilderness.

It feels like judgement.

CHAPTER SIX

The Jetty

FATHER AND I RETURN TO THE FORT, AND I SPEND THE REST OF THE DAY trying to stay focused on my chores, trying not to think about his words. But most of all I try not to think about Alexis. It comes as no surprise when I am awarded latrine duty, and as I carry the stinking tubs to the dumping area, I conjure the smell of Alexis's hair to mentally mask the stench. I wonder what she is doing now, if she is being kept in the infirmary, quarantined from spreading the disease of curiosity. I wonder if she's thinking about me and am almost certain she isn't.

The afternoon's work leaves me with little appetite, and I barely touch my mother's corn stew. Father makes small talk, which I think is supposed to distract Mother from her worries, but I don't think it's doing any good. As she clears plates, Father tells me that Byrne made him promise that I would meet with him after dinner. It's just as well that he's telling me this now because had I known what was in store, I probably would have eaten even less of the stew. I nod dutifully, excuse myself from the table, and leave to fulfill my duty.

Tessa greets me at the door, all hooded eyes and barely hidden resentment. I really don't have time for her games right now. She leads me to her father's study, a room the same size as my father's library but with far less books. No books at all, in fact. Byrne greets me with a smile when I arrive. Didn't see that coming.

"Sit down, Son," he bids me. I sit across from him at his desk, little more than a varnished tabletop and four rickety legs. On the table is a Glock, disassembled, parts greasy with oil. I'd think it was placed there for intimidation purposes, but I know Byrne better than that. This is just what he does, as comforting to him as reading is to my father.

"I want you to know that I'm not relieving you of your command," he says. Not a total surprise but still a relief to hear. "Truth is, I admire your spirit. There are two kinds of soldiers: ones who follow orders without question and ones who improvise. The improvisers are the ones you pick to lead. They're the ones who win you battles."

A swell hits my chest, something that feels like pride. I try to remember my gut, the feeling that warns me of danger, reminds me not to get too caught up in his words, his praise. "I'm not going to lie, Bowie," he continues. "I'm not real happy with the stunt you pulled today. But what matters to me now, what matters to the Fort, is how you handle the situation going forward. Keep your mind on your duty, and we can all put this miscalculation behind us. How does that idea sit with you?"

"It sits with me just fine, sir."

"Good." He smiles, yellow teeth peeking beneath the fringe of his mustache. "I knew I could trust you to not let your hormones get the better of you. Dismissed."

I get up to leave and turn to the door, hesitating because I know there is more. "Oh, Bowie," he says. I turn to face him. "My daughter is a prideful girl, like her mother was. Sometimes I don't know how I've managed to raise her myself these last few years. But beneath that hard shell, she's just a girl, with all the passion and worry and all that entails. The presence of this new girl has put ideas in her head, gotten her all spun out of whack. I'd like you to do your best to assure her that everything is going to be normal between you two. That she doesn't have cause to worry. Can you do that for me?"

"I'll do my best."

He nods and sends me on my way. Outside, the living area is quiet, Tessa being nowhere in sight, probably pouting off in her room. That's fine by me. Honestly, the job of reassuring her is the hardest thing I can think of trying to do right now. The thought of Tessa and her pettiness is the last thing on my mind. I leave the Byrne home as quickly and quietly as I can.

Tonight is my night at watch, and having nothing else to do, I arrive at the north tower early. Nagel is in the crow's nest, only too happy for me to take over. He gives me a cruel sneer for my trouble. He doesn't like me, and today's events have given him license to treat me with the contempt he's always felt. Worst of all for Nagel, I don't care how he feels about me. I ignore the look and go to make the climb, but he grabs me by the arm and turns me to face him.

"You may have Patrick fooled, Neville, but not me. If it came down to it, I'd be more than happy to put an arrow into the back of your skull."

"Shooting me in the back is the only way you'd hit me, Marcus."

That wipes the sneer off his face. He shoves me against the tower, and my shoulder blades hit the crossbeams, sending a painful jolt down my back. If he expects me to strike back, he's even stupider than he looks. Raising a hand against a member of the Old Guard is a serious offense, and Nagel could probably justify killing me if it came down to that. I just shake it off, flex my shoulders, and stand tall.

He levels a finger in my face. "Watch yourself, boy."

I stand there, arrow straight, at attention, eyes clear and mouth shut. He waits for me to give him a reason. I don't. Finally, he turns and saunters off. A real cock of the walk.

Once he is gone into the alleys, I turn and scale the tower to the nest. Only when I'm there, sitting with my rifle at the ready, do I allow myself the luxury of feeling shaken. There's no way I was going to give Nagel the pleasure of seeing me shiver, that's for damn sure. The feeling gets lost in the coolness of the night, and I rub my arms beneath my coat to help settle in. All the while I keep my eyes fixed straight into the shadowy tree line beyond the wall.

An hour passes as my mind drifts, running through the madness of this day. Despite the anxiousness it's brought me, it also fills me with a hum of excitement. Things are different now—not just here in the Fort but in my mind as well. Possibilities flood my thoughts like a stream after spring thaw, each cold rush bringing a new thought to light. I don't know whether to follow this river, to run with this curiosity, or to dam it behind the safety of all that I know. The mere fact that I am faced with such a choice is enough to make my bones restless.

The crunching of boots on underbrush snaps me alert, and I glance below, expecting to see one of the militiamen making their rounds. I catch the brief flash of a shape ducking behind one of the large pylons that support the wall. Taking up my rifle, I look through the scope, hoping the infrared will help me to parse through the darkness. At first there is nothing, just silent black and the shadow-green cast of the infrared. I bide my time, staying fixed on the pylon, waiting for someone to step out. After a few minutes, someone does.

Even as a green ghost image, I recognize her. Alexis. Her silvered eyes scan the shadows, hoping she hasn't been spotted. Then she glances up and sees the glare of my scope glinting in the moonlight.

"Crap," I hear her whisper. I stand, shouldering the rifle, and climb down as fast as my limbs will carry me. Moments later I am approaching her, and she gives me the guilty look of a prisoner caught trying to escape.

"What the hell do you think you're doing?" I scold under my breath.

"What does it look like?" Her tone is angry, petulant.

"It looks like you were trying to escape."

"Can you blame me?"

Come to think of it, I can't, not really. "And where were you planning to go, exactly? We're on an island. We'd find you eventually, or you'd die of exposure."

She folds her arms and looks away, avoiding my scrutiny. Finally, she looks back at me and says, "You want to know the truth? I wasn't trying to escape. I mean, I was, but I was going to come back. I was hoping I could get back before anyone noticed I was gone."

That plan sounds even stupider than just trying to escape. "I don't understand."

"Look, forget it, OK? Am I under arrest or what?"

"Where were you planning to go?"

Again, her eyes rove over me, vetting. Am I friend or foe? "I was going back to the plane."

This plan makes less sense the more she talks. "The plane is wrecked. Destroyed."

"I wasn't planning to fly it. There was something in there that I wanted."

My mind automatically assumes she's talking about some sort of weapon. That's just how I've been trained to think. "Whatever it is, it won't be any use against us." I point to the arsenal, standing tall against the sky, lording over us. "See that building? It's stockpiled with weapons. We've had tribes come at us before. None could match our firepower."

"Yeah, I get it. You're a bunch of gun nuts." She rolls her eyes, adding sarcastically, "Good for you. You must be very proud."

"I am proud!" The words blurt out; I have no power to control them. "We built a life here, and we have a right to defend ourselves."

"You don't have the slightest understanding of what rights even are." She shakes her head dismissively. "Look, you caught me, OK? Just turn me back in or whatever you're going to do. I'm done talking to you."

We stand there a moment, breath making angry clouds in the night air. She's right, of course; I should take her in, return her to the infirmary, and report the incident to Byrne. But I just can't bring myself to do that.

"You'd never find your way there anyway," I say, "not in the dark."

Her eyes settle on me, looking right through me. A lock of silver hair falls over her eye, and she pushes it back. "I would if you showed me."

My mouth suddenly feels bone-dry. "I can't do that."

"Can't—or won't?"

The challenge stabs at my pride. "Won't," I answer.

She sighs. "I get it. You're afraid."

"I'm not afraid."

"I think you are," she chides. "Afraid of your boss, that jerk with the beard. Afraid of mommy and daddy, of what they might think."

"I don't care what they think," I lie. "It's dangerous out there, especially for someone who doesn't know what she's doing."

"There's nothing out there. You said so yourself."

"There could be something out there," I say.

"Oh yeah? Like what?"

"Zombies, for one."

She looks at me as if I am the biggest idiot she has ever laid eyes on. "Zombies," she says incredulously. "You're serious. As in..." She extends her arms out straight, bent at the wrists, drops her mouth open, and staggers toward me, gasping and groaning. Her body moves in herky-jerky spasms, like a puppet on invisible strings. She rolls her eyes back in her head, leaving only the whites visible. It's a joke, but I can't help but find it a little disturbing.

"Stop it," I say. "It's not funny."

She drops the routine. "Oh, it's funny all right. Tell me...have you ever actually *seen* a zombie? Like in real life, walking around?"

If she's trying to make me feel like a fool, it's working. "No," I answer defensively. "I suppose you have?"

"I've seen plenty." An idea strikes her. "In fact, if you take me to my plane, I can promise to show you one. Several, even."

So, a challenge to my curiosity is the game she's playing. I have to admit it's a pretty smart tactic, despite the fact that she clearly does not think highly of me. That wouldn't normally bother me, but in her case, it does. True, I am attracted to her, but I thought that was because of her beauty and the novelty of her uniqueness. But now it seems I am more struck by her mind.

"All right," I hear myself saying. "I'll take you. But you have to promise me no tricks. We go to the plane, you get what you need, and we're back here before anyone discovers we're gone. No one knows that we did this, understand?" I repeat with emphasis: "*No one.*"

She smiles, flashing her perfect, pearly-white teeth.

WE MAKE QUICKLY FOR THE LATRINES, USE THE NIGHT VISION OF MY SCOPE along the wall to find Maya's hidden tunnel. It isn't hard; the scrap of artificial turf she's laid over it would be obvious to anyone—anyone looking for it, that is. I lift the flap of turf, likely taken from the storage bins, and motion for Alexis to climb into the dug-out hole. It reeks due to seepage from the latrines.

"You seriously expect me to climb into that thing?"

"Do you want to get out of here or not?" I answer.

Apparently so, because despite the awful smell, Alexis climbs into the slimy crawlspace, making it out the other end before I have even set in my first boot. I scurry through, and when I reach the other side, Alexis offers a hand and pulls me out of the hole.

"You'd think a big shot like you would just have a key to the front door," she says.

"There is no front door."

"Great." She brushes wet dirt off her loose-fitting fatigues. "Now I smell like hillbilly shit."

I don't need to know what a hillbilly is to get that she means it as a put-down; her derogatory tone says it all. This sort of sarcasm is not appreciated by the adults of Fort Thunder and usually results in a smack in the face or the assignment of some unpleasant duty. Wherever this girl is from, they are quite lax in matters of discipline. But I brush off her comments as I brush the caked-on muck from my pants. "This way," I say, making for the woods.

Scant minutes and the Fort is all but gone behind a curtain of trees. Alexis stays close, grabbing my arm, spooked by the darkness of the thick woods. I can't say I mind. I use the scope to make a cursory scan of the area to make sure there aren't any fallen trees or other unsuspected obstacles, but mostly I go off of memory until my eyes adjust. Am I doing this to impress her? Probably. But the fact of the matter is that I know these woods like the back of my hand.

When we reach the small field on the far side of the woods, the moon is providing enough light that I shoulder my rifle, no longer needing the scope. Alexis relaxes, able to navigate on her own. She lets go of my arm, and I immediately miss the feel of her hand.

"Hey," she says. I keep my eyes and feet forward. "Look, I'm sorry for being such a bitch back there. This whole thing has me pretty freaked out, you know?"

I slow my stride, allowing her to fall in step with me, but I don't say anything. Not because I'm angry with her but because I don't know what to say. It's not a feeling I'm used to—being tongue-tied around a girl. Usually I feel like the one in control, and I certainly don't feel that way with Alexis.

"What I'm saying is that I appreciate you doing this for me."

My shoulders shrug, almost unconsciously, bobbing the rifle. "Just curious is all," I say.

"Curious about me?" she asks.

"About a lot of things," I answer. And that much is true. But the truth is —yes—mostly about her. What are her passions? Her fears? I want to know everything about her, devour her like a meal set before a starving man. Everything about her is a mystery. Her skin. Her hair. The sheer, formfitting clothes I found her in. But mostly it's her mind I want access to, her innermost thoughts. And most of all, I want to know what she thinks about me.

"Well, when we get to the plane, you'll know more."

"So you tell me." I try to adopt a playful tone, something to put her at ease but which will still allow me to probe her for info. "But I saw inside that plane, and it gave me more questions than answers. All I saw were two dead bodies and—"

She tenses, and I realize that I've already put my foot in my mouth. "Oh," I say, catching myself, "I'm so sorry."

"No, really, it's OK," she says. "I had forgotten about them. That they were still in the plane."

How could she have forgotten that her parents' corpses were still in the plane? Sure, a lot had happened to her in the last few days, but I would think that unpleasant fact would still be at the front of her mind. Is this some strange cultural thing I'm not understanding?

But this is a subject I'm not going to breach—not now, anyway. "When we get to the plane, I can go in and get what you need. Just tell me what to look for."

"No, really, I can handle it."

"You don't understand," I warn. "The plane came off of the cliffs and fell onto the jetty. Even if there are no zombies down there, it's going to be dangerous. It's no place for someone who isn't familiar with this island."

"You mean it's no place for a girl," she says sharply.

It's true. I don't think it's any place for a girl. "Is there a problem with that?"

"Yeah, there is," she answers. "Where I come from, we don't have these antiquated notions about sexuality. Boys and girls are treated exactly the same."

"That's ridiculous. Boys and girls are not the same."

"It's called *equality*." Her voice has taken on a lecturing tone. "But I can see you don't have the slightest idea what I'm talking about, do you?"

"I know what equality means." My voice is heavy with irritation.

"I'm talking about how it applies to the sexes." She sighs, as if there's absolutely no point in discussing this with me any further. "You know what, forget it. Keep thinking whatever you want to think. But when we get to the plane, I'm going in, and you're not going to stop me."

"Fine," I angrily concede. "If you get yourself killed, it's not my problem." I mutter this last bit just loud enough for her to hear. "Less hassle for me, anyway."

She whacks my arm, but there's a playfulness there, buried under a thin layer of anger. "Jerk," she hisses.

We reach the far side of the field where the ground slopes into the ravine. Alexis surprises me by handling the landscape skillfully, like someone who knows the terrain. It occurs to me that she has an athletic build and could probably handle her own in a game of soccer. I have never cared much for the few games we play at the Fort, though I've read about sports like basketball and baseball and I think I might be interested in playing one of those. But soccer is the most popular of the games we are allowed because it was never fully embraced by the American government. I'm not entirely sure I see the logic there, and rather than force myself to enjoy the game, I focused my athleticism into training. I'd say it's paid off well so far.

The journey is long, and I'm grateful for the need to concentrate because I don't know how to make conversation with this girl. Silence is the easiest option. But after a while even the silence feels strained, and I sense she is growing just as uncomfortable as I am. We are over the shale hill and approaching the ranger station when she finally breaks the silence.

"This is far," she notes. "I can't believe you carried me all this way."

"I had help," I answer.

We pass by the old cabins, and Alexis shivers. I don't blame her; the darkness makes them feel all the more haunted. We reach the road, but this time I don't make a show of entering uncharted territory, partially because it's no longer uncharted, partially because there's no one to impress. "I get the feeling that bringing me back wasn't exactly a popular decision," Alexis says as we travel along the road.

"No, it wasn't."

"Well, I'm sorry for any trouble I've caused you."

"Don't be," I say. And surprisingly, I mean it. Despite all the heat I've brought upon myself, being here with her, right now, is somehow worth it.

We come to the cliffs, welcomed by the waves crashing below. I don't want to linger here long as daylight has begun to peek below the horizon, but Alexis has other ideas. She stands at the cliff's edge, arches her back, and gazes into the bay and the wilderness beyond.

"It's so beautiful," she says.

Some dim part of me understands what she means. The tinge of orange flashing on the bay, the deep green wall of pines, the cold finality of the rocky shore—seen through certain eyes, the eyes of a girl, these things may seem beautiful. But to me the bay, and wilderness it separates us from, represents threat and the promise of danger. In my alert and ready-for-anything mind, those woods are crawling with hostiles, zombies, and who knows what else, and the water is there to be drowned or swept out to sea in. It is a harsh, cruel vista; we are taught to respect and fear nature, not dawdle and admire it. I don't understand how anyone could be brought into this world and not see it that way.

"We should keep moving." Alexis gives me a look, aware that the moment is lost on me. Still, I walk away from the edge, and she follows.

As we follow the cliffs, the wind blasts off the water, as if to support my unspoken point. I glance back at Alexis and see her rubbing her arms, not getting much protection in the threadbare army jacket she was given. Under my peacoat I'm wearing a thermal shirt, but it won't do much good against the biting wind. Which is why when I remove it and offer it to Alexis, I think that I'm losing my mind.

She looks at me, surprised. "I'm not taking your coat."

"You're cold." I hold out the coat, suppressing a shiver. "Go on, take it. I'm used to this."

"Fine," she says, taking the coat out of my hand. "But only to teach you how dumb your misplaced chivalry is."

This gives me a smirk. "Don't get all bigheaded about it. I'd do it for any girl."

As she puts on the coat—way too big for her, of course—I turn and continue on our journey. Alexis gives a pleasurable sigh due to the added warmth, undermining her bravado. It makes the fact that I'm now freezing my ass off almost worthwhile. Almost.

"So," she says, coming up behind me, "speaking of girls, is that one who's been mad-dogging me the whole time your girlfriend?"

"'Mad-dogging?'"

"Yeah. You know, giving me dirty looks."

"Oh. You mean Tessa."

"I didn't catch her name."

There isn't any doubt in my mind she means Tessa. Her icy glare could reach from one end of the bluff to the other. "She's my betrothed," I say rather glumly.

"Betrothed?" Alexis repeats. "You mean like an arranged marriage?"

"Yeah," I reply, as if her question is absurd, "that's generally how it works."

"Not where I'm from it doesn't."

Anger boils up from my stomach, where it's been simmering since the mention of Tessa. I stop and turn around to face this girl and her judgmental attitude. "You know what? I'm getting a little tired of hearing how much better things are where you're from. If your people are so great, where are they right now? Shouldn't they be coming to rescue you? Or are they a tribe of cowards?"

Her lips flatten to a hard, angry line. "It's not that easy. Things are complicated. You wouldn't understand."

"I think I understand perfectly. I think your people are the same group of cowards who hid behind false flags when everything went to hell. Your leaders betrayed you, and instead of standing up for yourselves, instead of standing up for what you believed, you let them starve you and turn you into slaves. You have no idea what it means to be self-sustaining, no idea of what it means to be truly free!"

She stands there, glaring, my words a slap to her fine-featured face. "So marrying someone you don't love—that's freedom?"

"It's duty," I answer. "Another thing your people know nothing about."

I whip back around, walking faster than before. At first, I don't hear her following. But then the patter of boot soles lets me know that she's there, trying to keep pace.

"Look. Things got pretty bad for a while, I'll admit. But when bad things happen, you don't just give up and run away. You stick it out and try to make things work."

"My father tried. All of our fathers tried. The system was broken."

"Maybe it was," Alexis says measuredly, "but things got better."

We don't say another word to each other until we reach the Densmore. I hear Alexis gasp as we come upon the bridge in all its mangled glory. In the pinkish light of the coming dawn, the tangle of girders has a strange sort of beauty, the way a spider's web might be beautiful to a fly before getting caught in it.

"What happened?" Alexis asks.

I shrug, thinking it should be obvious. "We blew it up," I answer tersely, still a little angry about our argument.

"Why am I not surprised?" she says.

Time is running short, so rather than stopping to argue further, I lead us to the bridge following the straightest possible route. The thrill of seeing it is gone for me now; I just want to do what we came to do and go home. We reach the mouth of the bridge, where it dives off the cliff into oblivion, and I search the jetty below for the wreckage of Alexis's plane. It isn't hard to spot, even in the Densmore's ruined shadow.

"Down there," I say, pointing. Alexis follows my finger to the crumpled silver fuselage below. "We'll have to climb down the cliff."

She looks at the cliffside, the rocky, unforgiving drop to the jetty. "Let's do it," she says.

Before I can offer another objection, she is walking over to the edge, readying to lower herself down the side. The starting point she has chosen is the steepest way down and will surely result in her slipping and falling. "Can I at least lead the way?" I insist.

A piece of cliff rock falls loose with a touch of her foot, and she reconsiders, pulling away from the edge. It takes almost twenty seconds before the rock hits the jetty. She swallows her pride, looks to me, and makes a sweeping gesture with her arm. "By all means, lead."

Testing the cliff's edge with my foot, I find a section that seems solid and will make for an easier descent. Satisfied that it will hold, I start down cautiously, checking my hand and footholds before moving downward to the next section of cliff. Occasionally the seaworn earth crumbles and falls loose, but my natural coordination keeps me steady. I've had plenty of practice on the cliffsides of Bluff Pointe and the treacherous rocks that make up the ravine.

Above me, Alexis observes and follows my descent move for move, step by step. Only once do I hear her breath hitch fearfully when her foot slides off of a loose stone. For someone who didn't grow up on the bluff, she handles herself with real skill, as well as Maya or any one of the cadets—

better than most, really. We reach the jetty with no major slip ups, and finding myself on level ground once again comes as a quiet relief. Looking at Alexis's face, I know she feels the same.

"Piece of cake," she lies.

Ten meters or so from where we stand, the plane lies upended, front half dipping into the bay, back half-broken against the rocks, like some giant bird that has fallen from the sky to a miserable death. Other than this sad sight, the jetty looks clear, but I scan the shrinking shadows for signs of movement or anything out of the ordinary. Ignoring my caution, Alexis plows past me, taking the jetty rocks with a quick series of nimble jumps.

"Hey!" I follow after her, struggling to keep up. Though not the challenge of the cliff, the jetty is dangerous and uneven, an unforgiving path of jagged slate ready to break your ankle or slip you right into the bay. We were taught at the Fort that all terrain is potentially dangerous, to never let our guard down, and to assume that every tree, rock, or crevice is an injury in waiting or worse. Alexis, it would seem, was instilled with no such fear of her surroundings. On one hand, I admire the confidence with which she takes to a challenge; on the other, I could easily see her getting herself, or both of us, killed. When she arrives at the plane, several seconds before me, she turns and smiles gloatingly, as if she has just won a race.

"You should be more careful on these rocks," I say, slightly winded.

"You're just mad because I beat you."

OK, maybe I am just a little.

She turns to the fuselage, not even glancing at the nose of the plane where her parents' bodies are still strapped into their seats, heads lolling in the water. Whatever she's after in there, it clearly isn't them. It's a level of callousness I can't fathom.

"Do you think we should—"

Before I can finish my sentence, she ducks into the still-open hatch, disappearing into the plane with a splash. The water she displaces causes the fuselage to teeter like a seesaw on the rocks, bringing back unpleasant memories of my rescue. But I'm not letting her go in there alone. I unsling my rifle and set it down on the rocks, rubbing my arms in preparation for the coming shock. Then I draw a deep breath and step inside the plane and into the icy water.

I wasn't prepared. The cold sends a shuddering shock through my body, and I can't help but let loose a cry. Alexis, waist deep in the water, turns back to give me a sympathetic look. Her cheeks are already turning a light shade of blue.

"You need to make this quick," I say. "Before we both go into shock."

Alexis wades toward the back of the plane, ducking under a row of seats that hangs from the ceiling, which was the floor before the plane was overturned. Her head is down, scanning for something beneath the surface, and finally, a meter from the back, she finds it. Drawing in a deep breath, she crouches, dipping herself fully under the water. Just watching her do it makes the air leap out of my lungs.

Long seconds pass with Alexis entirely gone from view. Bubbles rise to the surface and pop, letting me know that she's there under the water, but it doesn't make me feel any easier. *This is taking too long*, I tell myself, getting ready to dive in after her. I am rubbing my arms, preparing to go under, when the plane suddenly shifts and sends me stumbling back toward the cockpit. Toward the corpses floating in their seats.

Reaching for the walls, I slam my hands against the door frame that opens into the cockpit, halting my tumble. The thick, bowel-clenching smell of rot fills my nostrils, and I resist the urge to look behind me, into the glassy eyes I know are waiting there. I imagine them staring up at me, refracted in the water, smiling with their water-eaten skeleton grins. If I linger here too long, I have no doubt that they will grab me and drag me into the cockpit to rot with them forever.

The plane shifts again, righting itself in the other direction, and I am propelled away from the reeking cockpit. The movement knocks me off my balance, and I start to fall, arms flailing for something to grasp onto. As I am about to topple, Alexis bursts forth from the water like she was shot out of a cannon, her body colliding with mine, preventing me from going under. Her head connects with the bottom of my chin, and we both let out a yelp and stumble back a step.

"Sorry," she says as she's catching her breath, "I didn't see you there."

All around us metal groans, and the fuselage shifts uneasily on the rocks. Once the pain in my chin has ebbed, my powers of observation return, and I notice that Alexis is holding something in her hands. It is small and black and roughly the size of one of my father's books.

"Let's get out of here," Alexis says, before I can ask what she's holding.

The plane groans again, threatening to jostle loose of the jetty and into the bay's current. I nod to Alexis, take her free hand in mine, and hurry us both toward the hatch...

The world flips on its side as the plane comes loose and rolls. The hatch, mere meters away, is now fully in the bay and flooding with water. In minutes —maybe seconds—the entire fuselage will be completely submerged. And Alexis and I submerged with it.

"Hold on!" I yell, a gush of bay water hitting my mouth. Alexis's grip tightens in mine as I feel her caught in the incoming rush. It's like trying to push forward into a freezing liquid hurricane. I wonder if our deaths will come by drowning, hypothermia, or both.

The thought is enough to propel me forward with a burst of adrenaline. Straining with every muscle, I reach for the hatch, fighting through the crushing flow of pressure. Just as my fingers find purchase on the rim of the hatch, I feel Alexis slip away from my other hand.

"Alexis!"

Still holding to the hatch, I crane back to look for her, but she is gone in the rushing water. I have only a moment to consider what to do, and a moment is more than I need. Letting go of the hatch, I dive headfirst into the fuselage, allowing the flow of incoming water to shoot me like a missile. The gambit works too well. Our bodies collide underwater, knocking us both into a spin that tangles us into each other's limbs. It takes my brain a second to recover from the shock of the collision and from the murderous cold trying to shut down my senses.

My boot strikes something under the water, and I feel a little give that is unlike the rest of the fuselage's solid steel interior. It is a small, circular window that has loosened slightly from the damage of the crash and the pressure of the inrushing water. I kick again, and the high-density glass gives way, popping right out of the plane and into the bay, creating an improvised portal. It seems insane to consider squeezing ourselves through it, but at this point going through the hatch would be like trying to swim up a waterfall. This may be the best—may be the *only* option we have.

Through the murk I see Alexis's eyes beginning to glaze. Seconds from now I will lose her to the cold. I wave my hand in front of her face, and she snaps out of it, focusing on my silent direction. I point down to the kicked-through window and the black hole it has created, motioning that she should swim for it. It takes her a heartbeat to register my meaning, then she nods and swims with all that her muscles allow. I swim behind her, careful to avoid her kicking feet but ready to push her forward if she stops.

She reaches the window, and with an exhale of bubbles, manages to push her slim body through. I follow after, my broader body making passage far more difficult. Wide shoulders betray me, wedging me in the window, and I struggle freeing one of my arms to allow much needed wiggle room. I'm almost free when the world starts to go dim.

It's too late. I've been underwater too long, brain fading from the lack of oxygen. I can't get through, not before I lose consciousness and drown. This is how it ends for Bowie Neville, star cadet of Fort Thunder. Wedged in an airplane window like a rat caught in one of Marcus Nagel's long-neglected traps. Black spots fill my vision, blotting out all light. A warm flood of calm envelops me, and I stop struggling. Dying is not what I expected at all.

It's almost comforting.

A sharp pain shoots up my arm, and I snap back to consciousness. Through the murk I see Alexis pulling at me, freeing me from the window. I come loose, and the two of us float toward the light, following our bubbles to the surface. Below me I feel a pull as the airplane is sucked into the gloom. I don't look down for fear it will take me with it.

We breach the surface, both of us gasping. The air is biting and cold, but I do not care. I have never been so happy to be so cold. It means I'm still alive.

The jetty is a few meters away, and we swim for it. Moments later we are clambering up the slippery rocks, desperate to free ourselves of the icy water. It takes us both several tries, but I find an area where the rocks allow purchase and pull myself up, then Alexis. On our backs, we lie on a large flat rock, trying to catch our breath as it plumes from our mouths in puffs.

I look to Alexis, and she looks at me. We both laugh—the joyful relief of two people who have just escaped drowning. We laugh until our tortured lungs can't take any more.

Chill starts to set in, and I stand, rubbing my arms and my legs, trying get warmth back into them. Alexis stands, and I go to do the same for her. She pulls away.

"What are you doing?"

It occurs to me that my help is unwanted. "I'm sorry. I was just—"

"Thanks, but I got it." She removes my soaked coat and takes out the item we have just cheated death to retrieve: something housed in a small black case, the soft kind that we have for our rifles back at the Fort. There's a zipper along the side, and she pulls it, glancing inside the case. She pulls out a flat black object the size of a roof shingle. She swipes a finger along its smooth, featureless surface. Then she sighs with disappointment and puts it back in the case. "Water got to it," she says. "Might be able to save it if it dries out properly."

"What is it?" I ask.

"Probably my only hope," she answers.

She rings what water she can out of my heavy wool coat, then puts it back on with a grimace. Before I can question her about this mysterious object for which I have just risked my life, she turns from me and walks down the jetty back toward the cliffs. When she notices I'm not following, she turns back and says, "We ought to be getting back now, don't you think?"

I do not understand girls. I don't know if I will ever understand them. Right now, I feel like tossing this one back into the water. "So you wouldn't save your parents, but you'll save...whatever that thing is?!"

"Those weren't my parents," Alexis says. She turns back to the cliffs and continues on her way. I stand there a moment, then pick my rifle up off the rocks and follow.

Scaling the cliff is easier than getting down, but I save further questioning for when we reach the top. Not waiting for Alexis to catch her breath, I ask, "So if they weren't your parents, then who were they?"

She looks at me warily, as if determining whether or not I am trustworthy. You would think by now I would have gained her confidence. "Bodyguards," she says at last.

It takes me a second to process this. "Why do you need bodyguards?"

"Look, Bowie, I appreciate all your help. I really do. You've gone way above and beyond. And it's for that reason that I can't tell you everything. Not at this point, at least. The more I tell you, the more danger I may be putting you in."

"I don't understand."

"Good. That's for the best. I'm not saying that to be mean. I'm just being honest. The less you know about me right now, the better."

Her words are meant to assure me, but they don't. Alarms go off in my brain.

All of my instincts warn me that this is wrong, that I have thrown in with the enemy. The thought that I have betrayed Fort Thunder is something I can't live with, so I raise my rifle and level it at her. "Enough games," I order. "Now talk."

Alexis looks shocked, then her lip upticks slightly. "Or what? You'll shoot me?"

"Are you a hostile or aren't you?"

"Haven't we already been over this?"

"I'm asking again." I rest my finger on the trigger. "Are you a hostile spy?"

Her eyes narrow. She stands arrow straight, fearless. "I'm not the one pointing a gun. If anyone's the hostile here, it's you."

She turns on her heel and walks off into the forest. I watch her go through the crosshairs of my rifle scope, knowing full well that I don't have the stones to fire on her.

So I put down the rifle. She doesn't even bother to look back.

I shiver, wishing that I hadn't given her my coat.

WE DON'T SPEAK THE ENTIRE JOURNEY BACK. REACHING THE LAST CLUSTER of trees, we come into view of the Fort, and my heart jumps into my throat. In the crow's nest of the southern tower is a sentry. Morning watch has begun, and my absence has been noted.

I duck behind a pine, pulling Alexis with me. Before she can protest, I put a finger to my lips. She gets the message to be quiet.

We hold up there a moment as I consider our next move. "Stay behind the trees," I whisper. And we do, creeping from tree to tree all the way back to the wall that borders the latrines. A quick, stinky crawl through Maya's tunnel and we are under the wall and back inside the Fort.

Alexis brushes at her soiled knees, blanching at the smell. "The Seavers are going to wonder why I'm so dirty." Her face scrunches. "And what do I say about the smell?"

"Say there was leakage by the latrines and you slipped and fell. It wouldn't be the first time that happened, trust me."

She makes a sour face and shakes her head. We stand there an awkward moment, not knowing what to say to each other. I'm still mad at her, and she's still mad at me, no doubt. Realizing that she's still wearing my coat, she takes it off and hands it to me. I throw it back on, grateful for the added warmth even if it's still a little soggy.

I feel something hard in the inside pocket, then remember. I pull out the mysterious slipcased object. "You forgot about this."

"Hold onto it," she says.

"I don't want it," I counter.

She sighs, her face softening for the first time since the bridge. "Please," she says, her eyes pulling at parts of me I didn't know I had. "I know you're angry with me right now. And you probably don't trust me. But I trust *you*, Bowie. You're the only person in this whole crazy place I think I *can* trust. And I need you to find a nice, dry place for that device and keep it safe until I can take another look at it. If you do that for me, I swear I can give you answers. That is, if you think you're ready for them."

"I'm ready for anything," I answer.

A smile cracks across her lips. I can't help but feel that the smile is at my expense. "OK, rock star, whatever you say."

"What's a 'rock star'?"

"Jeez, they didn't even tell you about rock stars?! You're named Bowie, for god's sake!"

"I was named after a James Bowie. He was a great pioneer," I tell her. "He made the Bowie knife."

She laughs. It's a beautiful laugh, even when it mocks me. "Yeah right. I'll bet you anything you were named after *David* Bowie. He was a rock star that wore crazy costumes and sang cool songs about being from outer space. But whatever. Keep that thing I gave you safe, and I'll teach you all about David Bowie later."

I want to argue the point further, but we have to break this up before someone comes to use the latrines. "Fine," I say hurriedly. "Whatever. I'll hold on to it."

She looks relieved. "And don't show it to anyone. Not a single person. Promise me that."

"I promise."

Alexis nods her thanks and walks off toward the infirmary. I watch her go, admiring the shape of her body and the purpose of her stride. She is beautiful—there's no denying that—but it's really the way she carries herself that makes my soul ache. There is no one who matches her spirit here at Fort Thunder. Not even me.

Tucking the object back in my coat, I walk back to the post I abandoned. Of course, I find Rafe there sitting in the tower, searching the tree line for invisible threats. I holler up to him. He jerks his head down at me, startled.

"What the hell happened to you?!"

I put a shaky hand to my stomach—a performance, of course. "Been throwing up all morning. Must have been something I ate."

He lingers in the nest a moment, eyeing me suspiciously, then climbs down the ladder several rungs at a time. Upon reaching the ground, he inspects me, as if I'm a subordinate under his command. I don't like it one bit, but in the interest of moving this along, I hold my tongue. "Why are you all wet?"

"I told you," I say indignantly, "I got sick. I had to clean up."

There is nothing unusual about my cover story. Stomach ailments are common, thanks to the high spoilage rate of our food. There is one refrigerator in the mess, but it fills up real quick, and personal supplies are kept in our larders. That means a lot of dried fruit and vegetables during the winter, and it also means the occasional sour stomach.

Rafe is well aware of this reality and has suffered more than his fair share of food poisoning. Still, he looks at me like I'm a liar. Which, in fairness, I am. "You still should have come and gotten me. Papa Byrne would have been furious if he found the tower unattended."

"So Papa Byrne doesn't know?" I ask, trying not to sound too eager.

"Not that I know of."

"Well, then there's no reason to tell him," I say.

"Tell him what?" asks a familiar female voice. I turn to find Tessa slinking up behind me like an animal creeping up on prey. She's wearing concern, but there is nothing genuine behind it. A spider looking to catch me in her web.

Regardless, I disarm her with a smile. "Not to worry, darling. I was just telling Rafe that something I ate didn't sit right with me. Just a bad bit of potato...I'm all better now."

"Oh, poor baby," Tessa purrs. She moves close to kiss me, then reels back suddenly. "Oh my, Bowie. You really do reek."

"Then I better wash up," I say. "I'll catch up with you two later." I don't like turning my back on them, but the longer I stay here, the deeper the hole will get. Best to leave now and let them say what they will. Gossip I can handle; I have long accepted that being the best means weathering the jealous whispers of my peers. But now it isn't just myself to worry about. Now there is Alexis to think of. For her sake, I will remain cautious and vigilant, even if she doesn't give a damn about me.

With that in mind I pass by the infirmary to make sure she snuck in OK. The building is dark and quiet, so I can only assume that our excursion went undetected. As accepting as they are, I'm sure the Seavers would be greatly troubled by her disappearance. Thankfully, it appears she got in and out without detecting her notice. Just another way she manages to impress me.

That is where my luck runs out. As I approach the family dwelling, I see that the gas lamps are lit, and I can see the silhouette of my mother pacing inside. I come in the door, and sure enough, she is standing in the kitchen, waiting for me. Her eyes are sunken with exhaustion and worry.

"I went by the crow's nest." Her voice is flat and unreadable. "You weren't there."

"I got sick," I lie. "I was out at the latrines."

"No you weren't," Mother says definitively. "You were out with that girl."

CHAPTER SEVEN

The Zombie

"I wasn't," I answer feebly. But Mother isn't having it.

"Sit down, Bowie," she orders.

I take a seat at the table. She takes a seat across from me, wearing a look of distaste. I realize she's reacting to my filthy coat and remove it, draping it on the back of the chair next to me. Must remember not to leave it there.

"You do realize how much danger you're putting yourself in. How much danger you're putting all of us in."

I don't answer. Not because I'm being defiant but because I don't have an adequate answer. She has me dead to rights, and there's nothing I can do. So I deflect. "Where's Father?"

"He's resting today," she answers sharply. I know what that means. The headaches are getting worse. "And thank goodness for that. He'd be beside himself if he knew what you had gotten up to last night."

"He already gave me the warning speech, Mother," I say.

"Well clearly it didn't stick." She sighs, taking me in with a shake of her head. "Bowie, if Patrick Byrne can convince the council that girl is having a negative effect on you, it might be all he needs to have her excommunicated."

"The council can't decide on anything," I answer curtly. "All they ever do is argue. I don't see what use they are at all."

"Please, Bowie, don't say that." My mother's tone has changed from lecturing to imploring. She gets this way when she's trying to make a point sink in. "The council is very important. It's a system of checks and balances that ensures people like Byrne can't seize power on the might of their weapons alone. It assures that we have reason."

"Well, I don't see much reason in it," I say. It has always been my dream that one day, when I am leader of the militia, I will do what Byrne could not and disband the useless council. Then I would rule with a strong, fair hand. It's a dream that seems more distant than ever.

Her anger returns. "How can you say that when they're the only reason keeping that girl from being cast out into the wild? Do you *want* that to happen?"

Honestly, my feelings about Alexis are so conflicted that I don't know *what* I want. Mostly, I want this conversation to be over. "I can handle Papa Byrne," I say. "All I need to do is show him that she has value. That she's not redundant."

"And you think that if he wants her gone, he can't find a way to *make* her redundant? Like he did to the Logans?"

Again, my throat hitches at the sound of their name. The Logans. It floods bits of memory into my brain that I have worked very hard to forget. "They left for the mainland," I say, lying to myself. "They were taken by zombies."

"Oh, Bowie." My mother's face slackens with sympathy; her eyes well up on my behalf. "You have to stop blaming yourself for what happened to Michael Logan."

My lower lip begins to tremble, but I will it to stop. I haven't let my mother see me cry since I was eight years old, and I don't intend to start again now. "Michael fell off the wall when we were playing. It was raining, and he slipped. It wasn't my fault."

"No, it wasn't your fault," my mother confirms. "But what you need to understand is that the Logans were doomed at Fort Thunder from the very beginning. Because of who they were. Because of the color of their skin." A tear struggles free of her left eye and scrolls down her cheek. "Because they were *black*."

When I see the face of Michael Logan in my mind, all I see are the eyes, wide with terror, as he falls from the rain-slicked battlement. It never occurs to me that the face I am looking into is darker than mine. All I see is the fear. And the betrayal.

My mother wipes another stray tear and sighs, leaning back from the table. "The Logans were good people," my mother continues sadly. "They were instrumental in the founding of Fort Thunder. They were there when the walls came up, and they broke their backs in the building of our houses. But most importantly, they were instrumental in the drafting of the law. Sam Logan, Michael's father, sat right next to your father on the council. Cecile, his wife, was my best friend, as Michael was yours. They were real people with wonderful laughs and strong convictions, and they were always there as voices of reason and diplomacy. But Byrne and Nagel and a few of the others couldn't see past the color of their skin. You see, the rest of the Lucky Thirteen families were all white, not a person of color among them. Your father even overheard Pat Byrne refer to the Logans as 'impure.' Called them 'niggers' in hushed tones among the more closed-minded of his men, a word used to demean people of the Logans's race."

I had heard the word before, spoken by Rafe and some of his cronies. But it didn't hold much power in a world where black people didn't exist anymore. "So what are you saying?" I ask my mother. "That Papa Byrne put Michael up to climbing that wall?"

"I wasn't there that day, Bowie. Only you and Michael were. I don't expect you to remember all the details from ten years ago. But it does seem awfully convenient that the one thing that would ensure the Logans would leave the Fort—namely, their only son being crippled—gave Byrne the leverage he needed to label them as redundant. He got exactly what he wanted, and believe you me, we've been a poorer community ever since."

This conversation is taking me to troubled places I don't want to go. I am tired and frazzled, and I want nothing more now than to be in my bed. There is a noise in the other room, and my heart freezes, realizing that my father is awake. He steps into the kitchen, and I wait for my mother to tell him all about my nocturnal activities.

Father smiles at me, his face trying to hide the pain eating at his skull. "You're back late," he says. "Or early, rather."

"Bowie and I were just having a little chat," mother says pleasantly.

"Oh? And what about?"

"Nothing much," mother lies. "He was asking me advice on girls. Regarding Tessa."

Father nodded. "That one is certainly a handful. But really, Callie, let the boy get some sleep. He looks ready to keel over."

Mother shoots me a look that says that we're finished and that I should run along now to bed. I am only too happy to take her suggestion. Once in my room, I plop down in bed and let the night's exhaustion run over me. Daylight is already peeking through the shabby blinds of my one grubby window.

I turn on my side, eyes falling on the soldier who stands on my nightstand. His dark features stare back at me, and I am reminded again of his original owner. Michael Logan.

Sleep comes so quickly that I forget I've left my coat out in the kitchen, along with the sleek, mysterious device hidden in its pocket.

I REMEMBER A FEW HOURS LATER, AND IT PULLS ME AWAKE WITH A JOLT. Pulling on fresh fatigues, I step out of my room only to find that my coat is no longer on the chair where I left it. Mother must have taken the filthy thing with her to do the morning wash. I could run down to the basins and try to claim it, but it would only draw more attention to my suspicious behavior. Face it, there's no clean way around this one. All I can do is hope that mother finds it and returns it to me without bringing my father, or anyone else, into the matter. Which is a very, very long shot.

Not able to eat breakfast, I take my mind off the matter the best way I know how—by shooting at zombies. We don't have real zombies at the firing range, of course. We just paint ghoul faces on some of the dummies to make them look scary. Everyone's favorite we call Old Gus on account of him looking more like a feeble old man than a proper zombie. Then again, as Alexis unkindly pointed out, I wouldn't really know what a proper zombie looks like.

The range is deserted when I get there, which isn't surprising as I'm the only cadet with a free period right now. There's a few assault rifles hanging in the gun cabinet, which is left unlocked during the day. Aside from the arsenal kept in the armory, the militia allows a certain amount of loose firearms to be kept around the Fort, unlocked and unsupervised for training and in case of emergencies. It's a policy that men should have access to a gun at all times, as a reaction against the strict firearm laws that kept people from being able to defend themselves back in the old times. *"That was the first sign of trouble,"* Byrne likes to say, and my father rolls his eyes whenever he says it. Regardless, access to guns is the birth-given right of Fort Thunder men, and most of us boys have been firing guns nearly as long as we've been walking. But only the cadets are expected to regularly train.

My eyes travel down the row of rifles, admiring them, taking in the lingering smell of oil and carbon. We keep our weapons in top form, as you would imagine. There are four weapons to choose from: an M16 (the most common weapon for cadets), an AR-10 (Byrne's weapon of choice), an AK-47 (too messy), and an AK-101. I choose the 101 because I'm a little sore from yesterday, and I find that the recoil on it is smoother. Some of the other cadets don't like the 101 due to it being Russian, but I don't see how where it's from should make any difference to us. We are a country unto ourselves.

Old Gus is waiting for me down the range, so I load the rifle, shore myself up against the wall of sandbags, and get to shooting. Gus jostles around as my rounds hit him, but today I can't seem to make him dance. I've loaded a full clip into him and am preparing another when Byrne comes strolling down the range toward me.

"Save a little something for the rest of us," he says, smiling. Strapped on his shoulder is the AR-10. Big surprise.

I make room for him along the sandbag, and he sits, sliding his bulk next to me. From his breathing, I can tell that he's out of shape; leadership has made his muscles soft and his bones stiff. But he's still one hell of a crack shot, which he no doubt intends to remind me.

"Let me show you how it's done," he challenges with a smirk. The AR-10 is already locked and loaded, so he wastes no time letting it rip on Old Gus. If I made the dummy dance, Byrne has the thing spazzing like a fool on a hot wire. His firing is precise and brutal, showering the target in rounds that inflict maximum damage, fraying the tether and sending a limb spiraling off into the air. He shreds the fresh canvas over the chest, right where the heart would be, and, laughing, makes a hole of the crotch. Then, just to prove what an alpha badass he is, he takes off Old Gus's head with one clean shot. He never gets tired of that move.

Looks like I'm going to need a new dummy. "Gee, thanks," I mutter.

Byrne smiles cruelly, puts down his still smoking weapon. "Don't get all raw now. You were pussyfooting around that thing. Shooting all sloppy."

"Got a lot on my mind, I guess."

"I'll bet." The smirk fades from under his beard, and he looks at me with fatherly concern. I used to find that look comforting. I'm not feeling that much anymore. "I think," he continues, "that you and I maybe oughta talk about that girl. The hostile."

My heart jumps a beat, and I fear that he knows, that Rafe figured out where I was last night, or worse, that my own mother squealed on me. But then I relax, play it cool, act like I've got nothing to hide. "Not much to talk about," I say with a shrug.

He sizes me up in that way adults do when they know you're lying. "You know, you might not believe it, but I remember what it was like. Being young. You've been cooped up here all your life, around all the same faces, and this girl comes out of the sky, looking the way she does. I sympathize, Bowie, I really do. She's a beautiful girl. I don't mind saying it, even if I do see a little black in her features. A hint of nigger blood."

The word makes me bristle. I can't hold my tongue. "Is that a bad thing?"

Byrne chuckles bitterly. "Oh boy. Your father's getting to you, ain't he?"

"You didn't answer my question." I lay my rifle flat on the dirt and sit facing him. "I remember the Logans, and they were black. And I don't remember anything wrong about them. In fact, I remember them as good people, no worse than any of us."

"You were just a boy then, Bowie."

"So?"

"So you don't remember things how they really were." His voice is rising above his usual calm, his face set stern. "Samuel Logan was a sneak and a usurper. He was plotting to dismantle the militia as soon as he reckoned they'd outlived their use. He was a two-faced politician, the exact type of person who had driven our once great country into ruin. And his wife was no better. An opinionated, uppity bitch who thought herself better than the rest of us. Can you imagine? A nigger—a nigger *woman* no less—looking down her big, flat nose at you?" He shakes his head, as if the very thought is beyond justification. "I never liked that family, not one bit, and there were plenty here who agreed with me. I tell you, I don't believe in God, but it was some sort of divine intervention that Michael fell from the ramparts that day."

"Was it," I ask pointedly, "or was it something else?"

"Be careful, Son," Byrne growls. "Dig too deep into old graves and you might not like what you find. Remember where you stand, Bowie."

From the coldness of his eyes, I can see that to push this further would be unwise. "I stand where I always have," I say, "where I always will. In defense of Fort Thunder."

A smile cracks beneath the mask of his beard. "Good," Byrne says, patting me hard on the shoulder. "I'd hate to see your head get all twisted on account of a girl. Especially when you've won the heart of the prettiest girl in all the Fort."

It dawns on me now what this is really about. It's about Tessa. Just a father looking out for his little girl. The fearful clutch on my heart eases. I haven't been found out, not in any real way, at least. This is all due to Tessa bitching in her daddy's ear. "Don't worry about me, sir," I assure him. "I promise you'll be proud to call me your son."

"I am, Bowie. Always." He sits up with a grimace, his bones causing him grief. "That's why I came out to talk to you. I have a mission I need my best cadet for. Something important I can't entrust to just anyone."

"Of course." I readily accept. "What is it?"

"The men have been reporting geese on the northeast quad, nesting in the rocks of the great ravine. None of the Old Guard are steady enough shots these days, despite what Marcus might tell you, and I'm concerned that they'd spook the damn birds right off the island. You're the best marksman we have right now outside of myself, and I'm getting too stiff in the joints. It sure would boost morale to have some meat this winter, don't you think?"

I take a moment to process this request. There haven't been any birds nesting on the island for years, at least none that anyone has laid eyes on. "This is big news," I say. "Have you told the council about this?"

"Please," Byrne scoffs. "What do any of those jabberjaws know about hunting? Besides, I don't see any reason to get everyone all riled up if the damn birds have already flown off."

Makes sense. I nod. "I'll round up the cadets."

"No, no cadets." He takes out his tobacco pouch and pinches some chaw. "I need you to do this alone. I don't want to take any chances on one of the others mucking it up. Set out at sundown. That'll be your best chance of catching the geese unaware."

Something about this doesn't smell right, but I'm in no position to be turning down orders. "I'll set out immediately," I say.

Byrne nods his approval and spits out a brown wad of chaw. Trying not to show my disgust, I stand and gather up the 101 and what's left of my rounds. Byrne stands too, and in a shocking move, hands me his beloved AR-10.

"What's this for?" I ask.

"Luck," he answers, spitting again. Something tells me I'm gonna need it.

Accepting the weapon, I turn, heading back down the range.

"Hey, Bowie."

I turn back to him.

"Happy hunting."

ON THE WAY BACK HOME, A CHILL SETTLES IN, AND IT'S NOT JUST THAT I'M without my trusty peacoat. I have a sinking feeling about this mission that all is not what it seems. Perhaps it's that, or perhaps it's the fact that the issue of Alexis's device is still unresolved. Walking through the Fort, I don't sense anything strange in the way people look at me; things seem to be in their usual state of balance. That's good. That means if my mother has discovered the device (which she most certainly has), she hasn't said anything to anyone. It gives me some small comfort to know that my mom is not a squealer.

I go back into our dwelling, and sure enough, the coat is there, draped on the chair, right where I left it. No one else seems to be around. I rush to the chair, pick up the coat, and check the inside pocket where the device was last.

The pocket is empty.

Well, that much is settled. I quickly check my room to see if, for some reason, Mother has returned the device or maybe left it on my bed, thinking it was some harmless item, no cause for concern. Yeah right. If only my mom were that stupid. There's nothing in my room but my bed, my clothes, and Michael's toy soldier.

I consider knocking on my parents' bedroom door to see if my father is awake, but I think better of it. I'm sure if he knew about the device, he'd be waiting for me in the kitchen, pacing worriedly. He doesn't know, which makes me all the more curious about the device. Whatever it is, it's important enough that my mother is hiding it from even my father. Part of me wants to go find where she is, confront her about it, but that will only cause a scene. And that's the last thing I need. Best to let this be handled behind closed doors.

In the meantime, I have a mission to see to. This matter will have to wait.

I GATHER MY GEAR AND HEAD TO THE SQUARE, WHERE I FIND THE OTHER cadets milling around the water pump. Rafe and Jessup are making a show of being chummy with Seth, putting their arms around him and giving him noogies while his brother stands by laughing. It's clearly just more bullying, but poor Seth isn't picking up on it. He thinks they really want to be his friend. I don't like it, and as the cadets see me coming, my eyes tell them as much. The monkeyshines come to a halt. "What's going on here?" I demand.

Seth steps toward me excitedly. "We were just getting ready to—"

Before he can finish, Rafe issues a loud hiss through his teeth. Seth clams up.

"Ready to do what?" I ask Seth.

Seth looks to the others. Devon is shooting daggers at his brother. Jessup is smiling obnoxiously. Gunnar won't look me in the eye. There's something going on here, something they're not telling me, and I worry that it has to do with Alexis or with the device. I am of a mind to press them further when a whistle comes down from the south tower.

I look up to see Wilkes glaring down at me. "Bowie, if you plan on making the northern quad by sundown, you best start hoofing it."

Byrne must have briefed him on my mission. I nod to him and then turn back to the cadets, addressing Rafe, Devon, and Jessup directly. "Keep playing your little games. Papa Byrne gave me a mission, and I've been instructed to go it alone."

"Good luck," Rafe says with a punch-worthy smirk.

With a hard look, I let him know that whatever nonsense he's trying to pull, it will be dealt with when I get back. Wilkes whistles as he climbs down from the nest, and Gunnar takes the initiative to help with the winch. They crank open the gate, and I walk through, AR-10 on my shoulder, a soldier at the ready.

"Look out for zombies," Devon calls out. The others giggle. I even hear Seth joining in. He thinks he's one of the boys now and not the butt of their jokes. Poor deluded kid.

The gate closes behind me, and I don't even look back. No point in letting them think their crap actually bothers me. I've got much bigger things to worry about.

About fifty paces into the woods, I sense someone following me. When I hear the light pad of boots crunching pine needles, I know who it is. She's good—I'll give her that. A lesser cadet might not have picked up on her. A strong downwind brings with it the stink of the latrines, confirming the identity of my stalker.

"Not today, Maya."

I turn around, and there she is, not ten meters away. But she's not smiling as if this were a game. Her eyes are downcast, serious. "Please, Bowie. Let me go with you."

"Did you hear what I said? I don't have time for this."

"I heard the others talking before you came into the square," she says. "They're planning something."

"I caught a whiff of that myself," I agree. "Nothing I can't handle."

"Just let me shadow you. Trust me, I've gotten real good at it. You won't even know I'm there."

"I knew you were there just now, didn't I? Besides, if they do try to pull some nonsense on me, what are you going to do? You're just a girl."

Her lips twist into a scowl, and I can see I've angered her. "Of all the people on this stupid island, I never expected you to pull that crap on me. You know I'm as good as any of the boys in your crew. Certainly better than Jessup and that fat tub Devon."

She's right, of course. "Look," I say with a softened voice, "you're a good soldier, Maya. If it were up to me, if things were different, I'd make you a cadet in a heartbeat. But things are the way they are, and I'm in no position to change them. In case you haven't noticed, I'm in a lot of hot water right now. The last thing I need is to drag you down with me."

"I can handle my own."

"Not against this, Maya. You can't just roll back the clock twenty years and make things different. The Fort was set up this way, with men and women in the roles they're in. Do I like it? Not really. But it is what it is."

"If someone *could* change things, it would be you."

For the first time, I understand the depth of her admiration for me. The way she looks at me now, I believe she would follow me to the ends of the earth. To her own death. "Maybe one day I will," I tell her, "and when that day comes, I swear I'll allow you to be whoever you want, Maya. But that day is not today. So please, go back home and try to pretend you're the girl your father wants you to be. And dream of a better time."

She stands there, the space between us seeming like a chasm that will take years to cross. Finally, she nods, accepting my orders. Like a good soldier. "Just be careful," she warns.

"Always."

She turns, and I watch her head back toward the Fort. She disappears into the trees, and I wait a bit to make sure she isn't sneaking back to follow me. Then I realize that I'm rapidly losing the light, turn, and head due north.

I take the journey at a steady jog, racing against the slowly dropping sun. At the ravine, the trail becomes more challenging, so I stop to catch my breath and make note of my surroundings. Fall has brought the color forth from the leaves, signaling the coming chill of winter. There's a bite in the air that warns me that it might come sooner than I think.

The fastest way to the northeast quad is to stick close to the ravine, which means navigating the treacherous, uneven boulders. For an inexperienced traveler, this route would be risky as there are ankle-breaking dangers in every slanted rock and hidden crevice. But I've been familiar with this terrain since I was a boy; every gap, every grade, and every crumbling ledge or uncertain shelf is burned into my memory. On a day when I had more time, I'd even embrace the challenge, leaping from boulder to boulder, imagining myself as one of the great explorers my father likes to wax on about. But today the urgency of my mission and the doom cloud hanging over me take all the fun out of it. Today it's just a pain in the ass.

I reach the area specified by Byrne, a small valley set deep in the forest with boulders ringed around the incline, forming a sort of natural arena. Once when I was hiking with Father, he likened it to an amphitheater—an outdoor gathering place where people would listen to live music or watch others performing plays. The arts, as Father would wistfully refer to them. In earlier times, my father campaigned to have music and performance brought back into our culture, as society had soured a lot of our people on that sort of thing. Television, movies, videogames, pop music—in most people's minds those things played a big role in the downfall of man, so no one was too eager to set down that road again, removed as we might be from it now. But my father always believed that we had lost too much. "*Thrown the baby out with the bathwater*," he'd say. I never gave it much thought. I played soldier and later had my drills and exercises. That was more than enough entertainment for me.

But standing here, looking down into the valley, I can see my father's point. I find a flat boulder and take a seat, imagining some sort of play being performed below me. Hell, maybe I'd even be in the play, the main star. Father would probably insist on Shakespeare, so maybe I could sway him to put on *Romeo and Juliet*, with myself and Alexis in the roles of the doomed lovers. Yeah right. Like Tessa would ever allow that. With my luck, it would probably be *Hamlet*.

There is a rustling in the trees, and I tense to readiness. If birds are really nesting in the rocks, I don't want my sudden movement scaring them away. Years back the bluff was home to geese, but we got greedy and hunted them off. Of course there are gulls and other scavenger birds, but they are really hard to shoot down, not that we don't try just for fun. There are other species, sparrows and stuff, but they've learned to steer clear of us and stay high in the trees. Too small to eat anyway. But a gaggle of geese could keep people in meat for a good part of the winter, provided that they can be caught. I am a good shot, so I'm up for the task, though I'm not convinced that sending out only one hunter is the most surefire strategy. Then again, I'm not convinced there are geese here at all.

My eyes scan the rocks for wings, beaks, anything. My ears strain at the faint breeze, listening for a quack or a honk, that telltale guttural clucking. I hear nothing. I'm just about ready to make a sweep of the valley when something lumbers out of the forest below.

A zombie.

Heart hammering, I crouch into firing position, trying to get a read on what I'm looking at. Fifty meters or so below me, a figure shambles awkwardly among the rocks, as if stricken with some physical affliction. At this distance, I can't make out details, so I take the rifle from my shoulder and look through the high-powered scope. With a twist of the viewfinder, the lurching figure snaps into focus, the infrared imaging it in a ghostly green hue.

For a zombie, it seems awfully small and not particularly fearsome. In fact, with its stumbling legs and flailing arms, it seems downright comical. Its hair is matted with mud and sticks out from the head like the frayed end of a rope. The face is so caked with filth that I can barely make out any features aside from the whites of its eyes and an occasional tongue flickering out to lick the dirt from its lips. This zombie doesn't look capable of making it out of the ravine, let alone climbing the walls of the Fort, and I think I understand now why Alexis laughed at the mention of them. Putting the sad thing dead in my crosshairs, I ready to take it out of its misery.

But getting a closer look at those dumbfounded features, something clicks into place. In my excitement, I hadn't noticed that this zombie looks familiar.

So instead of taking the headshot, I take aim at the rocks at its feet. Then I fire. The bullet ricochets off the rock, and the zombie hops back, startled, eyes alert and searching the woods.

"Hey!" the frightened zombie yells. Now it's confirmed. I'd recognize that squeaky, uncertain voice anywhere.

The zombie is Seth.

I stand, slinging the rifle back over my shoulder. Seth sees me and waves, flashing me his goofball smile. "Stay there," I order. He can tell from the stress of my tone that I'm not finding any of this funny. He stands there, looking cowed, as I descend into the ravine.

As I get closer I see the seams in his "zombie" disguise. He's wearing a costume of old torn clothes and some natty, dirt-caked wig. Something a child would throw together to scare other children. Up close, he looks even more ridiculous than he did at a distance.

"What the hell is going on here?!"

Beneath the muck, Seth looks both scolded and defensive. "It's part of the exercise! I was just doing what I was supposed to!"

"What exercise?"

"The zombie hunt. Rafe said you knew about it. He promised there wouldn't be real shooting!"

Now I'm really getting angry, but not at Seth. "Rafe didn't clear it with me."

"But he said the orders came straight from Pap—"

There is a *BOOM* and Seth's head explodes and blood and brains and bits of skull spatter my face and he falls to the ground and there isn't much of a head left at all and I yell something, I think it's his name, and I fall to the ground and try to pull his skull back together but there aren't any eyes. Oh god, what happened to his eyes...

BOOM! Another shot, striking low, by my feet. I whip around, slinging the rifle into my arms, scanning the trees with the scope. Judging the angle of the shot, I figure it came from behind me at an angle of one hundred and seventy degrees, maybe five. But I may have judged wrong as all I see in the scope are half-dead branches swaying in the gentle breeze.

Then I see it. Sunlight glinting off a gun barrel. Even at this distance I can tell it's an M16, standard issue for cadets. I follow the black barrel of the gun down to the sights, where eyes are trained on me, readying to take the shot. It's easy to identify the eyes. Only Rafe is both cruel and cowardly at the same time. Giving it no further thought, I pull the trigger.

Click. Nothing. I pull the trigger again. *Click. Click.* The clip is empty.

Byrne gave me a clip with only one bullet. Why would he...?

There is a *BOOM* and I raise my arm and there is pain and then only black.

CHAPTER EIGHT

The Tablet

I AM IN A SWAMP.

I have never seen a swamp as there are none on the bluff, but I've read about them and had them described to me. I'm not sure where this swamp is, on the mainland or not, but I know why I'm here. The brackish water I slosh through is strangely warm and steam rises from the marshland in bursts of heat, giving me a strange thrill. Unseen, high in the mossy trees, swamp birds cry out, their shrill voices wavering like ghosts. I reach for my shoulder, but my rifle is no longer there. Panic floods me. How will I succeed in my hunt if I haven't got a weapon? I reach around my back and am relieved to find my boomerang there, tucked into my belt, lying flat against my skin. Not ideal for hunting birds, but it will do. I pull the weapon from my belt and hold it at the ready, feeling the weight of it in my hand. It seems much heavier than before.

The trees thin out into a clearing, and the bird cries stop. Here the steam has thickened to a foggy soup, and my eyes struggle to scan through it. Around me are haunted shapes, probing skeletal fingers I can only assume are the reaching branches of dead trees. Suddenly I feel eyes upon me, and I whip around, but all there is to judge me is more trees and fog. I curse the silence, but no voice issues from my throat, just a dry, empty croak. I am about to turn around when a mocking gobble comes from above, and the fog clears enough to grant me a glimpse of my tree-bound tormentor. It sits on a lone branch, high on a tree that stands taller than the rest, hunched in a tangle of black feathers. Red-rimmed eyes glare down at me from a head no bigger than a potato, which bobs on the end of a long, ropy neck. It caws at me with a beak sharp enough to peck through wood and flares its wings out like a vampire's cape. This is the first vulture I've seen outside of my father's wildlife encyclopedias, and it looks ready to feast on me whether I'm dead or alive. As I raise my weapon and ready to throw, the winged beast shrieks in challenge.

Sensing what I am about to do, the vulture takes flight, swooping toward me, black wings flapping.

Panicked, I throw, but the boomerang arcs high and wide, spiraling past the bird without clipping so much as a feather. Reaching me, the creature rears back, screeching, gnarled talons raking me across my raised arm. I swat at it, but it only drives the thing further into a frenzy, shrieking and tearing, ripping strips of flesh from my shoulders and chest. Its knife-beak pecks at me, snapping centimeters from my nose, and my voice finally returns with a pathetic cry of defeat. Terrified, I run, swamp water sucking at my legs, and behind me I hear the horrible bird mocking me with a shriek. I don't care about the bird or even this mission. All I want is to be away, to be out of this swamp and back in my dry bed. All I want is to be home.

If I can make it home. The more I try to run, the more the thick, sucking mud clings to me, weighing me down, forcing me to a slow trudge. Looking down at my waist, I see that I am sinking, and panic grips me as I search for dry land. But all there is as far as I can see is swamp in every direction. I keep pressing forward, mindful that with every labored step I sink a little farther into the muck, hoping to find a rock or a branch or anything to climb onto. Finally, ahead I see something floating on the surface of the water, and though it doesn't look like much, any break in the miasma is enough to give me hope. Pushing hard, I wade toward the floating object, reaching it after several muscle-straining minutes.

Struggling for breath, I look down and see the flat black object Alexis rescued from the plane. Reaching for it, I wonder, how did it get out here? I can't imagine it'll be much help to me out here, but at least I can bring it back to her if I get out of this alive. My fingers brush the smooth surface of the slate-like object, bringing it suddenly to life.

There is an image on the flat side of the object, like a reflection in mirror glass. But looking closer, I don't see myself reflected back but another face entirely. It takes me a moment to recognize him with a face full of dirt and wearing that matted wig.

Seth. It's Seth's face that smiles back up at me. He still has his eyes. Didn't something happen to his eyes...?

"Wanna see a zombie," Seth asks, "for real this time?"

Something tells me I don't, so I stumble back, leaving the object floating on the surface of the mud. Not that it stays there. With a hiss and a gurgle, the swamp swallows it, the water around it churning into a violent whirlpool. I turn to run, but the vulture is there, screeching and ripping at my face with its talons. My feet slip out from under me, and I fall back into the whirlpool, cold water filling my ears with a rush. Struggling, I try to swim out, but something pulls at my leg, yanking me deeper and deeper into the muck.

Looking down, I see Seth there under the water, eyes leering at me from what is left of his skull. But then I realize that it's not Seth at all; it's my childhood friend Michael, looking to me with eyes full of betrayal. He has come for me, come to make me pay for my crimes against him, against Seth, against my father, my mother, my people. It's time to answer for my sins, and there is nothing, and no one, who can save me.

Michael (or is it Seth?) opens his mouth, issuing a cluster of bubbles. Yet somehow, in the rising trapped air, I can still hear a voice.

It's calling my name.

"BOWIE!"

My eyes snap open to a blinding white. A light brighter than the sun is glaring down at me, directly into my face. Mercifully, a silhouette comes into view, blocking it. At first, I can't make out any details, but then a face forms, gentle, smiling gratefully. A face I've seen in dreams far more pleasant than the one I am waking from.

I try to speak, but pain in my throat stops me. "It's OK, don't try to talk," Alexis says, tucking a fallen lock of hair behind her ear. As it passes my face, it brushes my nose with a tickle. I'm in far too much pain to enjoy it. "I'll get the others."

She rushes out of the room, and I realize I'm in the infirmary. Recent terrible events come rushing back. Seth. Gunshots. Rafe. The hunting assignment was all a trap, and judging by Seth's final words, it was all set up by Byrne. So why am I still alive?

My right eye throbs wickedly, and I reach to touch it, but my upper arm feels even worse when I move it. It occurs to me that I used it to shield myself from a bullet, which likely passed through my forearm on the way to my head. I fight through the pain and reach for my eye, but all I feel when I get there is softness. Gauze. That would explain why I'm looking through a half-haze. My right eye has been bandaged. I only hope it's still there underneath.

The door opens, and in step my mother and father, followed by Doc Seaver and Frankie. They all wear looks of concern and relief. Alexis stands behind them, peeking through their shoulders, but Frankie gently shoos her back and closes the door. Now it's just me and the adults.

"Oh, Bowie," Mother gasps. "Thank god you're alive!"

She rushes to my side, and my father smiles at me, fighting through pain of his own. "We're so grateful you're all right, Son. We thought we might lose you for a minute there."

There is a cup of water sitting on the side table, and I reach for it, wincing. Mother gets the cup for me and puts it to my lips. Cool water soothes my ragged throat. After several greedy gulps, my mother pulls it away, assuring that I don't make myself sick by drinking too much too soon. I appreciate the sentiment, but god, I'm so thirsty.

"What..." I force through the tightness of my tortured throat, "What happened?"

Father and Mother exchange a nervous glance. The Seavers cast their eyes solemnly downward. "We'll talk about that later, Son," my father says.

"No," I demand, "now."

My father looks to my mother again, and she nods. He gathers a breath and tells me, "There was an accident at the ravine. At least, I believe it was an accident. Some of the boys were out there doing maneuvers, and they said you came out of the woods and shot Seth. They said you mistook him for a zombie."

Anger surges in me, bringing with it waves of pain. "Not true," I croak, my voice a wind through dry leaves. "Didn't shoot Seth. Was a setup. Rafe shot Seth."

Nervous glances are passed around by the adults. The anger worsens. Do they not believe my word over that snake, Rafe? But then my father moves closer to me, and I can see that he does believe me. By the low voice with which he talks, I gather that we are all under scrutiny. Not surprising, considering the architect of this entire event is one Patrick Byrne. "I believe you," my father continues. "Of course we all do. But as you can imagine, this is no minor incident. This was a carefully planned and orchestrated incident, and there's a reason for that. Byrne couldn't risk having you killed by the others, even if it was made to look like an accident. The cadets killing their leader, even by friendly fire, would throw all of his training into question as far as the council is concerned. It could even jeopardize his standing as leader of the militia, which is the last thing he wants. By making it look like you were the one to kill Seth, he can claim you went rogue, even if the shooting is ruled accidental. This way is cleaner as the council will have no choice but to banish you, and Byrne's authority will never be questioned."

My father's theory, wild as it may be, does make sense. Starting at a very young age, we are trained on firearm safety, and no cadet is even allowed to carry a gun until he has completed over one thousand hours on the shooting range under strict supervision. With drills and chores, this takes most cadets over a year to complete, but I finished mine in under six months when I turned fourteen. It's always been a point of pride for me, and I'm ashamed to say I've bragged about it on more than one occasion. Now I wonder if it will be used against me. If an accusation of carelessness will be leveled at anyone, it will be me and not Byrne. And as far as the orders he gave me that brought me to the ravine, well, it'll be my word against his.

Guess whose word holds more sway with the council?

My already low spirits sink even further. Sensing this, my father puts his hand lightly on my shoulder. It's the one place on my body that doesn't hurt. "It's OK, Son. We'll find a way through this, I promise. One way or another."

I wish I could believe him. The more I think about it, the worse it gets. A twinge in my brow reminds me of another problem, one that could mean redundancy even if I am somehow cleared of Seth's murder. "My eye?" I ask.

Doc Seaver steps forward, his kind, well-worn face offering me a modest smile. "We were able to save the eye, thank goodness. Bullet grazed the eyelid and brow, and you'll have a nasty scar, but you won't lose it. You might have a little trouble with the arm when it comes to shooting, but with therapy I'm confident we can get you back up to speed in that department."

Though I doubt I will be allowed any therapy time, I am grateful nonetheless. Facing banishment with a bad eye and an arm that won't shoot is all but a death sentence. "If I shot Seth," I mutter, "why am I the one who's shot up?"

"The way Rafe tells it, after you shot Seth, he tried to get your attention, and you panicked and shot at him. He didn't think you meant to do it, figured you were just spun out about Seth. He said he had to take a shot at you before you fired on him or the others. Said he only fired in self-defense and that he wasn't trying for a kill shot."

"Tell that to my eye," I grumble.

Father asks the others to leave, which they do. I catch another glimpse of Alexis in the other room as they leave. My father notices. "You really need to keep your mind off of her," he advises. "That's really not going to help your cause."

I nod in agreement, and we talk strategy. Even if I hadn't been injured, I'd be taken off duty until the council met to decide my fate. This suits me just fine. As far as I can tell, my cadets are trying to kill me, so the less time with them the better. As for my accusation toward Rafe, Father doesn't know if it's wise that I use that as my defense. He thinks it will make it seem like I'm trying to deflect my guilt onto him, which is something the council tends to frown upon. Blame-shifting was a practice common in the old world, and we are a people who believe in taking responsibility for our own actions. Easy thing to believe when you're not being set up, but I see my father's point. It would be one thing if I had any evidence, but right now, I don't. If there was a way to find the bullet that killed Seth, maybe, but Father says that there was no reason to suspect foul play, and poor Seth was already buried.

I think of Vanessa O'Reilly, Seth's mother, imagining her stricken with grief. I also imagine her wanting to see my head on a spike, and when I ask, Father all but confirms it. Best stay away from her for the time being. I wonder if Devon knows it was Rafe that killed his brother, or if he's been rooked along with everyone else. Not a deep thinker, that Devon. He's probably calling for my head along with his mother and god knows who else.

We conspire until the subject is exhausted, and I tell Father that he should go home and rest. Judging from the pain worn into his face, he's in no mood to argue. We say our goodnights, and he assures me that I'll be safe in here and that Paul Haverford will be guarding the infirmary. Not exactly comforting to know a farmer is all that stands between me and the mob, but I wouldn't trust any of the militia, that's for sure. Maybe Wilkes could be trusted as he was always the most even-keeled. Still, Paul Haverford will have to suffice.

It doesn't matter; I won't be sleeping anyway. Before he leaves, Father slips an object into my hands. "A little insurance," he says. I recognize it without having to look; the smooth, curved wood tells me all I need to know. My father walks out the door, and I slip the boomerang under the covers, keeping it ready and by my side.

Somehow, I must have dozed off because the sound of the door unlatching snaps me awake. I bolt up in bed, boomerang drawn back, and try to make out the shape that stands in the doorway with my one good eye. When I see the way the light catches her hair, I know. My pulse quickens, not from danger but from seeing the way her eyes look at me.

"Bowie," Alexis whispers, "it's me. I'm sorry, I didn't mean to—"

"It's OK," I rasp. "Come in."

She creeps in the room and closes the door behind her. Seeing there's nowhere for her to sit, I scoot over on the bed, sending a flash of pain up my side. Alexis notices the wince on my face. "Are you sure?"

"I'm fine. It's nothing," I lie. "Come on. Sit."

She comes over to the bed and sits, her body pressing slightly against mine. Even through the pain it gives me a rush to be so close. In the darkness, I can just make out her profile looking down at her hands. "I'm so sorry, Bowie. For all of this."

"This isn't your fault."

"I think it is," she says grimly. "The other morning, right after I snuck in, Frankie Seaver woke me and suggested I get involved with the Fort to warm people up to my presence. I tried to discourage her, but I couldn't exactly tell her that I was out all night with you. So I agreed, and she took me with her to work in one of the gardens."

None of this sounds particularly incriminating. "So?"

"Well, there were other girls there already, girls my age. One of them was *your* girl, Tessa. I told Frankie that it wasn't a good idea, but she insisted. Said that the best way to get in Byrne's good graces was to be nice to his daughter. I thought she was out of her mind, but what could I do? I said I'd give it a shot, so I went over and asked the girls if I could help them with their work. Naturally, the others looked to Tessa, but she just smiled at me and said it was fine. I mean, I didn't believe her, but I figured she was playing nice, so I went along with it. Besides, as far as I knew, she had no idea about you sneaking me out. I figured the worst I'd get was some catty girl talk. That I can handle. Trust me, girls are the same no matter where you're from.

"So I grab this stick that passes as a rake and start raking in the dirt. Frankie says that they're trying to get a last crop of potatoes in before winter, so I'm like, fine, and just keep my head down and rake. This goes on for a while—just Frankie, me, and the girls raking—and then this other woman comes along. Real pretty, striking blue eyes. Like yours."

I nod, knowing who she means. "My mother."

"Yeah, I figured. Anyway, your mom asks to talk to Frankie in private, and the two of them go off a ways to the fence so we girls can't hear them. I see your mom keep glancing over at me, and I'm getting paranoid, like she knows something. Like maybe she found the tablet I gave you."

It takes a moment for me to realize what she means. The device. I remember now my coat and its empty inside pocket. "Yeah," I confirm, "I think she might have."

Alexis accepts this with a tight-lipped nod. "Yeah, well, we never get to that. As soon as the two women are off talking, Tessa slinks right over to me and starts giving me a hard time. She says she's on to me, that she knows I'm after you, and that you'll never fall for my 'nigger' charms. I mean, she seriously calls me a nigger. Where I'm from, using that word is serious. You don't just go around saying that shit. Not that it bothers me—my father is black, and I'm damn proud to be who I am. If it were up to me, I'd look more ethnic than I do."

Even in the darkness, I find her skin color perfect how it is. I wouldn't change a thing. "I'm sorry," I tell her.

"No, I'm the one who is sorry. I don't know what came over me. I just hauled back and let the rake fly, right into Tessa's face. Knocked her clear on her ass. Then she got up and came at me, and it turned into an all-out brawl. Took Frankie and your mom to tear us off of each other, and by that time a whole crowd had gathered. It was a total mess."

"OK," I say. "So you got in a fight? So what? What does this have to do with anything?"

"I think," Alexis continued, shakily, "I think that ever since you brought me back here, your loyalty to this place has been in question. Byrne has a lot a people talking in his ear right now, and his daughter's voice is awfully loud. Plus, to hear Frankie and Doc Seaver talk about it, your father and Byrne have never exactly seen eye to eye. Byrne probably figures the best way to get your father out of the way is to get you out of the way, especially if it looks like you're being led around by a girl who isn't his daughter. A girl from the outside world, no less."

"Well, whatever the reason, it doesn't matter much now," I say. "He made his move. What's done is done. Regardless of why, he wants me out."

"He wants both of us out," Alexis confirms, "and something tells me that Byrne is a guy who gets what he wants."

We sit there a while, soaking in the truth of her words. The weight of all this tires me, and I doze off again, and when I wake, Alexis is gone. It's probably for the best. No point in giving Byrne more kindling to throw on my funeral pyre.

Outside the infirmary people are talking, and I recognize the loudest voice as belonging to Vanessa O'Reilly. She's hysterical, demanding that I be tried for my crimes. And who can really blame her for that? But as much as I sympathize with the poor woman, I am in no shape to stand up to an angry mob and am relieved when my father comes in with Wilkes and August Christiansen flanking him, rifles on their shoulders. I can tell by the way the militia men are looking at me that they believe Byrne's story, but they believe in Fort law and won't drag me out there to be torn apart by the mob.

"You think you can walk?" my father asks me.

Whether I can or not, I nod and swing my legs out of bed. The pain is bad but not as bad as it was last night, and most of it's in my head and arm. I stand, and my legs are a little wobbly, but they work. Father steps in to help, and I swing an arm over his shoulders.

He turns me around, and I look right into the face of my best friend's father. "I didn't do this, August," I say. "No matter what Rafe says, I didn't do it."

August's face remains stony behind his reddened beard, but something in his eyes tells me that he believes me. Or at least, he's *willing* to believe me. If

Wilkes shares this sentiment, he doesn't make it known. "Save it for the council," he says gruffly.

Taking his unfriendly advice, I leave it at that. I'm just grateful they didn't send Nagel in here to fetch me. I'm sure that one has already made up his mind.

With my father's support, I am escorted out of the room and through the infirmary. Doc Seaver and Frankie are waiting out there, giving me their silent sympathy. Alexis is nowhere to be seen, and I can only assume she's off in one of the other rooms. Best not to give the militiamen anything to talk about. Not that I think Alexis would give anything away in the way that she looked at me. But better safe than sorry.

The crowd that greets us outside the infirmary doors is smaller than I was expecting. The O'Reillys are there along with their closest friends, the Ericksons, twins and all, as well as the cadets and the rest of the militia. Rafe stands next to Byrne and doesn't have the stones to look at me, which is hardly surprising. I catch sight of Nagel, high in one of the towers, and he smiles down at me and pulls back his arrowless bow, as if taking aim. He lets the invisible arrow fly with a twang, but I don't give him the satisfaction of flinching.

We start through the square, but Seth's mother runs out from the crowd and gets right in front of me. I remember being a kid and her making me cookies for being nice to her son when no one else would. Now I'm the one being blamed for his death. "Murderer!" she screams and spits right into my one good eye. Saliva drips down my face in a thick wad.

"I didn't kill your son," I tell her. "I would have never hurt Seth."

There are angry shouts from the crowd, and Devon steps forward and gently holds his mother back. Vanessa's husband died a few years back, so Seth's death must be a devastating blow. All the poor woman is left with now is her fat disappointment of a son—a son who will never amount to anything in the militia no matter who is in charge. I look Devon dead in the eye and try to suss out what he's thinking, or more importantly, what he might know. All I can read there is hatred, so I have to assume he believes what he's been told. No big loss as he was never much of an ally to begin with, and if he wants to come at me, he's welcome to try. Even with my injuries I'm sure I can take him.

Things are getting tense; Vanessa's screaming at me, blaming me, and resisting as Devon attempts—failing, as always—to pull her away. Finally, Byrne comes over, and Vanessa defers, stepping back and clearing him a path to me. He looks me over with disappointment.

"I had high hopes for you, Bowie," he says with false regret. "Not just for the militia. You were going to be family."

Behind him, across the square, I see Tessa lurking by the storage containers. I expect to see her smiling triumphantly, her plan seen to fruition, but that isn't the look she's giving. Maybe it's the welt on her forehead, a gift from Alexis's rake, but she doesn't look like someone who is pleased with herself. She looks like someone who has allowed things to go further than she wanted them to. Someone with regrets.

But her father needs to be my focus now, so I turn my attention back to him. "I have a family," I rasp with what little defiance I can.

"Yes, well, you should have thought about them before you shot another cadet."

Nothing would make me feel better than to spit out the truth—his plan, Rafe, all of it— and expose him here in front of everyone. But I remember my father's warning and keep my mouth shut. If the truth is to come out, I will have to find a way to prove it or risk looking like I'm trying to pass the blame. I have to come at him with facts, not accusations. Unfortunately, I am coming to realize that facts are in short supply here at Fort Thunder, but blame is plentiful.

It's almost as if Byrne is waiting for me to make the accusation, goading me even. When I don't, he gets back down to business. "The council will meet on your matter tomorrow morning. I don't see any reason to delay. I'll expect you and your father to be present."

"Of course I'll be present!" Father snaps. "I'm *on* the goddamn council!"

"Council bylaws strictly forbid a relative of the accused voting on the matter of their banishment." Byrne clearly had rehearsed this line. "You are welcome to provide counsel and be present, but you will not be an active participant in his judgment."

"I know the damn laws, Patrick," my father hisses. "I wrote them."

"And for that we will be forever in your debt. Now take your son home, Harlan, and get some rest. You both have a very big day tomorrow."

With that, the crowd in the square disperses. Vanessa O'Reilly melts into a blubbering mess, but Devon manages to somehow walk her out of the square. Father, our escorts, and I are allowed safe passage back to my home. When we reach it, Mother is waiting with hot soup and a face full of worry. August volunteers to stand watch in case anyone gets any ideas about harassing us. I'm not too worried about that as mob justice carries harsh penalties here at the Fort, but then again, there's never been an incident like this before. I'm setting a whole new precedent.

I eat hungrily as it's been awhile since I've had a proper meal. Mother brings some soup outside for August, which I'm sure he's happy to accept. There's a chill settling over the Fort, a sign of early snowfall, possibly as early as tomorrow. It only seems fitting that my freezing out should be accompanied by actual snow. Unfortunately, that makes the prospect of banishment all the more unpleasant and survival the more unlikely. Had this happened in summer, I'd have a fighting chance of setting up camp or at least some time to forage. If it starts to snow, I'll be lucky to make it to the ranger station before freezing to death.

When my mother returns, she clears the emptied soup bowls and takes her seat back at the table. She looks to my father, and he nods, and I know I'm in for some kind of serious talk. When he pulls the tablet out of his jacket pocket, I know why.

"Your mother found this in your coat," he says. "Do you know what it is?"

"No," I answer. "I mean, I know it's called a *tablet*, but that's all."

His eyes search mine, finding the truth. He places the tablet flat on the table. "As you know, the world we left behind had experienced a great boom in technology. People were able to use devices like this to communicate, to find information, to entertain themselves. They could connect with each other over vast distances, all over the world. It changed everything. Suddenly it seemed like the sum of all knowledge was available to everyone, right at their fingertips, able to be taken anywhere, accessed anytime. But there was a price to be paid. Because that kind of access and connectivity meant that the government had all of that access as well. They could spy on you, learn anything they wanted to know with a swipe of a finger. The notion of privacy was destroyed, and only those who dared to live off the grid, out of the gaze of the satellites, could claim to truly be free. Everyone else became a slave to this technology. To convenience."

As much as I appreciate the lecture, I know all of this. He's talking about computers, digital stuff. "So this is a cell phone?" I ask flatly.

"For all intents and purposes," Father answers. "This device was designed specifically for reading books." He scoffs, picking up the tablet as if it is an absurdity. "Can you believe that people actually chose this over reading a real book? Ridiculous."

"I don't know. You make it sound like it could be any book ever written. That doesn't sound so ridiculous to me."

My mother cracks a small smile and tries to avert it from my father, but he catches it and grumbles, "Yes, well, the question remains as to how this came into your possession."

I could go into a whole story, lie to cover up the expedition I took with Alexis, but what would be the point of that now? Still, the less they know the better. "Alexis gave it to me for safekeeping," I answer with a soldier's brevity.

This seems to satisfy my father. "Yes, well, I don't know how she managed to sneak it in here, but she was right to hide it. This is a very dangerous item, as I think you well know. But, as it turns out, it might also be the key to our salvation."

"But it doesn't work," I point out. "Alexis tried it, and it was broken."

Father looks to Mother, and she reaches across the table and takes up the tablet. Searching a moment, she runs her finger along the side, pressing a button I hadn't even noticed was there. The flat face of the tablet lights up, and my eyes immediately lock on it. Nothing here at Fort Thunder has that kind of glow. It's impossible not to look at it. "I remembered an old trick from before of putting these things in rice," Mother says. "It seems to have worked."

A circular icon spins on the tablet's screen, giving way to a small window with a blinking icon. Text beneath it asks for a password. "As you can see," Mother continues, "the device is locked. We'll need Alexis's help if we hope to use it."

"Use it for what?" I ask.

My father's eyes settle on me, determined and steely. "To contact the mainland."

This takes me a moment to process. I know what he means, but I've understood the world a certain way for so long that a part of me still won't believe it. "But there's nothing there."

In my mind, I imagine the world I've been told awaits on the other side of the bay. A world decimated by war, an irradiated wasteland crawling with zombies and hostiles, the only semblances of civilization being ramshackle villages and savage, wandering tribes. This is the world every child that is born in Fort Thunder believes exists beyond our island, past the sad wreckage of the Densmore. This is the gospel we've been handed at birth. It informs who we are, keeps us united, and forms the very core of all we believe.

And it is a lie. I knew it the moment I set eyes on Alexis. Nothing so beautiful could come from such a world. In her face, I see none of the pain and horror I've been promised is outside our walls, waiting for its chance to invade. I see nothing of the war I've been training to fight all of my life. That war is a fable, no more real than the stories in my father's old books.

But I need to hear it from him. "Bowie," he says after a long gathering of thought, "the truth is we don't know anything about what waits on the mainland. Things were bad when we left, and we never looked back. The things you and the other children have been told are what we believed *could* happen, but as to *reality*...well, that we don't know. We cut ourselves off from all that. Isolated ourselves. Things could have gone how we imagined—how we *feared* they were going—or society could have pulled itself back from the brink. Alexis would seem evidence that it did, and that is why she is a threat. If we allowed you and the others of your generation to form your own ideas about the mainland, to get *curious*, well, then some of you would leave. Maybe all of you would leave. And then where would we be?"

"I wouldn't have left." And that's the true irony of all this. Even if I was given some inkling that the mainland wasn't an apocalyptic wasteland, I still would have stayed. I would have remained firm in my faith in our society, loyal to what we built here, and true to my people—loyal to Fort Thunder, come what may. But now I see that whatever waits out there is no worse than we are. We were the hostiles all along, just as Alexis said.

My father and mother share a look that is both prideful and sad. Mother reaches across the table to take my hand. I can feel her trembling. "You're a good son, Bowie Neville. And you're going to be a great man. All your father and I want is for you to have a chance to be that great man. We don't care where you end up or who you end up with. We just want what's right for you. And right now, we feel that what's right for you is to leave."

"It's looking like I'm not going to have a choice," I say.

"I'm afraid it's not that simple," says Father. His face is showing strain, not just from the stress of the situation but from the pain I know he's holding at bay. "We can't trust the council to banish you and just leave it at that. For one, if they banish you, they know your mother and I will opt to go with you, which leaves a power vacuum Byrne will exploit."

"You're not coming with me!" I look to Mother for support. "I won't allow that! I'm sorry, but this is my problem, and I'll face it alone!"

Father holds up a reasoning hand. "Now, just hear me out. In the event that the council votes for banishment, your mother and I will stay. But there's more here that concerns me. You see, I'm not convinced that Byrne is going to be content just letting you live out there by yourself on this island. He's going to come after you. Not with the council's blessing, of course, but the council won't know what he and the militia are up to. They won't know if he's hunting you. And if he finds you—and trust me, he will—no one will have any way of knowing what happens to you when he does."

My throat tightens. "So you're saying he'll kill me."

Father's face is set tight, grim. "Him or one of his men. The point is, no one will ever know. If he lets you live, if he lets you peaceably coexist on the bluff, he runs the risk of you returning and seizing control of the militia. And if he just lets you stroll off the island when the bay ices over, then he risks you gathering forces on the mainland and coming back to level the Fort. Either way, from his way of thinking, letting you live is a risk he can't afford."

Hard as it is to admit, my strategist mind sees the sense of this. And it's true—if Byrne lets me live, I will come back. Not just for my mother and father but for my people. "So," I say, "what are we going to do?"

Father and Mother exchange a last look. Mother lays the tablet flat on the table and taps on the screen. "You're going to ask Alexis for help."

I SNEAK OUT A FEW HOURS BEFORE DAWN. AUGUST IS EASY TO GET PAST AS my mother made sure his food was laced with herbs that promote sleep. I don't put a lot of stock in the power of my mother's herbs, but old August is sawing serious logs when I creep out my front door and over him. I just hope I can get back before he wakes up.

Arrangements have been made with the Seavers for me to meet Alexis by the storage units. This was all done earlier, without my involvement, naturally. The Seavers are putting themselves on the line by doing this, but they have always been good friends, more loyal to my father than to Byrne and his men. Seeing as Doc is the only true medic the Fort has, it would take a lot for him to be banished, but I wouldn't put anything past Byrne at this point. I'll repay the Seavers's loyalty one day if I'm able. If I make it through this whole thing alive.

I find her at the farthest end of the containers, through the maze created by the empty spaces between units. This is a favored make out spot for teens as it's hidden away and easy to see or hear someone coming. Tessa and I made out here once, but I can't say truthfully that I had a good time. She just stood there, making my tongue do all the work, like it was all on me. I'd like to try kissing someone else to see if all girls are like that, as I suspect they're not. I wish I was coming here to make out with Alexis, but something tells me that kissing is the last thing on her mind. Still, when she sees me, she smiles.

"So," she says, "why the secret meeting?"

I pull the tablet out of my coat. Her eyes light up. "You found it!"

"My mother found it," I tell her, "and she showed my father."

Her face tenses, troubled. She takes it from my hand. "Did they tell anyone else?"

"No."

"Good." She finds the button on the side, presses it. The screen lights up, and she looks at me excitedly. "Oh my god, it's working!"

"Well now. Isn't that pretty."

My blood freezes. I glance up at the sound of the gravelly voice, and Alexis does the same. But I already know who it belongs to. Cable straining against the pulleys of a compound bow only confirms it.

On top of the storage units, Nagel leers down, armed and ready to shoot.

CHAPTER NINE

The Armory

IT'S NEARLY MIDMORNING BEFORE BYRNE AND THE COUNCIL COME INTO the armory.

After he caught us, Nagel held us in the square with the help of Wilkes and a woken August. Nagel chewed out August for falling asleep, and Wilkes went off to fetch Byrne. When he arrived, he was fresh and groomed, as if he never went to bed and was waiting for this all night. Like he knew it was going to happen. He took the confiscated tablet and didn't seem the least bit surprised by it. He asked me where we got it, and Alexis said she snuck out on her own to retrieve it from the plane. Byrne didn't look like he believed her, and rightfully so. Then he ordered us locked in the armory, and that was that.

Even as distressed as she is, I can see that, on some level, Alexis is impressed with the high, steepled building with its endless rack of guns, reaching skyward like some monument to a god of firearms. As we sit here, tied to chairs at the council table, she looks around with a sort of fearful reverence. "I have to hand it to you," she says after a long, gawking minute, "your people certainly are dedicated to their ideals."

I struggle at my bonds, trying every trick I know to get loose. Not that it would matter. Even if I could pull free, the armory is still the most secure building in Fort Thunder; that's why Byrne locked us in it. The weapons surrounding us on all sides are not loaded; the mountains of clips and bullets are all kept in a locked metal shed, accessible only outside of this building. In all the years I have been alive at Fort Thunder, not one person has managed to break into the armory, steal a weapon, and arm it. There are no stockades at the Fort because there isn't any need for them. Jails and prisons are seen as emblematic of the old world's sickness, and people here are trusted to govern their own behavior, and if they can't, they are banished. Until now, no one has ever needed to be locked up. So in a way, Alexis and I are real trailblazers. Hooray for us.

We don't talk much after that. There isn't much to say. I figure with Byrne's discovery of the tablet our banishment is all but assured now. This "trial" will be nothing but a formality, and my time is better spent thinking of what to do once we are outside the Fort walls.

When the council finally does arrive, I am surprised and hopeful to see my father among them. Mother, of course, is absent as women aren't allowed on the council. In fact, as far as I know, no woman has ever stepped foot inside the armory. Alexis is the first female to do so—yet another first—not that I bother telling her. The cadets are also all accounted for, no doubt called to testify as witnesses. The only one among them who bothers to look at me is Gunnar, and I can't tell if the look he's giving me is one of sympathy or disappointment. As for the council, they are stony as ever, and nothing about these proceedings suggests they will soften.

Nagel and August come over to untie Alexis and me, Nagel handling me with deliberate roughness. I can see him holding back a smile as he forces me to stand before the head of the table. Wilkes brings Alexis to stand next to me with considerably more gentleness.

The council, Byrne included, take their seats at the table. From this angle, I am able to admire the polished, redwood tabletop; I can even see myself reflected in its shine. Father takes the head of the table, another surprise, with Doc Seaver and the agriculturalists, Alan Erickson, Walter Kassidy, and Paul Haverford, at his right. Custodian Russell Clark sits at the very end, as if the stink of the latrines earns him the farthest spot down from the head. To Father's left sits Byrne and his militiamen—Nagel; Wilkes; August; and Jessup's father, Nicholas Mitchell. A seat sits empty at the end, representing the place Matt O'Reilly would be if he were still alive. There is no seat left for Samuel Logan. The excommunicated don't get placeholders to honor them.

My father picks a gavel up from the table and bangs it three times. "This meeting of the council of Fort Thunder is hereby called to order," he says.

Glances are thrown around the table by men who are uncomfortable with what they've been called here to judge. My father continues, "The business at hand today is very serious, the most serious of all matters, and I ask that you treat it with the gravity it demands. As it involves my son, I relinquish my chair as head of the council to Patrick Byrne. He will guide the proceedings from here on out."

He passes the gavel to Byrne, who handles it with the reverence of a sacred artifact. He stands, his face a solemn mask, and bangs hard on the table. "Gentleman of the council," he begins, "I agree with councilman Neville that this is a matter of utmost concern, and recent events have compounded the situation to the point that, in my mind, it can only be resolved in one way." He points the hammer end of the gavel at myself and Alexis. "With the banishment of this outsider as well as her accomplice and accused murderer, Bowie Neville."

I look to the cadets, who stand to the left, lined up behind the militia. Their faces are still as stone, eyes forward. Even Rafe keeps his usual smirk in check. Byrne turns to them. "We will begin with the most pressing matter, the murder of Seth O'Reilly."

"Objection," my father interrupts. "No one is calling this a murder."

"The killing of a cadet, whether by intent or by accident, is a murder by our law. When we founded this society, we agreed to do away with the grey area mentality that allowed for so many criminals to go free or benefit from reduced sentences. There are no degrees here at Fort Thunder. If one person kills another for any reason at all, then it is murder."

There are mutters of agreement from the council members as the agreements of the past, information that hasn't been called for since before our walls were raised, shake loose in their minds. For these men, this is the first—and likely last—murder trial they will preside over. Byrne checks down the table to see if there are further objections. There aren't. I can't help but feel that most of these men just want this unpleasantness over with, and I can't really blame them.

"Right then," Byrne confirms. "I call upon Rafe Nagel to give his testimony of the tragic events that occurred two days ago in the northeast quad."

Rafe takes a sharp step forward, stands arrow straight, playing the good soldier. "That afternoon, Bowie was given a classified mission that myself and the others weren't privy to. We had no idea where he was going or what he was doing. As I was left in charge, I decided to run an exercise where Seth would dress as a zombie and I and the others would hunt him. Not for real, of course, just a drill—our guns weren't even loaded."

"If your guns weren't loaded," I interrupt, "then how did you shoot me?" I gesture to my scarred and damaged eye. "Did I do this to myself?"

"Objection," Byrne says sharply. "The accused will not speak until asked to."

"Then I'll ask the question," my father demands. "How was Rafe able to wound my son if the guns they were using for the exercise weren't equipped with live rounds?"

Rafe looks to Byrne, and I can see a nervous sweat forming on his lip. Byrne offers him a nod, as if permitting him to go on with something they've rehearsed. "I loaded my rifle after I heard the first shot," Rafe says. "I had been watching it all from higher up along the ravine. I had no idea that Bowie intended to shoot Seth. If I had, I would have stopped him."

Without realizing I've done it, I scoff. Father shoots me a look, and I straighten. Being flippant will get me nowhere with the council, so I must endure this fabricated nonsense with decorum. Even if it kills me to do so. "I will ask the council to allow my son his version of the events," Father says.

The men exchange glances and nods. "Permitted," Byrne concedes.

Taking a moment to gather myself, I stand straight and keep my eyes locked on my father. Looking at him will help me get through this with the evenhandedness I need and hope the council will respond to. After a deep breath, I begin. "That afternoon, I was tasked with a mission. Papa...I mean Commander Byrne told me that some of his men had recently seen geese nesting out on the northeast quad—"

"Hold on one moment," my father interrupts. He looks to the militiamen. "Is this true? Did any of you see geese on the northeast quad? Because this is the first I'm hearing of it."

"I saw 'em," Nagel says. The other men look to the table, avoiding my father's gaze, but Nagel looks him dead in the eye, as piercing as one of his arrows. "Took a shot at one of 'em but didn't have the range. Didn't want to spook the others. When I got back to the Fort I told Patrick. Said he oughta send our best shooter out there an' try." Nagel turns to me and smiles wickedly. "Bowie here's our best shooter. A real crackerjack with a rifle."

I am not grateful for the compliment. That Nagel should corroborate Byrne's story about the geese comes as no surprise. Those two are as thick as thieves. I'm just surprised that Nagel was willing to paint himself as a poor shot to do so. My father isn't buying it either, but with no other choice, he instructs me to continue. "Like I was saying, my mission was to go to the ravine in the northeast quad and look for geese. Commander Byrne explicitly instructed I do this alone as he was concerned that the more cadets present, the bigger the chance the birds would get spooked and fly off. When I got there, I didn't find any birds. What I found was Seth O'Reilly wandering down in the rocks, made up like a zombie."

"So," Byrne interjects, "when you saw Seth, made up as a zombie, were you scared?"

"No," I answer.

"But you did fire on him. We checked your rifle—my rifle, in fact, which I had leant you—and it had been fired. There can be no question about that."

"I did fire the rifle." I try to keep my anger tempered. "When I first came upon Seth, I wasn't sure what he was, so I fired a warning shot at his feet. If anyone had bothered to check the northeast quad, I'm sure I could prove it. All I did was spook him. I even spoke to him."

"Well, if it wasn't your shot that killed him, whose shot did?"

I see what Byrne is doing. He's baiting me, trying to get me to lay the blame on Rafe. It's like my father said: if I try to pass my guilt onto someone else, the council will frown upon it. Yet without laying blame, I am as much as admitting guilt. There is a term for this situation; one of Father's books is named after it. *Catch-22*. It's a book about war. I read it, and I can't say I fully understood it. But I understand the term.

It's hard not to direct my accusing gaze at Rafe, but I resist. "I don't know," I answer. "Shouldn't someone have checked Seth's body for the bullet to see where it came from?"

"I did a thorough investigation of the scene," Byrne says. "There was nothing to indicate anything said by the witnesses wasn't true. And I wasn't about to delay burying the boy and cause the poor family further distress. The burden of proof is on you, Bowie."

That's the real kicker, isn't it? I can't prove I didn't do it, so it's my word against Rafe's. And let's face it, the deck is stacked against me. This game is rigged. All I can really do now is stay quiet and not make it any worse for myself. "That's all I have to say."

Byrne nods, giving me a look that could almost pass as respect. "Very well, I think we have what we need to make an informed decision on this matter." My father looks pained as he speaks, as if Byrne's words are driving the sickness farther into his brain. "Now we will move on to the matter of this."

He pulls the tablet from the inside pocket of his military vest and places it on the table for all the council to see. Surprise registers on many faces, young and old alike. Byrne saved this revelation for maximum impact, and judging by the shock in the room, it worked.

"For the uninformed and those who've forgotten, this device is known as a *tablet* or *e-reader*. It is a digital device that can be used to communicate with hostile forces outside of Fort Thunder." Byrne turns his steely gaze to Alexis. "It was found in Bowie's possession early this morning, during a secret rendezvous with this girl." He directs his eyes back to the council. "Now, I don't know how or when this item made its way into the Fort, but it calls into question the nature of our female guest here. I believe she intended to use it to call in hostile forces; that she is in fact the spy I feared her to be; and that Bowie, willingly or otherwise, is her conspirator."

"Now, hold on a minute!" Alexis steps forward, face flushed with indignation. "Do I get to say anything about this?!"

"No," Byrne answers curtly, "you do not. You are not a member of this community, and therefore you have no say. Furthermore, you are a woman and a treacherous one at that. I think this item here speaks for itself, and I move that the council vote to banish you immediately. As for the matter of Bowie Neville, he now faces charges of both murder and conspiring against the community. One of these charges alone would warrant banishment, but two makes this case, in my mind, cut and dried. And that doesn't even take into account the matter of his injuries, which could very well make him redundant. So, good council of Fort Thunder, what is your vote?"

It's not even close. Nine for, two—my father and Doc Seaver—against. Even August Christiansen sides with his militiamen. Friendship only runs so deep in Fort Thunder, I guess.

Before the council can be adjourned, my father reaches for the gavel. "There is one further matter," he demands. "If my son is to be banished, I ask that my wife and I be permitted to join him."

"Very well." Byrne looks ready to be done with this well-orchestrated charade. "We will vote on it. But I ask the council to consider that Harlan Neville is a founding member of this community and has extensive knowledge of our inner workings. To allow that knowledge to fall into the hands of our enemies could be disastrous. I ask that you vote to keep Harlan and his wife here for the good of our community. Grant his request at our peril."

Again, the vote is brief. Father isn't allowed a vote, but even then, he fares a little better than Alexis and I did. Here he gets the support of August as well as Doc, Paul Haverford and Walter Kassidy. But it isn't enough. He and my mother are condemned to live out the rest of their lives behind the walls of Fort Thunder, de facto prisoners. It never occurred to me to think of my home that way until now. All these years I believed we were living in freedom, but now I realize this place is a jail of our own making. A prison built on fear.

"And with that," Byrne says, "our business here is concluded." He takes the gavel from my father's defeated hand and strikes the table hard with a *whack*!

OUTSIDE THE ARMORY, A CROWD MILLS ABOUT, AWAITING THE VERDICT. Among them, of course, is a near catatonic Vanessa O'Reilly. Someone must have given her an herbal sedative or maybe snuck her some hooch from one of their personal stills. The rest of the people just look tired.

"A verdict has been reached," Byrne says, puffed up officially, "and justice has been served. Both parties have been found guilty and banishment will commence tomorrow at dawn. I ask that you go about your business and leave the families in peace."

Vanessa falls to the ground, howling sorrowfully, and Devon rushes to her side. Things get a little chaotic, and I lose track of Alexis, catching a glimpse of her silvery hair as Doc whisks her back to the infirmary. It's probably best if we are separated for now. She glances back at me, and our eyes share a desperate moment. Then she is gone, and I see Tessa standing there in her place, her face a silent accusation; this is what I get for betraying her. I realize now that, with or without Alexis, the betrayal was inevitable. I never loved Tessa, and I never would have. At least I have escaped the lie I would have been forced to live by being her husband.

My family and I are allowed to return home without incident. No guard is posted at our door as none is needed now that the issue is settled. All I can do now is banish myself without Byrne knowing, which he knows I'm in no shape to do. With my wounds, I need at least one good night's sleep if I am to stand a chance at survival. Rest will be precious and fleeting when I am out in the wilderness, running for my life.

In fact, the trial has left me exhausted, so when I return home, I go right to bed. When my father wakes me, I can tell by the grey light at my window that it's late afternoon. Out in the kitchen, Mother is prepping the evening meal: olive bread and black beans, a favorite of mine. I will do my best to enjoy it despite the bitter taste in my mouth.

"We have a small problem," my father says when we are both seated back at the kitchen table. From where I sit, we have a *big* problem, but I refrain from pointing out the obvious. "If you are going to survive this, we're going to have to get you that tablet."

Mother takes the bread out of our clay oven, and I'd be lying if I said that the smell of it doesn't take my mind off my problems, just for a second. "Byrne has the tablet," I say. "Or he's destroyed it. It can't help me or Alexis now."

My father shakes his head. "He hasn't destroyed it. Not yet. He left it in the armory, and as far as I can tell, he hasn't gone back for it. Maybe he doesn't see it as a threat, or maybe he wants it for himself. The point is, he left it there, and we need to get it. Tonight."

"How on earth are we gonna do that?"

As if in answer to my question, there is a knock on the door. My mother answers it, and Maya steps into the dwelling. She looks as surprised as me that she's here.

120

"You wanted to see me?" she asks my father.

He looks to her and smiles. "Maya," he says calmly, "thank you so much for coming. I'm afraid I asked you here because we need your help."

She looks to me, then back to my father. I have no idea what he is going to ask of her, but we all know it's serious. Nothing about Maya's face suggests that she's taking it lightly. "Is this for Bowie?" she asks.

Father nods.

It takes her only a second to answer. "Anything."

WE SET OUT AROUND TWO IN THE MORNING, WHEN THE NIGHT IS AT ITS darkest. After our meeting, Maya was sent home, and I ate a final supper with my family. There wasn't much talk over the black beans and olive bread. At this point action has more weight than mere words; even my mother, usually chirping with small pleasantries, understands this. We must remain firm in our resolve, and I have to keep my mind on what I must do. From here on out, focus will be the key to my survival.

Maya and I approach the armory from the back-alley maze of the dwellings, coming up behind it as if sneaking up on an enemy. There is only one way into the armory—through the front door—so there is never a sentry posted around back. We have no idea who will be posted out front, and it will be the luck of the draw. I just hope for Maya's sake it's not Nagel.

With our backs to the armory, we creep along the side of it, toward the front. The cover of the dwelling shields us from the sentries in the towers on the off chance that any of them are awake at this hour. The long years of peace have made even the hardest men complacent, and there isn't a one of them who won't sneak forty winks during a tower shift. With my banishing, they might be more alert tonight than most, but old habits die hard, and we make our way undetected. I find myself once again admiring Maya's stealth and soldier-like poise under pressure, but her greatest challenge lies ahead, around the corner we so silently approach.

We reach our position, and Maya looks to me for instruction. I nod. Lightning quick, she peeks her head around the corner, then pulls back and leans against the building. I can tell by the look on her face that she's not too pleased by what she saw.

"It's Jessup." Even at a low whisper I can hear the disgust in her voice.

"I'm sorry," I say at the lowest decibel possible. "Could be worse."

"Not by much," she answers.

Though I sympathize with Maya, the truth is that we're lucky. There was a good chance that a cadet would be stationed at the armory because, despite its importance, there isn't much need for it to be guarded. Getting in is impossible without keys, and only three of the militiamen even have them. Luckily, one of them is Maya's father, and even more luckily, he was off duty tonight, which means he was drinking. Stealing his keys was probably the easiest part of this for Maya. The hardest part is still ahead, waiting right around that corner.

"You don't have to do this," I whisper. "Still time to back out."

She shoots me a look of dismissal, knowing this is the only chance I've got. I nod, wanting her to know how sorry I am to ask this of her. She takes a breath, sucking in cold and steeling herself for the unpleasant task to come. Then she steps around the corner.

I crouch low so I can watch what happens next without being spotted. Peeking around the corner, I watch Maya saunter up to the barely awake Jessup. She swishes her hips, doing her best imitation of Tessa, and I have to stifle a chuckle. The poor girl just doesn't have it in her. But Jessup, being a runt, doesn't get a lot of attention from girls, and as I've said, Maya's not so bad to look at once you get past the dirt. She even cleaned up a bit for the task at hand—I probably should've told her that I noticed. Girls feel more confident when you notice things about them; at least, that's what my mother always says.

Jessup's eyes widen with surprise as Maya approaches, and she slinks right up next to him, talking in a low purr. I can't hear what they're saying, but Jessup clearly doesn't know what to make of this unexpected encounter. They talk quietly awhile, and I begin to fear that the runty cadet isn't going to take the bait. God knows he's talked a big game around girls, insisting that he has them all figured out, acting like a real ladies' man. But we all knew it was just a load of bull and he was making up for the fact that his small size would surely work against him when the time came for him to settle on a mate. Luckily for Jessup, there are only so many options, and some poor girl would probably get stuck with him. Who knows, maybe it would be Maya.

Finally, Maya convinces him to slink off with her to the storage bins. It's terrible that Maya's first real kiss is going to be with Jessup and that she'll have to endure his no doubt awkward groping, but I really didn't see any other way around this. It makes me proud that I can inspire such loyalty in someone who owes me nothing. I only hope I can live up to it.

Once the happy couple is out of sight, I keep low and hurry to the now unguarded armory door. Taking Wilkes's keys from my pants pocket, I fumble with the ring, panicking that I'll forget which three unlock the two deadbolts and doorknob lock. The keys are all shaped differently, which helps, and pushing the panic out of my mind, I recall what Maya said to me earlier as we were prepping in my kitchen. Square head for the top deadbolt, clover-shaped head for the bottom, and hexagonal for the doorknob. I slip the keys into their locks in that order, each time rewarded by a satisfying click. The doorknob turns as I unlock it, and after a gentle push, I am once again standing inside the armory.

It's dark inside, which comes as no surprise as none of the hanging lights are on at this hour and there's not a window anywhere in the tower. I reach back in my pocket, switching out my keys for a small, square item that's waiting for me there—my father's old flip-top lighter. It's a relic from the old times, when he used to smoke poisonous sticks called *cigarettes* which made people smell terrible, according to my mother. The Fort's generators are constantly needing maintenance, and on those regular blackout times, we rely on candles and gas lamps, hence the need for matches and reusable lighters. But the small silver object I hold in my hands is never used for such prosaic purposes; this is something Father keeps to remind him of what we left behind. Of the cancer we gave ourselves willingly, as individuals and as a whole.

It takes me a few flicks of the lighter's rusty wheel, but I manage to conjure a flame. It flickers in the cold night air, casting long shadows up the wall, light glinting off the endless black barrels, rifle stocks, and scopes. The sight of firearms brought me much comfort as a young boy, but now they feel like the eyes of my enemy. For a second I fear that they'll twist free of their hooks and fire on me of their own accord, riddle me full of holes. I think that it's better if I don't look at them and get on with what I came here to do. Still, I can almost feel them there in the dancing shadows, watching.

Turning my attention to the council table, I search for the tablet, nearly missing it there in the dark, feeling my heart miss a beat. The reflection of the lighter's flame flashes back at me from the tablet's flat surface, and I hurry over, scooping it up off the table. Right now, this may be the only thing that stands between certain death for me and Alexis, so I slip it into my jacket pocket with the care it deserves. Then, remembering the other task I came here to do, I turn to the wall behind the head of the table.

There are several pistols here to choose from, but I need something small and easy to conceal. The best candidate is a nickel-plated snub-nosed revolver that hangs conveniently on a nearby hook. I take it off the wall and hold it in my hand, testing the weight of it, palming the grip, checking the sights to make sure they're aligned. Satisfied, I stick that in a different pocket so it doesn't scratch up the tablet. Hopefully, bullets for the pistol aren't hard to come by as we won't have a chance to get at the locker tonight. Most adults keep a box or two of bullets in their dwellings in case of an emergency. I know my father has one or two in his desk at home, so here's hoping there's matching caliber bullets in there somewhere.

With my mission accomplished, I flip the top down on the lighter, extinguishing the flame, then slink back to the door to check the crack and make sure Jessup or anyone else hasn't shown up. The coast is clear. I sneak back outside, close the door shut behind me, and set about the process of locking up. My nervousness makes me mix up the order, and I start with the clover-shaped key in the top lock. Stupid. I start again, leading with the square key and getting it right. The final lock in the doorknob clicks into place, and I sneak back around the corner of the building and into the alleys between dwellings.

Now to let Maya know that her seven minutes in hell are over. I pick a small stone off the ground and pitch it high at the storage bins, our agreed upon signal. It hits one of the tin roofs with a small bang, loud enough to startle but nothing that couldn't just be an item in one of the bins shifting lose. Almost immediately Maya emerges from the storage area, wiping her mouth, Jessup trailing angrily behind her. He whispers some harsh words at her, something about being a tease, but Maya waves him off with the back of her hand and keeps walking. Jessup bitterly returns to his post at the door, completely unaware that the armory has been breached in his absence. Maya turns the corner and meets me in the alley.

"Well, that was miserable," she confirms with a whisper.

"Too bad," I quietly joke. "I would have pegged Jessup as a good kisser."

She sticks out her tongue in disgust, scrunches up her face. But honestly, to my eyes, Maya has never looked more beautiful. I am grateful to call her my friend.

Somehow, I manage to sleep away the remaining hours before dawn. Mother wakes me with a porridge breakfast, and we all gather silently in the kitchen to eat. I can see from their faces that there hasn't been much sleep and that their night was filled with worry and discussion. As far as I'm concerned, the time for talk is over. From here on out action is what matters, and in some small way, that brings me comfort. Action I can deal with; if I have to talk through any of this any further, I think I'll lose my mind. Let's just get this over with already.

There is a sharp knock on the door, and my mother answers. August Christiansen stands there, his bearded visage more solemn than usual. "It's time," he says.

"Just give us a minute," my mother requests. August nods.

She comes over to where I'm sitting and helps with removing the last of my bandages. I had gotten so used to the one over my eye that I almost forgot about it. As the gauze is taken away, my wounded eye adjusts, the blurriness coming gradually into a sort of soft focus, as if seeing through a curtain of haze.

Doc says my eyesight could remain this way for some time, maybe even forever, but I'm just grateful to still have the eye. I reach up my hand and trace the two scars that frame my eye, intersecting at a point just below my right brow, like a triangle. In a strange way, my face has become a version of the Fort Thunder symbol of the eye in a pyramid. The word is *irony*, and I can see from the look on my father's face that it isn't lost on him.

With that, I leave my home for what is likely the last time. Parents by my side, I walk into the square, outfitted in my navy peacoat, leather-patched fatigues, and laced military boots. In my pocket, I have a pair of my father's worn leather gloves to protect my weaponless hands from the elements, which, judging from the cold and the gathering clouds, are fixing to be brutal. We'll be lucky if we make it to the ranger station before the first flurries hit.

By the gates, every member of the Fort Thunder community has gathered, most of them still wiping the sleep from their eyes. This is a twice-in-a-lifetime event, and even the strongest of our family's supporters wouldn't dream of sitting this out in protest. Of course the militia and cadets make a strong presence, standing tall at attention, rifles slung at the ready. Devon stands slightly apart from them so he can comfort his mother, who is glaring at me with reddened, hate-streaked eyes. My heart goes out to the woman, and I hope she finds peace, but my banishment will do nothing to settle the ghost of her son. His murderer is standing but two meters to her right.

Alexis and the Seavers arrive moments after we do, escorted by a leering Nagel. The Seavers have given Alexis a tattered fur coat to supplement the now clean clothes I found her in. She looks a little comical with her pink hooded sweatshirt peeking through the old matted rabbit fur, but nothing on her face indicates that she's finding any of this funny.

I catch Tessa slinking around in the back of the crowd, wearing a look that could be read as righteousness or shame. Odd as it may seem, I feel sorry for Tessa. Who will she turn to after I am gone? To whom will she offer her hard-edged affections? Rafe would be the obvious choice as I'm sure he's being groomed as my replacement, but Tessa never had eyes for him. Not that her preference will be taken into consideration when it comes time to make her a match. I'd hope Gunnar for her, but I wouldn't wish her on him. Gunnar is too kind a soul, and even here, in the face of my ultimate humiliation, I can see in his conflicted, downturned eyes that he is still my friend. I don't even want to think of what I might have to do if Gunnar is sent after us.

Byrne steps forward to greet us, although I don't think *greet* is the proper word. He looks me over the way he looks over a weapon before he cleans it. I am an object to him now, me, who he once called son. Now I am the enemy, a threat to be neutralized. He leans in close to my face, taking in my scar, and the first flakes of snow land and melt on his beard.

"There were items missing from the armory this morning," he growls.

"I don't know anything about that," I lie. "I was home all night."

Byrne glances angrily back at Jessup, who is no doubt shouldering the blame for the missing items. Since Maya is standing alone in the crowd and seems under no scrutiny, I have to assume that Jessup made no mention of their tryst as he would catch serious hell for abandoning his post. I'm happy his cowardice can be counted on. "Bring the girl over," Byrne shouts to Nagel. "I want the two of them searched."

Happy to comply, Nagel grabs Alexis hard by the arm and walks her forcefully over to where Byrne and I are standing. I keep my eyes locked on Byrne, not wanting to show weakness through my concern for Alexis. All he will get from me is stony resolve.

To call the patting down Nagel gives me rough would be an understatement. He almost pushes me over with his calloused hands, searching my back and underarms for the missing items. I remove my coat and hand it to Byrne for inspection, and without my permission Nagel lifts up the back of my shirt. "Want me to take off my pants too?" I spit back at him.

Finding nothing, Nagel sneaks in a final shove, then moves on to Alexis, treating her as roughly as he treated me. The sight of his meaty hands probing her sets my blood to a boil, and I can see from his sickening grin that he's enjoying it. He turns his head to me as his hands rise under her breasts, cupping them and taunting me with a flicker of tongue. I'd rip that tongue out and feed it to him if I were able to. For her part, Alexis handles the molestation bravely, not giving the pig the satisfaction of protest or even a squirm. She makes me proud.

"OK, Marcus," Byrne orders. Even he finds Nagel's enjoyment of this distasteful. "That's enough." He turns his attention back to me, bitterly handing me my coat. "You might not have the tablet on you, but someone took it, and you know who. So tell me."

"Or what?" I look around at the faces that have come to see me exiled. "You'll banish me?" I refocus on Byrne. "I don't know what happened to the tablet. Maybe one of your men got homesick for the good old days and took it. Did that ever occur to you?"

Byrne grits his teeth and leans close enough to give me a whiff of his sour breath. "Don't play games with me, boy. You won't like how I play."

"I already know how you play," I answer. "Now, we going to get on with this or not?"

He considers me with cold steel eyes, then backs off, smiling. "Fine." He turns to the crowd, who are hanging on his judgment. "I didn't want to do things this way, but the boy leaves me no choice. After the meeting of the council, I was able to access the device and found information there as to its recent use. It had been used to reach the mainland, for the purpose of alerting our enemies to our whereabouts. We have been compromised, and the sad truth is that it comes from one of our own. We are betrayed from within."

"That isn't true," a voice says in the crowd. My mother steps forward, wearing her resolve like an uncomfortable mask. "I did use the device before my son was discovered with it, but it wasn't to give away our location. I used it to help my husband."

A collective murmur rises in the crowd as they try to process this admission. Byrne looks to my mother, a knowing smile peeking up from under his beard. "And what sort of help did your husband require that he couldn't get here at the Fort?"

"I'm dying," Father says, coming to stand at his wife's side. "Cancer. I've been dealing with it for some time, but it's worsened considerably in the last few weeks."

"I see," Byrne says, pretending to give the moment proper weight. "Can our own Doc Seaver confirm this?"

"I can," Doc says. "I identified a swelling in the lymph nodes a few months back, and I think it's moved on to his brain. Untreated, I'd say he only has a few weeks to live."

More muttering from the crowd. I feel a chill work its way through my bones, and it's not from the snow that's started drifting down from the sky. Of course, I'd suspected that my father was ill, but confirmation, to know that he's dying, is still a difficult stone to swallow. We have often had our differences, but life without my father is impossible to conceive. Even separated by banishment, I could still take comfort in the knowledge that he was alive, safe with my mother, even scanning the horizon for my eventual return. But this—this is a death sentence. No one recovers from cancer here at Fort Thunder. My father is a dead man walking.

"So," Byrne continues, "by Fort law, that makes you, Harlan Neville, redundant. Isn't that correct?"

"It is," my father answers fearlessly, "which is why I ask again that I be allowed to face banishment with my son. You've said it yourself; I'm of no use to the community at this point. I have weeks, perhaps days, to live. Let me spend them with my son."

Byrne paces while anxious whispers are exchanged in the crowd. He's making a big show of taking this under consideration, and it gives me a feeling of dread. This whole thing feels like a put-on, a scene orchestrated by Byrne for the benefit of the people, all leading to a conclusion that has already been predetermined. And the hole opening up in my gut tells me it's a conclusion that I'm not going to like, not one little bit.

"It's true," Byrne says, "you are of no further use to our community, as much as it saddens me to say. But as we discussed at the trial, it could be disastrous to Fort Thunder if you should somehow fall into the hands of our enemies. I simply cannot take a chance at that happening, however unlikely it seems."

"Don't be ridiculous, Patrick," my father says dismissively. "I'm a dying man. What possible threat could I be to you now?"

"Not to me," Byrne adds with false righteousness, "to the Fort! With your extensive knowledge of our community, you could supply our enemies with—"

"We don't have any enemies," my father says, cutting him off. The crowd hushes. "You know it. I know it. Most of your men know it. The truth is that there's never been an enemy at those gates—not a real one, anyway. The truth is that the only enemies we have are ourselves."

Byrne stands there, iron straight, cruelty pushing up the corners of his mouth. "If that's true," he says, "then let me show you how I deal with my enemies."

Too late I see that he's reached for the pistol at his belt. A shot fires, and my father's eyes go wide, caught completely by surprise. A dark stain spreads across his chest. He falls.

My father. My father has fallen. There is chaos. Shouting. Bodies clutter my view. I hear my mother cry out. I move toward her voice, but a hand grabs my arm.

"Bowie! No! It's what he wants!"

I am caught in the crush. Panicking people. Shouts from the militia, trying to restore order. It's madness. I've never seen it like this before. No one knows what to do.

"Dammit, Bowie, look at me!"

The hand on my arm pulls on me hard, turning me around. Alexis's eyes are urgent, desperate. She gives every syllable equal weight, as if I can't hear. "We...have...to...go!"

Through the tangle of the crowd, I catch a glimpse of my father's eyes. The curtain is descending quickly, but there's a little light left, a last bit of who he is. He shakes his head. Don't do it, he says wordlessly. Don't come to me. Run, before it's too late. Run.

So I run.

In all the madness, none of the militia can reach Alexis and me before we make it into the maze of dwellings. As the gates were never opened, Byrne probably figured he had all the time in the world to deal with us after he pulled this little coup. But he forgot about the tunnel by the latrines, or maybe he never knew about it to begin with. Either way, his overconfidence makes it possible for us to escape. I'll file that away for further reference.

By the time we reach the latrines, I can hear Nagel barking orders to the cadets to find us. Rafe probably knows right where we're headed, but he's too far behind. We come to the patch of turf that covers the tunnel, and when I pull it off, it sticks to the wet, freezing ground. At least the cold has hardened the soil, so it won't cling to our clothes. Alexis jumps in it without hesitation this time, and I follow after. Hurried moments later and we are outside the Fort walls.

Alexis makes for the tree line, but I stop her. "Wait." She looks at me as if I'm crazy, but I'm too busy looking at the snow-dusted ground to explain what I'm doing. Time is short, and my already rock-heavy heart sinks somehow lower as I fear what I'm searching for is lost. Then I see it—a piece of curved wood sticking in the snow by a tree stump. I threw it over the wall last night in the hopes I'd be able to retrieve it after we were exiled. By pure luck I happened to do it over by the latrines, never imagining that this would be where we made our escape. I pick it up off the snow and hold the cold, comforting weapon in my hand.

The sight of the boomerang gives Alexis some small comfort. "Smart move," she tells me. I tuck it into my belt. I'll congratulate myself later when I pull it out of Patrick Byrne's cold dead face.

We run for the forest, gaining as much distance as we can. Snow is falling now—thick wet flakes—which is good for covering our tracks. It is unlikely that anyone will come after us right away as the militia will need time to get the Fort under control; that buys us some time to figure out our next move. Several kilometers into the woods and I finally succumb to the need to rest. I shore myself up against a pine, suck in deep breaths, and come to terms with what just happened.

Patrick Byrne killed my father. Gunned him down in cold blood and seized control of the Fort. He's in complete control now. The man who killed my father.

And soon he'll be coming after me. After *us*.

My father is dead.

CHAPTER TEN

The Station

"WHAT NOW?" ALEXIS ASKS.

The sound of her voice jolts me out of my headspace. I realize I've been standing here a while in the nearly silent forest, thinking only of avenging my father. Of killing Patrick Byrne. The tree cover is sheltering us a little from the falling snow, but the ground is filling up quickly, and soon walking will be difficult. We are going to need to find shelter quickly, and there is only one real option as far as that's concerned. Unfortunately, it is likely the first place that Byrne will look for us. The old ranger station.

There was another plan, but with my father dead that's all out the window. The ranger station is the only logical choice as it places us near the jetty, the best place for us to cross until the bay is frozen. It was my father's will that we get off Deacon's Bluff as quickly as possible. It is unlikely that Byrne will choose to follow us far into the mainland. The longer we stay on this island, the easier we are to catch and kill, but crossing the jetty in a heavy snowfall may prove as deadly as anything Byrne sends our way. At the very least we need to ride out the night and hope for better crossing conditions in the morning.

"We head for the bridge," I tell Alexis. "There's that old ranger station on the way. We take shelter there for a bit, then we cross by way of the jetty."

"Won't they look for us there?"

I nod. "I'm hoping that we've bought ourselves some time. Byrne can't be sure we've even left the Fort, so it might take him a bit to mobilize. He probably figures he has time, that there's nowhere we can really run. He'll look for us there, but it won't be for a few hours, and by then the snow will be as much a hindrance to him as it is to us. And besides," I add grimly, "we really don't have any other options."

The answer doesn't seem to thrill Alexis, but she nods her concession. "OK then. Lead the way."

I check the trees and what little sky there is to get my bearings, figuring we ran due east from the Fort. That's good; it means we can follow the cliffs south and then creep back inland to the station. It'll be cold, but it'll get us there without taking us near Fort Thunder. I gesture in the direction of the tree-hidden cliffs. "That way."

"Bowie," Alexis adds, "I'm sorry. About your father. He seemed like a good man."

"He was," I say, "but I was always too stupid to see it."

Alexis wants to say more to me, offer me some measure of comfort, but I don't want to hear it. My father is dead, and all I ever did was disappoint him. I should have listened to him. I should have read more of his books. Maybe if I had, maybe if I'd listened to what he was trying to teach me, he'd be alive and we'd all be together right now. Maybe if I'd focused on learning and not on being a soldier, I could have been a healer like Doc and helped ease his suffering. Maybe I could have even saved his life. But I didn't. I was prideful and stupid, and now he is dead. The way my luck is going, I'll be dead soon too.

We head farther east, the ocean wind howling snow into our frozen ears. The Seavers were kind enough to outfit Alexis with a ratty scarf, so she at least has that to protect her. I'm not so lucky. My peacoat isn't much of a match for the air of the Pacific, nor are my father's gloves, and by the time we reach the cliffs, my face feels ready to crack right off of my skull. The sight of the ocean, so vast and unyielding, offers me no sense of wonder at all.

The snowfall here is thick and wet; there can be little doubt that we're facing a blizzard. Alexis and I make our way along the cliffs, our boot soles slipping on the slick, snow-spattered rocks. We must be careful in our haste not to fall and injure ourselves; a broken leg or even a sprained ankle would be disastrous. If it came to that, I would take Alexis by the hand and throw the both of us off of the cliffs and into the ocean. Better to drown in the freezing water than to sit here helpless waiting for Byrne and his men to find us.

It comes time to cut back into the forest, and we're both grateful for what little shielding the pines offer us from the snow. The path here is gone, obscured in the white, but I know the way by heart. We trudge through the growing drifts, soaked through to our calves, pressing on without a word shared between us. I am grateful that Alexis isn't trying to make conversation; it's all I can do to keep my mind on our task and not on my father. As it is, I almost miss the sign to the ranger station when we reach it.

"Oh, thank god," Alexis says, breaking the silence. "I don't think I can make it much farther."

This worries me as tomorrow the going will be even rougher, but no need to bring that up now. Best to keep hope alive as long as possible. That's something you learn as a soldier.

A half a kilometer later and we reach the ranger station. We pass by the other cabins, their sad, open-faced structures offering no shelter from the storm. The ranger's cabin still stands as it was built sturdier than the others, but its roof is full of holes and its windows broken, so we will be fighting the wind. Still, it's got four walls, so I'm grateful.

Inside, the cabin is coated with two decades worth of dust. There is a rotted-out desk set against one of the walls, pouring the contents of its innards out onto the floor like a smashed pumpkin. There are already a few small snow piles from the holes in the roof. It makes our crude Fort Thunder dwellings seem like the palaces described in history books.

"Homey," Alexis says. It might sound like a joke if she wasn't so defeated.

There is one bright spot in the gloom; an old stone fireplace is still standing against one wall. I immediately go to the rotting desk and start kicking it apart, breaking up the wood to use as kindling. Eager to do her part, Alexis goes to the handle that opens the flue, and before I can stop her, she wrenches it open with a yank. Twenty years of soot explodes out of the chimney, enveloping her in a thick black cloud.

The soot settles, leaving Alexis standing there, covered from head to toe. Even the radiant luster of her hair is dampened to a sickly grey ash. She looks at me, at her wits end, and I am almost certain she's going to burst into tears.

Right now, I wouldn't blame her. But once again she surprises me by breaking out into gales of laughter. I can't help but join in. Here we are, the butt of life's cruel joke. After all we have been through and will continue to endure, at this very moment the only sane thing to do is laugh.

When we have exhausted our amusement, she looks down at her filth-ridden clothes. "So much for my outfit."

I give the situation some thought. Going over to one of the piles, I scoop up two handfuls of snow, then turn to Alexis. "Arms out," I instruct. She does as I ask, and I run the snow all over her, cleaning what soot I can without soaking her entirely. It's no soap and water, but it does a decent enough job. Not thinking, I move my hands close to her breasts, and she steps away from me uncomfortably.

"I'm sorry, I wasn't—"

"No, it's fine," she says. "Thanks. I can handle the rest myself."

She goes to a snow pile and cleans off more soot while I stand there a moment self-consciously. I shrug off my embarrassment and get back to the task of building a fire. The wood from the desk is mostly rotten and wet, but there's enough dry material to be drawn from the scrap to fill the fireplace with a small pile. Once it's full, I remove my right boot and retrieve the small item tucked there, up against the ankle. My father's lighter. I didn't want to risk it being confiscated during the search, so I hid it there, figuring they wouldn't look inside my boots. The gamble paid off. Now this lighter is all I have of my father outside of his memory.

It takes a few tries, but I manage to get the beginnings of a blaze started in the hearth. Some musty manuals I find in a small closet behind the desk help feed the flames with their pages. Father used to talk about the troubled times in history when the ignorant would burn the books that they felt were offensive, but I don't think he'd mind us tearing up these rotting old tomes. Nothing in them is worth more than our lives, he'd reckon.

The smoke given off by the modest fire is stale and unpleasant, but enough of it wafts up the half-clogged chimney to allow us to breathe. The heat, on the other hand, could not be more welcome. Alexis and I scoot as close as we can to the chimney, warming ourselves, palms up and as close to the flames as the heat will allow. Sitting there, in the glow and the warmth of the fire, we can almost believe we are safe. Almost.

"Won't they see the smoke?" Alexis asks.

"They'll see it. Doesn't matter. It's not like we're hiding." I pull off my coat and lay it on the flagstone that radiates out from the fireplace. "At least this way we'll be warm. That's one advantage we'll have over them." Realizing that my shirt is soaked through, I stand and remove that as well. I catch Alexis's eyes admiring my body in the warm light of the fire.

"Nice abs," she says with a wry smile. "You must work out." I give her a quizzical look. "Sorry, just making a little joke there. It's something we say back home when someone's really obsessed with physical fitness."

One of the things often told to us about the old world was that people allowed their bodies to get soft and fat from complacency. That is not something that is permitted at Fort Thunder. Even the heavyset men like Byrne and August Christiansen are muscled beneath their bulk, and a stocky kid like Devon will have the baby fat burned off of him in a year or so. Exercise and fitness is built into our lifestyle, something that comes to us as second nature. I find it curious that Alexis's people have managed to survive without making this the norm.

Following my lead, she takes off her hooded sweatshirt, but that's as far as she's willing to disrobe. I take the boomerang from my belt and sit down next to her, absently scraping at the flagstone with the weapon's tip. As the fire warms me, I feel the icy wall I've built around my emotions start to melt. I can't hold it back any longer. I start to cry.

Alexis sits next to me, watching me silently as the tears flow. I feel her hand touching my bare shoulder, and while I would otherwise tingle at her skin on mine, now it brings me only small comfort. "It's OK, Bowie," she tells me. "Let it all out. Just let it out."

The wave passes, and I regain control, wiping the wetness off my nose with my scarred forearm. "It's not just that he's gone," I say when my voice can function without trembling. "It's that I was powerless to do anything."

"No one could have done anything." Alexis takes her hand from my skin, and I miss it immediately. "Byrne was going to kill your father no matter what happened. You rushing in to help would have only gotten you killed."

"I'm a soldier. That's part of the deal."

"You're not a soldier, Bowie." There's a sharpness in her voice that I do not like. "Not anymore. Sure, you've been trained. And up until now you've been loyal and the best of your peers. But you were drafted into a war that wasn't real. The freedom you think you stand for is just another system of control. You're free of that now—you don't have to fight for it anymore. And trust me, that's a good thing."

She tells me this to make me feel better, but it doesn't. All of my life all that mattered to me was being a good soldier. The last thing I ever imagined was that I'd end up a traitor. But then again, I never would have imagined that "Papa" Byrne would betray me or that he would kill my father. I feel like such a damn fool for believing in him. I feel like a fool for not listening to my father, for not reading his books or being willing to see what he was trying to show me about Fort Thunder. The doubt was there in him the whole time. I was just too blind, too caught up in myself and the self-satisfaction being a star cadet granted me. The truth was that all I cared about was myself. And now my father could offer me no more of his wisdom. Now there was nothing.

After a long silence I say, "I failed him."

"Oh, Bowie." She puts her hand back on my shoulder. "You didn't fail him. He was so proud of you, I'm sure. How could he not be?"

I put my hand on hers, and our fingers lock. She puts her other hand to my face, turning it toward hers, and I allow it, welcome it. Then we are looking into each other's eyes, and I see tiny flecks of orange dancing in the green of hers, reflections from the firelight. She is so very beautiful, and then she smiles, and I forget where I am, forget all about the cabin, the snow, my father, our lives. She moves her lips toward mine, and we are kissing, the softness of her mouth an impossibility next to the roughness of mine. I put my hands on her arms, and this time she doesn't resist, and I am pulling her closer, pressing her body against my bare chest. Her hands find the back of my neck, pull gently at my hair. All the while our tongues twist in each other's mouths. She pushes me down, back flat against the flagstone, and time melts away as we lose ourselves in exploring one another, giving our bodies over to desire. It's all that we have.

Hours later, a sound jolts me awake. I look over on the floor to see Alexis curled in my coat, sleeping close to the fire. The pleasant memory of what has transpired fades like a dream, and I sit up, waiting to hear it again. It comes: a soft sound out there in the woods, beyond the thin cabin walls. Could be snow sloughing off tree branches. Or it could be something else.

I jostle Alexis lightly on the shoulder, and she wakes. She smiles dreamily at me, but before she can speak, I put a finger to my mouth. The seriousness in my eyes tells her all she needs to know. She stays quiet, and we both grab our clothes off the hot flagstones and dress quickly. Once my boots are on, I pick up my boomerang and say in my quietest voice, "Wait right here. And stay low to the floor." She nods and rolls onto her stomach, hands flat on the wood floor, ready to spring.

Judging from the light coming in through the cabin windows, it's sometime around noon, perhaps a little later. It seems that, for now, the storm has let up as there's no snow coming in either from the windows or ceiling. This is good news for us but also good news for our enemy as they should have no trouble making it out here to hunt us. And with our recent distraction, we've given them plenty of time. One strategy would be to hole up in the cabin and wait, but if I know Byrne, the plan will be to set fire to it and either smoke us out or let us burn. I am not one to just sit back and wait for death to come to me. I prefer to meet it head-on.

So I hide the boomerang in the sleeve of my jacket and step out the door.

Outside, the woods are quiet in that way they get after a heavy snow. The sky is still dense with clouds, and there are a few small flakes, so I know that the storm isn't over. But for now, we've been granted a reprieve. Ahead of me by twenty meters or so is what's left of one of the old cabins, little more than a few planks of rotten wood sticking out of the ground in a freestanding wall. Plenty of cover to hide a shooter. Palming the tip of my boomerang, I stand there and wait. Listening.

Crunch. The sound of a footfall on snow. Then a straining sound, cable against steel. I know that sound, what it means. A shape emerges from behind the freestanding wall, and I duck into a roll as an arrow whizzes by, slicing the air where my head had been a moment before. It thunks into the side of the cabin, and I see Nagel pull another arrow from the quiver on his back. He can load that compound bow of his faster than most people can load a gun, and if I don't get back inside in the next second or so, I'll be skewered.

Staying low to the ground, I roll back toward the cabin, hoping that I've positioned myself close enough to the door as I won't get another shot at this. There's no use trying to throw the boomerang at this point; I'll never hit Nagel from this low angle. To make matters worse, he's moving toward me, smiling from behind his taut cable, arrow loaded and aiming right for my head.

Incredibly, I roll back into the cabin and manage to slam the flimsy door shut with my boot. Nagel's arrow hits—*thunk!*—and the arrow tip pierces the door. For a second I sit there, its point mere millimeters from my eye, catching my breath. Behind me, Alexis gasps.

"Good to see you still have yer reflexes," Nagel taunts from outside. I can tell from the sound that he's keeping his distance, not approaching the door directly. Smart move on his part as he has no idea what I have set up as defense. Which is nothing, but I'm not about to tell him that. "I tell you what, Bowie," he continues, "you come on out of there now, nice and calm, and we'll see what we can do 'bout making this easy on you. And the girl."

"If it's all the same to you, Marcus," I holler through the door, "I think I'll pass."

Even at a distance I can hear a dry chuckle. "You got stones, boy, I'll give you that. Always had 'em. Can't say I ever cared for you much, but I always did think you got stones."

"Come on in here, and I'll show you," I answer. "I'll smash one of those stones right upside your ugly head."

"Now, now. Don't be rude, boy. Ya see, the ruder you get, the less inclined I am to go soft when it comes time to dishin' out punishment. There's many ways to die, boy, as I'm sure you know. There's fast and there's slow. There's quick and there's painless. Now, I know I have a bit of a reputation, but I got no taste for torture. Can't stand all the screamin' and cryin'. But believe you me, you make this difficult, you give me a lot of your lip, and I'll make it hurt. I'll make it hurt real bad. Trust me, you'll wish you went out like yer daddy when I'm good and done."

The mention of my father sets my blood to a boil. I crouch, boomerang in hand, hatred in my eyes burning holes in the door. "Don't you talk about my father!" I yell. "Scum like you has no right even saying his name!"

"Yer daddy was a coward," Nagel mocks. "Always was. I never wanted him around to begin with. But Patrick insisted we needed him. Truth was, I think Patrick was sweet on that mother of yours. I gotta admit, she is one fine hunk of a woman. And now, with yer daddy worm food, ol' Patrick'll finally get his turn. Heck, maybe if he gets sick of her, he'll let me have a go at her as well. What you think, boy? You think your mama's up fer a ride on my meat stick?"

Hands clenched into raging fists, I move for the door, but a hand lands on my shoulder, holding me back. Alexis. "He's goading you, Bowie," she says in a low voice. "He knows if he makes you mad enough, you'll come out guns blazing. And then he's got you."

She is right, of course, and a part of me already knows it. I am letting Nagel get to me, letting him use my anger against me. I have to be smarter than that. I need to get my emotions in check and handle this situation with a clear head. I need to stay cool, like a soldier.

"I always thought those arrows were your way of overcompensating, Marcus," I sneer. Two could play at this game. "All talk and no action."

"I'll show you action, boy!"

We don't have much time before Nagel figures out that I didn't have time to rig the door with traps. With Alexis shadowing me, I go to the window at the back of the cabin and, ducking below the sill, do a quick peek up to see if anyone is positioned out back. Taking a mental snapshot, I duck back down, processing what I have seen. The trees there are close to the cabin, offering ample cover for more hunters, and I'm pretty sure I noticed the barrel of an M16 sticking out from one of the trees. I try to put myself in the mind of my enemy; what would I do if I were leading this mission? It stands to reason, with Nagel out front, that the rest of the hunting party would be stationed around the cabin, most of them likely cadets. Byrne wouldn't want all of his militiamen in one party—he's probably waiting with them somewhere farther out, maybe the jetty or even still back at the Fort. He's arrogant, and he doesn't think he needs to come at me himself, not as long as he has his loyal dog Nagel. At least, that's what I hope.

"Pretty sure we're surrounded," I whisper to Alexis. "Three cadets, maybe four."

"So what do we do?!"

If I'm right and cadets are hiding and awaiting Nagel's orders, that means if we can get out of the cabin undetected, we might be able to sneak by them. And there's only one chance we have to get out undetected.

In the center of the cabin is a moldy throw rug made of some kind of woven fabric. I step to it, pulling it off the floor, revealing the worn floorboards beneath. Years of rot have left gaps between the boards, like a mouth of rotten teeth. One good kick will send my foot right through. But I can't let Nagel hear me doing it. We need to bring a little noise.

"So what's it gonna be, Marcus?" I holler at the door. "Where's that action? Or are you just gonna wait out there all night like the coward you are?"

There is a high-pitched whistle, a signal, and I pull Alexis down with me onto the floor. The cabin erupts with gunfire as the cadets blast from outside, their automatic rifles turning the rotted wooden walls into kindling. Splinters fly everywhere, showering us in dust and pulp, and Alexis wisely covers her eyes. The noise is deafening, and it provides me with the perfect cover for what I need to do. While the nervous young men empty their clips, I crouch at the gap-toothed boards and slam my foot down as hard as my leverage will allow. It takes a few blows, but on the third, my foot breaks through into the narrow crawlspace, hitting the dirt below.

The firing stops. I freeze there a moment, my leg still awkwardly planted in the hole as I wait for more gunfire. My guess is, we have a few seconds as the cadets reload their rifles. I step back out of the hole and motion to Alexis. "Get in."

She doesn't need to be told twice. Once Alexis has gone into the hole, I lower myself in after her and pull the rug back over us to cover it. The crawlspace between the ground and the floor of the cabin is tight, barely high enough to accommodate me at a crouch. Alexis, being smaller, fares a little better. The air down here is musty and stale, like breathing in cold dirt. It sits thick in the lungs. Doesn't matter; we won't be down here for long. Huddled close to Alexis, I scan the darkened area, trying to figure the best direction in which to crawl. Nagel is by the front of the cabin, which is dead ahead of us, and there are likely others stationed on all sides, but I have a feeling that's all about to change. Sure enough, a few seconds later, I hear the door of the cabin swing open and hard-soled boots come clomping in overhead.

We hold still, waiting for Nagel to make his move. "Come on now, Bowie," he says to an empty cabin. "No point in hidin'. I'm gonna find you, and the madder you make me, the worse it's gonna be. Don't just think about yourself now. Think about yer girlfriend."

Clomp. Clomp. He steps farther into the cabin, and I picture him above us, bow loaded and drawn. I keep that image in my mind as a reference, using it to plot our course. If we can pass underneath him, we stand a chance of sneaking out from under the cabin and might even be able to make it into the woods before the others spot us. And I feel a lot more confident going up against a cadet or even one of the militiamen than trying to take on Nagel. Alexis has her eyes on me, waiting for my signal, and I gesture forward, to the narrow strip of light that indicates the front of the cabin. Right under Nagel's boots. Alexis nods, and I put a finger to my lips, letting her know we really need to do this quietly. She returns with a look that says, *just how stupid do you think I am?* Then she gets on all fours and starts crawling, quiet as a ghost, toward the light at the front of the crawlspace.

"I'm not playing around boy!" Nagel's voice booms right over our heads, and one of his boots clomps forward, showering dust on us through the cracks in the floorboards. I hold my breath so none of it gets up my nose, but Alexis isn't so quick on the draw. She jerks still, body tensing as she tries to stifle a sneeze. It's no use—her nose betrays her. She buries her face in her sleeve and lets a muffled sound go, little more than a wisp of air. Barely a noise at all. Above us, I hear a floorboard creak. Nagel heard it.

"Now hold on a minute," he says excitedly. "Is that a little mouse I hear?"

Alexis glances back at me fearfully. I frantically urge her to move forward with my eyes. She turns back and crawls quickly and quietly toward the light.

"Squeak, squeak, little mouse," Nagel taunts from above. As we scurry forward, his boots clomp over to the rug, kicking it off of the hole in the floorboards. "Looks like I found yer little mouse hole." There is a *shing* of metal as he draws the machete he carries from its scabbard. The bow isn't the only weapon favored by Marcus Nagel. He likes his kills up close and personal.

Unable to stop myself, I glance back at the hole. Nagel's upside down face leers back at me, ponytail dangling from the top of his head. "There you are!"

Turning back to Alexis, I see that she has stopped to look back. "MOVE!" I yell. No need to be quiet now. We need to get out of here, fast. Alexis gets the message. She scampers forward, and I follow, fast as my crawling limbs will allow.

Behind us, Nagel laughs, the sickening sound chasing us through the crawlspace. For a second I hope that he's dumb enough to crawl in after us, but no such luck; the clomping of his boots follows from overhead, and his shadow falls on us from above the floorboards. The cracks run parallel to our path, which makes it real easy for Nagel to stab at us with that machete of his. Which is exactly what he does. His first attempt lands at my waist, jabbing through my peacoat, missing my belt by mere millimeters. I freeze, drawing in a tight breath, trying to shrink myself away from the blade. Nagel pulls it back up through the crack, scraping it against the floorboard.

Wood creaks above me as Nagel stomps overhead, passing by me to where Alexis is still crawling for the light. He's coming for her. I grab her feet, yanking her to a stop. She yelps.

"ROLL!"

Turning her legs like a wheel, I push her to the left. Nagel's blade shoots through the floorboards, hitting the dirt where she lay a moment before. Alexis rolls onto her back, face up, and glances fearfully to her right. The blade retracts through the crack, readying to plunge again.

"Crafty little mice," Nagel taunts through the cracks. "But you can't run from the cat forever. And when this cat catches you, he's gonna play with you for a nice long time."

I have never seen a cat, but I know enough to get the point. They always struck me as strange, cruel animals to keep as pets. Nagel comparing himself to one makes perfect sense. Only he's not nearly as cuddly.

Alexis starts crawling in the direction I rolled her, to the left side of the cabin. Smart move. Nagel will have to choose a direction in which to hunt, so that gives us a one in four chance that he'll choose wrong—if we can keep quiet and not give away our position. Left is as good a direction as any. I follow Alexis's lead, crawling along the dirt like a spider, and the blade comes down again, missing the sole of my boot by millimeters. All I need now is a wounded foot to hobble me and make me even easier prey. I scamper away from the blade as it retracts, trying my best to minimize the noise of my escape.

One of the advantages of heading in this direction is that the floorboard cracks run perpendicular to us now, making us harder targets for Nagel's machete. Still, one good jab and it's all over. In the corner of my eye, I see him stab through the cracks in the direction we were previously headed, which gives me hope that we've shaken him long enough to crawl out of the cabin. But then I hear his boots clomp hurriedly back to the hole for another look into the crawlspace. Had I known he'd be doing that again, I would have waited there to cut his damn throat with the sharp edge of my boomerang. Fat lot of good it would be trying to throw it at him in this tight of a space.

This time, I don't look back. I hear him grumble something when he spots where we are, and I know we've got seconds before he's over us again. Thankfully, Alexis is already pulling herself out of the crawlspace ahead of me, where the gap opens into the woods. I don't think I could handle seeing her struck with that machete. My mind might just snap for good.

Footfalls stomp overhead, and I scamper as fast as my limbs will allow. No need to be quiet now; Nagel's got me in his sights. I am almost to the crack of light, to the freedom of the outdoors, when I feel something thin and cold slice into my left forearm, right through my coat, just below the bicep. Clenching my teeth, I hold in my cry, not wanting to give that ponytailed bastard the satisfaction of hearing my pain. But, boy, does it hurt. I watch as Nagel pulls the blade back up through the cracks, cutting a small riverbed into the exposed flesh, which quickly fills with blood.

Ahead, Alexis ducks in from the outside, eyes widening when she sees that I'm cut. I shake my head, wanting her to forget about me and run. But she stays there, frozen with fear. Or maybe it's something else. Either way, I wish the stupid girl would run.

A soft chuckle filters down from above as Nagel inspects the blood on his blade. My arm stings, but this is just a flesh wound, and my anger is more than enough to drive me forward. If that jackass thinks a little cut is gonna get me to give up, he's got a lot to learn. The pain that radiates through my arm now is nothing but a good motivator, and I am just about to charge forward when Alexis's eyes widen and she holds up her hand, warning me to stop. I do, and Nagel's machete plunges down again, this time a hair's breadth from my face. Of course—how could I be so stupid? Nagel anticipated exactly what I was going to do, and if it hadn't been for Alexis, that machete blade would be planted in my skull right now. I owe her my life.

My startled reflection stares back at me on the flat of the blade. An idea comes to me, and I back away, scooting back onto my butt. Once I've dug in some leverage, I aim both feet at the blade and kick the flat part of it as hard as I can with the soles of my boots. Nagel howls overhead as the shock travels back up the now bent machete blade. He tries to pull it back through the crack in the floorboard, but the bend I've put in it won't allow for that, and the weapon remains stuck. He might be able to wiggle it through eventually, but I'll be out of this crawlspace by the time he does. I scoot to the side, circumventing the blade as it jabs up and down with Nagel's frustrated attempts to free it. Moments later I arrive at Alexis's smiling face and the fresh outdoor air.

"Clever boy," she says. She touches my arm, wanting to get a look at my wound.

"No time for that," I say. "We've gotta go—"

"Don't move, Bowie!" We both turn to the sound of Rafe's nervously pitched voice. He's emerging from the woods, M16 trained on us, trying to not look scared. Alexis and I stand to face him.

"Step aside, Rafe," I say. "You don't have the stones for this, and you know it."

"I'll show you stones." He levels the rifle, readying to shoot...

With one motion, I drop the boomerang into my palm and let it fly. Panicking, Rafe fires wild, and I pull Alexis into a snow bank as bullets riddle the ground where we stood a moment ago. Rafe ducks the boomerang, and it goes whistling over his head toward the thatch of pines behind him. My former second-in-command smiles, getting a bead on us once again.

"You missed," he sneers.

Not yet, I didn't. A whipping sound signals the boomerang circling back around, and too late Rafe realizes what has happened. It connects with the side of his head with a hard *whack,* and he cries out and lowers the gun. I'm rushing toward him already, the boomerang giving me the second I need to be on top of him before he can fire again. Reaching him, I grab the rifle by the barrel, my father's gloves protecting me from the hot metal as I yank it out of his hands. His big brown eyes go wide with surprise as I smash the stock of the gun into his face, breaking his nose in an explosion of blood and sending him sprawling on to his back in the snow. With his weapon commandeered, I flip it back into the cradle of my arms and stand over him, barrel aimed dead between his stupefied eyes.

"Don't even think it, Bowie."

I turn to find Devon standing next to Alexis, a pistol held to her head. He's shaking and nervous, but I can't risk taking him down as long as he has her at this close range. I move the barrel of the M16 away from Rafe's bloodied face and hear him sputter a sigh of relief. I kick him in the thigh, and he cries out like the whiner he is.

Gunnar emerges from the woods, M16 slung low, eyes downcast. It's killing him to be a part of this, but we both know he doesn't have a choice.

I'd like to tell Gunnar that it's OK, that he's doing exactly what I'd be doing in his position—following orders. But now isn't the time or place for that. Here and now, we are enemies. Still, I don't raise my weapon at him, nor does he raise his on me. We are just shadows separated by an invisible wall.

Nagel comes running around the corner, bow in hand, and smiles when he sees the stalemate. He has no reservations loading his weapon and drawing it on me. "Put down the gun, Bowie. I'll put one between yer eyes before you get off so much as a shot."

Instinct screams to fire on him, to take my chances and die by the consequences, but the thought of Alexis stays my hand. As long as she's alive, I want to live as well. I drop the M16 in the snow, and Rafe crawls out from under me, wiping the blood from his nose and glaring at me with white-hot hatred. He goes to reach for the rifle.

"Leave it, boy," Nagel orders. "You're not gonna need it just yet." Doing as his father says, Rafe leaves the gun where it lies. It's clear from his confused face that he's clueless as to why this order was issued. I am too and have a really bad feeling about it.

Nagel comes right up to me, grinning, and once again I get a face-full of his rotten breath. "You made me work for it, boy. Not that I don't appreciate a worthy opponent, but I promised you what I'd do if you didn't play nice."

"It didn't matter what I did, and you know it," I spit. "The truth is that you're a sick fuck, and you're gonna do what you're gonna do. So go ahead and do it already."

His eyes light up, thrilled by my defiance. He requivers his arrow and punches me hard in the stomach with the following movement. I double over, the wind knocked out of me, but I won't give him the pleasure of seeing me fall to my knees. Even as I struggle to regain my breath, I keep my eyes on him and my face stony. If he thinks a sucker punch to the gut is going to get me crying for mercy, he's got a lot to learn about Bowie Neville. He grabs me by my hair and yanks my head up to face his once again.

"See, it's not about what I'm gonna do, Bowie. And it's not about you either. See, I've got some boys here who don't have a lot of experience with women, so I figure, what with yer pretty little friend over there, what better time than the present to start their sexual education? You following my meaning, boy?"

I'm following, all right. Judging from Alexis's horrified face, she's following too.

"What would Byrne have to say about this, Nagel?" I ask. "Would he be OK with you forcing a bunch of boys to rape a woman?"

Nagel makes a show of looking around the snow covered wilderness. "Do you see Pat Byrne anywhere around here? Cuz I sure as shit don't. He sent me out here to run this operation the way I saw fit, and that's exactly what I'm doin'. I don't think any of these boys're gonna complain, and you certainly won't be talking. You won't be doin' much of anything but being dead. But first, you're gonna watch."

With a sweep of his leg, he takes me out at the knees, driving me into the snow. "Stay down," he orders. He snaps at Devon. "Bring the girl over here." Devon does as he says, leading Alexis over to where we are, nervously looking to his leader. Nagel grabs Alexis roughly by the neck and pushes her down on her back. "Now," he says to Devon, "keep your gun on Bowie. If he moves an inch, shoot him. Remember what he did to your brother."

I see Rafe flinch at this remark. He and I both know who the real killer was. But Devon still thinks I'm to blame, so Nagel's propaganda does its job, and he jams the barrel of his pistol into my temple. Devon's never been more to me than a bully and a malcontent, but I can believe he's got stones enough to shoot me if I try and make a move. So I don't.

Nagel shoulders his bow and looks to Rafe. "All right, son, time to make you a man."

Rafe looks horrified, unprepared to do what his father asks. "Wait...you mean—?"

"Well, what the hell do you think I mean?!" Nagel shakes his head with disgust. "You think I'm gonna let my own boy have sloppy seconds?! This here is a rite of passage, and I'm giving you the sweetest bite of the apple! So go on and take it!"

Like a scolded child, Rafe walks over to where Alexis lies in the snow, looking up at him with a mixture of hatred and fear. As much as I hate Rafe, as much as I know he hates me, I know that this isn't what he wants. He's a bastard, but not the kind of bastard his old man is and wants him to be. He crouches down and reaches for Alexis, and she slaps and claws at his face. He backs off, looking to his father for more instruction.

"Christ on a cracker, boy," Nagel reprimands, "you gonna take that shit from a *girl?* Hit that bitch! Show her who's boss!"

It takes everything I have to not let the rage overtake me, to not charge at Rafe and get myself shot. Out of the corner of my eye, I see Gunnar blushing ashamedly, unable to watch this sick bit of theater. Rafe steels himself, jaw clenched, and descends again on Alexis, brandishing a fist. She screams and claws at him again, and he hits her, and she claws some more, and he hits her again, hard, on the side of her face. She yelps, and I feel my body tense involuntarily, flush with adrenaline, ready to fight. Devon senses it and presses the pistol in harder. "Don't try it."

Tough as she is, Alexis can't hold up the front. The pain of Rafe's blow takes the fight out of her, and she starts to cry. It's a heartbreaking sound, and its effect can be seen on the faces of all the cadets, most of all Rafe's. He doesn't have the stones for this, and he knows it.

"Dad," he says to his expectant father. "I can't. I'm sorry."

"You sure as shit are sorry!" Nagel hollers. He storms over to where Rafe crouches over Alexis, grabs him by the scruff of the neck, and pushes him into a snowbank. "You need to see how it's done?! You need a lesson?! Well, I'll give you a lesson, boy! You just sit right there, and I'll show you how to take a woman, you dickless piece of shit!" He positions himself between Alexis's legs and pries them open as if they were no more than a stuck winch. She screams—a sad, hopeless cry—and he reaches for his belt. "Been awhile since I had a piece this fresh."

Alexis turns her pleading eyes to me. But I am helpless to intervene. There's no way I will reach her before I am gunned down, but I cannot just sit here and watch. I'd rather be dead. So as Nagel slips a hand into his dirty boxer shorts, my leg muscles tense, and I ready to charge. It will be the last thing I ever do, but at least I won't have to live with this...

CRACK! A shot fires, and I think that Devon must have pulled the trigger. But I am still here, tensed in a runner's crouch. Nagel jerks back, freezes, eyes registering blank surprise. There's a small hole in his temple, a trickle of blood, and then he falls over, off of Alexis and onto the snow. He lands in such a way that I can see a chunk of his skull is gone, blasted clean off. Inside is wet and pink. His limbs spasm, a few last twitches of life, and then he is still. Alexis chokes out a small sob, then scoots out from under his dead body.

Out of the woods steps Maya, in her hands the snub-nosed pistol we stole from the armory. Its barrel is still smoking from the shot she fired into Nagel's head. She is quite the shot, it would seem. Guess all that secret target practice with a slingshot paid off. But judging from the look of horror on her face, it didn't prepare her for killing.

I don't think anything could have.

This gives me the distraction I need to yank the gun from Devon's hand before he can fire. I rise to my feet, knocking him down with a well-placed elbow to the chin. He hits the icy ground hard, out for the count. With my next move, I aim Devon's pistol at Gunnar, who still hasn't processed what happened. This only leaves Rafe, and I'm pleased to see that Maya has already got him dead in her pistol's sights. She has more than proven her skill and willingness to use it. Rafe wisely stays seated in the snowbank.

Gunnar looks to me, reading the situation. He knows that I couldn't bring myself to shoot him, but he throws down his rifle anyway and puts his hands up. I nod to him, and he nods back. Our communication is understood; he's not going to force me to do something I don't want to do, but he can't risk coming over to my side either. He is loyal to his family, and I respect that. For now, this uneasy truce is the best either of us can hope for.

Right now, my chief concern is Alexis, so I hurry over to her, sidestepping Nagel's body, and help her to her feet. "Are you OK?"

She nods, shaken but unharmed. Shrugging off the attack, she straightens out her clothing and catches her breath. But her eyes can't help but wander to Nagel, fearing that he may spring to life at any moment. If I didn't want to waste the bullet, I'd shoot him again just to make her feel better. Make myself feel better as well.

A static hiss comes from his body, a sound I recognize from my training. Though our communications are limited, the Fort does employ a handful of walkie-talkies for long range maneuvers. Nagel has one of them in the pocket of his ratty old army jacket, and I can guess who's calling on the other end. Keeping my pistol on Gunnar, I step over to Nagel's body, reach into the jacket, and pull out the squawking device. Byrne's voice crackles on the other end.

"Marcus, I'm hearing shots fired. Report."

While it's tempting to answer and tell Byrne his lapdog is dead, now is not the time. We need to get away from here quickly, preferably as far from the militia as we can get. I twist the knob on the walkie-talkie, silencing and pocketing it. I glance over to Maya and move toward Rafe. She understands what I'm doing and moves her sights to Gunnar, freeing me to aim my gun at my wide-eyed second-in-command.

"My father..." he stammers. "That bitch killed him!"

"My sympathies," I lie. I keep the gun trained on his face. "If you want, I can see to it that you can join him right away. But I imagine he'll be just as disappointed in you in death as he was in life. Shall we find out?"

Rafe's face falls, sinking with the truth of my words. Some small part of him is glad his father his dead, glad to be finally free of his abuse. Maya did him a favor, and on some messed up level, he knows it. "Now," I continue, "tell me where the others are."

He looks to Gunnar, who isn't offering any help. "Why don't you ask your blond buddy over there? Make him the traitor!"

"Because I'm asking you." I press the barrel into his forehead. It's going to leave a mark. "And don't make me ask again."

A moment passes as Rafe struggles with my request. Finally, he confirms what I already suspected. "They're at the Densmore. Waiting for you to attempt a crossing if we were somehow unable to contain you."

"*Contain* us?" My voice rises with anger. "You were sent to *kill* us. Worse, what with your sicko father in charge." I remove the gun barrel from Rafe's forehead. I was right—it left a nice little red mark, like a miniature target. "I tell you what, Rafe. I'm gonna let you live this time. So you can tell Byrne himself that you and your daddy have failed."

With the help of the girls, I gather the cadets' guns, leaving them unarmed. Between us now we have three M16 rifles, four pistols, and a couple of hunting knives. I also manage to go around front and collect my boomerang. The one weapon we leave behind is Nagel's compound bow. He was the only one who knew how to use it anyhow.

They can bury it with him.

CHAPTER ELEVEN

The Peak

NEEDLESS TO SAY, WE DO NOT HEAD IN THE DIRECTION OF THE DENSMORE. With Byrne guarding the jetty, we need to find another place to cross, which leaves only the narrow finger of Bluff Pointe. Of course, if the bay isn't properly frozen over, the icy waters will sweep us out with the current into the Pacific Ocean, but we'd likely be dead by then anyway. It's a threadbare strategy at best, but right now it's the only one we have, so I lead us due north in the direction of the pointe.

Whether by luck or design, we do not encounter any enemies as we follow along the winding ravine toward our destination. The fact is that Byrne just doesn't have enough men or cadets to pepper the whole island, but we can expect to encounter someone before we reach the northern tip. He will have anticipated that this will be our backup move; I will not underestimate my former mentor as a strategist. With the great rocks of the ravine providing some cover, I feel confident that our course of action is sound, or as sound as it can be. After we have traveled a quick five kilometers or so, I pull the party over to rest in a tight cluster of boulders that can offer protection from sniping eyes.

"Thank you," I say to Maya, who leans against a rock, catching her breath. She still looks shell-shocked by what happened back at the ranger station. She's a soldier now, no matter what anyone says. A killer.

"I... I didn't know what else to do."

"Yeah, well, I'm grateful you did," says Alexis. "You saved my life, saved me from a fate worse than death. Thank you. I'm Alexis, by the way."

Alexis offers Maya her hand. Maya blushes slightly and takes it. "Maya," she says. I can see that Alexis's exotic beauty affects her as it does me. It dawns on me that Maya's disinterest in boys runs deeper than the choices the Fort offers her. She is attracted to women, a fact that would have resulted in her banishment had it ever been found out. Not that it matters now. "I'm a friend of Bowie's," she finishes after Alexis withdraws her hand.

"Yeah, I gathered that." Alexis makes sure to add gratitude and warmth to her voice, and it's probably more than Maya's ever gotten from a girl close to her own age. "You really put yourself on the line here, Maya. For Bowie and for me. I can't imagine what it's cost you."

From the way Maya's eyes fall, I gather she isn't quite ready to weigh the full cost. As if needing to distract herself, she reaches into her camouflage army jacket (ironically, a hand-me-down from her father, who is now hunting us) and pulls out a small black object. "Here," she says, handing the tablet to Alexis. "Bowie said you were going to need this."

At the sight of the tablet, Alexis's eyes light up. "Oh my god, this is brilliant!" She takes the tablet from Maya and runs a finger along the edge, finding the small button. She presses it, and the screen on the tablet glows to life. On it, a circular icon spins, searching for some sort of signal. Finally, text appears, reading COULD NOT FIND CONNECTION. "Dammit," Alexis sighs. "I was afraid of this. We're out of range here."

"Out of range of what?" I ask.

"A satellite signal." She looks around the ravine, at the deep, tree-shrouded valley we are in. "Maybe if we found higher ground..."

Maya looks to me, and I know what she's thinking. We are only a few kilometers from Callie's Peak, the highest point on the island. If there is any signal to be found, it's there. Not the wisest move in terms of making it quickly to the pointe, but if this tablet can really be of use to us, it's our only viable option. "I think I have an answer," I say, "but we have to move quickly, and it's a bit of a climb. You think you both can handle it?"

Both girls nod. "All right then," I confirm, "let's go."

The climb to the peak proves even less pleasant than I was anticipating. I take the girls up the easiest way I know, but with all the snow and ice to wade through, even the mildest incline is treacherous. Alexis slips at one point, and I barely manage to grab her arm before she falls off the side of a cliff into a cluster of waiting rocks. The heat of her breath as I pull her close excites me, reminding me of our time back in the cabin. Once the fear has left her eyes, she smiles, gets her footing back, and removes herself from my arms. "Easy there, tiger," she chides. "Keep your mind on getting us safely up this mountain, please."

Maya has no time for our foolishness. She reaches the crest of the peak before we do, taking in the view of the island as she catches her breath. Moments later, the three of us stand together, in awe of the three-hundred-and-sixty-degree view that greets us.

"I gotta hand it to you," Alexis notes, "your people sure picked a beautiful place."

Her saying that makes me feel sad. It is a beautiful place, and this will likely be the last time I'll be able to appreciate it. This island is my home, for better or worse, and now I must leave it, whether by escaping or dying. Who am I without this land, without these people? Where else in the world could I possibly belong? Suddenly I feel very lost. A man without a country.

But at least I'm not alone. "Well," I say to Alexis, "this is as high as it gets."

She nods and pulls the tablet from her jacket. Again, she starts it up, and again she waits for a signal. For a while we all stand there, staring at the spinning search logo as if mesmerized by it. I have almost given up when text appears, reading CONNECTION FOUND.

The screen fills with icons, and Alexis swipes at them excitedly. "Oh my god, I can't believe it worked! I thought for sure we were just too out in the boonies!" Her finger drifts over an icon that looks like a book, and she taps on it. Suddenly the screen is lined with bigger icons that look like book covers. "I promised you zombies," she says. She swipes at the icons, and they scroll away only to be replaced by new icons. A whole series of them appear, covers depicting harried people with guns and tactical gear—people who look like my people— fighting off rotting ghouls. The books have titles like *I Envy the Dead*, *March of the Zombies*, and *Zombie War Zero*. Works of fiction, meant for entertainment. Nothing more.

"So zombies aren't real," I say, feeling the fool.

"Not to my knowledge," Alexis confirms, "but they make for good stories."

And that's all that they ever were. Stories to keep us scared, to keep us from wandering too far away from home. Just a lie our parents told us to keep us afraid of the outside world. I feel so stupid for believing it, and I can tell from Maya's face that she feels the same way. Not that any of that matters now. The idea of zombies suddenly seems so silly and harmless.

Alexis pushes all the books away with a finger and taps on an icon that looks like the envelopes people used to use to send letters to one another, before the days of the internet. I make an educated guess that this is some sort of email, and sure enough, a blank page appears below a window with more icons over it. She taps some letters into a long rectangular box above the window, and a row of letters and symbols appear. I have no idea what they mean, but I think they're some sort of address. Then Alexis moves her finger to the blank page and starts furiously tapping in a message on a keyboard that has appeared on the bottom of the screen.

In the corner of the screen, a small rectangular icon blinks red, and Alexis glances at it, typing faster. She looks to me, eyes full of urgency. "What can you tell me about this island? I mean, do you have any idea where it is?"

"We're on Deacon's Bluff," I answer like a dimwit.

"I know, but that could be a name your people made up. Like, do you have any idea where this island is in relation to the US? Like, what part of the coast are we on?"

"My father says we're near a place that used to be called Oregon," Maya adds. "That's where he was born, anyway. Does that help?"

"Yes, it does." Alexis goes back to typing. "And it's still called Oregon, FYI."

Before we can ask what *FYI* means, Alexis finishes her email and taps an icon that is shaped like an arrow. It reminds me unpleasantly of Nagel. The message disappears as if flipped away by invisible hands, and another spinning icon appears that says SENDING...

The screen on the tablet blinks off. "Dammit!" Alexis presses the button on the side, but the screen remains blank. She presses again. And again. Nothing. "Shit!" Frustrated, she draws back her arm, readying to throw the cursed thing off the side of the peak to a cluster of jagged rocks waiting below. I grab her arm, stopping her.

"I don't think you really want to do that," I say.

She sighs and lowers her arm, tablet still in hand. "The power on this thing is dead, and god knows where we'll find an outlet. Hell, I don't even have the charger anymore anyway. It's totally useless."

"But were you able to get a message through to your people?"

"I don't know." She gazes out at the expanse, eyes hopeless. "Maybe. But even if I did, it could be days before anyone comes for us. The fact that no one was sent after the plane makes me think that they don't have any idea where I am. They probably think the plane went down in the ocean and that I'm long dead." She sighs. "It probably would have been better if we had gone down in the water."

Her hopelessness settles over all of us, like the dark clouds that cluster around the cold, bright sun, threatening more snow. I want to offer words of encouragement, but right now I have none. The fight is leaving me; I just want to sit down on this mountain and enjoy what little I can of my world before Byrne comes to take it away. But my thoughts won't allow me that sort of peace. Remembering the walkie-talkie in my pocket, I take it out, twisting the knob and turning it back on. The speaker squawks with static as I press the button and put it to my mouth.

"Byrne," I say to the device, "you there?"

For long seconds, there is only fuzz on the other end. Then a voice breaks in. "I'm listening."

I give my words some consideration. "Did you find Nagel?"

"I did," Byrne answers.

"He didn't leave us any choice," I say, a child making excuses. "He was gonna do things to Alexis. Terrible things! And then he was gonna let the others do it too and make me watch. Is that your idea of a fair fight?"

"There's nothing fair about war, Bowie." There's a pause on his end, a sigh maybe, if I could hear it. "I didn't teach you that, but there's the truth of it. War is ugly and unfair."

"Yeah, well," I answer, "it doesn't have to be. You killed my father; I killed your friend. By my count that makes us even. This could end now if you wanted it to. You could just let us go. We'll make our way off the island. No one else has to die."

"For one thing, we're not even." He keeps his voice tempered, but I can hear the anger in it, the venom riding just below the surface like a black current. "You didn't kill Nagel; that dyke daughter of Philip's did. That little bitch needs to answer for her own crimes."

I look to Maya, who is just beginning to deal with the enormity of her predicament. We both know there's no reconciling this, no going back. "Maya's my soldier," I tell Byrne. "She acted on my behalf. You put all of that on me, understand?"

"You're really not in a position to be giving orders, Bowie. Not to me, and not to those girls. I tell you what—you surrender to me without a fight, and I promise to go easy on those girls of yours. They are just women, after all. They know not what they do."

Alexis puts an angry hand over the walkie-talkie, looking into my face and not allowing me to even weigh this option. "No!" she says. "Do not listen to him! This is all a load of bullshit! He's just trying to get you to lay down without a fight, and then he'll kill you and do whatever he wants to us. There's no bargaining with him, Bowie, and you know it."

She's right. There's no bargain to be struck here, no way I can spare these two an unpleasant fate. Our only hope lies together, in us somehow getting off this island alive. I just wish I could believe that it was possible, but standing up here, seeing how far we have to go, knowing how fast we'll have to run...

The walkie-talkie is back at my mouth without me realizing it. "No deal," I say to Byrne. "We're not doing it your way. You're going to have to come and get us. Or we'll get you."

Again, a long stretch of empty hiss on the other end. Then, "So be it. Never let it be said that Patrick Byrne doesn't rise to a challenge. I'll see you all on the field of battle. I plan to bury all three of you by day's end."

"Plans change," I shoot back. But the signal has already gone dead.

I feel the eyes of Alexis and Maya on me, looking to me for leadership and courage. Inside I have never been more afraid, more doubtful of myself, but I won't show them that. They need me to show strength so that they can believe in the impossible, even if I don't. They are both so strong and so beautiful, and I must be worthy of their faith and trust. So whatever doubts I harbor, whatever fear gnaws away at my confidence, I swallow it like the broth from a bitter root. I stand tall and steel myself, rising to their expectations, becoming what they require. Their general.

"You heard him," I say to them. "There's to be no surrender. We head north, for the pointe." Each of us has an M16 now and a pistol (I have two), and Maya and Alexis have the knives. My boomerang is the only blade I need. Ammo has been distributed evenly, and though it isn't a lot, I reckon it'll be more than we need. There just aren't a lot of possible outcomes to drag this thing out, but I can't think about that right now. Have to stay positive.

Quickly I go over the business of firing and reloading, mostly for Alexis's benefit as she is not comfortable around the weapons. Maya, of course, knows exactly what she's doing, having spied on the cadets' training activities for years. I'm glad she did because without her I don't think Alexis and I would stand an icicle's chance in hell. We still don't stand a chance, but Maya evens up the playing field just enough to give me the faintest spark of hope. And a spark can start a fire.

When I'm satisfied we're ready as we can be, I look over my squad of three and make last minute spot checks. Steely, battle-ready eyes look back at me from soft, feminine faces. These aren't girls anymore. These are warriors. I couldn't be more proud of them.

Before we start down the mountain, I take Maya aside. "Look," I tell her, "there's a good chance that, at some point, your father will be out there with the enemy, shooting at us. Are you sure you're ready for that?"

The last of the softness fades from Maya's face. "It doesn't matter," she says simply. "At this point I'm dead to him anyway."

That hard fact sits in the air between us, like a weight. After that, there isn't much to say.

So we begin our climb down from my mother's peak, into the waiting battleground.

CHAPTER TWELVE
The Kill

WE'RE NOT EVEN FULLY DOWN THE MOUNTAIN WHEN THE SNOW STARTS again, pelting us mercilessly. By the time we reach the flatlands of the north quad, the drifts are up to our calves, soaking through our boots and making frostbite an immediate concern. The upside is that the snow will also slow down our pursuers, but then I remember the four snowmobiles tucked far back in Fort Thunder's storage containers. Not enough to carry all of Byrne's men, but more than he needs to cut us off before we reach the pointe. If we don't freeze to death before we make it that far.

The journey across the flats proves uneventful, which is good because we're sitting ducks out here in the open. Beyond is a thick pine forest, the last stretch of terrain before the island tapers off, providing us with a peninsula and a jumping off point for crossing the bay—should the bay even prove crossable. No point in worrying about that now, I tell myself, taking small comfort in the shelter the forest provides. Here, hidden under the canopies of snow-covered pines, the quiet can almost make me believe that we're safe. Best not get too accustomed to that feeling as death can still come out of nowhere and at any time.

My growling stomach reminds me that it's been nearly eight hours since Alexis or I have eaten. We come to a high shoulder of rock that is reasonably clear, and I set the group down for a few moments of rest and food. Maya produces some fig bars from her jacket, and Alexis and I gobble our food gratefully as we watch the light glinting its last on the snow and ice draped all around us. Night is coming and with it colder temperatures and decreased visibility. Though that may actually work in our favor.

As if reading my thoughts, Maya asks, "Do you think we'll reach the pointe before nightfall?"

Shrugging, I swallow the last of my bar. "Think so," I answer. "This last stretch always seems longer than I remember it, plus the snow is slowing us down. Might not be the worst thing if we waited until dark to cross."

Maya shakes her head. "I'd rather try while there's still light. If there are parts of that bay that aren't frozen, I want to see it coming. Getting trapped under the ice is just about the last way I want to go out."

She's got a point there, and I acknowledge it with a grunt. "Not to mention the fact that the longer we wait, the more chance Byrne has to get in front of us and cut us off before we even reach the pointe. No, we need to get through this as quickly as we can and just go for it. I reckon we can make it there by sunset."

"Sounds beautiful," Alexis says with more than a hint of sarcasm. "At least we'll have a pretty view as we fall through thin ice."

I shoot her a look that lets her know she's not helping. She gets the message and finishes her fig bar with no further comment.

The snow lets up a bit for the final stretch of pine forest. As I recall, the trees clear out into a small valley before the land rises back up to the pointe's rocky peninsula. It's an odd dip of terrain that'll be murder on our already taxed leg muscles, but it's the most direct route, and we can't afford to lose the light. Maya's right about crossing the bay before sundown as there's no real option in terms of trying to hole up somewhere until morning. Once we reach the tapered tip of this island, there will be literally no shelter and no place to hide.

As soon as we reach the crest of the valley, I sense that something is off. Looking down, I see that we'll have to come out of tree cover and cross what looks like a quarter kilometer or more of open area before the last thatch of pines that rises on the opposite incline. Any sniper hiding in those pines will have a clear shot at us the minute we wander out into the open, which we will be forced to do. It's exactly where I'd be if I was the one hunting us.

Silently, I motion to the girls to stand still and be quiet, which they do.

Maya quickly clues in on what I am thinking and points to a fallen tree nearby that will provide us cover while allowing us a good view of the tree line on the other side of the clearing. It could also expose us, so we have to get there carefully and without being spotted. I motion for Maya to go first, and she darts from pine to pine, staying low and out of the open wherever possible. She reaches the fallen trunk and, smiling, gives us the thumbs up. Alexis is next, and she follows Maya's lead almost exactly to the move, reaching the tree without incident. Maybe my initial reading of the area was a bit paranoid, but better to be safe than sorry. I follow in Maya's footsteps, crouching low, taking one pine at a time, my eyes always on the tree line in the distance.

The bullet whizzes by my face before I hear the *CRACK*! I dive into the snow as it strikes the tree behind me and to the left, dusting me with wood pulp and snow. Ahead of me, Alexis and Maya look on fearfully, waiting for another shot, but I know I'm too low now for the shooter to hit me. I flash them a smile. This is a good thing—far better to know that they're out there than to wander out into the clearing unaware. I'm willing to bet that whoever let off that shot was a cadet; a militiaman would have the patience to wait. Someone is gonna get their ass chewed out for that blunder, you can be sure.

Crawling on my knees and elbows, I reach the fallen tree and the rest of my team. Maya is already shoring herself up against the trunk, checking the scope on her M16. Good soldier. Alexis is just cradling her rifle like it's an unwanted baby and trying to get her breathing under control.

"It's OK," I say to Alexis. "I'm all right. They missed by a mile."

Maya sets her rifle across the top of the trunk, looking through the scope, scanning the far tree line. After a moment, she reports, "I think I see one of them."

"Can you get a shot?"

"No. Negative." She tenses on the trigger, then backs off the scope. "All I've got is the tip of a rifle. M16, it looks like."

"Let me see." She moves out of the way so I can look down her scope. She's right; it's another M16—which means a cadet—and she's also right that she doesn't have a shot. Best we hold off at the moment and not give away our position. If they knew we were hidden behind this fallen tree, the bullets would be flying already. There have been no shouts or communication of any kind since we've been spotted, which makes me think this is a small detachment we're up against, maybe only two or three shooters. That gives us a fighting chance.

But not if we stay here too long. Now that our general position has been noted, there will be radio communication with Byrne, and he'll be coming up behind us right quick. Then we'll be trapped—easy pickings. We need a move, and we need to make it fast.

Withdrawing from the scope, I look to Maya. "Here's what we're going to do. I'm going out there, and you both need to cover me." I take my M16 off my shoulder and lay it between Maya and Alexis. "Keep the shooters occupied."

Alexis shoots me a horrified look. "Are you nuts?! You'll never clear that distance before one of them takes you down!"

"I won't come at them directly," I explain. "I'm going to bank as far to the right as I can, use whatever cover there that's available to me. If you two keep them shooting at this location, I think it'll distract them enough to not notice as I make my way around."

"No offense, Bowie," Alexis scoffs. "But you're a little hard to miss."

Her point gets me thinking, and I scoop up a handful of snow, rubbing it between my gloved fingers. It's still very wet and a little sticky, perhaps just enough for what I have planned. "What the hell is that for?" Alexis asks, eyebrows raised skeptically. "Building a snowman?"

My answer comes with a smirk. "Camouflage."

Scooping up another handful, I slap the snow onto my thigh, patting it down as well as I can. Most of it sloughs off, but enough of it sticks to powder my olive fatigues with white. I do the same for my arms and chest and even my hair. Alexis watches me the whole time, the skepticism never leaving her face. I present my back to her. "A little help?"

I hear her sigh and dig into the snow, scooping up handfuls. "I still say you're crazy," she tells me, patting the wet, sticky white all over my back. After a minute or so, she scoots back to look at her handiwork. "That's the best I can do."

"Better than nothing." I check the pistol I am carrying, one of the automatics, a SIG P250 subcompact. Nice and small, ideal for concealment, which is what I need right now. It's got a full clip, locked and loaded. Not the ideal weapon to take into a firefight with automatic rifles, but if I'm lucky, stealth will be on my side, and it won't come to that. The fact that it means killing is something I shut out of my mind. There's no advantage to dwelling on it.

Besides, it's kill or be killed now. It's war.

Quickly I issue my final instructions, that the girls direct their fire at the tree line in an attempt to keep the enemy occupied. Meanwhile, I'll be creeping across the clearing as far to the right as I can, keeping my eyes on the trees for the muzzle flashes of the shooters, which should give me some idea as to their position. Once I'm across the clearing, the trees should allow me cover and the chance to sneak up on the enemy and take them out. If I make it across the clearing, that is.

"OK," I say, wrapping up our briefing, "let's do this."

The girls nod in unison, both of them with the assurance of true soldiers. It's mostly an act but one I appreciate nonetheless. As I creep off to the right, ducking low among the pines, Maya starts taking shots across the clearing in steady, controlled bursts. By the time I have crept to the base of the clearing, the enemy has returned her fire, both sides shooting blindly into the trees. Judging from the steady bursts of rounds, even Alexis has managed to join in. It feels just like one of the many exercises we performed as cadets, and I must keep reminding myself that this one is real, that it counts. Still, it's not hard to imagine that if I just blew the whistle, the game would be over, and my friends would emerge from hiding so we could all go home.

No. Mustn't think like that. Must stay focused.

Feeling that I'm far enough afield of the area of concentrated fire, I crouch low and start across the snow-covered clearing. It's hard to judge the distance of the shots as the small valley makes the sound echo, bouncing from my left to my right and back again. Several times I dive flat on my stomach, fearing I've been spotted, but, after heart-pounding moments, determine that it's just my ears playing tricks on me. Only once does a shot land anywhere near me, an eruption of powder and smoke a few meters to my left, but judging from the trajectory, I'd say it came from our side, Alexis or Maya firing a little too wild. I'd put money on it being Alexis. The girl has stones, but her experience with firearms seems limited at best. Which is fine, just as long as she doesn't shoot me by accident.

As I close the distance to the far tree line, I try to keep my concentration on sighting the muzzle flashes of my enemy's rifles. I catch some bursts to my far left in the general area that we caught sight of a rifle, which indicates that the shooter hasn't changed his position. So that's good, but there's a second shooter firing, and that's the one I'm worried about. Turns out I should be worried, as I see a burst of hot orange not more than five meters from where I am creeping, maybe twenty paces into the trees. This makes me think I'm dealing with a militiaman as they are typically more confident with their position, figuring that they won't need as much cover when dealing with inexperienced shooters. It's a miracle that he hasn't spotted me, so I'm going to have to move quickly and take him out fast.

Drawing up a quick map of the area in my mind, I drop a mental pin in the tree cluster I believe the shooter to be in and take the last stretch of clearing at a dead run.

Now he sees me. Shots explode at my feet, spraying powdered snow into my face. I charge through the cloud to the trees waiting just meters beyond, hoping that his next shot isn't better than his last. A round bursts as I dive into the cover of trees, bullets blistering the pines. Foxholing up against one of them, I freeze, catching my breath, waiting, pistol raised and ready to fire. No more shots come. For the moment, my enemy has lost me from his sights.

I look down at my clothes. Virtually all of my "camouflage" has sloughed off, but that's OK; it won't do me much good at this point anyway. In my mind, I replay all of the exercises we ran of this kind of scenario, of facing a shooter in a pinned down situation. Quickly, I reopen my mental map, recheck where I've pinned the shooter against my current location. I could start shooting to draw his fire, get right into it with a one-on-one shootout, but my SIG P250 won't be much of a match for his superior rifle, so I may want to think of another strategy. When he doesn't attempt to draw me out of hiding, it gives me an admittedly crazy idea. Wouldn't be the first crazy idea I've had today.

Without second-guessing myself, I crouch into a roll and take to the trees in front of me, positioning myself farther away from my shooter. Before I reach the nearest pine, his lack of firing tells me what I need to know, that he isn't exactly sure of my position. As he doesn't have me locked down, I am free to move, as long as doing so doesn't accidently put me in his sights. It's a chance I'm willing to take, as I'd rather have the element of surprise than try to take him in a direct firefight. I slink to a tree on my left and then another, keeping my mental map drawn, charting my movement while keeping my shooter's pin centered. Slowly, tree by tree, I make my way around the map until, by my reckoning, he is ahead of me, ten meters or so to my left. Then I peek out from behind my tree to see if I've been reckoning right.

My answer comes in the form of bullets. I duck back behind the tree as splintered bark explodes around me, showering me in pulp. The shooting is too good, too measured and precise to be a cadet. I'm dealing with a militiaman, and though I'd match my skills with most of them in a straight fight, this situation is going to require a less direct approach as I would be riddled with rounds before I ever even got off a shot. What I have to do is catch my opponent off guard and draw him out so I can get at him clean. The solution rests in the inside pocket of my peacoat, flattened against my heart and ribcage. I draw the boomerang out.

Back to my map. Judging from the direction of the gunfire, my mental pin is more or less where I place the shooter, give or take a couple of trees. While the snow has ceased temporarily, the wind still blows strong from the northeast, which will be a good or bad thing depending on how I throw. I've only got a few seconds before the shooter changes positions to get a better shot at me, and I need to root him out on my terms, my timing. The weapon in my hand has gotten me out of a few major scrapes, but I have never needed it more than I do now.

Taking the wind into consideration, I pull my throw just slightly, arcing the curved piece of wood northwest. Breathlessly I watch it spin, tensing when it nearly hits a pine, letting go as it disappears from my view. After that, all I can do is wait.

THWACK! Wood upon wood. A voice cries out, shots fire, cursing. If I am to have a moment, it's now. Boots crunch on snow and I step out, pistol raised. A short, confused man is out from behind his tree, firing to his right, wrongly believing that he's being attacked from that direction, that the boomerang came at him at a straight angle. It didn't. Too late he realizes, turns, and I have my shot. The eyes of Nicholas Mitchell go wide, and my finger tenses, planting a bullet right between them.

Mitchell drops to his knees, and I can't tell if his face is registering surprise or if that's just what death looks like. He falls face-first into the snow. I'm thankful for that. I don't think I could stand to look into those eyes any longer.

As if to honor the dead, the woods are silent with a ceasefire. Without thinking, I approach Mitchell's fallen body, watch with detached fascination as the blood pools from his head into the snow, making a shape like a question mark. So this is how it feels to have killed a man. Like nothing. Like emptiness.

No, I tell myself. This is war; the numbness I feel is battle stress, and sometime later I will experience the full weight of this, of having taken a life. I have to believe that. I have to believe that I'm a man and not some unfeeling, death-dealing machine. It goes against all of my training to think that, but I have to hold on to what makes me human. For my father's sake.

It occurs to me to take Mitchell's weapons, but we already have all the guns we can carry. I will need his ammo, however, so I am not spared the horror of rifling through the pockets of his corpse. Again, I tell myself this is good, necessary even. I should experience it. Feel the slack of the body, recognize that it once held life and I took that away. Feel the true weight of all this. But in truth I just feel numb and a little tired from adrenaline withdrawal.

After pocketing a few clips, I go to the tree and retrieve my boomerang. There's a nick in the bark where it hit, higher up than Mitchell stood. The thing didn't even hit him, just scared him out into the open. Makes the whole thing sadder for some reason. If he hadn't let it rattle him, he'd still be alive right now. And I would likely be dead.

Slipping the boomerang back into my coat, I crouch low so as to not make myself an easier target for whoever might be out there. And who is out there, I wonder? It stands to reason that Byrne would have assigned this mission to father and son, so I'm thinking that Jessup is out there among the pines, probably wondering why his father stopped shooting, why he hasn't heard a signal, a whistle to let him know that I'm dead. I could whistle, trick Jessup into the open, and take him down as easily as I did his father. It would be the smart thing to do, and that rat-faced jerk would more than deserve it, but after killing his dad, I just can't do it. Jessup isn't much of a match for me, even with a better gun, so I can afford him a moment of fairness before putting him down. Am I ever stupid or what?

"Jessup?" I call into the woods. "Are you out there?" No answer, just the rustle of wind through the pines. "Your father is dead. I killed him. Do you hear that? I killed your father."

Silence is my answer. Keeping my eyes to the west, to where the first shots were fired, I wait, holding my pistol. I watch the trees for any movement, readying myself to make another kill. Will it feel any worse to kill someone closer to my own age, someone I have grown up with, trained with, even laughed with on rare occasions? I tell myself that it won't, that it will be no different than killing his father, but this time self-deception doesn't come so easily. Jessup is a pawn in the game as much as I am, just a scared kid following orders. I guess that's all war comes down to in the end—scared kids following the orders of older men. Seems like a terrible waste when you look at it in those terms.

Well, I'm sorry for that, Jessup. I never cared much for you, in fact, I downright hated you most times, but none of this is your fault. For that, I'll put you down as easily as I can. Quick and clean, if that's at all possible. Quick and clean.

Now get out here where I can see you.

He does, but not in the way I'm expecting. In the trees, a little to my left, Jessup steps out, sees me, freezes. I level my gun, waiting for him to do the same, but his eyes are on the body of his father, taking it in with slack-jawed confirmation. His arms are shaking, and he's scared; there's no way he's getting that rifle up and aimed at me before I take him down. Which I could right now. But I don't. It's not that I'm afraid to kill him—I'm not. I want to give him a moment to process this: me, his father, what it's all come to. A moment to understand that this is where his life ends and that it didn't have to be this way.

Jessup runs. He turns away from me and tears off into the pines, and I curse myself for not taking the shot. I consider letting him go, but I know that would be stupid. Letting him go would just mean I'd have to face him again. I'm already regretting letting Rafe and Devon live. No, I've got to end this now, clean, like I said. Jessup is about to duck behind a tree when I shoot his right leg out from under him. He falls, howling in pain.

It's the crying that gets to me the most. I come up on Jessup carefully, ready to duck for cover should he start firing at me with his M16. But the fight seems to have gone out of him, and all he can do is thrash around in the snow and the blood and the pine needles and cry. Maybe it's because I killed his father, or maybe he's just a coward, but he doesn't so much as touch the rifle, just lets it hang on his side as he blubbers and whimpers. I'm torn between feeling sorry for him and being disgusted by him. He was trained for this—we all were. What makes him so special that he gets to face his death crying like a goddamn baby?

The blubbering mostly stops when I reach him, and I'm grateful for that. He looks up at me, snot running from his nose and lips, eyes red with hatred and tears. "You're an animal!" he spits at me. "You've got no honor. Just a wild dog!"

Strong words, coming from a rat. "You don't know the first thing about dogs, Jessup, and neither do I." His lower lip quivers as I level the gun at him. "This is war. I didn't start it, but here we are. That's all this is."

The hatred in his eyes softens, changes into something else. Fear. "Please," he begs. "Please don't do this. You don't have to do this! You shot up my leg. I'm no threat to you now! You can just walk away. I won't even tell the others which way you headed!"

"They know which way I'm headed."

That trembling lip starts shaking uncontrollably, and the sobs come again. At this point it's just making me angry. "For Christ's sake, Bowie, I'm begging you! Please! I couldn't even come after you if I wanted to! Hell, I'm probably redundant anyway! Please!"

He's right—with the way I took out his knee, he probably is redundant. Which makes my decision all the easier. I pull the hammer back on the pistol. "Sorry, Jessup."

A last flare of anger returns. "FUCK YOU!" he screams. That's good, Jessup. Show some stones in the face of oblivion. It doesn't make me respect him, but it does makes me feel a little better about pulling the trigger.

BLAM!

My wrist takes the brunt of the kickback, and cordite stings my nostrils. Jessup's head jerks back, and a spray of blood sprays the trunk of the pine he's shored himself against. He doesn't quite fall fully over, just sort of leans there, blood dripping out the back of his head on the snow. This time I know better than to look at the eyes.

The soft crunch of footfalls approaches to my left, from the clearing, and I know without looking that it's Alexis and Maya. I don't know how long I've been standing here, looking down at Jessup but really not looking. The wind picks up, rustling the trees with a lonely sound, and I hear no further shots fired, no evidence of more enemies waiting in these woods. Jessup and his father were the only ones posted here. That means the rest are still coming.

When the girls arrive, Alexis puts a shocked hand to her mouth, but Maya keeps her face set and stony. She might be doing it for my benefit, showing me she can handle it, but I think that it's just the way she's wired. For a second I worry that the kill has changed Alexis's opinion of me, cast me in a savage light. But then she puts her hand on my shoulder and sets my fears to rest.

"Are you OK?" she asks.

"I'm fine," I lie. That's what killers do; we lie to ourselves. I know that now that I'm a killer. "It had to be done."

Both girls offer me nods of grim assurance, but only Maya really knows how I feel. That's OK as I don't want Alexis to ever know this feeling if it can be helped. I make a silent promise to myself that I will try to protect her from it. If I can't save her life, I can at least save her soul.

Almost instinctively, I draw the walkie-talkie from my pocket and twist the knob, checking for breaks in the static, a clear frequency. I find one, put the talkie to my lips, press the button.

"Byrne? You out there?"

It takes a moment to get my reply. "I'm here."

"The Mitchells are dead," I say. "Took them both down myself."

"I see," he sighs. "Thank you for giving away your position."

"You knew where we were headed. I'm betting you're on your way already."

He answers with a dry chuckle. "You know," he says, "it's almost too bad I can't let you live. It would be a real treat to take you back to the Fort in chains and make you watch me take your mother as my own. She'll fight it at first. They all do. But in the end, I'll break that filly. I just wish you could be there to see it happen."

"I'll kill you before you ever get the chance," I counter. "And trust me, Byrne—that's what this will come to. Me and you. I promise you that."

Again, he laughs. "Bowie Neville," he says. "I wouldn't have it any other way."

CHAPTER THIRTEEN

The Ice

A KILOMETER INTO THE WOODS, I HEAR THE WHINE OF ENGINES, CARRIED on the wind like an encroaching swarm of giant flies. The three of us quicken our pace, neither girl needing my instruction. With no snowfall to slow them or to cover our tracks, the snowmobiles (Byrne calls them Vipers after their model name) should have no problem tracking us and even less trouble catching up to us. Our only chance is to reach the pointe and hope the ice is frozen enough for us to cross and not the Vipers and their riders. Basically, conditions have to be perfect, or we'll be dead within the hour. So no big deal or anything.

Thankfully, we're closer to the pointe than I initially judged. Clearing the last curtain of trees, we step out onto the rocky shoulder of the peninsula, the ocean wind blasting our ruddy cheeks. Alexis visibly shivers, and I resist the urge to warm her in my arms. This is no time for romantic gestures. Then again, there may not be much time left. But the truth is I don't have the courage. Easier to face the enemy than show tender feelings to a girl.

We climb over the last of the rocks and stumble onto the flat of the peninsula. The sandy scrubland creeps out onto the bay like a crooked finger, bending a little to the west, then curving back to a tapering point due northeast. Beyond that is water, just shy of a full kilometer until the far shore reaches it with its scar of stony beach, and beyond that, a forest of pines. I used to think I knew what awaited in those pines, but now I have no idea. Now they're just trees, ones that I must reach if I have any hope of surviving.

I look to the girls as we all jog out onto the pointe. "Follow the land for as far as it will go," I say between breaths. "No point in risking the ice until we have to."

"Won't that make it easier for them to shoot us?" Maya glumly points out. She's right, of course. Byrne knows the lay of the peninsula; all he has to do is set up his snipers to aim ahead of us, and we'll run ourselves right into the bullets. On the ice, we'll be far less predictable.

But we'll be out in the open. On ice that is barely frozen over.

As we run, I glance over the bay, trying to judge the stability of the ice by its appearance. The vast stretch of it is patched with white and grey, the wind blowing whirls of dusted snow around horizontal windows that gaze into inky black. The surface is smooth save for the long cracks that multiply and gather in the areas where the ice begins to break loose in floes before drifting out to sea. The tighter we stick to the peninsula, the more stable it seems, but again, that will be an easy trajectory for the snipers to predict. Our best hope is to zigzag across the slippery expanse and hope that we don't wander too close to where the cracks are at their most dense. I don't think Byrne will risk driving any of the Vipers out there after us, so we've got that much going for us, at least.

As if chasing my thoughts, the sound of the snowmobile engines echoes across the bay and slaps back at us. Still running, I turn and see the hunting party arrive at the rocky shoulder, the men and boys dismounting at the bark of a command. It takes a moment before I spot Byrne among them, flanked by Wilkes, August, and Gunnar. Rafe and Devon are there as well. I can tell by their slumped body language that there has been a reprimand. I imagine there will be a lot of pressure on the two of them to prove themselves at this stage of the fight, and for a second I almost pity them. Almost, and only for a second.

The large rocks of the shoulder form a natural barricade, perfect for covering snipers and giving them just enough elevation to make us easy pickings. If we're to make a move onto the ice, we'd better do it before they have a chance to get settled and put us in their crosshairs. Taking Alexis by the arm, I look to Maya, who is already waiting for my order. "Let's do it."

Maya is the first onto the ice, skimming across the surface as if her shoes were skates. Alexis proves equally coordinated, lean legs bending as she moves, left to right, left to right. The hand I keep on her arm proves more to my benefit than hers; I fumble along, sliding awkwardly, my feet threatening to slip out from under me with every move. If it wasn't for Alexis lending me stability, I'd already be flat on my ass.

There is a whizzing of air and three explosions of powdered ice less than a meter to my right. *POP! POP! POP!* The sound of the shots echoes across the bay, reaching us a millisecond after the bullets land. Alexis tenses next to me. "Don't stop," I say, adrenaline keeping my voice steady even as my brain chokes back panic. "Eyes forward. Don't look back."

A high powered round hits at Maya's heels, sending her skidding forward. My heart freezes in my throat as I wait for her to go down, but she rights herself without losing a step, amazing me once again. *CRACK!* Another round, .50 caliber, likely from a Western Coalition sniper, one of two we keep in the armory. Byrne has really spared no expense on this hunt. The ice at our feet splinters, the large hole left by the bullet emitting a spiderweb of cracks from its epicenter. The heart I've been holding in my throat drops to my stomach. I realize what they're doing now. They're not even trying to hit us.

They're trying to break the ice.

Confirmation comes in the form of more .50 caliber rounds, raining down in front of us in a widening semicircle at a distance of six or so meters. I yank hard on Alexis, stopping her. "Maya," I yell, "stop!"

She slows to a skid as the horrible sound of cracking ice surrounds us. Scant meters ahead a fissure appears, breaking loose a large chunk of our projected escape route. Instinct screams to go right, to stick closer to the inner bay, but that's just what Byrne will expect us to do. Which is why when Maya looks back at me for instruction, I gesture to the left.

Toward the open sea, where the ice is at its thinnest.

More shots, coating us in a fine spray of ice dust. A large chunk in front of us cracks away, revealing a pool of black, fathomless water. I would just as soon stand here and have my head blown clean off my shoulders than fall into that water. But as long as there's a possibility of survival, as long as there's a chance that I might be able to kiss Alexis again, I'll keep moving.

Pulling Alexis with me, I move us to the left, to the east and toward the ocean. Maya shakes her head, letting me know silently that she thinks this move is ill-advised, crazy even. I'm pretty sure it's crazy myself, but I'll take crazy over certain death. The shots follow us as we slip and slide, tearing up pieces of the ever-thinning ice. I don't let them rattle me. Just keep moving forward, I tell myself. Don't think of the ice. Don't think of the cold water, of freezing, drowning. Don't think of being trapped under the ice, pounding helplessly on the underside of a clear wall, icy water filling your lungs as your friends stare helplessly on the other side...

POP! A last shot hits meters behind us, the bullet hitting the ice a millisecond before the sound reaches our ears. That means we're farther out than I thought, perhaps even out of range of the snipers. The three of us are together now, forming an uneven line, and I take in the view to our left, of the yawning chasm of the Pacific and the sun glinting low and golden on the waves. Take in these moments of beauty, I tell myself. There may not be many left.

Beautiful or not, the floes we skirt are sectioned off like ships at a port queuing up for sea travel. Definitely ships we want to avoid. I push us several meters farther along the shore of ice, keeping us as close to the inner bay as I can. When no more shots come, I bring our party to a stop and glance over my shoulder.

Incredibly, we have put an impressive distance between us and the pointe. The men at the boulders have become tiny ants, scurrying to and fro at barked commands I cannot hear from this far away. A small group of them gather—three, by my count—and make their way down toward the pointe, following it out into the bay. Gunnar's height and blond hair give him away, and the smaller, dark-haired one has got to be Rafe, out for blood for what we did to his father.

"He's sending out a small party after us," I say. "Rafe and Gunnar, by the looks of it, and one militiaman."

The girls—women I should say—turn to look, both of them gulping cold lungfuls of air. The distant party approaches, rifles raised, and I watch Maya's face drop as their image becomes clearer. "It's my father," she says. "That's his jacket. The bastard sent my father."

Even at this distance I recognize Wilkes's well-worn camouflage jacket, the kind soldiers wore during the Vietnam War. That was a dirty war from all accounts, but not as dirty as sending a father to kill his own daughter. That's a depth even the most brutal of warlords wouldn't dare to sink to. But then it occurs to me that Byrne may have sent Wilkes out here to reason with his daughter, get her to turn on us, or maybe Wilkes himself volunteered in the hopes of saving her. Strange that I'd be giving Byrne any sort of benefit of the doubt, but there could be any number of factors at play here, and I need to consider all of them, not just for myself or for Alexis but for Maya. I owe her my life after all.

"You know," I say to her, "there may still be a chance you can back your way out of this. There may be a chance you can go home, that Byrne will cut you a deal on your father's account. You can say I brainwashed you or that you killed Nagel in self-defense. Lord knows he was a loose enough cannon. And I don't imagine many will miss him, least of all his son. We could make a show of you turning on us now, make it look like you came to your senses. You don't have to see this thing through with us, Maya. You don't owe us that."

She stares back at me, cold breath misting from her mouth, face incredulous. "This isn't about what I owe you, Bowie. This is about what's *right*. Let's say you're right and my father is able to somehow get Byrne to allow me back into the Fort. What is my life going to mean then? Everything I do will be watched. I'll be forced to marry one of the boys, who will hate me, and have his children. I don't even know if I like children, Bowie. And I certainly don't like boys. So what kind of life is that?" She shakes her head, her flat brown hair floating like burnt straw in the wind. "I'd rather die out here with my friends."

I look to Alexis, who nods her resolve. That's it, then. We're in this together, hell or high water. Or freezing cold water, as the case may be. "Let's keep moving, then," I say. "We've got a good head start. They won't catch up to us before we reach the—"

There comes a rush of air, a whooshing sound, a sound I have only heard once before, on a test demonstration August Erickson ran for the cadets sometime last year. In all the stress and confusion, it never occurred to me that the hunting party would be carrying a rocket launcher with them, but here we are, standing like fools as a rocket streaks across the sky toward us, trailing smoke. I put my arms over Alexis's and Maya's shoulders and dive. "GET DOWN!"

A concussive blast, a cushion of air. We are bounced in the blast, Alexis and Maya flying free from my arms. I land palms down on the ice, meters back from where I stood moments before. I'm just grateful the ice is still there. Grateful my hands are still there. I look up, but the air is clouded by powdered ice and smoke. The atomized ice crystals shimmer in the air, making me feel like I've been hit by some sort of magic spell.

"Alexis!" I yell into the gloom. "Maya!"

Someone coughs to my right, where Alexis had been moments before. I crawl over and find her sprawled on her back, fist balled to her mouth, hacking. Her eyes take me in but don't really register me because of the shock. I quickly inspect her body, looking for wounds, damage. She's shaken badly and filthy with soot but seems otherwise intact. "Are you OK?" I ask. She doesn't answer. I snap my fingers in front of her eyes, jolting her back to reality. "Alexis!"

"I'm all right," she gasps. "I'm all right."

I help her into a sitting position and scan the gloom, hoping that it settles quickly. A figure stirs in the swirl, and Maya emerges like a character out of myth. Her eyes are wide and dazed, but her legs are steady. Her rifle is slung into her arms, ready to shoot. When she sees us, she hurries over, kneeling at our side.

"We're OK," I tell her before she has to ask.

"What the hell was that?"

"Rocket launcher," I answer. "Saw one of them fired once, out in the woods."

"Why would they send a party out onto the ice just to blow us to bits?"

The smoke clears, giving me her answer. "They weren't trying to hit us," I say glumly, pointing ahead of us toward the shores of the mainland. "They were trying to cut us off."

Both women turn to look at the carnage wreaked by the rocket's explosion. The once glass-smooth ice is now a wreckage of tiny icebergs, bobbing uselessly in black water. The blast has shattered a rift in the ice more than eight meters across and twice that wide. We can try to get around it, but even the parts that are crossable are horribly cracked and no doubt unstable. And we can forget about feinting west again—the ice on the seaside is all but gone into the Pacific. We are trapped, stuck waiting here for the trio Byrne sent after us to arrive.

"Well, I'm not going down without a fight," Maya says, checking to make sure her M16 is locked and loaded. "I've got a bullet here with Rafe Nagel's name on it."

I consider asking her if she's also got a bullet with her father's name on it when his voice calls out across the ice. "Maya!" he shouts. "Talk to me, girl!"

"I've got nothing to say to you, Dad," she answers. "The time for talk is through."

"Just hear me out," he continues. The three coming toward us are much closer now, maybe fifteen meters away, moving steadily. "Nothing that you've done so far can't be fixed. Papa Byrne understands that you're just a girl and that you fell under the spell of Bowie Neville and the outsider witch. There's no shame in being a weak-minded girl, Maya. You're only being true to your gender. Give yourself over to me now, and I promise we can find a place for you again. Turn the other two over to us, and you'll be welcomed back a hero."

As the words reach Maya's ears, her face transforms into someone I don't recognize. I can't tell if she's offended by what he's saying, by the inference of weakness, or if she's considering his offer. With the way things are at the moment—Alexis and I on our butts, no weapons drawn, and Maya over us, locked and loaded—she could easily do what he asks, turn her gun on us, take us captive, or even shoot us. Maybe what I'm seeing is someone weighing the rest of her life, the long and the short of it, on this one defining moment. I'm looking at a fully grown woman standing at the crossroads, a woman holding the fates of all three of us in her hands. Either choice she makes, this will likely be the last I know of Maya Wilkes, my ally, my friend. She looks down at me, and I nod, letting her know that whatever choice she makes, I understand.

"Run," she says. "I'll hold them off."

"Maya, no!"

"RUN!"

There will be no arguing with her, that much is clear. I stand, knees bent, crouching low, and pull Alexis to her feet. Maya offers her a final, sad nod of female solidarity. Alexis, for her part, can only say, "Thank you."

And then we run.

The hole made by the rocket forces us to the east, our right, which puts us back in the line of sniper fire. Shots ring out across the frozen plain, bullets chasing us, whizzing by our heads, kissing our ears with their deadly heat. A burst of rounds opens up behind us, Maya firing at her father and his tight conscription of cadets. I have to believe that's she's only providing cover for us, not actually trying to shoot her father dead, as abandoned as she may feel. There's still love there between them; I heard it in his voice as he tried to bargain with her, and I've seen it in her eyes from the beginning. Somewhere, in some other reality, they have reconciled and are living a happy life together, father and daughter. But this is not that reality.

Wilkes and the cadets return fire, their bullets strafing past Maya and nipping at our heels. Instinct demands that I keep my eyes forward, on the hole in the ice now mere steps away and off the spiderweb of cracks at our feet. But the sound of the fire fight causes me to stop, to glance back just for a moment to see if Maya is still standing. It proves a crucial miscalculation. The soles of my boots skid out from under me, and I fall on my ass into a spin. My gloved fingers scrabble at the glassy smoothness of the ice, finding no purchase, no friction to slow me down. I call out to Alexis, but she's too far away to stop my trajectory. All she can do is skid to a shaky stop and look to me, wide-eyed, as I go spinning to the lip of the hole. Before I even reach the water, the thin ice at the mouth cracks under my weight, and I plunge into the now widened hole.

I try to hold my breath, try to keep the freezing water out of my lungs. The cold hits my chest like a blow to the ribs. My body flushes suddenly hot, as if using up all its heat in one desperate burst. The need to breathe is so automatic that, despite knowing what will happen, my lungs revolt, and I gulp liquid cold, taking water into my nose and throat. Even though my eyes are closed, I can feel the water at my eyelids, trying to freeze my eyeballs into my skull. I won't look up to the horrible sight of the ice above me, the shadowy shape of Alexis trying to see me through the frozen surface. I don't want her to see me. I want her to run. Run, Alexis. Leave me here to drown. Go home to where you are safe. Don't let my death be for nothing.

Numbness comes, settling into my limbs. I only realize I've been thrashing because I stop and experience the strange serenity of floating. The cold is still there, but it's distant now, like a faraway voice. For a moment, I think I hear my father, his voice carried by the endless current, calling me out to sea. Why did I think this would be so bad, drowning? Why was I ever so afraid of death? It seems so peaceful to me now, so welcoming—the end to all of my troubles, all of my suffering. My body flushes with heat—there's a word for it that I've forgotten—and my brain begins to shut down, little lights being turned out in a darkened room. All that's left now is to sleep without dreams, to let go, to die. To give myself over to obliterating black...

Again, I hear my name, muffled. Let me go! Can't you see I'm ready now? I feel a pull at my neck, something grabbing me by the collar of my coat, and then I am yanked back into the terrible light. Reflex forces the water from my lungs in a painful expulsion, and I cry out with a gasp, more agony than relief. I feel the rage of being torn from a beautiful dream. Female voices squabble in my ear; I recognize them, of course. Blinking cold fog out of my eyes, the faces of Alexis and Maya come into focus, looking down at me, slack-jawed, panicked. I cough up the last of the liquid with an agonized hack.

"What..." I blubber. "What the hell are you doing?!"

"Saving your life," Alexis answers petulantly. "I couldn't get you out of there myself—if it wasn't for Maya, you'd be gone by now."

I sit up, trying to fill in the blanks of the last few minutes. Meters away, I see Wilkes, Gunnar, and Rafe making their way toward us on the ice, no longer hindered by Maya's cover fire. They'll be upon us in less than a minute. I reach for the M16 at my back, but it is gone under the ice, likely drifting out to sea. My pistol still rests on my hip, and I draw it, but when I aim it to fire, the hammer jams from the cold water. Useless.

"It's OK," Maya assures us. "I've got a plan. Just stay low. And stay out of the way."

Maya unloads her weapons, leaving them for me to take. I try to question her, but the cold has returned to my body with a vengeance through the wetness of my clothes, forcing me into hitching, uncontrollable shivers. Alexis puts her arms around me and pulls me close to her body, attempting to warm me. It's wonderful but woefully inadequate.

Maya approaches her father's party, hands raised in surrender. "You win, Dad," she says. "I surrender. I'll go without a fight."

Wilkes and the others are close enough that I can see the looks of confusion on their faces. They're as baffled by Maya's play here as I am. Wilkes nods to them, and they raise their weapons at me and Alexis. We respond in kind, Alexis taking Gunnar, me taking Rafe. This is what is known as a Mexican standoff, though I have never seen an actual Mexican in my life.

"Easy now," Wilkes says to us. "No need to make the death toll any higher." He lets his own rifle hang, approaching Maya with open hands. "We can end this peacefully. Just let us take you in, and you can face justice with dignity and honor."

"A little late for honor, don't you think?" I say to Wilkes. "I don't see much honor in what you've allowed Byrne to do." I look to Gunnar, knowing that the redness in his face is more shame than the cold. "You've let him turn my brothers against me. You stood there and did nothing as he gunned my father down in cold blood. Is that the justice I can expect?"

"You were never a brother of mine," Rafe snarls.

Wilkes shuts him down with a glare. He turns back to his daughter, and his face softens, heart breaking at what she's become. What she's been forced into. I can't see Maya's face from this angle, but I can only imagine she's looking as sweet as she can. "I'm sorry, Daddy," she says through a sniffle of tears. "Take me home. I promise I'll be good. I'll be what you want me to be. I'll do whatever you want. It'll be like it was back when Mom was alive. We can be a family again. I can be the daughter you need me to be."

Beneath that handlebar mustache, Wilkes's lip quivers. I have never seen that man's face crack before; it's frankly unnerving. "Oh, baby..." he stammers. "Oh, my sweet baby girl."

He pulls Maya into a hug, and they stand there, swaying in full embrace, both of them sobbing. Despite all of the horror and death, it's a beautiful moment, and I think all of us, Gunnar and Rafe included, are struck by it. After all, what are we if not family? I think we're all fooled for a moment into believing that we can put this madness behind us. That maybe things can somehow still be OK.

Then I notice Maya's hand worming toward the grenade hanging on her father's belt. Her tiny finger slips through the ring of the pin, pulling it loose without making a sound. With equal skill, she pops the lever into her hand, palming it, arming the grenade.

Now I see her play. Dimly I wonder if we are far enough back to not get caught in the blast. I count five seconds, five very long seconds, then push Alexis down on the ice, cover her ears, and pray for my own.

It isn't so much a sound as a concussion. Alexis and I are pushed back by the blast, almost back into the hole, which is less than a meter away. Ice rains down on us in tiny glinting particles, a shower of invisible diamonds. There is shouting, but it is all muffled through the fog of damage the explosion wreaked in my ear drums. I'll be lucky if I'm not deaf. Good thing I don't have to worry about redundancy any more.

I lift my head, taking stock of the situation. In the haze of smoke and fog, I see shapes moving, scrambling, hear the panicked shouting of Rafe and Gunnar as they try to make sense out of what just happened. Even though this fight has made us enemies, I am glad my old Viking friend is still alive. Then again, it only means that I may have to kill him later, but now is not the time to worry about that. Now is not even the time to mourn Maya, who, along with her father, is gone, obliterated into pieces that I, thankfully, cannot see as the water has claimed them. All that's left where Philip and Maya Wilkes once stood is a massive rift, an expanse of water and shifting floes, tiny icebergs making their way out to sea. The fissure snakes its way east, making it impossible for anyone to cross, cutting Alexis and I off from our pursuers. If we run now, head for the mainland, and keep our heads low, we will be out of range in a manner of moments, and there will be no chasing after us. Maya has delivered us freedom.

Taking Alexis's shaking hand in mine, we stand together, facing Deacon's Bluff in proud defiance, in honor of our fallen friend. We speak no words as none are required, and I probably couldn't hear them anyway with the ringing in my ears. Across the rift, through the drifting, obfuscating smoke left by the blast, Gunnar and Rafe stare back at us, shell-shocked. Without even realizing I'm doing it, I give Gunnar a military salute. It's not for him, of course; it's for Maya. And Gunnar understands this, returning with a nod.

Then we turn, and again we run, skirting the hole and making our way east, to stable ice, and on to the mainland. No more shots are fired as we run, at least none that I can hear. I'd like to believe that my former friends are showing their respect for Maya's sacrifice and allowing our escape, but the truth is that, with the smoke and the rift in the ice, there's no point in wasting the bullets. They wouldn't be able to confirm the kill even if they hit us. The chase is over.

At least, that's what I tell myself. But in my heart, I know that our reaching the mainland won't stop Patrick Byrne from coming for us. He will not stop until he sees us both dead.

CHAPTER FOURTEEN

The Mainland

OVER THE YEARS, I HAD THOUGHT ABOUT WHAT IT WOULD BE LIKE IF AND when I stepped foot on the mainland for the first time. I never imagined it would be running from my home, hunted as a fugitive, with a mainlander woman clinging to my arm for support. That honestly never even occurred to me. Stepping upon the rocky scrub, gazing forth into the shadowy pines no different from the ones I have known, I am filled with a feeling of sadness. In my mind, I pictured this moment as one step in a grand adventure, a triumphant moment in a great battle, a reclamation of a world left behind, a homecoming of sorts. But not this. I never imagined this.

Alexis, for her part, breathes a frosty sigh of relief. To her, this means escape, freedom. She turns back to the bay, to Deacon's Bluff and the tiny specks of men gathered angrily on the rocky shoulder of the pointe. We're too far away now to hear cries of anguish or barking reprimands, but somehow, I know they are happening.

She looks to me, trying to judge how she should react. Should she grieve for Maya? Should she be grateful? Relieved? I can't begrudge her whatever she feels. She didn't know Maya as well as me, and I was just getting to know Maya myself. And that's the worst part—that now I'll never see what she was to become. Alexis must read all of that in my face because she says exactly the right thing. "I'm so sorry, Bowie."

There's a lot of sorry going around today. Choking back the urge to cry, I nod, put my watering eyes toward Deacon's Bluff and my mind on our immediate troubles. "We have to keep moving," I tell her. "This isn't over. Byrne's not going to let a little thing like a body of water keep him from hunting us. Not after what we took from him today. He's lost his three best friends, his lieutenants. There is no way he just lets us walk away from this."

"Sure," Alexis says doubtfully. "But what's he going to do, walk around that massive hole in the ice and hope he catches up with us? We'll be miles away before he gets here, and judging from those clouds in the sky, the snow isn't over. There'll be no tracks to follow."

"August Christiansen is the Fort's best tracker, and Gunnar is no slouch either," I inform her. "Plus, they've got the Vipers." I clarify, "The snowmobiles."

Alexis points to the massive fissure in the ice left by the blast. "They're not getting them across that! There's no way!"

"You're right; they won't." I turn my eyes to the south where the top of the Densmore Bridge peeks beyond the cliffs, just a hint of rust in the far distance. "What they'll do is double back and cross under the Densmore, along the rocks of the jetty. The ice will be more solid there. It's why he was waiting for us there earlier; he knows it's the easiest place to cross. The rocks fortify the ice, make it more stable. They'll make it across, and then they'll try to get out ahead of us as we make our way east. There's really only one direction for us to go."

Alexis shakes her head. "Well, we won't go that way. We'll stick to the coast and head north. Eventually we'll hit Canada, and then..."

A strong wind comes off the bay, causing her to shiver involuntarily. She knows that heading north is a fool's risk. Another storm is coming, more frozen air from the north, and if I know anything about how this area was settled, it'll be days before we see another living soul. There is not enough shelter along the coast, and we will not survive the cold, so east with a lean to the south is our only real option. Which, if my theory is correct, will put us directly in the path of Byrne and his hunting party. But it's a risk we have to take.

"Unless you know something I don't, I think we'd better head east," I say. "There's still a lot of woods between us and Byrne, and I am willing to bet he doesn't remember the terrain as well as he thinks he does. He's overconfident, and we can use that against him."

I can see from her faraway look that Alexis has her doubts, and in truth, I can't blame her. Though the scorecard would show more deaths on Byrne's side than ours, there were three of us, and now one of us is gone. I've never been good at percentages, but at a glance that doesn't seem like a great number. I hate myself for thinking of things—of Maya's death—in these sort of terms, but it's what I need to do now to keep focused. If I stop to think of all that I've lost right now, I'll just lay down and die.

We are about a kilometer into the mainland when the storm returns with a vengeance. Heavy, wet snow piles down on the already thick layer covering the ground, and if not for the cover of the pines, we'd be up to our waists in it by the end of the hour. Staying close, Alexis and I struggle through the worsening drifts. Ice-cold winds blow from the north, plastering the wet snow to our already frozen faces, our meager scarves creating only a thin protective membrane. The sun is all but gone now, making things all the colder as we sink into shadow, a pair of wraiths lost in a whirlwind. We will need to find shelter soon if we are going to survive the night, and I am determined to not let Maya's final gesture go to waste.

Alexis, however, is rapidly running out of steam. At one point, she falls into a drift, and when I try to pull her back onto her feet, she resists. "Bowie, I can't," she gasps, destroyed with exhaustion. "I have to just lie here a while. I have to rest."

"If you lie here a while, you'll die," I answer sharply. "I'm not letting that happen."

"Isn't there anywhere we can find to get out of this mess?"

I look around us as if it'll help, but all I see is darkness peppered with flurries of white. But it does seem that the ground starts to rise a bit to our left, which could lead to a hill or, better yet, a mountain, and mountains can sometimes mean caves. It's a long shot, for sure, but I don't know this terrain and don't have anything but my instincts to go on. My instincts will have to do for now.

Bending down, I haul Alexis out of the drift and onto my back, having her throw her arms around my neck. She hangs there like the primates I've seen in pictures clinging to their mothers. I can't believe how little she weighs, less than she did when I rescued her from the plane just a few short days ago. It seems like years ago now.

We trudge like this, Alexis hanging on my back, for what feels like hours but is probably only twenty minutes. The muscles in my legs feel like they are on fire, a feeling I should welcome in the cold. I remember my father explaining the concept of hypothermia to me, the experience of feeling warmer when, in actuality, you are freezing to death, and it starts to not sound like such a bad way to go. I don't think Alexis would object too much if I just lay us both down and let the snow claim us. I'm giving the whole idea serious consideration when my eyes fall upon a small clutch of boulders set into the side of the hill, forming a natural sort of awning. It's not a cave, but it could provide us with enough dry ground and shelter to ride out the night.

"Over there," I say, my voice ragged from strain. "I think I see something."

Alexis lets go of me and stands on her own, her legs wobbly but somewhat recharged. I'm grateful to be free of the added weight, though I'd never tell Alexis that. Mother taught me to never talk about a woman's weight, though I think that sort of superficial concern is the furthest thing from my companion's mind at this moment. She trudges on ahead of me, reaching the boulders first and inspecting them as a viable shelter. The large rocks lean into each other, creating a narrow space between them and the mountain that is mostly dry and out of the wind. A nook barely big enough for two people to fit in, but big enough nonetheless.

We set about clearing the area as best we can, and I venture back into the pines to retrieve some branches to make us a wall. Alexis helps, and after we have a good number of branches, we thatch them into a crisscross pattern and pull it over us when we crawl into the nook. With the wall's protection and the doubling of our body heat, we might manage to get a little warmth back into our limbs and maybe even get a little sleep.

Alexis folds herself into my arms, more from necessity than attraction this time. That's OK; I'll take what I can get. "Christ, I'm freezing," she says, shivering against me. "I don't know if I'll ever feel warm again. What I wouldn't give to be in Hawaii right now. Or even Vegas."

Those are names I recognize, places beyond my tiny world that I thought were gone, reduced to rubble, desolate wastelands. This idea, these images I have carried so long in my mind, seems simplistic and childish now. A deep resentment rises within me, and I start to feel angry at my father, at my mother, at all the adults who have lied to me for so long. How could I have been so stupid to believe the lies they fed me? How could I have been so blind to the truth, so willing to be led by the nose, a good little soldier, never questioning my orders, my mission? My entire existence has been built on a lie, and somehow, even after all that has happened today, this is the thing that causes my stomach to hitch. That I am nothing, a total failure.

Alexis feels my anguish. "It's OK," she assures me. "Let it out. Cry all you need to."

"I just feel like such an idiot," I say between sobs.

She rests her head on my chest, giving me the space to let the tears flow. "You're not an idiot, Bowie. All children believe what their parents tell them. No matter who they are or where they were raised. We're all brainwashed to some degree."

I let loose a bitter chuckle, wiping the water from my face with wet gloves. "You seem to have things figured out pretty well," I say.

"Are you kidding me?!" Alexis laughs. "Let me tell you something. I don't have anything figured out. I'm just as big of an idiot as you are—maybe even a bigger one. My life was handed to me on a silver platter, and it still wasn't enough. I had to have life on my own terms. So of course, I did what any over-privileged kid with anger issues did—I rebelled. It was little things first. Hanging out with the wrong crowd. Dating the wrong kind of boys. Then it was smoking, shoplifting. Doing drugs. Being reckless with my own life as well as others'. Why not? I was the daughter of a senator. I could get away with anything."

"A *senator*?" That word rings an alarm in my mind. It's a word I have been programmed to reject. A word used to delineate a leader of the old government, my sworn enemy. Despite all that has happened, I still have an automatic response to that word, and that response is disgust.

"That's right," Alexis confirms. "My father is the US senator for the state of California. Why do you think I was being so cagey to Byrne when I was being questioned? If he knew I was the daughter of someone in power, he would have killed me right on the spot. And you probably would have let him do it."

"No," I say, desperate to believe my conviction, "I wouldn't have."

She looks at me with a faint smile, then nestles back into my coat. "It's

OK. I wouldn't have blamed you. You've been brought up to believe the government is evil. And you know what? You're not one hundred percent wrong. Some of the time governments do bad things. That's true of all governments, no matter how big or small. You can't always trust them. All you can do is hope that good people rise to power for the right reasons. Because in the end, that's all that governments really are. People, Bowie. People just like you and me."

It's hard for me to imagine that the monster I've been programmed to hate is really made up of people, but then I'd never imagined that the leaders I looked up to, like my idol Papa Byrne, were monsters themselves. Maybe we're all monsters. "If you're the daughter of a big-shot senator," I ask, "how the hell did you end up here?"

"Protesting." Alexis laughs, a laugh as dry as fall leaves. "Isn't that perfect? It wasn't the drinking or drugs or fooling around that did it. It was all over a protest I was involved in that got out of hand. Some friends and I went up to Alaska to chain ourselves to an oil pipeline, one of the biggest in history. The oil company's security fired on us, accidentally killing one of our protestors, a friend of mine. It was all over the news, a huge scandal for the senator's daughter. That's why I was on that plane. Those people were my father's private security, come to take me home." Her lips pull down at the edges, and I can see the pain tugging inside of her, the guilt settling like a stone in her gut. "Well, I don't have to worry about it anymore, at least."

"I'll get you home, Alexis. I promise."

She smiles at me, a consolation prize, then settles back in. "Don't make promises you can't keep," she says, her voice drifting. "Now shut up, and go to sleep."

Her body slackens, and sleep comes for her quickly. For me, it's not so easy. My mind is on my father, my mother, Maya, Jessup's face as I put the bullet in his skull. Too many faces, too many eyes following me. I could run all the way to the end of the earth, and I'm certain they'd still be following me, right until my final breath.

I try to lose myself in Alexis's warmth so that sleep will come. Finally, it does.

HOURS LATER, I CAN'T SAY HOW MANY, I AM WAKENED BY A SOUND

outside our shelter: footsteps on snow, but quieter than I expect. That is not the heavy crunch of the army-issue boots worn by Fort Thunder soldiers. The steps are light, nimble; if I wasn't so keyed up for any noise, I might have mistaken them for snow falling from branches. I tense, reaching for a pistol, trying not to move enough to wake Alexis from her sleep. If she wakes, she'll make noise, and then we'll be discovered for sure.

Several minutes pass as I sit there, pistol gripped tightly in hand. My heart pounds so loudly that I'm surprised it doesn't wake Alexis, what with her ear pressed so close to it. But she remains blissfully unaware of the prowler outside our den. Just as I am preparing myself to get the jump on whoever is out there, the steps fade into the distance, and I am convinced that our hiding place went unnoticed. After a few more minutes of silence, I gently rouse the girl sleeping in my arms. She starts to mutter something, but I put a finger to my mouth.

Instantly she catches my meaning and stays quiet. I gesture to the outside, mouth to her that I heard someone out there, and she nods, reaching for her M16. When I feel she is ready, I take the barrel of my pistol and gently push aside some of the pine branches that make up our "door." Through them I see nothing, just a deep snowfall and countless pines. Mercifully, it appears the snowstorm has stopped, and there's even a little warmth in the air.

Which just means an easier hunt for Byrne and the others. I open the hole wider, checking the periphery for any sign of someone out there, the slightest glint of metal, a shadow ducking behind a tree. But all that is out there is woods and snow.

Well, if there are snipers lying in wait, they're about to get their chance. Looking to Alexis one more time, I nod, and she returns with one of her own, indicating her readiness. Then I lean back against the rocks, put my boot soles against the pine barrier, and kick.

The barrier falls away, revealing us to the wintery world beyond. All is as silent as before. The hail of bullets I half expect do not come. We step out of our makeshift shelter, feeling the ache in our bones of a night shouldered up against cold rocks. I stretch my neck and back, sending a ripple of popping sounds out across the silent forest.

After it appears we are indeed safe, we take turns relieving ourselves behind nearby trees. When Alexis is done, she walks back wearing a disagreeable look on her face. "What I wouldn't give for a clean bathroom and a hot shower." As she nears me, I notice her stepping through a line of tracks, small footprints leading past our shelter and off into the woods in an easterly direction. This must have been the lurker I heard mere minutes before.

I point out the tracks to Alexis, and she takes them in grimly. "Well," she says, "I guess that means we don't head that way."

"Actually, I think that's exactly what we *should* do. Whoever left these tracks had no idea we were here. They won't expect us coming up behind them."

"But what if they lead us right into the others?"

"I don't think they will," I say. "I don't think this is militia at all. Those aren't the tracks left by our boot soles." I lift up my boots to show her my treads. "See? Not ours."

"So that means they're native." This doesn't seem comforting news to her.

"Then we're saved, right? I mean, these *are* your people."

"Yeah," she answers with more than a hint of uncertainty. "See, it's a little more complicated than—"

A whistling sound cuts her off, some sort of signal issued from the trees. We both crouch low, waiting for incoming fire, but nothing comes. Another whistle rings out, a response to the first, this one farther away.

Quickly, we move into the trees, and I deliberately lead us along the tracks, following them up a small ridge and then down a winding slope. Ahead the trees thin out into a clearing, and as we draw closer, I realize that it is a frozen-over pond. There is a cracking noise, and as we approach, careful to use the trees for cover, I see a small shape out on the pond, working at the ice with a large stick. Even at a distance I can see that it is a child, too small to be anyone from the hunting party. Boy or girl, I cannot tell; the child's hair is long and wild, matted into great clumps that hang in front of a grunting, sweaty face. The clothes worn by the child are a combination of old, worn fabrics and patches of filthy animal pelt.

If I didn't know better now, I'd swear I was looking at a zombie.

The stick breaks through the ice with a *crack*, and the child hops up and down, grunting with glee. Judging from the high pitch of the voice, I guess that it's a girl, but the jury is still out on that. The tiny savage slings a pole from her back, pulls a wriggling worm from the folds of her ragged skins, and threads the worm to a hooked line at the end of the pole. "Ice fishing," I say to Alexis with some astonishment. "She's ice fishing."

I start to move toward the pond, but Alexis grabs my arm. "Bowie, maybe we should just hang back a bit."

"It's just a girl," I say dismissively. "And we haven't had real food in over a day." It's true, and worse, the meager rations Maya brought us are all but gone. This may be the only chance we have at food in the foreseeable future. "I'm just going to go talk to her. See if we can't maybe lend a hand. Besides"—I pat my pocket where the pistol lies comfortably—"I've got this covered." I hand my M16 over to Alexis, and she shoulders it, looking comically weighed down by two weapons. "This way she won't be spooked. But you cover me from here, and if something goes down...well...you know what to do."

Alexis looks at me horrified. "You want me to shoot a little girl?!"

"Hopefully, it won't come to that," I answer. "Now do you want to eat today or not?"

She grumbles something in response, or maybe it's her stomach answering for her. Either way, I step out of the thatch of pines providing us with cover and make my way down toward the pond. The girl doesn't see me at first as she's understandably preoccupied with fishing. But the crunching of my boots on snow alerts her, and she jerks back from her fishing hole, holding out the dripping pole like a defensive weapon.

"It's OK," I call out, raising my hands to show I'm unarmed. "Don't be scared. I just want to lend you a hand..."

The girl hisses at me through yellowed teeth, and I begin to think this maybe wasn't such a good idea. She sticks her fingers in her mouth and whistles, the sound so shrill it makes my eardrums spasm. I stand stock-still, arms still raised, smiling the best I can. "All right. It's OK. I get it. I won't come any farther. No need to freak out..."

A whipping sound comes at me from the side, and before I can move, I am struck by something hard to the neck. It takes a moment for the pain to hit, but I feel a hot trickle of blood and put my hand to my throat, fearing I've been shot. There is a wound there but nothing too serious, and glancing down at the snow, I see a small rock with my blood on it. Now I know what the whipping sound was. Someone pegged me with a slingshot, the primitive kind used by natives before this land was settled. The kind Maya used to practice on recyclables back home when she thought no one was looking.

"Bowie!" Alexis shouts behind me. "To your left!"

I go for the gun in my pocket, pivoting left in time to see someone drop out of a tree. It's a man, dressed in the same sort of tatters as the girl but much older and with a shaven head. In one hand he holds the slingshot, a skin pouch hanging on the end of a leather tether. In his other hand...well, there is no other hand. The snarling savage who races toward me has only one arm, but judging from the coiled muscles of his compact physique, one arm might be all that he needs.

Before I can get a bead on him, he whips the slingshot with his one arm, and it wraps around my wrist, yanking the weapon out of my hand. With his next move the one-armed man does a flying kick to my chest, sending me sprawling back into a tree. Remembering my hand-to-hand combat training, I stay centered, swinging at the man with my forearm, looking to connect with his chin. He rears back, hitting me hard with his single fist, right in the side of my face. I think I feel a tooth coming loose. I swing again, full fist this time, but he blocks with his arm and kicks me back again, slamming me up against the tree. He's a good fighter, and he knows it, and as he slams his forearm into my windpipe, crushing the breath out of me, he shows me what few teeth he has. As if he's enjoying himself. He draws something long and white from his belt—what appears to be some sharpened bone. He presses the bone-blade's tip to my side, one ounce of pressure away from skewering me through the liver.

"John! No!"

The tip of the man's blade eases off of my side. Another figure emerges from the trees, this one lithe and lean, taller than the man by more than a head. Long black hair frames a sturdy face, sharp-featured, hard-lined, and strangely beautiful. A woman, but not like any woman I have ever seen. She carries in her hand a gut-strung bow, and her leather clothes are finely stitched beneath a grey coat of matted fur. Her eyes, ice-blue, stare right through me.

"Who are you, boy?" she asks. "Not one of mine, and not from any tribe around here."

"He had a gun, Faye," the one-armed man, John, reports while backing off of me, blade at the ready. "It's right over there, on the ground."

The woman goes to inspect, but before she can reach the weapons, a burst of rounds startle her back. Alexis. The woman crouches low, draws her bow, targeting Alexis's vantage point. Something tells me this woman is a really good shot, better than Alexis, even considering the disadvantage weapon-wise. I see this going very badly very quickly, so I raise my hands again and look to the thatch of trees where I know Alexis is crouching.

"Alexis," I call out, "don't shoot! Put down the weapon!"

"Uh," she calls back. "I don't think I really have much of a choice!"

A few moments later, Alexis is led out of the trees by another savage, a large man holding a spear. Like the woman, his hair is black, his face hidden behind an equally black beard. His skin is a rich brown color that I haven't seen since, well, the Logans. But his features are different than theirs, more angular, hawkish. My guess is that he's Middle Eastern, but I'm only going by what I know from books. There were never any Middle Eastern people among the Lucky Thirteen, and Byrne always spoke of them as a violent, warlike people. The word he often used to describe them was *terrorist*. Said that they employed guerilla tactics to wage war on our government. I never understood why that made them enemies as we saw the government as *our* enemy, but those kind of questions were met with sharp, short answers. Still, at the moment, I am inclined to fear this man and what he might do to Alexis.

"Don't hurt her," I forcefully request. "Do whatever you want to me but leave her out of it. All I wanted was to ask for some food."

The warrior woman, Faye, smiles at me, but it's not friendly. It's the smile of someone taking pleasure in having the tables turned in their favor. "Food, eh? And why should we give you our food? Because you have guns?"

"No," I answer, keeping my voice even, trying not to show fear. "Because we're lost out here and hungry, and it's the human thing to do."

Faye laughs, sharp and cutting. The dark-skinned man joins in as does One-Armed John. Smiling, the feral girl comes up the shore of the pond and folds herself inside of Faye's furs. I assume they are mother and daughter, but the girl is so filthy I can't discern a resemblance. When the woman is done laughing, she jerks a head at John. "Tie them up," she orders.

With some skill, the one-armed man pulls some hemp rope from a threadbare backpack and manages to tie my hands behind my back. I pull at the bonds, but his knot, executed with his one hand and his teeth, is as good as any I've made during training. He does the same to Alexis, and we are bound together, she behind me in a train formation. Faye inspects the work and nods, pleased. "Abrahem," she says to the dark-skinned man, "get rid of the guns." She looks over to the pond, to the hole in the ice made by the feral girl. "Evie's hole should do nicely."

Wordlessly, Abrahem does as she asks, gathering our weapons and dumping them into the hole in the frozen pond. One-Armed John pats us down for more weapons, finding none. I am glad he is the one tasked with this job because his single appendage misses the boomerang lying flat against my back. It won't do me much good now, but at the right moment, it might.

Once the last of our guns are gone under the ice, Alexis and I are gathered into a tight cluster. Evie, the feral girl, comes out from under Faye's furs and dances around us, grunting and hooting in what can only be interpreted as amusement. I don't find any of this funny.

"Come on," Faye says to me, "we're going on a little walk."

CHAPTER FIFTEEN

The Tribe

WE ARE LED ALONG A NARROW PATH THAT SHADOWS THE SMALL RIVER feeding the pond. The soft gurgling of the ever-flowing water gives the false impression of tranquility, but I don't allow my brain to buy into it. Our captors do not speak to us on our walk, which suits me fine, nor do they treat us roughly, though judging by the way One-Armed John glares at me, I bet he'd like to.

The path we travel is well worn from use; even the fresh snow has been trampled down to a mushy brown, and I imagine the blanketed surroundings are regularly cleared away during warmer seasons. Ahead of me, Faye walks with the confidence of one who has come this way hundreds, maybe thousands, of times. A true master of her terrain and the equal of any man.

A good twenty minutes passes this way, the savages leading, Alexis and I trudging silently in bondage. The path diverges from the river and rises up a small hill, and ahead I see that we are coming into a large clearing, perhaps some sort of field. The air is acrid and thick with smoke, the unmistakable haze of burning wood. Evie runs off on her own, grunting happily and disappearing over the hill. Cresting the hill in her wake, we view the savages' settlement. I am shocked to realize that they have no wall.

What stands in front of us is less a settlement and more a loose encampment of clustered tents and shacks. As we are led down the path that winds through the camp, fearful eyes watch us from behind hanging flaps and from crudely cut and shuttered windows. The dwellings get more tightly situated but no less random as we move deeper into the center, then finally it all opens up into something that could be seen as some sort of village square. Here there is a great pit full of charred remnants, the scene of many a bonfire, and I scan the pit quickly for signs of human bones. Beyond the pit is a massive tent, five times the size of any other, held up by at least ten bordering poles and two taller poles in the center. The tent's canvas is blackened and greasy, but thick vertical stripes of red are still visible through all the soot. I recognize this sort of tent from my studies—the kind that housed circuses in the old days. Father even said he had been to a circus once as a boy, said the clowns scared him. Somehow, I doubt there are any clowns inside this circus tent.

As we round the bonfire, hardscrabble faces emerge from their crude dwellings to take us in. Men, women, and children of all sizes and shapes, the newly born to wizened and white-haired. There's one woman who is older than any person I have ever seen who seems to have skin made of tanned leather. Many a limb is missing, and I notice several that are twisted and deformed, the sort of imperfection that would never be tolerated at Fort Thunder. But the thing I am struck by most is how few white faces I'm seeing. There are a few, for sure, though the streaks of filth make them hard to immediately identify, but here they are a minority. The villagers have rich, varied skin tones and a wealth of ethnic features, sometimes a combination of many. The word for this is *diverse*, and though I was taught it at Fort Thunder, I don't think I ever knew what it meant—people of no unifying race looking at me as some blond, blue-eyed freak.

Faye raises a hand, and we are brought to a halt before the great tent. She turns to the onlookers, projecting an impressive air of leadership. "These prisoners are under my protection," she states clearly. "They were found in our woods and will be dealt with appropriately when we can determine more about their intentions. There will be a meeting of tribal leaders immediately, but in the meantime, no one is allowed in the main tent unless authorized. Is that understood?"

There are nods all around, a general air of respect for her command. Surprising considering what a rough-hewn group they are. Faye opens the flap of the tent, and we are ushered inside by John and Abrahem. I hear grumbling from the onlookers as we pass from view.

Inside, the tent is arranged like a meeting place, with rough wooden benches and tables situated in a loose circular pattern. The center area is cleared, and we are brought into it and forced down to our knees into the dirt. With Abrahem and John flanking her, Faye lords over us with cold, judging eyes.

"I'll be back within the hour," she informs us. Her eyes focus on me. "I think there's someone here you'll be interested to see."

"We look forward to it," I answer. Faye smiles at my sarcasm and takes her leave. John and Abrahem leave with her, but I see their shadows lingering outside the tent. Any ideas I might have of escaping are best left unconsidered.

I look over to Alexis to see how she's faring, to find in her the hope that I'm lacking. All I see there is worry.

"It's OK," I lie. "If they were going to kill us, they would have done it already."

"Maybe," she says, "or maybe they just have to check with the other leaders before a verdict can be handed down. That's what it sounded like to me."

Her reasoning is sound, but I make a point not to agree with it. I also make a point not to say what I fear the most—that these people are cannibals and intend to eat us. Tales of mainland cannibals were as common in my youth as zombie stories, and now that I think on it, they were more or less indistinguishable. And though the idea of undead creatures roaming the forests seems silly to me now, the eating of human flesh is an entirely possible, even plausible, reality, especially among starving peoples. To hungry eyes Alexis and I must seem very appetizing. I wouldn't be shocked to find this meeting of leaders is nothing more than an exchange of recipes.

I keep these thoughts to myself, and we wait out the minutes in silence. My knees are starting to ache badly when the flap opens and a group of new faces enter the tent.

Correction: mostly new faces. There is a face among them I recognize, though it has changed much over ten years' time. Grown longer, more defined, and hardened around the edges. But it is a face I would recognize even a hundred years from now. I've seen it many nights, haunting me in my darkest, most guilt-riddled moments.

"Hello, Bowie," Michael says. "It's been a long time."

I open my mouth, but no words come out; I am struck speechless. Michael steps forward, his stride aided by the use of a wooden cane. I see now that his right leg, broken by his fall all those years ago, never healed properly. The kneecap is twisted at a bad angle, and his right foot leans inward, hindering his step. But the rest of him seems to have healed just fine. He turns to the others, a motley group of oldsters that counts the leather-skinned woman among them. They hold themselves in a way that reminds me of the council at Fort Thunder. "May I request a few moments alone with the prisoners?" Michael asks them.

The old ones exchange glances and nods. The leather-skinned woman holds up a wrinkled hand. "Take all the time you need, Michael. We'll await your verdict."

Michael dips his head in a deferent bow. "Thank you, chief elder."

The elders leave through the tent flap, and I catch a glimpse of Faye waiting outside, guarding the tent. Something tells me she'll be waiting there for us should we try to make a run for it. Michael hobbles over to us, coming to stand before me face-to-face. Even hunched over a bit on his cane, he's taller than me by a few millimeters. "What are you doing here, Bowie?" He glances over to Alexis, who looks just as surprised by this exchange as me. "And who is she?"

"I've been banished," I answer. "Byrne killed my father."

If this news affects Michael, his eyes do not show it. "I'm sorry to hear that. I guess you now know how it feels. To have your own people turn on you."

His words cut deep, made all the worse by the fact that I deserve every jagged syllable. But I'm not going to give him the satisfaction of knowing that. Not yet, at least. "You seem to have done all right for yourself," I say with some defiance.

Surprise registers in his eyes, the same hazel eyes I last saw looking to me with betrayal as he fell from the wall. A slight smile curls in the corner of his mouth, but like me, he keeps his feelings guarded. Still, I detect a small amount of respect in his face as he tucks a stray dreadlock behind his ear. He turns his attention to Alexis, who seems uncharacteristically cowed in his gaze. I almost sense a hint of attraction, and it makes me feel jealous. "I don't recognize you from my days at Fort Thunder, and judging from your appearance, I highly doubt you were welcomed into the community. So who are you?"

"I'm Alexis Deveraux," she answers. This last name — not the one she gave to Byrne back at the Fort — must be her real one. Smart girl. "I'm a US citizen."

"What is a US citizen doing with the golden boy of Fort Thunder?"

"*Exiled* golden boy," I add.

"Yes," Alexis cuts in, keeping Michael's attention on her, "and that's my fault."

"It's not your fault," I grumble. "You opened my eyes to the truth."

Now Michael is back to me, and this time he can't force back a malicious smile. "Well, well. I never imagined that Bowie Neville would be taken down by a girl."

"Nobody took anyone down," Alexis interjects defensively. "Bowie's in this mess because he tried to help me. If it wasn't for him, I'd have died on that island. He protected me against his own people, put his life in jeopardy, and it cost him his father's life. He's a hero."

Right now, facing the friend I betrayed, the last thing I feel like is a hero. "Look, Michael," I say, "I understand how it must feel to have me here as your captive. Whatever fate you decide for me, I'll accept it without protest. But Alexis has nothing to do with any of this. I brought her into Fort Thunder, and that's why we're here. That's why we're running. So do what you will to me, but let her go. She's innocent."

"Hold on now," Michael says, face set with concern, "what do you mean 'running'? You just said you were exiled."

"We were," I confirm, "but Byrne kept pursuing us outside the Fort. He blocked off the jetty and then chased us all the way to the pointe, out across the ice. Marcus Nagel is dead. Phil Wilkes and his daughter, our friend Maya, are too." This next part comes hard. "I killed both Nicholas and Jessup Mitchell. Shot them both down, right there in the snow."

A look of horror settles on Michael, which is nothing compared to how it feels to have done it. Those faces will be there now on sleepless nights, replacing eight-year-old Michael Logan's. If there's a small solace I can take from this, it is the relief of knowing he survived, that he even, in some small way, prospered. Less guilt I have to take to my grave. "So as you might imagine," I continue, "Byrne isn't taking any of this lightly. He wants me dead, and I don't think he'll stop until he kills me himself. And I wouldn't want to be the person who takes that pleasure away from him, so it's probably in the best interest of your people to let me go and face what's coming on my own, away from your village."

Michael processes this with some disbelief. "He won't cross the bay. In all these years, he's never once come across to the mainland."

"He's never once had a reason to," I say. "Now he does." The words settle in the tent like a heavy fog. "You know what he's capable of, Michael. Time hasn't softened him one bit. He's out for blood now, and he isn't going to stop."

"We have numbers," Michael counters.

"Yes. And Byrne has guns."

We stand there, at a stalemate, Michael considering what I have told him. After what feels like an eternity, he turns and hobbles out of the tent, slapping the flap closed behind him tersely. Now, all there is to do is wait.

"That went well," Alexis intones sarcastically. "Friend of yours?"

"Former," I confirm. "Someone I let down years ago. He has every reason to hate me. So no, I wouldn't say that it went all that well." It has already occurred to me that I haven't seen Michael's parents since our arrival. I can only assume that they're dead and that asking about them won't help our case any, so I keep it to myself.

The tent flap opens and the warrior woman, Faye, enters. In her hand she carries a sword, a long thin blade with a brass grip big enough for only one hand. The blade is polished to a keen shine, and she carries it with the confidence of one who knows how to use it. She steps into the round where Alexis and I wait, on our knees, limbs bound. Standing before me, she holds the blade for my inspection, centimeters from my face. "Do you know what this is?"

"A sword," I answer, trying not to sound glib.

"Not just a sword," she answers, "a Confederate saber used in the American Civil War. Did they teach you about that war back at your little stronghold?"

I nod. "Eighteen sixty-one to sixty-five. A war between the North and the South over the ownership of slaves. Lincoln was president. The North won."

"Not very nuanced, but acceptable," Faye confirms. She places the shining tip of the blade under my chin. "Then you understand the irony of this sword being here, with this tribe. A tribe where everyone is truly equal regardless of their race or gender."

"It's a blade," I say, perhaps unwisely. "I don't think it cares who wields it."

She presses the sharpened tip up against my tightening throat. "Then it won't mind if I cut you open and let you bleed out onto the dirt."

"You sure you're cleared for that?" My voice struggles over the pressure of the blade and my mounting fear. "As I told Michael, there's someone who wants me dead already, and he's not going to be happy about someone beating him to it. Especially if that someone is a woman."

"Bring it on," Faye says with a cruel grin. "I'll be happy to face any of your people out here, on our turf. I'll show your leader what a woman can do." She gives the blade a tiny amount of pressure, and I feel a hot trickle of blood dripping down my throat...

"Faye, that's enough." The old woman has returned and is standing at the flap of the tent. Her eyes, set and stern, carry far more command than her quiet rasp of a voice. "These two are not to be harmed. In fact, I want them cut loose."

Faye withdraws the blade, offering me a challenging smile. "Yes, Mother." She strides behind me, never losing the cockiness of her swagger despite the parental reprimand. I feel the blade slip between my wrists, and after a few seconds of rough sawing and almost cutting me, the bonds slough loose. I stand, rubbing my chaffed and sore wrists, keeping my eye on Faye as she frees Alexis. She takes a little more care with Alexis's restraints. I'm just glad that it's understood that Alexis isn't from Fort Thunder and doesn't share in my transgressions.

Michael has also returned along with the other tribal elders, two men and two women. Once Alexis and I are fully freed, the white-haired woman approaches us fearlessly, trusting us to behave.

"My name is Mars," she says. "I act as the voice for the coalition."

"Mars?" I question. "Like the god of war?"

"I never liked the name I was given—Marsha. Terrible name. So I shortened it to Mars. After the planet and the promise of new frontiers, like the one we've built here. But the irony isn't lost on me, if that's what you mean." She gives me an amused smile. "Now, if you'll both follow me, we will adjourn to the longhouse and try to sort all this out."

With Faye at our rear, we are brought out of the tent and joined by more guards, Abrahem and another girl, younger and smaller than Faye, both carrying crude spears. All of us follow behind the elders, who walk slowly, their aged bones not allowing much in the way of mobility. It occurs to me that I have never been in the presence of people this old. Doc Seaver is the oldest person I know, and these people seem a good twenty to thirty years beyond him. With the natural debilitation of their age, they would be declared redundant at Fort Thunder, and I start to wonder what will happen to Doc or Frankie—or my mother, for that matter—when they reach this age. Will Byrne exile himself when he grows too old to effectively fire his trusty AR-10? Somehow, I don't think so.

We walk across what I assume is the village center, their square, and I can't help but take in the wide variety of people who ogle back at me with contemptuous eyes.

"We settled here at River Bend almost twenty years ago," Mars informs us. "Left the States for likely the same reason your people did, Bowie, but not under the same circumstances. See, your people left because of the policies of a leader we supported. Of course, no leader is perfect, and he had his share of detractors, people that were unhappy with him beyond just the color of his skin. Maybe your parents were in that lot, or maybe they were racists. I don't know. But every action has a reaction, and when that leader left office, another rose, one who stood for everything the other man didn't. And there were people who were hungry for that point of view, ready and willing to embrace all of their hidden prejudices. Well, this new leader fed their hatred and welcomed their anger, violence. Whipped them into a frenzy. There were riots. Mass deportations. People who had been decent citizens for generations thrown into detainment camps under suspicion of being terrorists. The great melting pot had become just that—a seething cauldron of hate. And those of us who weren't willing to stand with this leader or allow him to roll over us were told if we didn't like it, we were free to leave. He even set aside a piece of land for us here in the Pacific Northwest, in this nature preserve. This was a man who had no use for nature anyway. So we were shown the door. A de facto deportment. It was no small irony that it was just across the bay from the island where your people had settled two years prior."

It is impossible for me to not think of my parents as I listen to Mars's words. I know in my heart that my parents were not racists. When my father spoke about the reasons they had left, it was always politics—his distrust of the system, that money and corporations had taken over, and that he believed in his heart that people needed to be independent and not look to their government to help them. My father believed in self-sufficiency above all, and the color of someone's skin meant nothing to him or my mother. For god's sake, the Logans were their best friends. I know for a fact that Michael's father was vocal against minorities allowing the system to coddle them. He believed in self-sufficiency just as much as my father or Byrne or any of them. That was the bond that united our people, and no philosophy of racial superiority was ever a part of our belief system. Of course there were words and talk, but until recent developments opened my eyes to the truth, that's all they were: words and talk. I was never taught to be racist. I was taught only to be a good soldier. All that I am guilty of, even in my betrayal of Michael, is wanting to be the best I could be.

We come at last to the longhouse, a long, narrow hut made of wood planks with a thatched bark roof. I have seen pictures of similar huts in books that detailed the lives of Native American tribes that settled in this area before the whites came over to decimate them. In fact, it occurs to me now that much about this village harkens back to those native tribes, as if this new tribe is deliberately evoking the land's original people—a reclamation of sorts.

The hut has no door, just a doorway that enters into a small square atrium. Mars stops at the doorway, allowing the other elders to enter first. Then she gestures for Alexis and me to follow. I go in first in case this is some sort of trap. Inside I find the longhouse to be simply a long, narrow room with several rows of wooden benches separated by a middle aisle, all facing a small stage area, like what I know of the inside of a church. Thankfully, there doesn't seem to be any sort of religious iconography, just a simple meeting place and staging area for a speaker. It's how I have always imagined a town hall might look in the mythic lands I know only as *suburbs*.

The elders are taking their places on the stage, sitting cross-legged in their loose-fitting, rough-hewn robes. I turn to check on Alexis and, finding her behind me, notice Mars denying entrance to Faye and the other warriors. Some terse, hushed words are exchanged, and Faye looks none too happy with the decision but concedes to her mother. It seems that we are being trusted to sit before the elders without a conscription of guards. This would never be allowed at Fort Thunder, of that I can assure you.

Once the words are exchanged, Mars comes in and indicates that we should be seated at the benches. We follow Mars to the staging area, and as she quietly confers with the other elders, Alexis and I take seats in the front row. The hushed talk between the elders carries on for a bit as we get settled, and I can make out some words but not full sentences. Understandably, there is still some disagreement among them, but Mars seems to have things under control, proving herself every bit as authoritative as Patrick Byrne or even my father. It makes me realize how stupid it is that there are no women on Fort Thunder's council, and I wonder how things might have been better had my mother or Frankie Seaver been given a voice.

Finally, the talk is done, and Mars takes a seat in the center of the group, cross-legged like the others. "So," she says, directing her gaze at me, "we've discussed it, and we've agreed to help. If what you say is true and Patrick Byrne is coming here to claim you, he will meet with resistance on behalf of the Coalition of Liberated Tribes."

It takes me a second to process this. "But I don't want your help," I say. "I want you to let me go to face Byrne on my own. I don't want him coming here at all!"

"He may be coming here whether you leave or not. Or he may never come at all. We won't know until it happens. In the meantime, it's best that we prepare."

With this decree, Mars whispers quietly among them, and they disperse to parts unknown. Mars remains seated. I get up from my seat, thinking we will be taken back outside, but Mars waves a hand at me, indicating that Alexis and I should stay. "You will help us with preparations, but first we will have a meal. Can't face the enemy on an empty stomach."

Two of the elders return, a tall, bald man and a short, wire-haired woman, carrying with them three small bowls. The woman places her bowl into Alexis's waiting hand, and the man gives me another bowl and Mars the last. Steam rises from the greyish broth within, but the clay of the bowls somehow isn't too hot to the touch. The elder pair take their leave as Mars looks to Alexis and me expectantly. "Go on," she says, sipping from her bowl. "Eat."

I feel Alexis's eyes on me, waiting for me to try the stew. Gazing into the bowl, I see small pinkish chunks swimming among the soupy greyness. My mind cannot shake the stories of mainland cannibal tribes, and my stomach lurches involuntarily at the thought of swallowing bits of human flesh. But at the same time, I do not want to offend my host. Raising the bowl to my lips, I tip a tiny bit of the stew into my mouth, careful not to take in any of the chunks. The stew is hot and thick and not entirely unpleasant, rich in a way our vegetable-based stews never could be. But while some deep, primal thing within me has been stirred by the taste of meat, I think of where the meat comes from and resist. As the bowl comes away from my face, I see Mars's eyes on me, testing, slightly amused.

"It's possum," she says. "The stew. It's possum. Not what you were thinking."

"I wasn't thinking anything," I lie, taking another sip from the bowl. Next to me, Alexis slurps with some hesitance, and a quick glance at her face reveals a grimace. I guess the idea of possum stew is not exactly appetizing to a palate as refined as hers.

We eat in silence for a bit, only the soft sounds of our sipping to fill the long, vast hall. When Mars has eaten enough, she places the bowl down on the stage beside her and folds her hands in her lap, the picture of calm. She closes her eyes and in a soft voice says these words: "Thank you, David, for the nourishment you have provided. With the strength you have given me, I pledge to help others, to offer assistance, sanctuary. This is the promise I make with the blessing you have bestowed on us, your people."

The three of us sit there in the wake of the strange prayer. Alexis and I both finish our food and place our bowls beside us, not knowing if we should attempt to replicate the words Mars recited upon finishing. Instead, all I can offer is "Thank you for the food."

Mars nods. "You're welcome."

"Yes," Alexis says, adding insincerely, "It was really good."

Mars smiles knowingly. "There's no need to lie to me, dear. Our food is crude even by our own standards. It's one of the things we all miss from the old world."

Another silence settles into the room, and I feel compelled to ask,

"Those words, the ones you spoke after finishing your meal. What were they?"

"David's Blessing," she answers. "It's a sort of prayer."

"Who is David?"

"David was my husband. He gave his life for us by giving us his flesh."

In my mind, this can only mean one thing, but I don't give voice to it. Instead I choose to say nothing, just look down solemnly at my hands, at the ever deepening lines of my palms. Just when I think that I can't stand another moment of silence, Mars speaks.

"It's OK. There's no need to feel bad for what you are thinking."

"But I wasn't..." I stammer.

"You were, and I don't blame you for it. Because you aren't wrong. The stories you were undoubtedly told are true. At least in part."

Her eyes remain fixed, but it feels like they are looking through me, past this building, this village even, into the distant past. "The winter of twenty nineteen was a brutal one. We ran out of food quickly, and when we asked the States for help, we were denied. Told we had made our choice, so now we had to die by it. We knew of your island, so a small group of us went to your settlement to ask your people for help. I'm guessing you would have been around two or three at the time. Anyway, as you probably know, we were not greeted warmly by your leader, Patrick Byrne. There was some arguing among your people, I think, but Byrne and his militia prevailed, appealing to the fears of your people. A tried and true tactic. At that time, my husband and Faye's father, David, was the tribal leader, and he wasn't going to take Byrne's no for an answer. So instead of leaving the island as Byrne commanded, we stayed.

"Needless to say, Byrne didn't like that. He had his men open fire into our group, killing several of us, wounding others." She holds up her forearm, revealing a scar very similar to the one I recently acquired. "I was lucky. My husband was not."

I allow the moment gravity before I respond. "I'm sorry," I say. "I'm sure if my father could have had his way, we would have helped your people."

Nothing in Mars's face indicates that she believes or is comforted by my words. "David didn't die on your precious island," she continues. "He was gut shot, which, as you know, is a miserable, agonizing death. But he wanted to die here, among his people. We got him back across the bay and into to this very longhouse, where he slowly expired. There was nothing we could do, no crude medicine we could conjure to ease his passing. But even suffering as he was, David thought only of others. He ordered that when he died, we were to eat his body to keep ourselves alive. So that is exactly what we did."

I should be feeling horror, but all I can feel now is shame. These people came to us, starving, needing our help, and we turned them away. Worse, we turned our weapons on them, gunning them down in their weakened state. These are the ideals I devoted myself to—selfishness and lack of mercy. And all this time I thought of these people as monsters for doing what was necessary to survive. At the Fort, we often referred to ourselves as *survivalists*; it was a term we wielded with honor. But these people are the true survivors. We are just bullies with guns.

The rest of the meal passes in silence. I finish my possum stew, and I'm grateful for it, grey greasy broth and all. Alexis chokes hers down, and I don't sense the same sort of gratitude from her, which is understandable. Her people's sins are not the same as mine.

As we are setting our bowls down, Michael comes into the tent, walking as fast as his cane will allow. "Evie's returned from her scouting mission," he reports. "Bowie's right. Byrne and his hunting party have crossed the bay and picked up our tracks. They'll be here in an hour, maybe less."

"Well then," Mars answers, "we'd better get ready."

CHAPTER SIXTEEN

The Battleground

Outside the longhouse, the village is already in a commotion. Word has gotten out that the battle is coming to the people of River Bend. I can see from many of the faces that not all are happy to be thrust into this fight, and more than a few of the families are leaving, which no one, least of all me, holds against them. More surprising is all the people who stay, including Michael, Faye, One-Armed John, Abrahem, and, as promised, Mars. Being of no use in battle, the council of elders elects to stay in the longhouse until their fates are decided, but Mars insists on meeting the enemy head-on, from the front lines. This frail old woman has more courage than most of the grown men I have known in my lifetime. She reminds me in many ways of my mother, should she ever reach such an advanced age. I am proud to fight alongside her, to die if I must.

There isn't time to set any elaborate or convincing traps, so it is decided to simply shore up our positions and claim whatever advantage we can. Faye, Abrahem, and others climb up to the roofs of some of the rickety shacks around the village, armed with bows and spears, ready to fire down on the enemy. They'd be better served by walls and a watchtower, but this was not a village built upon the principle of defense. The only enemies they ever expected to face were the elements and maybe themselves.

Darkness starts to fall, and I take my place with Mars and Michael at the bonfire in the village square. There was some talk about not building the nightly fire, but Mars rejected it. "Let them know where we are," she said. "We're not hiding."

I manage to convince Alexis to wait with the elders in the longhouse, which she is not even remotely happy about. It took me ten minutes to convince her that, despite being tough as nails and somewhat proven, it would be best if she sits this one out until there are no other options. I remind her that this isn't her fight and that she isn't a savage like us, but she still acts like a child being sent to her room. I'm not very confident that I can keep her safe and that Byrne won't come after her if things go south, but I've got to do whatever I can. I've come this far because of her, and I'm not losing her to a stray bullet.

Michael and I find ourselves next to each other, warming our hands over the same lick of flame. "So," I say to him awkwardly, "I haven't had the chance to ask about your parents."

To my surprise, he doesn't seem angry that I've asked. "Both gone now," he says. "Dad died our third winter here—pneumonia. Mom lasted a little over a year more, mostly for my sake I think. I don't even know what she died of. Just woke up one morning, and she had gone in her sleep. I guess she didn't want to go on living without him."

"I'm sorry."

He shrugs at my meager condolence. "Don't be. Believe it or not, we were happy here. Happier than we'd ever been at Fort Thunder. My father saw the writing on the wall with your people years before we were exiled. He knew that Byrne and a lot of his men were bigots and that it was only a matter of time before they conjured an excuse to cast us out. What broke his heart was that it came at my expense."

"I'm sorry about that too," I say.

The words hang in the air to be swept up by the fire in wisps of smoke. Useless. But Michael turns to me, flames dancing in his brilliant eyes. "You were still a kid, Bowie. You didn't know what was going on. None of us did. You can't be held accountable."

"I was jealous of you," I confess. "I wanted to be the best, and I knew that I wasn't. You were. You were better than me, and I betrayed you because I knew I couldn't compete."

For a moment, Michael's eyes turn hard, as if something he has always believed has finally been confirmed. Then his face melts into a smile. "Yeah, I was the best, wasn't I?"

I smile back. "By far. It wasn't even a competition."

"Oh, I don't know." He chuckles. "Don't sell yourself too short now. I mean, the rest were a sorry bunch, but you ran a good game. And you played fair. Not like... what was his name? The dark haired kid with the chip on his shoulder?"

"Rafe," I answer.

"Yeah, Rafe. How is Rafe these days?"

In the distance, I hear them. Engines drawing closer, carried on the wind. "Why don't you ask him yourself?"

THE VIPERS CIRCLE AROUND THE VILLAGE, THEIR RIDERS WHOOPING AND firing the occasional shot into the air, trying to rattle the villagers, but this group is not so easily rattled. As the circle draws tighter, the snowmobiles can be seen in the light cast by the bonfire, but when Faye draws her bow back to fire, Mars holds up a hand, stopping her daughter from engaging. Personally, I'd want to take the preemptive strike, but I've seen enough of Mars's leadership to trust her instincts. There are plenty of stories of guerilla forces winning against enemies of greater military might, and I hope this will be one of them. Still, when I hear the concussive blasts of Byrne's formidable AR-10, I can't help but feel that I'm making my final stand.

When the militia finally ride up to the bonfire, I'm just grateful that the waiting part is over. I'm tired of running, and I'm tired of this fight. I want it to end, one way or another. As the flames cast their fiery relief on the face of Patrick Byrne, I resolve that only one of us will walk away from this village alive.

Only two men ride to our bonfire, Byrne and August. The rest of the hunting party is out there somewhere in the dark, lying in wait for the first signs of trouble. I can see from the bitter look on August's face that he isn't happy with this situation. My guess is that he tried to talk Byrne out of this crusade, reasoned that we would die on our own, exposed to the elements. A noble effort but one doomed to fail. I've known Patrick Byrne long enough to know that once he sets his mind to something, there is no convincing him otherwise, and his mind is set to killing me no matter how far I run.

The two men dismount from their vehicles and approach the bonfire, rifles at the ready. Byrne's lip curls up slightly under his beard, pleased at finding me alive. He looks around the bonfire, at all the tense, foreign faces. It's clearly been a long time since he's been in the presence of so many people of a different race. "Who is in charge here?" he demands.

Glances are thrown around. The people of River Bend are reluctant to give up their leader to a warlord. But Mars doesn't need their protection, and she doesn't fear Patrick Byrne. She steps forward, mere centimeters from the licking flames, and locks eyes with his across the fire. "I am," she says with the requisite authority.

It takes a moment for Byrne to process the wizened female form that addresses him so defiantly. "A woman?!" He chortles, the sound making my stomach roil. "You're serious?"

If the insult bothers Mars, she doesn't show it. "I know who you are, and I know what you want. I'm sorry you've taken all the trouble to come here, but the boy is now under the protection of the Coalition of Liberated Tribes. Under my protection. So why don't you pack up your guns and your vehicles and go on back to your island?"

This elicits another chuckle from Byrne. His eyes scan around the fire dismissively, as if looking for a more suitable candidate to address, one with the right pair of chromosomes. He lands on Michael, who has been at my side this whole time, his hands balled into fists. Byrne smiles with disbelief. "Michael Logan?! Is that you?"

Michael nods, jaw clenched. "That's right."

"I'm impressed." Byrne keeps his cruel eyes locked on Michael, sizing him up. "Didn't think you'd last long out here with your injuries."

"Sorry to disappoint you."

"Hell, son, you were never a disappointment. Always a credit to your race. It was your parents I had the problem with. You I had hope for. I would have made you my top cadet when the time came." He aims the comment at me, thinking it'll hurt me. It doesn't. "Unfortunately, I had to use you to get your parents out of my Fort. Hated to do it, really. But they couldn't keep their black hands out of my business."

"Well, then you'll be glad to know that they're dead."

"I'm sorry to hear that," Byrne lies. "We've had our share of losses as of late. I imagine Bowie has told you. Marcus Nagel. Nick Mitchell and his son.

Seth O'Reilly, a boy no older than thirteen. So you can imagine how I'm feeling right about now. I can't just allow you to shelter this criminal. He has to pay for crimes against his people."

"As Bowie tells it," Mars says, directing the conversation back to her, "he was framed for the death of the boy. And judging by what you did to Michael and his parents, it's what I would expect. And the others, well... my guess is that you sent them to kill him. Is that right Bowie?"

"That's right," I confirm.

"Well then," Mars continues, keeping her eyes locked on Byrne. "The way I see it, those killings were done in self-defense."

"And the way *I* see it," Byrne counters, "if you don't hand Bowie over to me, your blood will be on his hands. As well as the blood of all the people in this village."

The threat cuts through the crackle of the fire, clear for all to know. I can feel bodies tensing around me, readying for battle. Despite Mars's conviction to defend me—maybe because of it—I don't want these people to die on my account. So I step forward next to Mars, flames licking at my face. "I'll go," I say. "You can take me, but spare the lives of these people."

Mars looks to me, angered, but I shake my head, giving her my final decision. For his part, Byrne looks pleased by this offer. "Fine," he accepts, "but what about the girl?"

My throat tightens. "She's dead. She died from exposure, out in the snow."

Byrne sighs, not allowing the lie even a moment of consideration. "We found the tracks. We saw the shelter you built. She's alive, and she's here."

"She's not a part of this."

"Yes, she is." His iron gaze travels past me, looking for signs of Alexis in the crowd, finding none. "All of this is due to her, Bowie. The result of her interference on our lives. Had you just left her there to die in that plane, none of this would be happening. Surely you see that. I let you bring the enemy into our home, and now we've been compromised. Now, I'm willing to take my share of the responsibility for that, for being too fond of you to stop the problem before it began, but now I have to fix it. If I allow that girl to live, to return to the world we left behind, she will tell them about us. Tell her people what she saw, how we live. Do you think that they're just going to allow us to go on the way we've been living? You don't understand the old world the way I do, Bowie. The moment they feel we're a threat, they'll come for us, and they'll take away everything we've built. I can't allow that to happen."

The rhetoric rings false to my enlightened ears. I've seen too much now to believe in his paranoia. If the "old world" wanted to come for us, they would have done it already. What's to stop them? They have planes, satellites, endless resources—they've no doubt known about us all this time and haven't moved upon us in twenty years. All Byrne has to support what he is saying is his own fear, a fear he used to build a community. And he needs that fear to keep it in line, to keep people believing that he knows what's best, how to protect them. That fear is more crucial to Fort Thunder's protection than the flimsy wall that surrounds it. I see it all so clearly now.

"You two can bargain all night if it suits you," Mars interrupts, "but I'm not allowing you to take either Bowie or the girl."

Byrne smiles back at Mars from across the fire, his eyes narrowing with recognition. "Wait a minute," he says, gesturing with the index finger of his left hand, "you were a part of the group that came to us all those years back. I remember that self-righteous attitude. And that hair. A little grayer now, but otherwise the same ratty mess."

"I remember you as well," Mars answers stonily.

That awful smile creeps back onto Byrne's hair-shrouded lip. "Didn't I shoot your man?"

"Yes. You did."

"You must miss him very much."

"I don't see that as any of your concern."

"Let me make it up to you..."

Too late I realize what Byrne is doing. Why he was gesturing with his left hand, keeping her focus away from his right, the hand reaching for the pistol at his belt. I move to push Mars out of the line of fire, to take the bullet even, but his pistol's muzzle is already flashing. Mars's head jerks back, her eyes wide and unseeing, and the only thing I push out of the way is a body that is already dead. She hits the dirt in a messy heap, like a jumbled pile of sticks.

"There," Byrne smugly concludes, "now they're reunited."

The village erupts into chaos. Bodies fly into action. High to my right I hear a sharp *twang* as Faye lets her arrow fly. It strikes Byrne in the shoulder, and he cries out in pain, dropping his pistol before he can get off another shot. Without even realizing it I have my boomerang in hand, ready to throw, but Michael pulls me away from the bonfire.

"No!" he urges me as I turn to him, seething with rage. "You'll only get yourself killed!"

"I don't care," I snarl back at him.

"And what about Alexis?"

The invocation of her name quells my rage and I holster my boomerang. Pushing through an oncoming rush of battle-charged villagers, Michael and I make our way back to the longhouse to find Alexis waiting, clutching a sharp rock she's picked up off of the dirt floor. It's a pathetic weapon, but I admire her initiative. "What happened?"

"Things have gone to shit, that's what happened," Michael answers. Still seated calmly on the stage, the elders have closed their eyes and gone into some sort of meditative trance. If the current state of things in the village alarms them, they sure don't show it. Michael hobbles up onto the stage, passing right by them, and opens up a large cabinet that takes up a good portion of the back wall. Inside are weapons: knives, bows, spears and even a few swords. He tucks a knife into his belt and looks to Alexis and me. "Well? Are you going to arm yourselves or not?"

We join him on the stage, circumventing the meditating elders and joining him at the cabinet. Alexis drops the rock, her eyes lighting up at the sight of one of the swords. It's narrow and lightweight, an elegant weapon with a leather-bound grip. I recognize it from books on Asia and various weapons manuals. It is what is commonly known as a *katana*. Alexis takes it down from its cradle and chops the air several times, conjuring a satisfying *swish*. Satisfied, she draws it back into a battle-ready pose and smiles.

"Do you really know how to use that thing?" Michael asks.

"Not really," she answers, "but chicks always have these kinds of swords in movies. I'm sure I can get the hang of it."

"You'll cut your arm off," I say disapprovingly.

"So you're advising that I stick with a rock?"

She's got a point there, literally. Katana it is, then. "What about you?" Michael asks me. He reaches for a bow that is hanging on a hook. "Figure you're an OK shot with one of these."

"Better with this." I hold up my boomerang, "at least until I get a chance to upgrade."

Michael shrugs and withdraws his hand from the hanging bow. "Suit yourself." He faces us, armed now with only a knife and his cane. "I tell you what—if you come across an extra pistol, hand it off to me. I bet I'm still better with one of those than you are."

His challenge gives me a smile. "I look forward to testing that theory."

"How about this?" a familiar voice sneers. We turn to the front of the longhouse to find Rafe and Devon blocking our exit, M16s shouldered and ready. "How about I show you all how real shooting is done?"

My arm flexes, ready to throw my boomerang, but the elders sitting before us rise, forming a human wall between us and Rafe. Silently they join hands, ancient limbs forming a chain of courage and solidarity. Every time I think I've seen these people at their best, they shame my idea of loyalty even further. I don't think I ever truly knew the meaning of the word.

"Move aside, fossils," Rafe demands. "I won't ask you twice."

The elders give no answer. We cannot see their faces, so I have no idea if their eyes are open in silent judgment or closed in anticipation of death. Before I can move into a position to wing my boomerang around them, Rafe opens fire, mowing them down left to right. A hand yanks my arm, pulling me down to the floor of the stage as bullets destroy the weapons cabinet in a shower of splinters. Blood mists the air as the last of the elders fall from the stage or land in front of us. One of them, a woman with skin like tanned parchment, hits the floor centimeters from my face, her eyes staring and blank. Now I know they met death with open eyes.

Rafe's magazine empties, and I don't wait for him to reload. Almost of its own accord, the primitive weapon flies from my hand, but Rafe instinctively raises his rifle to block, bouncing the boomerang off into a corner of the room. He's learning, at least. No matter—my throw has given me enough time to close the distance between us, and I'm on him a moment later, grasping the barrel of his M16 with both hands. The heat from the recently fired barrel burns my palms, but I'm beyond that kind of petty pain at this point. I shove Rafe's weapon into his face, cross-checking him backward. He hits the dirt floor, kicking up dust, and I throw the gun aside, as it isn't loaded and I'd rather kill Rafe with my bare hands.

Despite my rage, I keep Devon in my periphery, ready to move at him if he tries to fire on me or my friends. From the way his hands are shaking, I'd say he's afraid, unsure whether to help Rafe or concern himself with Michael and Alexis. "Don't move!" he shouts, voice squeaking. I turn to see him leveling his rifle at Alexis and Michael, finger twitching anxiously on the trigger. On the stage, Alexis and Michael stand frozen.

Stupid. By taking my eyes off of Rafe, I have given him the chance to kick me in the shins. I tumble back, yelping, and Rafe scrambles to his feet. The pain is white hot, blinding, but I fight through it and charge back at him before he can pull the knife from its thigh-sheath. He barely has time to block my fist with his forearm, leaving his stomach free to receive an uppercut from my left. My fingers crunch on the Kevlar vest hidden beneath his army jacket.

As Rafe and I trade blows, moving around one another in a continuous melee, I try to remain conscious of what's going on near the stage with Devon, Michael, and Alexis. From what I can tell, they have flanked Devon and are creeping toward him slowly as he struggles with who to keep his aim on. Meanwhile I try to concentrate my blows to Rafe's face and neck as his flak vest makes my body blows all but useless. Despite that, I'm wearing him down, and he only manages a few hits to the side of my ribs. If he's doing any damage, I don't feel it. The rage has hold of me now, allowing my fists no pain as they pummel his face and neck.

I land a hard punch to his face, crunching cartilage at the bridge of his nose. Blood gushes from his nostrils, and he reels back, slamming his back against the rickety wall of the longhouse. Lunging, I plant my forearm across his neck, pressing his head against the wall, doing my best to crush his larynx and end it. His face goes red as he struggles for breath, eyes bulging, veins ready to burst his forehead and temples.

There is a straining sound followed by a *CRACK*, and for a moment I think I've broken his neck. But then the flimsy wall behind Rafe gives way, and we both tumble through it, broken wood tearing at our clothes. Cold air and bonfire smoke greet my face, and Rafe and I hit the dirt, reflexively rolling away from each other. I land on my back, the ground knocking the wind from my lungs. For a moment I lie there, staring up at the sky as my body struggles to right itself. All around me are the sounds of madness and chaos. The sounds of people dying.

The close burst of an M16 rifle jolts me out of my daze, and I sit up, facing the hole I have just made in the wall of the longhouse. Inside I see Alexis slashing at Devon with her sword and him firing wild, missing both her and Michael. She swipes the blade across Devon's arm in a shockingly graceful move, arcing his blood through the air. He cries out and drops the rifle, and Alexis draws the katana back, ready to decapitate, teetering on the edge of savagery. But she is unable, or unwilling, to deliver the killing stroke, allowing Devon to run out of the longhouse, clutching his wounded arm. He nearly trips over me as he stumbles past.

I turn to get a better look at the battle raging in the village square. At first it is difficult to make sense of all the madness, but gradually my mind puts the pieces in place. The near constant popping sounds coupled with the strobing of muzzle flashes lets me know that automatic weapons are being fired. Everywhere I look, figures clad in skins and leather drop, crude weapons falling with them into the dust. The villagers are being massacred. I would have thought their sheer numbers would have been able to overtake the few soldiers Byrne had with him, but in the light cast by the fire, I see that he has gathered reinforcements.

The frightened faces of non-militiamen Walter Kassidy, Paul Haverford, and Russell Clark are now among his ranks, the hapless men conscripted on a quick return to the Fort before setting out after us. Two agriculturists and a custodian drafted into this revenge campaign, men wholly unsuited for battle, firing wild across the bonfire at any shape or shadow that moves among the flames. My heart sinks at the thought of having to kill these men, but their inexperience isn't hindering their attack, and their added firepower is enough to give Byrne the advantage he needs.

I scan the area to determine who is left among the villagers. Most of them are scattered and running from the hail of bullets, but I catch a glimpse of Faye darting between some huts, bow drawn taut. She lets her arrow fly, and poor Paul Haverford finds himself on the other end of it. The arrow strikes him right in the neck, the shaft skewering his Adam's apple like some sick William Tell routine. The farmer grasps at his throat, his eyes widening in pain and shock, and then he drops into the dirt, his final field sowed. The other enlisted men are too blind with panic to notice.

Byrne steps back into the fire's nimbus, his eyes taking in the carnage, a cold tactician. He doesn't see me here on the ground, and I start to formulate a strategy to get at him, try to plot a route across the square that will put me behind him before he can notice I'm there. But my plan is cut short when Abrahem steps out of the shadow of a hut, rushing at Byrne with the Confederate saber—the same Faye threatened me with hours ago—held high over his head.

For a second I think Abrahem might have the drop on Byrne and this will all be over. But Byrne seems to sense the warrior coming, whipping around to face him and drawing his machete with the same motion. Blades clash with a *CLANG* so loud I can hear it over the steady report of gunfire. The two men engage in battle, thrusting and swinging at each other like warriors of an ancient time, both displaying equal parts skill and savagery. For every thrust Abrahem makes, Byrne parries; for every wind-whistling slash Byrne makes, Abrahem blocks. The clatter of their blades builds to a metallic staccato, a primal rhythm pushing the combatants deeper into battle frenzy with every glancing blow. The savagery with which they fight is like nothing I've seen, a dance as elegant as it is deadly. It stirs something in me on some deep, subconscious level.

Blades lock at the hilt, and the warriors lock eyes, faces a mere meter apart. Abrahem pushes out with a grunt, sending Byrne back nearly into the fire. The tribal warrior takes a moment, draws a deep breath, summoning some hidden strength. He holds the saber two-handed and razor straight, waiting for Byrne to make his move. Something about the hint of smile beneath Abrahem's beard makes me think that Byrne's next move will be his last.

POP! A lone rifle shot sounds, fired from the darkness behind Abrahem. The warrior drops to his knees, the bullet having struck him in the back of the leg. Abrahem drops the saber, and out of the shadows steps Gunnar, rifle in hand, face blanched with horror over what he has done. I feel a sharp pang of disappointment for my friend, but I know that were I in his position, I would have done the same. Byrne smiles wickedly, drops his machete, and replaces it with the dropped saber. He comes right up to Abrahem, holding the sword in an executioner's stance.

"No," I hear myself gasp, knowing full well that I am powerless to stop what comes next. Byrne swings the saber, striking the still-kneeling Abrahem at the side of the neck. Blood crests from the blow, but Abrahem's head remains attached. His body goes rigid with shock, and Byrne swings again, carving more flesh from the side of the warrior's neck. Byrne swings again.

And again. With every blow Abrahem's neck is hacked away until it hangs by a tether of sinew and spine. His now lifeless body begins to topple, but Byrne steadies it with his boot, not satisfied until he's finished the job. A final swing and Abrahem's head drops from his shoulders. Byrne kicks the headless body into the soot.

Somewhere, Faye screams. Looking up, I see her on the roof of a tin shack, having witnessed the horrible death of her mate. Walter Kassidy spots her and tries to take her down, but his shooting is piss poor and his bullets patter uselessly against tin. Faye draws an arrow from her quiver and fires it a millisecond later, sending the whistling shaft directly at Byrne. If not for a reflexive raising of his right arm, the arrow would have hit its mark, right into his eye. Instead, it sinks into his forearm, causing him to howl in pain but leaving him very much alive.

I aim to fix that.

Pulling myself up, I move to rush Byrne while he's distracted. But someone grabs me by the boot and pulls me back to the ground. Rafe.

"We're not done yet," he hisses through blood-drenched teeth.

"Yes, Rafe," I answer, bringing my fist down into his face with a shuddering crack, "we are." I hit him again, smashing his front teeth into his blubbering mouth. "You were never a match for me. Never my equal." I hit him again, turning his already broken nose into a formless mound of pulp. "Even your father knew that. You were always an embarrassment. And that's how you'll die, like your father. An embarrassment."

Rafe laughs, spitting up blood. "Maybe so," I stay my fist, letting him have his final say before I drive what's left of his nose into his skull, "but I'm taking you with me."

Who is he trying to fool? Then I see it. A grenade, clutched in his hand, the pin pulled, lever lying in the dirt a meter away. Rafe laughs again.

I jump from his body, stumble into a run, but it's too late. The concussion hits me, catching me in the blast. After that is nothing.

CHAPTER SEVENTEEN

The Arena

"BOWIE!"

The voice echoes at me from a distance, loud but somehow soft at the same time. A woman's voice. Mother? I let it pass by me, a gentle wind.

"BOWIE! WAKE UP!"

Something strikes at my face, stinging my already pained flesh. I am shaken at the shoulders, and my bones ache from my head to my limbs. My eyelids flutter open, as if by some terrible obligation, despite my every attempt to keep them closed. The world outside my vision is hazy and filled with pain except for the shape above me, which gradually draws into focus.

Alexis.

The tense lines of her face melt into a look of relief. It all rushes back to me—the battle, Rafe, the explosion. My field of vision expands beyond Alexis, and I see filthy striped canvas far above her head. I'm back in the circus tent, where we were held by our tribal captors. Why am I here and not dead? Some small part of me feels disappointment at being drawn back into this misery. Here I was thinking it was finally over.

Alexis helps me into a sitting position. The tent is filled with people, militia and villagers alike. It has the appearance of some sort of bizarre town meeting, and for a second I think that I'm seeing things. But then I notice the guns being held on what's left of the villagers by the surviving members of my people. Gunnar is there, I'm grateful to notice, along with his father, both of them wearing troubled looks of regret. Devon is alive and accounted for, a bloody welt making itself known through the sweaty cluster of his hair. The anger he's been carrying ever since his brother was killed seems to have been replaced by a sense of confusion. Russell Clark and Walter Cassidy still number among the living, both looking somewhat surprised by that fact. And of course, standing out in front is Patrick Byrne. In the interim he's managed to pull Faye's arrow out of his forearm, but there's a makeshift bandage wrapped there as a reminder. I hope that arm pains him for the rest of his days.

Of the villagers, the only ones I recognize are Michael and Faye. They both look to me with great sadness in their eyes, and I can't say if it's for the losses they've suffered of if they're worried about me. Probably a lot of both. Well, if this is to be the place of my execution, I intend to face it standing, so with Alexis's help I struggle to my feet. Looking down at my clothes, I see that I am a little singed from the grenade blast but otherwise intact. I feel like I've been thrown down a mountain, but I'm not about to let Byrne see that. Summoning whatever reserves I have, I steady my wobbly legs and look the Devil straight in the eye.

The Devil saunters over to me, smiling beneath his greying beard. If my brain wasn't a little jumbled, I'd swear it was a look of admiration. "You've put up a good fight, son, I'll give you that. I never imagined you'd make it off Deacon's Bluff, let alone mount a defense. It's a testament to your training, if you'll permit me to take a little credit."

"I don't permit you anything."

This gives Byrne a hearty chortle. I'm glad he sees me as a joke. Keep underestimating me, old man. Right up to the moment my knife's at your throat. If I can get my hands on a knife, that is. I don't need to check myself to know that I am unarmed at present. Byrne wouldn't take any chances with me this close up.

A breeze wafts through the tent, and I smell something on it, biting and acrid. Gasoline. There's a shed in the back of the Fort Thunder storage areas that holds a supply of it, small tanks our founders took with them in our convoy. We knew we wouldn't be able to get more, so the stuff was hoarded and used only when the Vipers, rarely used themselves, needed fueling and for the occasions when we needed to run the generators. My father explained to me many times how gasoline was cause for much of the world's strife, so we did everything possible to avoid becoming dependent on it. Now Byrne is using whatever he carried over the bay to soak the tent from the outside, no doubt intending to burn it down with all of us inside. A terrible death. I look around and see children's faces among the terrified villagers, and the thought of innocents dying this way makes me feel sicker than the gas fumes. I don't see Evie among the children and hope she either escaped the battle or died fighting it.

"So is this your idea of honor?" I ask Byrne. "Burning women and children alive?"

"It all could have been avoided had you surrendered when I asked."

"That's a lie, and you know it," I answer sharply. "You're a murderer, Patrick, plain and simple. You murdered David, Mars's husband. You murdered Seth. My father. And now you're going to murder a whole tribe rather than face me like a man."

His face twitches, my blow to his ego touching a nerve. He comes closer, facing me eye to eye. I never noticed until now, but we're the same height. I might even be taller by a hair's breadth. He has bulk on me, that's for certain, but how much of it's muscle and how much is fat? I never imagined that I'd ever face him in hand-to-hand combat, but now it may be the only hope I've got to save these people. If I can take Byrne down, I'm certain I can get the others to walk away from this without killing the villagers. They aren't killers like Byrne, not one among them. They just need their mad dog of a leader to be put down.

"So," Byrne hisses, rank breath invading my nostrils, "you think you can take me?"

"I *know* I can." My smile taunts him. "You're old. And soft."

We stand there for what feels like hours, eyes locked. I can see his mind working, sizing me up, weighing my reach, my wounds, my will. Finally, he smiles back, reaches for the Velcro straps on his flak vest, ripping them loose. He shrugs out of his jacket, lets the vest fall to the ground, flexing the mass of his arms and shoulders, showing me the cords in his neck. I may have underestimated how soft he's grown.

"Let's do this, little boy," he says. Challenge accepted.

We square off against each other, moving in a boxer's circle. The tent has become our arena; the militia and their hostages, our spectators. As we move, I gather what strength I can back into my limbs, try to find my balance. The blast has thrown my equilibrium out of whack, so I try to compensate, make the necessary adjustments to my footing. Byrne's added weight will give him the advantage of leverage, so I have to remain light on my feet, move without throwing myself off-kilter. If he gets me down, he'll never let me up, so my best tactic will be to move in quickly and jab, wearing him down slowly, then move back out before he can zero in. The irony here is that this is a strategy I learned from him.

He makes the first swing with his right, not even coming close, but when I move in to jab, I realize it was a trick. His left is ready in wait, and he clobbers me with it right as I step into his arm range. He knows what I know, thinks the way I think because he taught me to think it in the first place. I stumble, pain shooting from my cheek and my jaw, spitting blood into the dirt. He moves toward me again, but I maintain my balance, blocking his blows with arms crossed in front of my face. His fists rain down on me as I back away, trying to get myself out of his range, and he sneaks a fist under my arms and into my stomach. The breath explodes from my lungs, and I lose my balance and fall onto my back. I lie there on the floor of the tent, sucking wind.

Glancing at the crowd tells me the fight is over, not that I needed confirmation. But Byrne doesn't descend on me. He stands there, barely winded, planted firmly in a boxer's stance.

"Get up," he says.

Against the protest of my aching muscles, I stand. Part of me wants to just give in and let him finish me, but the thought of Alexis and Michael and all the others being burned alive in this tent keeps me going. As long as there is a chance, I will keep fighting, no matter how much pain he inflicts on me. As long as there is life in my body, I will stand.

He moves toward me, teasing me with playful jabs, pulling me back into the fight. When he sees I'm not going to take the bait, that I'm going to keep him moving until he tires, he stops, drops his fists, and laughs at me. "Is that how I taught you to fight? By playing games?"

"You taught me to win, whatever it takes."

"Well, you're not going to win by dancing around like a sissy." He holds his ground, hands at his side, giving me every opportunity to come at him guns blazing. "Come to think of it, forget what I said earlier. This whole time you've been fighting like a coward. You could have met me in open battle at any time, but you've hidden, you've played tricks, and you've run off to others for help. Now you challenge me to a real fight, and all you want to do is dance."

"Sticks and stones," I answer.

This gets a smile from my mentor turned mortal enemy. "I'm only too happy to break your bones. Now come fight like a man."

He's right in one regard; I can't dance around him all night, as much as I'd like to. With a bone-popping flex to loosen my neck, I move in toward him, feigning with my left, hoping he thinks I'm favoring that side on account of my wounded eye. He doesn't have to know that the scar over my right eye has proven superficial and that I can see out of it almost as well as I could before I was shot.

Byrne raises his fists to meet me, and I swing my right under them, giving him a body blow just like the one he gave me. Then, without waiting for him to react, I swing southpaw, landing my left hard against his hairy jaw. He stumbles, and I hit with my right, then my left, then my right again, the last blow nailing him right in the eye. The goose egg is already forming as I pull back my fist, but Byrne only stumbles back a few steps and laughs.

"There's the Bowie Neville I raised!"

"I was raised by my father. All you taught me was how to kill."

"Your father was a coward," Byrne spits. "He never had the stones to back his convictions. I carried him—me and my men—all these years. Without us he would have been just another school teacher begging for scraps from a master he despised. I gave him a way out. I gave him purpose. And just like a dog, he bit the hand that fed him. So I had to put him down, like a dog. Just like I'll put you down."

Behind Byrne, my eyes fall on Devon, watching all this breathlessly like the others. "And what about Seth? Did he have to be put down too?"

"Seth was weak," Byrne says, his lips downturned with disgust. "It was only a matter of time before he was declared redundant. He also needed a purpose, so I gave him one."

A sickened look spreads over Devon's face as he struggles to accept what he's hearing. But I'm glad that at least now he knows the truth—that Byrne was ultimately responsible for his brother's death. I don't expect it to do me or the villagers any good, but maybe now that it's out in the open, Byrne's leadership will be put in question. That way I can die hoping that some small seed of change has been planted on my grave.

"You've given me a purpose too, 'Papa Byrne.' To drive your smug face into the dirt."

With all my strength I lunge at him, swinging hard with my left. He blocks with his right, and I see him wince as my fist hits his bandaged forearm, the wound left by Faye's arrow. I move to strike with my right, but he grabs my arm, whipping me around and putting me into a headlock. He knees my legs out from under me, dropping me into the ground, my head still locked in his arms like a bolt in a vice. He squeezes. Black spots form in my field of vision, growing larger, threatening to block it all out. And then I'll be dead. In the gawking crowd I find Alexis's face, focusing on it, wanting it to be the last face I see, the last thing I ever see...

No. That's not what she wants. She wants me to live.

My fingers grasp along Byrne's arm, tracing the bandage, rooting for a soft spot or indentation that would indicate the wound. I find it—at least, I think find it—and dig in with all my remaining strength. Byrne howls in agony and tries to hang on, but I wriggle and worm my fingers deeper into the wound, jabbing my fingertips into the meat of his arm. With a sound of agonized disgust, he lets go and pushes me face-down into the dirt.

Gasping, I roll into a crouch, coiled and ready. Byrne is clutching his arm and trying to walk off the pain, hissing and throwing curses. I'm not going to give him a chance to recover. I spring at him, battering him in the gut with my head, and the two of us tumble back onto the floor. His fist strikes the side of my head, and the black spots return, but I fight them back, stay focused. In a scramble of limbs, I manage to position myself on top of him, get my hands around his thick, hairy neck in a solid choke. For the first time ever, I see a look of real terror in his eyes; he knows I will not let go until he is dead. I am so happy that neither I nor anyone else got to kill him in battle. For him to die at my hands is so much more satisfying.

The cold barrel of a gun jams into the back of my neck. "That's enough, Bowie. Get off him now. We're done here."

August clicks the hammer back on his Glock so that I know he means it. Just a few more seconds and it would have been over. I look down at Byrne's reddening face above my hands. He's smiling back at me. Not an ounce of shame.

"I mean it, boy," August commands. "Get up!"

I loosen my hands. Byrne makes a sound that's part cough, part laugh. Raising my hands, I step off of Byrne and stand, August keeping the gun pressed to my neck the whole time. Byrne picks himself up off the ground and brushes himself off, smiling as if this has been nothing but a bit of friendly sparring, a fun little wrestle. Playing it off like I didn't just beat him.

"I thought this was going to be a fair fight," I grumble.

Byrne holds up his wounded arm. Blood is seeping from the bandage where my fingers were digging. "There's nothing fair about the way you fight, Bowie."

"Call it what you want. I beat you, and you know it." I look around to the crowd, to all the faces, ally or enemy. "They know it too."

"May that comfort you in your final moments." He doesn't offer the crowd a glance, because I've shamed him. "You and I are done here. You are free to die with your people."

"At least I'll die happy, knowing I've shown you as weak."

Byrne keeps his eyes fixed on me even as he signals his men to vacate the tent, which all of them do save for August, his chief lieutenant, who keeps his gun drawn. Once they are gone, Byrne walks over to his vest and jacket, putting them on and rearming himself. He motions to August, and the two of them head to the flap of the tent. Reaching it, August exits, but Byrne turns to give me a final look. "You'll die in agony," he tells me. Then he pulls a long cylinder from the inside of his jacket and cracks it, spewing forth a fountain of sparks. A flare.

Alexis rushes over to me, and I take her into my arms. Byrne allows us this with a bitter smile. Then he touches the flare to the canvas of the gasoline-soaked tent.

The flames crawl to a height of ten meters or more before Byrne even ducks out of the flap. Some of the villagers rush to the far end of the tent, looking to crawl out from under it, but more flares have been lit by the militia, and everywhere we look there is fire. In less than a minute, the tent will be entirely engulfed, and there is nowhere to run, no crawlspace through which to escape. Byrne made sure this was a deathtrap, coating the tent and surrounding area with enough gas to create an impenetrable wall of flame. Already there is screaming and panic in the air, at least in what little air isn't already thick with smoke. I pull Alexis close to my chest and shield her from the choking black, but she is already coughing from the inhalation. She looks up at me, her crystal-blue eyes watering small rivers. "Well, this sucks."

"I'm sorry," I tell her. "For all of this. For everything."

She shakes her head. "You did all that you could."

"I should have kept us moving. Running."

She places her hand against my mouth. "Don't do that. Don't spend your last moments feeling regret for things you couldn't change. Just spend them with me."

We kiss for what I imagine will be the last time. All around us, people are screaming, crying, choking, coughing, trying to find a way out and finding none. As I ready to close my eyes on the world for the last time, I catch sight of Michael moving frantically along the flaming wall of the tent, whacking it with his cane, hoping to open up an escape route. Poor, brave Michael—a fighter up until the very end. Though I admire his spirit, I am saddened that his final moments will be occupied by this pointless struggle. I wish he had someone, one of his parents, a sister or brother, a girlfriend. There he is, another person I have failed, sentenced to death. At least I got to tell him that I was sorry. And then paid back his forgiveness by bringing this hell down upon him and everyone he cares about. What a great friend I am.

"Hey," Alexis says with a cough, "you're doing that thing. Regretting. I can tell."

"This..." I hack, my lungs feeling like they are filled with hot stones. "This is all my—"

Something tears behind me with a *shriiiiiiiiiiiiip*! Glancing back, I see panicked people running back and forth, not noticing the blade that has forced its way through the flaming canvas and is cutting open a long flap. A moment later and the blade slashes again, cutting the burning flap free to reveal Devon standing there, machete in hand, his feet planted in a burning pool of gas, flames starting to creep up his legs. His soot-streaked face scans the tent wildly, his eyes landing on mine. "COME ON!" he shouts. "THIS WAY!"

Without another thought I grab Alexis by the arm and rush her to the hole made by Devon. Other villagers have seen the newly made escape route, and a small mob of them jam up the exit. For his part Devon remains at the hole, helping people through to welcome cold air and freedom. I hand Alexis off to Devon, but she resists, turning back to me. She can see by the look on my face that I'm not leaving. Not just yet.

"What the hell are you doing?!"

Ignoring her, I look to Devon. "Don't let her follow me." He nods. Alexis protests further, but I don't listen. I'm already gone back into the inferno. And I'm sure she knows why.

Michael.

I search for him in the mad rush of people exiting the tent but can't find him among all the soot-caked faces. Above me, over the whooshing roar of fire, I hear the sound of overheated cables snapping, whipping loose angrily as the tent starts to collapse. In a matter of moments, I and anyone else still in this tent will be covered in flaming canvas. Here in the heart of it, the smoke whips itself into a roiling black miasma. Panicked shapes of people rush out of the swirl, unaware that there's a way out as they are unable to see it. None of them are Michael. I try to help as many as I can, point them in what I believe is the right direction, but I have no way of knowing if they listen or do as I instruct because they are gone into the smoke as quickly as they come. Like figures emerging and disappearing back into the bottom of a lake.

"MICHAEL!" My shouting comes out a strained hack, more smoke than air. But I keep yelling anyway. "MICHAEL, THERE'S A WAY OUT! FOLLOW MY VOICE!"

My foot strikes something, and I look down. Through the haze I see Michael lying there on the ground, eyes closed. His cane lies next to his open hand.

I crouch low, pulling his head into my arms and putting my face next to his, hoping to feel breath. In the broil of this oven, it is impossible to feel anything but the blast of heat. Remembering my first aid training, I put two fingers to his neck and feel for a pulse. Nothing at first...but then I find it. Faint and fluttering but still there.

Not that it'll matter if I don't get him out of here before the tent collapses. As if in response to my thought, there is a sloughing sound above me and a rush of heat as the ceiling of the tent comes down in a shower of flame. Pulling Michael into my arms, I start to run, feeling bits of burning canvas land on my neck with a scorching sizzle. Somehow, despite the beating my limbs have suffered, I manage to carry Michael and myself back in the direction I believe Devon's hole to be, only my mental map and compass to guide me. There is a roaring rush as the tent collapses in our wake, flames licking my back, roasting my skin. Cables snap and whip at me from out of the smoke, one of them lancing my cheek like a hot brand. I fight through the pain and keep moving, keeping Michael in my arms and out of the fire.

For a horrible moment, I fear I've lead us in the wrong direction, that my internal map has failed me. But then I see a tiny sliver of moonlight on snow and Devon still standing at the flap, searching the whirlwind of black smoke and trailing embers. "BOWIE!" he shouts.

With the last of my effort, I dive for the hole. Cold air blasts my face and rushes into my burning lungs. Hands grab me and Michael, hauling us through, and over a moat of smoldering gas that has been dampened by clothing and snow. Michael is taken out of my arms, allowing me to stumble clear of the moat and drop into a roll on the hard, cold ground. Behind me, the massive tent finally gives in, collapsing in a deafening *WHOOSH!*

Rolling on my side, trying to both get air into my lungs and cough the soot out of them, I take stock of the situation. Thanks to Devon, a large percentage of the villagers, nearly all, were able to escape the collapsing tent. Some of them gather around him now, applying snow and dirt to his legs, which were badly burned by standing in the flaming moat of gasoline. Devon is taking his burns like a man, gritting his teeth through the pain as the villagers help him and thank him. I never imagined the day would come when I would see Devon emerge a fully realized soldier. All I can hope is that somewhere Seth is looking down on his brother, feeling the same pride I feel.

Close by, Faye is helping Michael, recovered and conscious, to his feet. Panic strikes me as I look for Alexis, not seeing her in the bustle of the crowd. Then I feel a hand on my shoulder and realize that she's been beside me the whole time. I roll over to face her, grateful tears rolling down her lightly freckled cheeks in twin streams.

"That was really, really stupid," she says with a snuffle and wipe of her nose.

"Had to get Michael out of there," I force out. "Couldn't let him down again."

She takes my reddened hand in hers. "I know."

The whine of snowmobile engines creeps from behind the roaring inferno of the tent, snaking around until one of the Vipers, and its bearded rider, becomes visible. Byrne. He takes in the triage scene with a tactician's eye, assessing whether any of the dazed and harried villagers are willing or able to mount an attack on him, which none of them are. Even Faye is too busy helping Michael and too far from a bow to be any threat. Byrne sees me alive and recovering, and it gives him a scowl, but it's Devon he zeroes in on, eyes blazing with rage. It's bad enough that I'm still alive, worse that a soldier has betrayed him so directly. He drives his Viper straight over to Devon, scattering the shell-shocked villagers helping him. Then he dismounts, drawing his pistol from its holster and putting a round in the chamber.

I try to get up, but my legs won't let me. The whole thing plays out in my mind before it happens, which makes it all the more sickening. Devon stands soldier straight despite his wobbly legs, ready for what will no doubt be a harsh verdict. Perhaps some part of him doesn't believe that Byrne will execute him right here and now, or perhaps he's not thinking anything at all. I hope it's the latter. I expect there to be some exchange between the two, some dressing down, but Byrne simply puts the gun to the side of Devon's head and fires. Blood spouts from Devon's far temple, bits of his brain splattering into the tent fire with a *hiss*. I'm grateful that his eyes shut by reflex before he was shot.

Before Devon even crumples to the ground, the other Vipers and the men riding them arrive on the scene. Every one of their faces blanches with horror when they see what Byrne has done. The men pull into a circle around their leader, snowmobile engines sputtering in neutral. Byrne ejects the shell from his pistol's chamber and turns to face them, looking like this murder has been nothing but a minor irritation.

"Jesus, Patrick!" August is aghast, finally at his breaking point. "Was that really necessary?!"

"He was a traitor and died a traitor's death." Byrne turns his gaze on me. "And speaking of traitors..."

Chambering another round, Byrne strides toward me, intent on finishing what he's started. I struggle into a sitting position, putting Alexis behind me but knowing it won't do any good. I'm sure once I'm dead, he'll shoot her too and then have his men shoot all the villagers, Faye and Michael included. Poor Devon's heroic gesture was just that—a gesture. Allowing myself and the others to live would be tantamount to defeat, and Patrick Byrne will not be defeated. Not while there is strength in his body and breath in his lungs.

He stands before me, looking down on my face for what he hopes will be the last time. I do not give him the satisfaction of looking scared. "Goodbye, Bowie." He places the barrel of the pistol to my forehead. It's still hot. "Say hello to your father for me."

"Put down the gun," a trembling voice orders. It is followed by the *click* of a rifle bolt being pulled into place. "I mean it. If he dies, you die."

I don't need to see behind Byrne to recognize that voice. My old friend Gunnar, come to my rescue. Please don't let it cost him his life.

"I'm not fucking around here, asshole. Drop the goddamn gun!"

If the cursing doesn't tell Byrne that Gunnar means business, nothing will. Giving it a final moment's consideration, he removes the gun from my head, holding the barrel skyward and raising the other hand. He turns slowly to face Gunnar and drops the weapon into the snow. "You're making a big mistake, son," Byrne says calmly. "Biggest one of your life."

Gunnar keeps his rifle trained on Byrne, but I can see the fear in his eyes. Which means so can Byrne. "I tell you what," Byrne continues in that calm, authoritative tone, "you let me pick my gun back up and finish what I came here to do, and we'll forget all about this. Hell, I'll even throw the girl in for you to enjoy before I kill her. How does that sound?"

"No deal," Gunnar answers, voice squeaking ever so slightly. "Now step away."

"Oh, Gunnar," Byrne says regretfully, "I wish you could see how disappointed your father looks right now."

"Actually," August says, stepping off his Viper and slinging his AR-15 into his arms, "that disappointment is for you, Patrick."

I can't believe what I'm witnessing—an honest to god mutiny. Even without being able to see Byrne's expression, I'm sure he's as surprised as I am. August comes to stand with his son, both their guns trained on their leader, and behind them I see a wave of relief spread across the other men's faces. This mad crusade is going to end here, whether Patrick Byrne wants it to or not. It's almost too much to process, a dream from which I am certain to be woken. But then Alexis takes my arm and helps me to my feet, showing me that it's real.

Byrne is not about to just accept this display of insubordination. "You sure you know what you're doing here, August? Is this a road you really want to go down?"

"I've been following you for long enough," the grizzled Viking says flatly. "I didn't leave it all behind to take up with a madman who kills children. Doesn't matter what your reasons are, I want no part of it. And neither will anyone back at the Fort. You're done, Patrick."

"So you're telling me this is your idea of a coup?"

"Call it what you want, I don't care. I'm getting the council back together when we get back to the Fort, and we'll settle it then. As far as Bowie and the girl are concerned, they can go where they like. Our business with them is done."

The two men stare are at each other for a long while, the only sound passing between them being the steady crackle of the tent fire. Finally, Byrne shakes his great, shaggy head and lets go a dry chuckle. "Fine. Take me into custody. Bring me to my court martial."

Without taking his gun off of the prisoner, August jerks his head back to the men, indicating that they should help with Byrne's capture. Russell Clark, still looking like he just got done scrubbing latrines, steps off his Viper and fishes a length of rope out of a small backpack. He approaches with the rope in one hand, a revolver in the other, cautiously, showing his uncertainty with each tentative step. Isn't there someone with a little more experience who might better handle this? I start to limp forward, intending to take the rope from Russell and tie Byrne up myself, but the beating my body has taken is making me too slow. Before I can stumble half the distance I need to, Byrne lashes out with an elbow, connecting with a sickening *crack* to Russell's jaw. The custodian goes down, and Byrne snatches the pistol out of his flailing hand.

"DROP THE GUN!" August shouts. "DROP IT N—"

POP! The pistol, now in Byrne's hand, fires, winging August in the shoulder, sending him spinning and sprawling to the ground.

"DAD!" cries Gunnar. Damn it, Gunnar, keep your eyes on Byrne before he—

POP! Another round, and for a horrible moment I fear my friend has been shot. But then I see Paul Haverford shouldering a rifle, eyes wide with amazement that he's just taken a shot at the leader of Fort Thunder's militia. He's missed, of course—Paul was never much with a gun, as I recall—but the shot was enough to throw Byrne off-kilter and keep him from firing on Gunnar. I've never loved old Paul Haverford more than I have at this moment.

Adrenaline hits me, and my muscles finally kick into gear. I expect Byrne to turn and fire on myself and Alexis, but instead he's bolting for the snowmobiles, several of which have been left unattended. He's making a run for it. I can only imagine that he intends to get back to the Fort and barricade himself in with whoever is left there to rule over. There's only one person left there that I truly care about, and I am not about to leave this madman alone with her, especially after all that has happened. He will not put his filthy hands on my mother.

Chaos swirls behind me as I chase after Byrne: shouting, people running back and forth, fire, more collapsing tents. Alexis calls after me, panic in her voice, but I don't stop or even turn back to look at her. I'll only have one chance to catch up to Byrne, and I can't let him out of my sight for even a moment. He reaches the clutch of Vipers, straddles one quickly, pulls the ripcord starter, and guns the throttle, engine roaring to life. Then, with a spray of snow from the snowmobile's back treads, he is off into the still, shadow-strewn woods.

I reach the Vipers a moment later, jumping onboard the nearest unoccupied vehicle. A few meters away, Paul Haverford sits on another, still cradling the rifle he just fired at Byrne. I can't tell if he's terrified of me, of the man I am hunting, or both. I pull the ripcord starter, getting nothing, pull again and get the engine idling.

"Best of luck to you, son," Paul says, implying he won't be joining the pursuit. He takes a handgun from his hip, a Walther P99, and I flinch, expecting him to shoot me. Instead, he tosses it over to me, and I catch it. It's already locked and loaded. "I'm no good with it anyway."

"Thanks," I reply. And then I'm off like a rocket.

The Viper's engine roars beneath me as I reacclimate to the vehicle, which proves to be quite easy. All I have to do to increase speed is give the Viper some gas with the hand clutch, and I am traveling along at a decent clip, following the tracks left by Byrne. Where he swerves, I swerve, leaning into it as I turn the handlebars, lifting my butt off the seat as I do. Icy spray fountains from under the skis, coating my boots. With a quick flip of a switch, I turn on the headlights, giving me a clearer view of Byrne's trail leading into the dense patch of forest up ahead. Thus far the trees have been spaced wide, allowing me ample clearance, but all of that is about to change. No matter. By the time I pass through the first phalanx of trees, rocketing between a pair of tall pines, the vehicle feels like a motorized extension of myself.

Knowing that he's being pursued, Byrne takes chances, riding his snowmobile down a treacherously steep dip and into a snowed-in gully. I follow, gripping tight to the handlebars as my Viper sways and wobbles its way down the dip. When it threatens to topple, I compensate by leaning in the opposite direction, slaloming down the incline as if riding a giant single ski. There is a cluster of large jutting rocks waiting in the gully, and I have to swerve with all my weight to avoid being dashed on them. Once I am back upright, the pursuit becomes more direct as the gully forces Byrne into a straightaway path and gives me a moment to catch my breath. The cover of pine forest darkens the first rays of sun cresting somewhere over the horizon, so I must depend on my headlights to keep him in sight. Giving the engine all the gas I can afford, I lean forward on the handlebars, using every ounce of my being to catch up.

I am closing in on him now, the roar of my engine mingling with his. He glances over his shoulder quickly, eyes locking with mine for a split second, rewarding me with fear and surprise. The front skis of my Viper are nearly touching his back treads, and I steady the Walther in my left hand while keeping my right on the handlebar grip. I am not a very good shot with my left, but at this close of a range, it should be no problem, so I put the back of Byrne's head in my sights and ready to fire. Sensing what I am about to do, Byrne brakes, forcing me to fire wild as my skis hit his treads. The handgun drops from my grip as I am forced to brake to avoid a collision. As my vehicle slows, Byrne's speeds up, leaving me in his quickly growing wake.

My option now is to keep in close pursuit or stop to pick up the gun and hope I can catch up with him. Unless I plan to kamikaze into him, I don't know how I will stop Byrne if I don't have a weapon. My boomerang was lost in battle, and Haverford's pistol was all I had. Seeing no other alternative, I slow the Viper to a stop, hop off the seat, and run a few meters back to pick the gun up off the snow. I'm back on my Viper scant seconds later, more than enough time for Byrne to put some real distance between us. The only thing working in my favor is the fact that ahead the gully tapers up a hill, which will slow Byrne down a bit as he climbs back to level land. If I can find a way to make up the distance, or better yet get a clear shot at him, this can end.

Byrne's Viper takes the hill, hitting it with enough velocity to plow upward at a good pace. I follow directly in his path, shadowing his every move, but I can't match the skill with which he takes the hill, and I drop even farther behind. He reaches the top and zooms quickly out of sight, leaving me to my excruciating climb. When I reach the top of the hill, he is gone from my sight. All I have to follow are his tracks, which swerve off into a dense thatch of trees.

This seems like he's leading me into a trap. If I knew the lay of the land, I might try to anticipate his direction and try to cut him off by taking a more direct route, but I have no idea where I am. None of this area looks familiar. I don't even recognize the terrain that led us to the village when Alexis and I were captured, which makes sense if Byrne is heading back to the bluff the way he came, south, by the jetty. Or he could be leading me off course through a terrain he suspects I won't be skillful enough to navigate. Following at his heels is the only sure way not to lose his trail, so that's what I do, right into the tightly packed pines.

The going is just as treacherous as I expected. Branches fly out at me in every direction, tearing at my coat, trying to yank me out of my seat. Dips and hollows buck my vehicle. Snowy stumps come out of nowhere, threatening to pitch my Viper into a roll. At one point, I am forced to swerve violently to avoid crashing into a tree the size of a sequoia that seemed to come literally right out of nowhere. Ahead of me I can hear the whine of Byrne's engine mocking me like some droning, motorized beast.

Then, just like that, the sound is gone.

My heart leaps a beat as I imagine Byrne downed in a ditch, his Viper tumbled onto its side, his legs pinned under it as he lies screaming for help, knowing I will bring only death. But as I follow his trail, the trees grow even denser, forcing me to slow to a crawl as the shadows grow heavier all around me. Finally, the trail ends in a small clearing, the tracks a jumble of snow and dirt, a messy figure eight, as if Byrne drove his Viper around and around in mindless circles. Not mindless, I realize, but intentionally confusing. In the low light of the tree cover, it'll take me minutes to figure out which way he's gone, if he isn't hiding somewhere ready to catch me off guard. Frustrated, I kill my Viper's engine, hoping my ears can pick up what my eyes can't.

The forest offers no sound but the wind rustling the pines and the occasional slough of snow falling from the branches. It was this sort of wintery quiet I would enjoy on solo patrols in my youth, a peace I'd find walking the woods that border Bluff Pointe or in the forest before the restricted zone. Places that now only remind me of death. My home, my father, my sense of peace—is there anything left for Patrick Byrne to take from me? If it were not for my mother, I would abandon this mad pursuit and go back to Alexis, try to find some new life with her, some new peace. But as long as Callie Neville is alive and Byrne can get to her, I will know no peace. So I sit here in the still of the trees and listen.

It comes to me from behind, the sound of steel whipping through air. I dive from my seat as the knife strikes me, glancing my shoulder, just missing its intended mark—my throat. The blade cuts through my jacket and slices my upper arm, but it's only a flesh wound, and I feel no pain. I'm too busy scanning the forest behind me for a sign of the knife's thrower.

There! A glint of metal tucked behind an icy cluster of ash trees. Knowing he's been spotted, Byrne fires up his engine and rides off deeper into the densely packed forest. I quickly scan the area for the knife he threw at me, but it's disappeared into a snowy thicket. No time to root around for it now. Letting it go, I start my Viper and speed off in the direction of my fleeing enemy, engine rising to a racing hum. In moments, I am hot on Byrne's tail again, my headlight catching his darting form as he swerves between narrowly spaced trees, hurdles over white-knuckle jumps. My attempts to follow him are spotty at best. Years of practice have made him a smooth, nearly effortless driver, able to navigate impossible turns and take wild chances. The best I can do is keep him in my sights and stay in control of my vehicle.

It becomes clear very quickly that I am going to lose him.

I begin to feel a tingle of warmth on my right cheek. I recognize it as sunlight coming through the trees, indicating a less dense patch of pine forest. Ahead of me Byrne banks hard into the direction of the sun, and for a moment I believe that my luck has changed, that he's grown wary of ducking between trees and stumps and he's going to try to outrace me in the open. I follow his lead, banking hard to the right, and after a last stand of trees, I am greeted by pink dawn breaking bright across the horizon, temporarily blinding me in its beauty. Then my eyes fall forward, and I realize what a huge mistake I have just made.

Byrne has led me to the side of a wide open gorge, one he knew was here and knew I would charge blindly into. I lean my body hard left, falling into a skid. With a spray of snow, I drop from the vehicle, tumbling onto the ground as the Viper rockets over the lip of the gorge. By the time I have stopped rolling, my snowmobile is gone, crashed onto the snowy rocks below.

It's over now—Byrne has won. With no breath to curse, I watch helplessly as his vehicle drives along the edge of the gorge, making its escape. Dimly I wonder if he will turn and look back at me, take a moment to confirm his victory and, seeing that I have not followed my Viper into the gorge, come back to finish me off. He will probably just keep riding as I have taken the fight out of him at this point. I'm sure I'll feel different about it later, but right now getting to keep my life seems a small consolation for losing him.

There is a screeching howl, the cry of some sort of enraged animal. Ahead, where Byrne rockets away, something small and feral has darted out of the forest, wielding a sharp stone. The beast-creature throws the sharpened rock right at Byrne's head, sending him pitching off of his Viper and tumbling into the gorge. The snowmobile careens back into the forest, causing the feral creature to roll out of its way, revealing herself as Evie. She jumps and grunts a primal cheer as the vehicle collides with a tree with a satisfying crash.

In a state of total disbelief, I stand and make my way along the gorge toward the site of the crash. Evie races over to me excitedly, attacking my bruised torso with a hug. "Thank you, Evie," I say with a wince, trying to gently loosen her grip. "Good girl. You're a good girl."

Taking my hand, she leads me over to the gorge, hopping and squealing happily, pointing over the edge. I do my best to calm her down and set her to the side. "It's OK, just stay here. Let me handle this. Stay right here."

A soft moaning drifts over the edge of the gorge. Evie seems to grasp what I am saying and stays put, looking like she's ready to jump out of her skin. Cautiously, I approach the edge of the gorge, ready for Byrne to jump out at me. He doesn't. I reach the edge and look down.

The gorge itself is a twenty-meter drop into a bone-breaking landscape of jagged rocks and boulders. If Byrne had fallen all the way to the bottom, he would surely be dead, but it would seem that fortune has once again favored my enemy. He is lying on a narrow shelf about halfway down, his back flat against a jutting outcropping of rock. One of his legs is broken at the knee and twisted under him, and his body is twisted at an odd angle, indicating a broken back. His head is bleeding from the wound Evie's rock gave him. I think I see a rib poking through the side of his flak vest.

His eyes focus up at me, and we stare at each other for a while, neither of us able to comprehend that this is where we are. Finally, Byrne tries to laugh, but all that comes out is a pained wheeze. "So this is it," he says, his voice a hoarse struggle. "Just gonna let me die out here like this? This is all you get?"

"What more do I need?" I challenge. "You're as good as dead."

"Not by your hand," answers Byrne.

"No, by a girl's," I point out. "I'll be sure to tell that to the others, don't you worry."

All sense of amusement fades from his face. I step away from the gorge, back to Evie, ready to lead us back to the woods and her village. But something just won't let me go. I turn back to the gorge and listen to the sound of Byrne's labored wheezing. A sound as empty and as hollow as my victory.

Against all of my better judgement, I search the edge for a suitable place to climb down.

CHAPTER EIGHTEEN

The Larger World

By the time I reach the rock shelf where Byrne lies, he's passed out, hopefully due to the pain. Evie watches me with animal suspicion as I scale down the cliff of the gorge. If she could talk like a proper person, I imagine she'd be telling me I was crazy to be helping my enemy and not just leaving him to die. But Evie doesn't know Patrick Byrne the way I do, doesn't know that a life as a cripple is a far worse fate for him than death. What looks like mercy on the surface is in fact a worse punishment; at least, that's what I tell myself. The fact is that I don't think I can stomach the way this recalls how I left Michael on the Fort Thunder wall, all those years ago. All I can hear in my head is my mother's voice telling me not to deny someone help if you are able. I wonder if she would still apply that to the man who killed her husband.

Or maybe I just want him to live a little longer so I can kill him myself.

I quickly realize that Byrne is too heavy for me to carry up the cliff, so I root through the pack that is hanging loosely on his back and find a length of rope. As Byrne drifts in and out of a pained sleep, I tie him into a quick harness and then take the other end with me when I climb back up the cliff. Once I am topside I find the nearest tree and use the trunk to give me a little leverage with the rope. The bark is rough, and there's a good chance it will wear the rope down, causing it to snap and send Byrne tumbling to his death, which is a chance I guess I'll just have to live with.

I call Evie over, and though she continues to look at me as if I've lost my mind, she lends me a hand, and after twenty minutes of strained exertion, we haul Byrne's sorry body up over the edge of the gorge. He's taken quite a few scrapes along the way and cries out with renewed agony, all of which suits me just fine.

As I had the cadets do when we rescued Alexis from the Densmore, I set about fashioning a sled with which to drag Byrne back to the village. I needn't have bothered. I haven't gotten the thing a quarter of the way built when a pair of snowmobiles come roaring out of the forest, having followed the trail left by our chase. Gunnar and Paul Haverford.

"I'm not letting you take him back to the Fort," I say before either of them can get in a word. "Not without me and not without some assurances. Otherwise I'll kill him right now."

"After you've gone through the trouble to save him?" Paul says with an amused smile. "Seems like a bit of a waste. Don't worry, son. Byrne's time as leader is over. Just by looking at those legs, I can tell he's redundant at this point."

I consider this a moment, then nod, satisfied. "Come on," Paul continues, "let's get back to the village and figure out what to do from there."

I find it hard to fathom that the village would have us back after the hell we brought down on them, but on the ride back Gunnar explains that Michael helped broker an uneasy peace on account that there had been a mutiny against Byrne, who was clearly the aggressor. Devon helping people escape the tent fire also went a long way to temper some of the immediate anger, and the fact that he paid for it with his life helped to garner a little villager sympathy. The hope is that by leaving Byrne's fate in the hands of the villagers, a war may be avoided, but I don't think there'd be a war either way. Mars wouldn't have wanted it. Still, I half expect to be met with spears and arrows flying, which makes what actually awaits us back at the village all the more surprising.

We hear them before we see them, and for a heart-stopping moment, I fear the sky is literally falling. Glancing up, I see them through the cover of pine: large black shapes flying above us, shaking the forest all around with their mighty rotors. I've seen enough pictures in training manuals to recognize helicopters, but nothing quite prepared me for the awe I experience just seeing them from below. To me they are creatures straight from a fairy tale.

Gunnar's own awe is more heavily weighted by fear. "That can't be good," he says over the Vipers' roar.

We pull into the village to find the helicopters already landed, their blades slowing with a whining judder. Men clad in black armored clothing and featureless helmets pour out of the open cabins of the massive beasts, high-powered automatic weapons cradled in their arms. With just this small conscription of forces alone, a mere four helicopters by my count, the entirety of Fort Thunder would be hopelessly outgunned and outmatched. If these people—this government—wanted us gone, they could have wiped us out long ago with little effort. We have our freedom because these people allow us to, and every notion I have ever held about being able to fend them off is nothing but a bad joke.

The villagers, most of whom are still dazed and reeling from our battle, seem to greet these new invaders with a sort of weary resignation. Something about the way they look at the copters and the armored men tells me that they've seen all this before. Once the troops are on the ground, a team of medics follow, and once it is established that there will be no further hostility, the medics immediately set about helping the wounded. Despite their imposing presence, I get the sense that the government trespassers are here to help, not invade. But then I remember Callie's Peak and Alexis's usage of the tablet in an attempt to contact home, and I understand what I am really looking at—a rescue mission.

They've come for Alexis.

Panic strikes as I fear the troopers, some of whom I recognize as women, may have already reclaimed Alexis, but then I see her helping a medic tend to a woman's wounded arm. Leaving Byrne in Gunnar's capable hands, I circumvent the confusion of villagers to reach her, and seeing me, she pulls me into her arms straight away.

"You stupid jerk," she admonishes, kissing my cheek. "I could kill you for running off like that."

"I'm sorry," I say, "it won't happen again."

She offers me a sad but grateful smile. There won't be an again, and we both know it. "So," I say as words continue to fail us, "this is something, isn't it?"

Alexis glances back at the helicopters self-consciously. "Yes, well, Daddy never does things halfway I'm afraid."

Before I have a chance to fully process what she has just told me, a man flanked by two weapons-drawn soldiers comes through the crowd, assessing the situation with cold detachment. The man is my father's age, his close-cropped hair silvering at the sides, and he is dressed in a clean grey suit and tie, the way men dressed for work in the world my people fled. His eyes immediately fall on me, sizing me up from top to bottom. I can't tell if I'm being assessed for threat or approval. He nods to his soldier guards, letting them know it's OK to lower their weapons, which they do. The man extends his hand to me.

"You must be Bowie," he says. "Senator Deveraux. It seems I owe you a debt of thanks for saving my daughter's life."

Tentatively, I shake the senator's hand. "You're welcome, sir."

He smiles, withdraws his hand. "You've got manners," he says, as if he expected less. "Someone out here raised you well." He looks around at the village, at the ruined huts, the smoldering tent. The bodies. "How could a boy like you come from people who would do this?"

"I won't make excuses for my people," I answer, "but we aren't all like this."

The senator nods curtly. "My daughter briefed me of the situation when we arrived. She said this was the work of Patrick Byrne, the militant. We have detailed files on him and many of the members of your group. So I know all about Fort Thunder."

My head reels with questions. "You... you knew about us?"

"Of course." He studies my bafflement, taking in the extent of my ignorance. "You didn't think you were just living out there without the US government knowing about it, did you?"

I think the answer to that question is clear on my face. The senator looks to his daughter, and she returns with a look of confirmation that, yes, I have been raised a blind fool. "Maybe it's best if Alexis makes things a little clearer for you, Bowie. In the meantime, I want you to know that I have clearance to take Patrick Byrne into custody. He's wanted for crimes in the States, and by stepping back on American soil, he's violated the terms of his own accord.

Not to mention that what he's instigated here will likely be seen as a war crime. I imagine you had plans for him yourself by bringing him back here, but I'm afraid I must insist he come with us."

At first, the thought of Byrne escaping my grasp fills me with anger. But then I take a moment to really think about it. Sending him back to the States, to a place he despised and fled, is almost as bad as any punishment I could devise. It's clear that he is wanted as a criminal and will spend the rest of his crippled, miserable life in a state-sponsored prison under the thumb of cruel guards, other hardened criminals, and worst of all, bureaucrats. I was taught all about the prison system, and the thought of Byrne—a great man of the wild—trapped in a cage for the rest of his days gives me some sense of satisfaction. The truth is I didn't have any sort of plan as to what to do with him anyway. Mostly I just want the satisfaction of seeing him destroyed.

"Just promise me that he won't go free," I demand.

"I wouldn't worry about that," the senator promises. "Now I'll let you two say your goodbyes. The choppers will be leaving in ten minutes." He gives me another long look. This time, there is something different in his eyes. A sort of respect. "I can't thank you enough, Bowie. If there's ever anything you need, please get in touch. I'd like to believe this can be a fresh start between our world and yours."

With a brisk nod to his guards, the senator takes his leave of us, seeing to the handling of his captured fugitive. Through the crowd I see Byrne, semi-conscious and moaning, being loaded onto a proper stretcher in preparation for flight. Alexis notes the concern worn into my face. "It really will be all right, you know. We'll make sure he pays for his crimes."

She takes my hand, drawing my eyes to hers. She leads me over to where some benches have been fashioned out of logs by the villagers. "Come, sit," she urges. She sits, and I sit next to her. "So I suppose you could use some answers."

"Answers would be nice," I confirm.

"OK, well, my understanding of all this is a little fuzzy, but I can give you the basic gist. Long story short, whatever you've been told about any sort of total government collapse is a lie. You know that much already. But what I didn't tell you is that we, meaning the US government, *allowed* your people to secede. Your people and others, including the people of this village. There are settlements and strongholds all around the borders of the US, on small offshore islands like Deacon's Bluff and on designated preserves like this one. There was a lot of strife in the US about people who wanted to secede, so finally it was just decided to allow it. Your people were the first to sign what is known as the secession accords, an agreement that basically states that your people are no longer beholden to our government, for good and for ill. That means you are not allowed back on government lands without permission, and you are not allowed to ask for any government assistance. In turn, we leave you alone. We even have no-fly zone restrictions."

"So how did your plane end up crashing on my island?"

"There was an engine malfunction, and we were forced to land. The pilot thought we'd stand a better chance of survival if we touched down on the bluff. We were never meant to pass over the island. It was simply the nearest body of land." She looks down at her hands, regret spreading over her face. "I take responsibility for that, for the death of my handlers. They were only doing their jobs and bringing me home. This is all the result of my stupid need to rebel."

I take her hand into mine. "I know just how you feel."

We sit for a while, appreciating our last moments together. Around us people tend to the wounded, trying to help the village onto its feet, but all I can think of right now is Alexis. Will I ever see her again? And if not, can I move on and eventually love another? The very idea seems impossible to me right now, as impossible as this village ever truly recovering from what it has suffered. Yet we will all have to try. I guess that's all there is to do in the end.

"You know," she says after this small stretch of forever, "you could always come with me. My father could arrange it."

I try to imagine the world Alexis is from—and myself in it, which is the most impossible thought of all. "As much as I'd like to," I say, "I can't. Not with my mother back at the Fort."

"I understand," she says, squeezing my hand. "But maybe... once things are settled, you might think about it? I mean, coming to visit anyway? Get a sense of the larger world."

There was a time when I would have said that I have enough of a sense of the larger world, but the boy who said that is gone, and the man who stands in his place understands just how little he actually knows. "Someday," I tell her. And I don't even believe it's a lie.

Her father returns after speaking at length to August, already patched up from his shoulder wound, about what will be done with Byrne. Gunnar's father handles himself like a true diplomat, and there seems to be no further debate on the matter. With everything settled, it is time for Alexis and I to say our final goodbyes, which amount to a hug, some rushed expressions of gratitude and promises, and a kiss that I wish could have lasted much, much longer. When it is done, she is whisked into one of the helicopters by her father's men, leaving me to watch as the mighty vehicle lifts into the sky with the whirring roar of blades. Alexis watches me through the window of the closed helicopter door, and I raise my hand limply to wave goodbye, a pathetically inadequate gesture. She wipes back tears, smiles sadly, and waves back. Then she is too far up in the air to see.

"She seemed like a great girl," Gunnar says. I didn't even realize he was standing next to me. "I'm sorry I didn't get to know her."

"She'll be back one day," I say. I turn and give him a sly grin, the kind I haven't given in weeks. "No woman can resist Bowie Neville's charms."

In a manner of minutes, all of the copters are gone, as if they had never been there at all. Medical supplies have been left for the wounded, but Byrne was the only one lifted away. This is the price of independence, I guess; emergency help is one thing, but the villagers must still live or die on their own. If I hadn't been raised with such a strong sense of autonomy, I might find it a little cruel that the government could forsake those in such need. But then again, autonomy is what they asked for, and it's what I've asked for by standing with my people. So I guess we'll have to figure things out on our own, at least for now.

It comes time for us to go, and there is one last thing I must attend to. I find Michael over by the ruins of the circus tent, pulling his cane out from under a flap of smoldering tarp. He sees me coming, offers a curt and knowing nod. "So I guess this is it."

"Doesn't have to be," I say. "We could use a guy like you around."

"Yeah." He scrunches his nose at the thought of my proposal. "I don't think so, Bowie. This is my home, where my parents wanted me to be. I really don't see a place for me back in your world, even without Papa Byrne's influence."

Can't say I blame him for feeling the way he does. And honestly, it makes me feel better about things to know that, should we need allies on the mainland, Michael will be here. A friend.

Suddenly, I remember something, the last item I took from home before I left. It was small enough to stash in the thigh pocket of my fatigues and not be detected by Nagel's search. I reach into the pocket and root around with my fingers, finding it tucked into a fold. Why I felt compelled to bring this totem, I'll never know, but now, returning it to its rightful owner, well...it feels like *providence*.

Michael's eyes light up like a boy of six as I present him with the action figure. "I don't believe it." He takes the figure from my hand as if grasping a lost treasure. "*Sergeant Stone*. I've dreamt about playing with this guy for over ten years."

"Consider it a gift," I say, "from one old friend to another."

He turns the figure over in his hand, going over every detail, where the paint is chipped, where the mold is rough and uneven. With a trembling lip, he pulls me into a hug. It feels good to have my friend so close once again. "It was good seeing you again, Bowie."

We break our embrace. "Maybe the only good thing out of all this."

Both of us turn to assess the world around us. Faye is already inspiring her people, bringing smiles back to shell-shocked faces. She's going to be a great leader. "We'll be fine," Michael assures me. "We're tough, and we've weathered worse."

Gunnar stands over by the snowmobiles, motioning to me that it's time to go. I give Michael a final pat on the shoulder, then I leave him to rejoin my people.

EPILOGUE

The wait at the gates is excruciating.

We drove the Vipers back along the northern route, back the same way the militia and their leader had come. As I imagined, the ice along the jetty was far more stable, and the ride across was easy and without incident. Passing in the shadow of the Densmore, I took in the great bridge, but now it seemed somehow slighter, diminished. Knowing what I knew now, about the sprawling cities beyond my tiny world, I had to believe that the Densmore, even in its full glory, was a mere footbridge compared to monoliths like the Brooklyn Bridge and the Golden Gate. Nothing more than some iron girders and concrete, an easy passage to a small coastal island that families picnicked or camped overnight on. The kind of bridge you passed over in your car as you took in the sights. That's all it was, and left in ruin it was even less. A sad, rusted relic.

Returning to Deacon's Bluff, I felt nothing. The sight of familiar environs gave me no feelings of nostalgia or homecoming. By leaving this place I had outgrown it. Whatever comfort and familiarity it offered was no use to me now. As my snowmobile carried me through well-charted forests and time-worn trails, I knew that my return here would not be permanent.

Before we set out, August assured me that I would be welcomed back, that the council, whom he would now lead, would not oppose my return, and that I may even be instated as head of the militia—what was left of it, at least. I didn't refuse the suggestion outright as I wanted to implement new policies and specifically address those forbidding girls from joining the militia; it was the one thing I could do to truly honor Maya. Beyond that I had little desire to hold the position, and that fact made me sad. This was the moment I had been waiting for my entire life, and now it was tainted. But maybe that's what life was. Moments overshadowed by the promise of expectation.

So here I am, standing before the gates, waiting for them to open. August said that communication with the Fort had been cut off once the hunting party left the bluff, so there is no way to know what has transpired during our absence. Alan Erickson doesn't seem the sort of man to stage a bloody coup, but power changes people, even mild-tempered farmers. For all I know we'll be greeted by a firing squad led by Tessa, mowing us down right where we stand. I can't imagine she'll be happy to see that I have returned and her father has not. Poor Tessa. If she hadn't tried so hard to destroy me, I could almost feel bad for her.

"Hello?!" August calls out when our return is met with silence. "Anyone there?!"

A small face pops up in the crow's nest. It's Wilhelm, Gunnar's little brother and August's youngest son, apparently promoted to watch. This is a good sign. "Dad?!" the twelve-year-old boy shouts down.

The Christiansen men, August and Gunnar, smile. "We're home, Son," August calls back. "Now go fetch some men and open these gates."

Wilhelm does as his father tells him. As the minutes pass and we wait, I hear the excited voices of people gathering on the other side of the gates. No doubt my presence among the returning party has been noted, and there is hurried discussion as to what this means. The last thing I care about now is what people have to say about my return. Let them talk. All I care about is that my mother is alive and well. It is the only thing that matters.

While we endure this endless moment, August turns to me. "You know," he says warily, "this might not be over, Bowie. They could patch Patrick up and send him back to us. I don't know how their laws work now, but I sure as hell wouldn't trust any assurances given to you by some politician. Politicians lie. I'm sure that much hasn't changed."

I hold August's gaze with confidence. "If he comes back, I'll be ready for him."

Finally, there is a screech of metal as the winch is engaged, and the gates are rolled slowly, painfully back. Excited faces greet us, the ragged remnants of my people, now mostly women and children. Among them is Tessa, whose hopeful face falls to despair the moment her eyes meet mine. She doesn't even bother to look for her father. Just turns away and disappears into the crowd.

Wilhelm has gathered his mother, Tif, and the two of them race forward to embrace August and Gunnar. I want to share in the joy of this reunion, but I can't until I see my mother. My mind races with horrible imaginings, that Byrne had her put to death before he set out or that she took her own life or fell ill out of grief. Surely at any moment someone will come forth and confirm the worst of my fears. As the moments stretch into eons, I brace myself for the terrible news that I am an orphan and my return was for nothing.

I hear her gasp before I see her. The crowd parts, and my mother stands there, hands pressed to her mouth, tears streaming down her face.

"Bowie," she says, forcing the words through her tears. She tries to say something else, but I don't hear it. I'm pushing through the crowd, fighting against the current. Trying to reach her. For a gut-wrenching moment, I lose sight of her and fear that she was only an illusion, a mirage playing tricks on my hope-starved mind. But then her hands are upon me, pulling me into her arms, and I smell that sweet blend of coriander and paprika, the spices she overuses to make her winter curry. I have never loved that smell as much as I do now.

"I'm sorry, Mom," I say in her ear as she clutches me tight. "I couldn't just leave you here. I had to come back."

"It's OK, Son," she says, "I would have done the same."

"I've done some terrible things," I confess with a hitch of my throat. "Killed men. Boys. My friends."

"It's not your fault, Bowie. None of this was your fault. It was going to happen sooner or later. I'm just happy that you're here. That you're alive."

We stand that way, clinging to one another, as our world swirls excitedly around us. When it seems we have hugged for as long as two people can bear, she withdraws from my arms, takes me in, smiling gratefully. "Your father would be proud of you."

"I know. I couldn't see it before, but I do now. I only hope that I can live up to his memory. That I can be the man that he was."

"You already are," Mother says.

The gates close behind us, and the walls of Fort Thunder swallow us in their shadow.

THANK YOU FOR READING

Did you enjoy this book?

We invite you to leave a review at the website of your choice, such as Goodreads, Amazon, Barnes & Noble, etc.

DID YOU KNOW THAT LEAVING A REVIEW...

- Helps other readers find books they may enjoy.
- Gives you a chance to let your voice be heard.
- Gives authors recognition for their hard work.
- Doesn't have to be long. A sentence or two about why you liked the book will do.

———

Don't miss out on your next favorite teen or new adult read!

———

**Join the Fire & Ice mailing list at
www.fireandiceya.com**

Perks include:

- First peeks at upcoming releases.
- Exclusive giveaways.
- News of book sales and freebies right in your inbox.
- And more!

ABOUT THE AUTHOR

Sebastian Bendix is a Los Angeles based writer and musician, as well as host of midnight horror film series, Friday Night Frights. He attended school at Emerson College for creative writing and spent his formative years in Boston playing in popular local band The Ghost of Tony Gold. Upon moving to LA he transitioned back to writing, stepping into the world of horror fiction, where he has found success both online and in print with numerous stories published in genre imprints. Bendix self-published his first horror/fantasy novel *The Patchwork Girl* in 2013, and his second novel, *The Stronghold*, is a  ripped-from-the-headlines thriller scheduled to be published by Fire and Ice in Fall 2017. Also an avid film lover, Bendix has a sci fi/horror script that has been optioned and is in development.

sebastianbendix.com
www.facebook.com/therealsebastianbendix
Twitter: @sebastianbendix
Instagram: @sebastian_bendix

Made in the USA
Las Vegas, NV
28 December 2021

39682051R00152